War at Waversea Book Two

Burned by Sin

A Dark Why Choose Academy Romance

DEDICATION

For those who love without words, speak through touch,
and trust even when we've been given no reason to.
Love doesn't need to be loud, it just needs to be real.

Thank you to all the incredible women who shared their time, stories, and strength with me during my research. Your honesty and fire inspired Harper, and I hope I've done you justice.

Please check the Trigger Warnings below before diving in.
If you're a dark romance lover, you can skip through. You belong here.

- Orphaned FMC
- Stuck in the middle of a physical rivalry
- 1:1 Bullying
- Stalking
- Blackmail
- Gaslighting
- Invasion of Privacy
- Ableism / Discrimination
- Privilege Dynamics
- Eyes Open/Eyes on Me sex
- Open Door Sex
- Possessive behaviour
- Substance Use
- Party Culture
- Mentions of childhood trauma
- Battles with Depression
- Flashbacks/Nightmares from one of the MMC's

RHYS

CHAPTER ONE

People confuse me. Their emotions. Their reactions. Even now, as I repeatedly flick a coin high in the air and catch it, coming up heads every time, I can't wrap my head around it.

Clayton took my money and ran. Chasing whatever miserable existence he might find beyond the sunset. Still, it's not far enough. His memory lurks around campus, his name whispered too often, even after I threatened to start cutting out tongues. I just can't seem to snuff him out.

Flicking the coin in the air again, my fingers slip. The tiny disc clatters to the ground, rolling towards the lockers which held thick layers of paint a few weeks ago. Remnants of paint thinner linger in the air, a colossal effort needed to erase the damage. But despite the lockers gleaming in all their mundane glory, the stain remains in my memory. The one *she* blamed me for.

The coin wobbles to a stop, heads up once again. Always heads up, as if that's the only fate I can control. The only one that is predictable enough. Dragging my hands down my face, I brace my elbows on my knees, a layer of sweat drying on my skin. It won't be long before muffled voices sound down the hallway, the team begrudgingly arriving for their five am drill. I've been heading out in the middle of the night as a freaking courtesy to the rest of the world. If I encounter a single person, I'll end up in a jail cell.

Swooping low, I grab my coin and my bag, before heading out the back way. The hallway's still dark, shadows stretching long across the tile. I keep my head down, slipping past the trophy cases and posters for a fundraiser next weekend that I'm absolutely no way in hell showing up to, no matter what my father says. He's furious with me, after the Board came down on him like a horde with pitchforks for losing Clayton's scholarship funding. So furious, that he wouldn't even entertain the idea of whisking me out of here. He'd rather leave me to suffer in a mess I didn't create, but didn't fix either. I let Harper and Clayton walk away from me that day without a second thought for my own preservation.

By the time I push out the door, the cold air slaps me across the face. Thank fuck. I need anything sharp enough to cut through the numbing ache in my chest. I can't stand the weight of it, hoping each lone basketball session or day spent high or sleeping will help to carve it from my system. It doesn't. Only one thing might, my fingers tingling to reach for my cigarettes and lighter. There's an empty spot on my ribs, begging to be filled with a scar. But, as pointless as it is now, I made Harper a promise once. If she wants to cut me open, burn me to ash, and crush out the rest of my pathetic presence, she'll have to do it herself.

Campus is blissfully quiet this time of morning, the rest of campus tucked up in bed, unaware of the fiend stalking close to the buildings and avoiding the streetlamps. With my hood up and bag slung low, I reach my frat house in record time, my shoes crunching over the crisp grass. As opposed to a few weeks ago, before I kicked everyone out, there's no light on in the kitchen. No pre-practice protein shake being whipped up, no lackey completing my coursework.

The hallway echoes with a grand silence I'm becoming accustomed to. I can't let anyone see me like this. Brooding, wallowing, *thinking*. I walk through the empty shell, kicking aside the crushed beer cans I've tossed aside and not bothered to pick up. The only room I'm wasting my time to keep clean is my bedroom, my lone sanctuary in this world. Throwing my bag aside, I leave the blackout curtains drawn tight and head into the bathroom.

This is my routine now. Work myself raw on the court or in the gym until my muscles scream. Shower, grab a pre-packaged snack and collapse into bed, letting the hours bleed together until I can't tell whether it's day or night. If I wake up, it's always too early. If I sleep, it's rarely dreamless.

Resting my hands on the counter, I stare into the cold, blue eyes in my reflection. The dark circles surrounding my eyes are getting worse, my hair a mess of sweaty cowlicks. My muscles are pumped from the workout, yet my frame is leaner due to the terrible diet I've adopted. Snack when needed, get takeout when remembered. Even my tattoos appear duller. No wonder not even my own mother came back for me.

I stand a little straighter at the unusual thought. Now there's a sign that my mental state is slipping. I point blank refuse to think of my mother. The only person in the entire world who knows the extent of my father's cruelty. I don't begrudge her for taking the chance to escape and never looking back. I inherited the selfish bastard trait from both of my parents.

Running the faucet, I splash water up the mirror so I can no longer look at the sorry excuse of a man I've become. I can alter my exterior, I can throw on a mask of indifference, but I can't pretend Harper hasn't permanently altered me. She's the other woman I'm fighting against thinking of, although it's proving near damn impossible.

Aside from the gif that went viral, smearing my last name in the eyes of the students and the press, I've only seen Harper once since that afternoon. I was heading to a meeting in the Dean's office, and she was exiting the library. If she saw me, she didn't show it. Her eyes were vacant, no doubt from refusing to wear her receivers and completely tuning out the world around her. Her solemn expression caught me off guard, rendering me frozen in place to watch her lifelessly wander back to her dorm like she was running on autopilot. Quite frankly, she looked more broken than I felt, and I don't understand why.

Why would she be so cut up over Clayton Michaels? He had nothing to offer her. His baggage was a burden he could barely carry. I thought perhaps, given time, Harper might have twisted the truth, turning me into the hero who freed Clayton of his financial burdens. I've given him more of a second shot than this shithole ever could. But that hasn't happened. She hasn't come knocking, hasn't come searching. It would appear, from the moment Clayton left, he took all of the color with him and in this monotone reality, Harper can't see the good in me like she did before.

Ugh, I'm particularly dismal today. Foregoing the shower, I flop onto my mattress and throw my arm over my eyes. I try to think of anything other than those large green eyes glistening with tears, those perfect cupid lips forming the words that have become my prison. Rhys Waversea is nothing. Not a bully, not an asshole, not even that guy who stole my soup once. *Nothing*.

When my mind conjures her love-heart face anyway, I don't even fight it. What's the use? No one's coming to tell me to snap out of it. No one's coming to see if I woke up this morning. No one's coming.

Her hips buck and rise, eager to meet my every thrust. I stare up at her beautiful face, the trickle of her hair over her pierced nipples. I'd forgotten how well she can ride me, her thighs spread wide over my hips, her body in tune to my every whim. Lifting my hand from where it's cradling her hip, I beckon for her face and pull her down to me. As always, she responds so well.

"Go slow. I want to savor this," I breathe across her lips. They brush mine, the faintest touch before she rolls her hips over my cock again. The guttural moan that bursts from me is jarring, slamming me back into reality.

I gasp and shoot upright, scanning my empty bedroom. I'm alone, painfully so, my chest heaving. Sweat beads my brow and when I peer down, it's my own hand I find gripping my cock within an inch of its life. The poor fucker is purple and straining against the loss of blood flow. I slowly uncurl my fist a finger at a time, hissing as I nudge each of my pierced rungs. Damn, I went too hard. No, *she* went too hard in fucking up my brain.

Not bothering to look outside or at the time, I shower until the stench of desperation is wiped clean away. Rhys Waversea doesn't fantasize. He doesn't *pine*. He just takes what he's owed and leaves the clean up for someone else. Except this time, it's becoming increasingly difficult to deny the cold, hard truth. I'm going to have to clean up my own mess, quite literally.

With a towel slung around my hips, I dig my phone out of my sports bag, finding it on low battery. I avoid looking at the thing at all costs these days, deciding a bit of self preservation is in order. I can't spiral into a chasm of unending fury about a gif if I don't see or read about it. Especially when the hacker I paid an extortionate amount to came up blank.

Any surveillance near the gym was wiped, the hack into the school laptop was encoded in a way that when tampered with, it threw up a screen filled with my name running on repeat. There's no mistaking there were multiple intended victims of the locker vandalism, a scheme carefully conjured to strike with three arrows in one blow. It stings worse to imagine it was someone clever, someone patient enough to wait until my attention slipped, someone who knew exactly which nerve to strike to unravel me.

It takes a moment to realise the hand holding my phone is shaking. I'm a mess of pent-up anger, pointless misery and a solid case of blue balls. I need to snap out of it. Searching for the service I need, I shoot a message to the first page that loads with the instruction to get over here ASAP. And now we wait. And not think.

Except this morning's dream is adamant on haunting me. It's not the first time Harper has been lurking on the fringe of my mind. In fact, she never truly leaves, but her presence is more tangible than usual today. The silky caress of her skin brushing against mine, her breathy moans swallowed by the thundering of my shower, her giggle echoing around the basketball court, sending an arrow of lust straight to my cock.

Only to wake with the desire to hate-fuck my own hand as the treacherous bastard refuses to go down until I give him what he wants. I have a feeling Palm-ala and the images behind my eyelids aren't going to work for much longer, and then what? I might as well use the pierced fucker as a hat stand since he refuses to even consider joining inside anyone else. It's only her now. The girl who ruined me without my consent. The girl who cracked me open, convincing me I had more to give, and then called me worthless in front of the entire world.

I may be cruel, but Harper Addams is a savage. And yet I want her more than ever.

The doorbell sounds, driving me to the bedroom window to look outside. A white van is parked at the end of the pathway, 'The McLean Machine' printed across the sliding door. *Damn, that really was fast.* Across the street, a group of easily fifty people have gathered to see if I'll leave my domain today. Looks of hope catch my gaze through the glass, a few girls dropping to their knees to beg me to let them come back in. I turn away on a scowl, thumping across the wooden floorboards to quickly dress and jog down the stairs.

Might as well get this over with.

Throwing the door open, I grip the white polo top of the man standing on my porch and yank him inside before slamming the door closed again. With the material still in my hand, I push him against the nearest wall, causing the plastic caddy of cleaning products in his hand to crash to the floor. 'Eddy McLean' has been embroidered into his shirt above khaki shorts and embarrassingly tall socks.

"This is your own business, McLean?" I snarl, trying to get a read on him before I permit him to remain in my house. To see me in the sorry state I'm in.

"Yep. Started the company from scratch when I realized entitled frat boys like to party and pay big bucks for someone else to handle the clean up." His flat chest puffs out, not a waver of nerves in that he just insulted my entire lifestyle. I study his face for a long minute in silence, which he waits out without trying to squirm away. I respect his work ethic, to see an opening in this hard world and capitalize on it. Now, for the final test...

"Do you want to suck my dick?" I quirk a brow. Eddy blinks a few times, but manages to keep his tone level.

"No, thank you."

I shift my fingers, flattening them just beneath the open buttons on his polo shirt.

"Are you sure? I may be biased, but it's a real beauty."

"I'm not sucking your dick," he deadpans, pursing his lips tightly shut. Well, that's good enough for me. There's nothing worse than trusting a cleaner in your own home, only to find them stepping in behind you in the shower. I'm speaking from experience.

"Good answer," I lightly tap his cheek a couple of times. "Go on then, clean this entitled frat boy's house."

Picking up his products, Eddy heads into the kitchen without another word. I stare after him as he gets to work washing out a plant pot I've been using as an ashtray, deciding I might just like him before stomping my way back upstairs. Standing in my bedroom doorway, I stare at the room without really focusing.

Fuck me, I'm bored. Bored of this room. Bored of the constant monologue in my head. Bored of having her scream my name whilst asleep, and knowing she's walking around out there forgetting I even exist. I've let her forget me. I've damn near forgotten myself.

Turning down the hallway and entering the room at the far end, I pull off my tank top and push my feet into white sneakers before heading over to the treadmill in front of a flat screen TV. Flicking on some bullshit for purely background noise, I power up the machine beneath me, pressing the touchpad for the belt under my sneakers to quickly increase to max speed. The burn is instant, my steps thundering whilst I chase a feeling I can't explain. It's somewhere between gratification and passing out, but once I've entered my home gym, I'm not leaving until I've reached it.

I'm trapped by my own limitations, forced into a cage my mind has created and unable to break free. Only thoughts of Harper swirl around there, with hints of emotions I don't understand. Whoever said time heals all is full of shit, because with each passing day the binds restraining me only tighten further.

I should hate her for this turmoil, but I can't even bring myself to do that. I can't feel anything, yet I can't not feel either. It's fucked up and all-consuming, my blackened soul withering away into ash. Everything seemed so much simpler the night Harper dominated me.

The thought jars me so physically, I have to grab the chrome handrails either side of me as my feet are dragged backwards. Grunting, I manage to slam my closed fist on the emergency stop button and collapse into a heap on the rubber that still wheels me back onto the hard floor, slamming my head into the wall in the process.

That night, Harper changed my concept of gratification. She controlled me, commanded me. Childhood memories flood back, a reminder that I vowed to never let anyone have power over me again. Yet I can't deny the freedom I felt watching Harper use her curves to lure and seduce, her green eyes to own and possess as I was drawn into everything that makes her special. Her smart mouth, her lack of fear. How she embraced my faults and freed me of the blame. I did it before, I could do it again.

Even just considering submitting to her has the binds around my chest lessening, my mind clearing for the briefest moment. I don't know what's wrong with me or how to fix it, but if I let Harper make those choices, I can be relieved of trying to figure it all out. If only for a little while. She won't pander to my ego or stroke my self-esteem. She won't offer false words or try to change me. She'll give me the cut-throat truth and deliver whatever punishments she sees fit. She could utterly destroy me, and I think I might just let her.

CHAPTER TWO

Turning the final page of the weighty paperback in my lap, I slouch back with a small smile playing on my lips. I do love a happy ending. If only they happened in the real world too. Taking a moment to bask in the warmth spreading through me, my eyes drift across to the chipped, blue wardrobe opposite and the feeling vanishes.

McAllister Halls are for those who need extra support or grants to pay their tuition at Waversea. As in, their funding is approved on a low income basis as opposed to mine, which is on a disability award. This also evidently means that all of the new, high-tech renovations went absolutely anywhere else. The furniture is barely holding together on aged screws, the mattress beneath me thin and lumpy. Yet, there's nowhere else on campus I feel comfortable anymore.

Kenneth is typing away at the desk to my left, no doubt still talking to himself too. We've fallen into a strange but easy routine. I hide from the taunts, since the entire student body have taken it upon themselves to seek revenge for my disrespecting Rhys, and Kenneth enjoys having company in his room once again. He doesn't even mind when I leave my receivers in my bag, happy to chat to the side of my head.

If I'm being honest, I'm a little worried about him. He wears Clay's hoodie like he's holding onto a lifeline, the pitiful gaze in his eyes pulling at my tender heartstrings. I don't know what Clay meant to me or what we could have been, but Kenneth seems to have lost his idol. Even so, I'll be pulling that hoodie off him if he refuses to wash it soon.

Placing the book beside his laptop, I stretch my arms above my head and yawn. The sun has set on another long day, and although I should be revising my notes from class, I reckon I'll head back to mine for an early night. At least sleep can give me a brief reprieve before it all starts again tomorrow. The jeers over breakfast, shoulder barges in the hall, being left the broken microscope in class, pages ripped from the books I return to the library. Small annoyances that are becoming harder to simply ignore.

Not that I'm one to run from a fight, let alone hide away, but I'm healing. At least, I hope I am. Losing Clay and Rhys in one day has left a hole in me that I didn't realize they were filling. I wanted a normal student life, to stay wrapped in my silent world, but now I've got exactly that, it hurts. A constant ache of loneliness I can't over-come. I've been isolated before, I should be used to it. At least I have Addy and Kenneth to grab food from the cafeteria and check out books from the library. A bookworm without books is just...a worm. *Ew.*

Waving a hand to catch Kenneth's attention, I sign *'heading home'*, to which he grins widely at and copies. It's sweet how he wants to learn to sign with me, I've never had that before. Although I get the feeling Kenneth latches to people quickly, clinging on like a stray puppy with unwavering loyalty to whoever feeds his need for attachment. Grabbing my backpack, I head out into the dark.

Just as I reach the bottom of the stairs, my phone buzzes, a message from Addy mentioning some last-minute dance training ahead of some fundraiser performance this weekend. I pout, but I don't begrudge her for getting back to her life. She's been amazing since...that night. Making herself available whenever I needed a shoulder to flop against, cancelling practices to eat ice-cream and binge crappy TV shows with me. Until the guilt rolled in that my temporary slump is the reason she's missing out on rehearsals, so I started hanging out at Clay's - I mean, Kenneth's, instead.

Shuddering against the chill that night has brought, I hug my new sheepskin coat around me. One of the perks to a self-appointed pity party, a much needed online shopping spree. My breath puffs out in orange-tinted clouds under the streetlamps, groups of smokers huddled beneath, their cigarette embers glowing gold against the dark. I briefly wonder if Rhys is amongst them, and then remember I don't care. I hurry past and slip into the cafeteria just before it closes, ignoring the scowls thrown my way as I grab a paper bag of doughnuts definitely not intended for just one.

Most of the cheer squad, the catty ones anyway, are risking hypothermia by sitting cross-legged on the fountain in the tiny outfits they seem to live in. Klara catches my eye to hiss something between her teeth, but I walk past with my middle finger high in the air. If I wasn't so determined to see my degree through, Klara would have bested me weeks ago with the literal shit stuffed into my locker or the marker pen scrawled across my textbooks. It's bad enough she signs a 'K' on everything so I know she's responsible.

My fingers are already going numb from clutching the bag, so I hook it into the crook of my elbow and breathe into my palms while weaving through the courtyard, past shuttered windows and shadowed archways until Bolton Halls rises ahead of me. The automatic lights flick on at my approach, the heater by the stairs blowing out a lazy, barely-warm breath that makes the concrete smell faintly of dust and old detergent.

I fumble with my keys at the door, twist the lock and push inside. Then, I jump out of my damn skin at the dark shape slumped on the edge of my bed. A noise leaves my throat and I don't even want to know what it sounded like. The figure doesn't move. The hallway light spills in, revealing the ink rippling over his bare arms, and the sea of demons and angels staring up at me. Rhys sits there, elbows on his jean-clad thighs, hair falling forward and his face buried in his hands.

For a long second, I simply stand there and watch him. His posture screams defeat, but I'm not so easily fooled. Not by him, not anymore. He doesn't move, not to look at me or to state his business after all these weeks. Rhys has been a ghost, many wondering if he is still even on campus. Once my thrashing heart has somewhat settled, I roll my eyes and pull out my phone, switching to the microphone app. Walking to my dresser with more confidence in my strides than I truly feel, I place the device down and flick on the lamp.

"Get on with it then. What do you want?" With the accuracy of a blade, Rhys' pale eyes flick to me, his hands falling limply between his legs. Black circles shadow his eyes, creases framing his mouth from the frown that's secured there. But most of all, he looks haunted. Strained even. I'm still not falling for it. "I assume you're here to exact whatever twisted revenge you've been cooking up in your recent absence."

"I'm not here to torment you," he mumbles with a shake of his head and returns his gaze to the floor. It's a sorry sight. I force my spine to stiffen, pushing all of my effort into maintaining the barrier I've been building.

"No, you let your disciples do it instead," I snarl. Rhys' head tilts at this, tension pulling between his brows.

"Who?" he rasps, and if I wasn't mistaken, a trace of his old self filtered back to life. It's gone in my next blink. Pushing myself to sit on my desk, I sigh dramatically.

"It's too late to act like you're capable of caring, Rhys. Get out of my room." Silence follows, the seconds dragging by as if my pulse is ticking off each one. His richly expensive scent reaches me from where he sits, imbedding itself into my furnishings and confusing my senses. The only movement in the room is my foot shaking impatiently. I try to wait him out, figuring he'll crack first, but his limbs are loose and he doesn't seem to be in any rush. Slapping my thighs in exasperation, I jump down to the floor and stand before him with my arms crossed.

"What the hell do you want?!" I call out, attracting the attention of a fellow student making her way towards the bathroom. She quickly scurries along at my scowl, but back in the direction she came. It won't be long before the whispers are passed room to room and we have an audience. For that reason only, I slam the door closed.

"I want..." Rhys mutters, his voice is so quiet that I'm forced to toss my phone onto the bed beside him. He goes unnervingly quiet again, fixated on a spot on the floor until I kick his shoe with my boot. "I want you to punish me."

I can't contain the responding laughter that leaves me. It's somewhere between deranged cackle and what-the-fuck-is-my-life hysteria. Of all the grand entrances I expected Rhys to make back into my life, of all the bombs I was waiting for him to drop, he has successfully surprised me once more. I should applaud his ability to fuck with my mind in six words.

Dropping onto Addy's bed, my head tips back to the ceiling, searching for some divine intervention that doesn't arrive. I had rehearsed for the anger or misery that would come with seeing him again. I wasn't prepared for amusement. He doesn't flinch at my reaction, only tilts his head a fraction and finally lifts his eyes to meet mine. Devoid of life, much like the first time I ever met him but worse. There's no air of superiority now, only a perfected wounded puppy expression that looks misplaced.

"Thanks for the offer, but no."

Rhys' face twists with confusion but his eyes speak outrage. *There it is.* The arrogant asshole who thought he could break into my room and have me bending to his every whim. I can't quite wrap my head around what he wanted. For me to shove my boot into his balls and choke him to the point of passing out? In Rhys' terms, pain is pleasure and he doesn't deserve either.

"Why not?"

"Hmmm, let me think," I tap a finger on my chin. "Because whatever this is," I wave my hand over the whole of him, "you're not finding an easy way out of it. And because my hatred is too rewarding for you."

Rhys stares at me so intensely, I have to force myself not to look away. My skin prickles beneath his scrutiny, a shudder fighting its way to roll through my spine. Hold your ground, Harper. This man has ignored you for weeks, not even bothering to check if you're safe. At the very least, I thought what I had with Rhys would have sparked some small consideration. I'd already lost Clay, and Rhys couldn't even give me that.

"Do you want me to beg for it? Grovel at your feet, would that make you happy?" Rhys grits out. His anger is stirring, the entitled side of him that can't be denied rising to the surface. Good, I've been waiting for this fight.

"Give me a break. You don't care about my happiness. You just want me to alleviate whatever bullshit you can't handle feeling. But I'm not going to save you this time. Work it out for yourself." I push to my feet and open the door, gesturing it's his time to leave. Rhys may not have been the one to drive Clay from campus, but he gave him the means to do so. In my mind, Rhys is as equally guilty for taking him from me. For leaving me utterly exposed and alone.

"I'm not leaving," Rhys states, yanking his hoodie over his head and proceeds to get beneath my covers, curled up like a wounded dog with no fight or life left in him.

"Well, you aren't staying. I'm going to the bathroom, you need to be gone when I get back." Grabbing my wash bag, I walk the length of the hallway and close the door to give myself a moment to process what the fuck is happening. Pressing my forehead against the wood, I wonder if he will go but even without the steady breathing washing over my phone's mic, I know his stubborn streak will win out. Rhys has no intention of going anywhere.

I should be screaming or punching his miserable face for the recent taunts I've had to endure. For disappearing while I had to be on high alert for whoever targeted us. For showing up and thinking he can control the narrative again. So why am I hiding in the bathroom, trying to settle the thrashing of my stupid, fragile heart?

Pushing away from the door, I wash my face, patting cool water on my neck. My hair is faded now, brunette roots showing amongst the dusty pink. My eyes appear just as drab, lifeless green like a woodland desecrated by winter. Rhys wants punishment. The man who gets off on pain, who will enjoy my efforts far too much. I need to make him suffer in other ways, to pay for the part of me that's still breaking.

Pushing off the basin, I march back to my room, disregarding the multiple bodies who have gathered in the hallways, trying to get a peek through the crack in my door. Word spreads quickly around here. I'm quick to enter and shut out those who drift closer, curious to see if the King of Campus really is among us. There's nothing king-like about the broken man in my bed.

"Fine. Here's your punishment," I grind out. Rhys sits up as I jab a finger in his bare chest. "You're going to attend every class on your timetable. In the ones we share, you'll be my proactive and contributing lab partner. You'll write your own notes, complete your own assignments, join me for study sessions in the library like every other student. No more bullying freshman, no more self-entitlement. And..." I swallow, collecting myself, "and you'll find a way to have Clay's scholarship reinstated."

"What is any of that going to prove?" Rhys's face twists with pure disgust, which was my intention. Punishments aren't meant to be pleasurable. I roll my eyes, slapping my hands on my jeans.

"That you can be a decent human being?! That you're not going to run away because of something an internet troll said. I really thought you had thicker skin than that."

The air shifts before I've finished. Fury radiates from him in a wave so sharp it feels like a cut, all coiled restraint snapping loose. He moves suddenly, violently dragging me into his orbit. My breath catches as I'm hauled forward, forced onto his lap, straddling him before I can shove back. The blanket between us does nothing to dull the heat of his grip, his hands clamping my face so hard I can feel the tremor in his fingers.

His pale eyes are wild, glassed with a depth of agony that strikes me harder than his strength does. The sheer intensity pouring off him roots me to the spot, my pulse hammering as his chest rises like he's holding back the roar of something feral.

"I ran away because of what you said. Those words came from you." The truth tears out of him like they've been festering, raw and violent. My dorm light hums above us, the only sound against the ragged drag of his breath. His grip trembles against my jaw, not loosening, not steady either.

"That day at the coffee shop. You cut me open, pressed hope into my veins like a toxin. I started to believe it myself, that I could be more. Be better for you. Until I heard what you said. I'm a leech, draining the life from everyone around me because I have none of my own. Survives on the weight of a name I didn't earn. That's what you said."

My stomach twists. The wrath I was clinging onto slips away, a harsh reality coming to light. As if I've been peering through blurred glasses which have just been cleared. I've spent so long grieving what I almost had with both Clay and Rhys, what I lost so suddenly, I didn't consider that I hurt him first. I was blinded by what Clay had shown me, enraged that he thought I could have had a part in it, and I hurt Rhys.

The heater kicks on at the far wall, rattling through the following silence, but it doesn't warm the ice spreading through me. His chest heaves beneath mine, every inhale clipped as if it's requiring a valiant effort. I catch the faint twitch in his jaw, the way his knee bounces once, betraying the restraint he's holding onto with white-knuckled desperation.

"Rhys. I thought...I thought that you..." My throat scrapes, words catching as his fingers flex against my face, urging me to meet the full brunt of his rage.

"You assumed I went back on our agreement." His stare doesn't waver, locked on me with such desperation, it nearly knocks the wind from my lungs. "I don't make promises, but I intended to keep that one. For you."

I can't quite catch the sob that escapes me, the entire world being ripped out from beneath us. Even now, I still believe Rhys played a part in the events of that day. He made the deal, he's the reason Clay isn't here. In whatever way, he deserves to suffer for that, but I'm not faultless. It was me who created the barrier between us, who threw the first shot that brought this all crashing down. Where we could have come together, strong and united, we fell apart. I ripped us apart.

Apologies are due, but I need to be careful with Rhys. His ego isn't so easily stroked, and his defenses are higher than ever.

"Yet here you are," I whimper. Releasing my face, his hands drop to my neck, thumbs brushing my throat as our foreheads touch.

"Yet here I am, begging you to finally remove the blade and let me bleed out."

My fingers shake as I peel myself from him to unhook the button on my jeans, fumbling to strip down to my underwear, because for the first time in weeks I can feel everything I've been stuffing down, and the pressure is too much to bear anymore. Shifting my phone onto the bedside table, I clumsily climb beneath the sheets. Rhys welcomes me in, his warmth seeping into places long since forgotten.

He doesn't claim me with roughness. Instead, his thumbs trace tiny circles along my spine that are laced with regret, his forehead seeking out mine until the tremor in his hands slows and I can hear a new, quieter rhythm beneath the hammering of my pulse. When he leans in, it's gentle at first, lips barely grazing mine as though testing whether the world still exists. I should put a stop to this, should continue denying myself of these pleasures that teeter the edge between heavenly and sinful. Rhys is a flame that I can't stop touching, testing how long it takes until I burn. And because of me, that flame nearly went out.

I meet him halfway, turning the kiss into a hunger that is heavy with grief, as if every missed chance and stupid fight and ugly word is dissolving between our mouths. I let myself sink into it, let the anger I'd clung to like armor fall away piece by piece. There is something offensive and beautiful about two broken people finding the same patch of warmth. I raise my hands up to his jaw and guide him back to me, press the pad of my thumb across the faint scar beside his ear until he inhales and relaxes.

For the first time since the gif, since the locker, since we became fractured from within, my walls start to crack. I lay my vulnerability bare for Rhys to do whatever he wants with it. That's my apology. To forgive, to nurture or to break me in the same way I wronged him, that's his choice now.

Breathless, we lay, simply clinging to each other and sharing the tiny space we've carved out for ourselves. A place without judgement, without the need to explain what this is. It just is.

Sleep doesn't come. Addy arrives home late, the outline of her head bobbing to music in her headphones. If she notices the extra body or expensive cologne contaminating our shared space, she doesn't make it obvious, flopping into bed and doom scrolling until she passes out.

Rhys' lips trace my cheek, his nose following my jawline, his hands following a slow and sensual path across my body. Eventually, when the heater clicks off and the first rays of morning start to bleed through the curtains, he shifts us, curling against my back with his chin tucked into the hollow of my shoulder. His arm over my waist grows heavy, his breathing fanning my hair. Held in his embrace, I can almost believe we might survive what we have done to each other, but we're not the only ones who need to heal and this isn't the only relationship I need to fix.

CLAYTON

CHAPTER THREE

"Hey, Kellyanne, you got the list of tonight's inmates?" I grumble, arriving at the reception desk.

"Don't let Dr. Hollister hear you say that. He takes great pride in this hospital." Kellyanne cocks a brow and leans over the desk she's manning. Her dark eyes skim over the length of me before settling back on my face with a knowing smile. I know the receptionists talk. Despite my lack of conversational skills, they've taken a particular interest in commenting on my appearance, questioning my jagged past and guessing what I'm running from. Rumor also has it there's a wager running for who on the roster can bed me first. I scoffed when the security guard told me, and quickly became horrified to find his own name was on that list.

Turning to leave, Kellyanne rushes around the desk in a bid to hold my attention.

"Oh, before you go," the nurse chuckles to herself, standing with her hip popped and a finger twirling in her hair. "Mrs. Mitcham has been eagerly awaiting your next shift. She'll possibly throw herself out of bed so you'll have to lift her again." At the mental image of Mrs. Mitcham's tight smile against her leathery skin, I grimace.

"Thanks for the heads up," I say dryly. Note to self, start my round on the far side of the building and hope Mrs. Mitcham is asleep by the time I circle back. She's sweet enough, really, always offering me a boiled sweet each time I tuck her back into bed. It can happen multiple times a night, though somehow never when the others cover my round. Rumor has it she was a hooker back in the day, a suspicion I can confirm by the way I find her face down, ass up, whenever she's sprawled across the floor. *Shudder.*

I shouldn't complain. The medical director, Dr. Hollister, took one look at me sleeping in a bus shelter and hired me on the spot because of my build. He even found me a room to rent down the road and gave me a two-week advance to get me on my feet. I don't usually accept charity and couldn't help being suspicious of his generosity, but a favor I can work off is different. This is a fresh start. Honest, hard work for a decent man who's shown me respect. One day, I'll be in the position to help someone in need too.

And yes, I could have fleeced Wavershit for all he's worth, finding myself a luxury apartment just to spite him. It's the least I deserve after the hell he's put me through, and that was before Harper appeared on the scene. I refuse to think of her, of what they might be doing. If she's safe with him, if he's protecting her with the same vigor as I would. She's not mine to protect anymore. She was never mine in the first place.

Alas, my mom's old debts are cleared, her care and accommodation is covered for the next five years, and I'm making an honest living. Clipboard in hand, I bid Kellyanne goodnight and stroll toward Falcon Ward. Running a hand over my beanie, I breathe in the sharp chemical tang of disinfectant and push down the pang of longing I never thought I'd feel for one of Peterson's classes. Every time I try to shove the thought aside, it comes back harder, forcing me to press a fist against my chest through the thin cotton of my T-shirt.

Black cargo trousers hang heavy on my legs above sturdy boots, a baton and can of pepper spray clipped to my belt. Overkill for a so-called "night porter," if you ask me. But with this shiny new hospital planted right in the middle of Detroit's most dangerous neighborhood, I suppose it's necessary.

As expected from glancing at the list, around half of the new patients in tonight have obtained gun shots or knife wounds and I find myself wondering yet again if I'm here to keep the gang members out or so-called victims in. A concept I struggled with at first, my fingers itching to protect the truly vulnerable and throw the troublemakers out on their injured asses. But as Jaye Dean, one of the matrons explained, the goal here is to keep the violence at bay long enough for the sick to get better, and whatever happens once they leave isn't our concern.

Rounding corners from one empty hallway to the next, I flick various switches for the lights to dim and allow those in both communal and private rooms a short reprieve to sleep. Occasionally, a nurse will pass between the rooms with a wheeled trolley, checking heart rates and administering timed medications. There's an eerie silence that oddly soothes me, knowing those in pain are gifted a brief rest from the real world. Pain and deceit festers outside these walls, curling around the bricks and rasping at the windows.

A harsh, hacking cough drags my attention to a room set back from the rest. The door is slightly ajar with a lamp on inside, shadows moving across the walls. The name on my clipboard for room sixteen reads Anastasia Grant, suffering from bronchitis. Low muttering meets my ears as I inch forward, curiosity leading me onwards. Through the gap in the door, my eyes fall on a stick of a woman enveloped in a curtain of her black hair. Despite simultaneously sweating and shivering, it's not her holding my attention but the two young boys curling into her sides. Their shaggy hair and scruffy faces drive a spear through my heart, knocking the breath out of me as I turn away.

A familiar tightness crushes my chest, the same rising panic that I've been battling during every shift. I can't save them all. I can't save anyone. My role is to protect the walls of this hospital, to sleep well and keep in shape, only to come back and do it all again. That's all.

Stepping back into the corridor, a metal trolley crashes into my shin and I quickly reach out to steady the wide-eyed nurse stumbling behind. Her hands have latched onto my forearms, the small watch clinging onto her blue tunic swinging violently as she breathes out a shaky laugh. But no humor can pass my lips.

"Do you know what the story in there is?" I nod my head back to the way I came, withdrawing my arms when she doesn't immediately let go. Her brown eyes flick beyond me and a small frown pulls at her mouth.

"Single mom," she murmurs. "The hospital only provides meals for her, but she gives the food to her sons, so she'll never have the strength to get better." With a small shake of her auburn-covered head, she steers the trolley around me and continues her round. I swallow thickly to sink the knot stuck in my throat and stroll into the empty waiting room opposite. I almost stumble, the collapse of my chest threatening to overwhelm me.

Switching off the boxy TV in the corner which was playing to itself, I collect the discarded magazines no one would ever choose to read willingly and put them back in a stack on a low table. Pulling a crumpled twenty from one of my many pockets, I smooth the note over my thigh and push it into the vending machine. Piling a few sandwich boxes, packets of crisps and chocolate bars into my arms, I slip back across the hall to lay them out onto an empty wheelchair I spot and silently glide it into the room without being seen.

No, I can't save them, but I can at least feed them for one night. Their future beyond that is in someone else's hands. Resuming the job I'm being paid for, I stroll out of Falcon Ward before starting on the next, shifting from room to room without anyone noticing I've been there at all. The silent savior no one wants or needs.

The rest of the night is uneventful, each level of the hospital filled with the bleeping of heart monitors and soft snores filtering through blue curtains. Occasionally there's a cry of agony or distant alarm, to which clusters of nurses rush and I promptly jerk out of their way.

Approaching the final ward, I sanitize my hands as I always do when moving from one to the next, then press the red button to open the double doors. An empty nurses' station sits to my left. Blue tunics and navy Crocs disappear into the room at the end of the corridor, a red light flashing above the door. My shoulders slump as I'm forced to head in the opposite direction, starting with the room at the far end.

"I'm not sure when he'll be here, Mrs. Mitcham, but—" drifts out as I push the door open.

"It's okay, Kaylah. Thank you. I'll take it from here."

Kaylah steps aside, revealing a very empty bed. I bend to retrieve Mrs. Mitcham from the floor, staring at the ceiling to avoid seeing how her hospital gown has ridden up her wrinkled thighs. I have nothing against the female figure, but when someone old enough to be my grandmother is trying to shift my hand from the back of her knees to other places, a line needs to be drawn. After placing her back in bed, I tuck the covers beneath the mattress tight enough to hold her until a doctor comes in the morning. Her pruned fingers caress my bicep.

"You know, I'd still be able to show you a good time, for the right price." She winks over her glass eye.

"How about I pay you not to throw yourself out of bed, Mrs. Mitcham?" I manage a friendly smirk. A small, fragile laugh leaves her, shifting the white wisps of hair on her bony shoulders.

"I've told you, call me Sarah. I want to hear my name on those full lips of yours." I flinch as her thumb brushes across my mouth. Whoever I was in a former life, I must have been a hell of a dirty bastard to deserve this.

"Get some rest and stay put. You'll break your new hip before you even get the chance to use it." That earns me a wiggling eyebrow, and I curse myself for not choosing my words more carefully. With a wave of my hand, I stride out and pull the door shut behind me. Kaylah is at her desk filling out yet another incident form. Leaning my forearms on the counter, I huff in frustration.

"Stop giving that woman my work schedule." Kaylah doesn't care about my rough tone, she's too busy laughing behind her hand and failing miserably to hide it. Rolling my eyes, I push upright and walk off. "Her death is on you if she falls too hard one day."

Her giggling fades, a solemn quiet following as I head toward the elevators. Maybe I shouldn't always be so sombre. Although the barriers I've cemented in place would never allow it, maybe I should attempt to joke with the staff, potentially make a few friends. It's not like I've got anything left to lose. The thought drags a frown across my face, plummeting my mind back in time as the elevator descends.

I've replayed that night with Harper over and over. Her in my arms, in my bed on repeat, searching for some sign I missed. A clue that she'd been dangling a carrot in front of me, waiting to stab me in the back the second I let my guard down. But there's nothing. Either she was a skilled liar, or I'm a classic lovesick fool. Odds are, it was a bit of both, but it doesn't matter now. The life I've stumbled into is the best I could have hoped for.

With my record and lack of qualifications, just having a roof over my head and a paying job is a miracle. I'm done fantasizing about achievements, or hopes of companionship. The idea that someone might be able to drag me from my grieving and adore the person I was always supposed to be has gone. I've had a target on my back for longer than I can remember, whether it was from the streets where I grew up, the JDC or Waversea Academy. I don't know what it feels like to simply be accepted, until Harper gave a hint of it. Then ripped it away.

Stretching my neck, I pass the front reception where I started and drop the clipboard onto the counter. My shift's almost over, so I waste time strolling through the hall of consultation rooms. No one will be in them this late, and there's no point stepping back onto a ward for the little time I've got left.

I find a dark corner, drop onto a seat and let my forehead fall into my palms, the world narrowing to the small square of shadow around me where no one can see the tremor under my ribs. In these minutes of quiet, I can finally let go of the urge to keep moving, to let the ache inside breathe a little. Loneliness is different at night, a weight that has nothing to do with hunger or cold, and everything to do with the hollow space where a voice used to be. I'm left rehearsing conversations that will never happen and bargaining with ghosts for chances I will never get back. Moments I can never relive.

Pulling off my beanie to push a hand through my hair, I prepare to head back when a noise reaches me. A metallic crash so quiet, I could believe it was a trick of the mind but the churning in my gut urges me to check it out. Tugging my beanie back in place, I curl my hand around the baton on my hip and creep along the rest of the corridor on silent feet.

A flash of light appears beneath a door on my left before disappearing. Gritting my teeth, my hand hovers over the handle while I force my shoulders to rest a little, and throw the door wide open. A cowering black hoodie lurches back, his flashlight shining in my face to obscure his facial features from view. I hear a soft curse as he takes in my size, the baton in my hand and raised clenched fist with the other.

"I don't give a shit what you're doing. Get the fuck out of here before I throw you out." I reach for the light switch since his light is giving me an instant headache, the room brightening to see him crouched beside the open medicine cabinet.

"P-p-please, my mom is s-sick. We can't afford the medicine she n-needs." His voice surprises me, my eyes realizing this boy could barely be older than twelve or thirteen. Although, evident by the picks hanging from the cabinet's lock, he's had to grow up a lot quicker. Mousey brown hair pokes out from beneath his hood in tight curls, his mocha skin littered with freckles.

For a long moment, I just stand there. This wasn't what I expected for my first break in, and the fighting tactics I usually rely on seem a little excessive for a teen. Finally, I huff, and place the baton back in my belt.

"You have to go." Stepping aside for him to leave, his eyes flick back to the cabinet, indecision passing through his young features. "Don't do it, kid. Believe me, it's not worth it." I shake my head, banishing the memories trying to rise. The justice system doesn't care for age or circumstances. A criminal is a criminal. But still, the desperation in his eyes resonates too closely to an emotion I battle with every day. "Look, the medical director that runs this place in reasonable, maybe he could-"

"M-my mom has terminal cancer," his voice wobbles and a tear leaks from his eye. "There's nothing anyone can do, but she's in so much pain. I can't see her like that anymore." The breath that saws out of me is slow and shuddering, a searing ache ripping through my ribs and settling in my heart.

I look at my feet, combatting the emotions swirling in my chest. Being a night porter is my job, my chance at a fresh start. I can't throw it away, especially if I were to get caught and fired. I'd be done. I might as well fill my pockets with morphine and codeine too because I'd need to make money somehow if I let him do this. Fuck, why am I even considering that?! But then again...I know how it feels to watch your mom suffer and not be able to help.

From a young age, I'd seen it all. Desperate people forced into lives of crime to get by, men who join gangs to protect their family and mothers standing on street corners just to put food on the table. I know what it means to be ruthless when needed, but the streets also taught me about compassion.

To know if the kids from down the hall who are loitering in my doorway, are actually locked out because their mom hasn't returned yet. To realize the woman in the bungalow down the street isn't oddly paranoid, but has agoraphobia and needs her letters slipped under the door, not left in the mailbox at the end of the path. To understand the homeless man sleeping on the front steps isn't insane enough to believe the birds will talk back to him, but is actually an ex-marine suffering from PTSD. A coffee and a pouch of bird seed each morning was all he needed, not judgement and abuse.

I know these streets, and perhaps not personally, but I know these people. They are my community. I'm one of them, so why am I pretending to be anything else?

"Can you run fast?" I finally ask, clocking the security camera in the top corner of the room without really looking at it. The boy nods quickly, his brows pulling together slightly. On a slow breath, I rest against the doorjamb as casually as I can manage.

"Pull your hood lower. There's a scalpel on the counter above you. When I tell you to, grab it, take what you need and run at me. There's a fire exit directly opposite this room, run as fast as you can and don't look back. And don't come looking for more. Next time I won't let you go." More tears have gathered in his eyes, but he nods slowly. Running a hand over my beanie, I say *now* the second my own arm blocks him from my vision. I hear him shift, the rattle of pills being shoved into his pocket as I stand upright and feign shock.

He's right, he is damn fast as he runs for me as instructed. I brace myself low as if to tackle him, but once close enough, I grab the scalpel between us and ram it into myself below the collar bone. Jerking back, his eyes widen with shock before darting past. He's out the fire exit and enveloped into the night while I continue to play my part for the camera, sinking down against the desk beside me and holding a shaky hand up to the blood seeping into my t-shirt. It does sting like a bitch, but nothing I can't handle.

Once I've given enough time for the *surprise attack* to be processed, I reach across and hit the security button beneath the desk before slumping back. Now, I wait to be discovered and hope he got away in time. That his little legs carried him far enough, that he avoided being seen. Fuck, what if he's caught and he spills everything?

Before long, I don't have to fake the tremors raking through my body as I realize what I've done. More than that, what I've risked for a kid I don't even know. Yet I can't bring myself to regret it. A part of the old me clicks back into place, the one from before my life went to shit. The one who was loyal to the streets.

No matter how much I try to deny it, these people are my family and the streets are my home. Joined by hardship, we must fight together to survive. Once, I would have given anything for those who needed me. That's the Clayton I need to find again, because that fucker would never have let Harper Addams close enough to hurt him.

CHAPTER FOUR

Tapping my pen on the open textbook before me, I check my phone once again for...well I don't even know what. I deluded myself into believing Rhys would actually turn up. I haven't seen him since the night we spent holding each other, but I'd told him to be here. *Monday morning, Peterson's class, don't be late.* That was the instruction. So far all I've proved is I'm still an idiot when it comes to him.

Peterson places a test tube rack of clear liquids onto all the other tables before approaching mine with an unconcealed grimace. Even the faculty has been treating me differently, following some big review that the Clayton incident sparked. It was decided that the students have too much scope for boredom and as such, our timetables have been intensified. Friday basketball rallies are cancelled until further notice, a curfew has been put in place. Staff have been ordered to be vigilant, and far more assertive.

The review also saw all investigations against Peterson dropped, concluding that Rhys was the culprit behind my implant attack. The decision doesn't sit right with me, especially with the way Peterson has been singling me out lately. I get my equipment last, often the shoddy pieces, and my assignments have been given shorter deadlines than everyone else. I accept it all without complaint, simply grateful that he has started wearing a mic clip on his lab-coat pocket so I can hear him clearly, since I don't have a partner or anyone to swap notes with anymore.

I don't know why I feel so miserable about that. I've never needed to rely on anyone before. But I suppose now I've sampled what companionship could be and how it can end far too suddenly. Who'd have thought all those days reading in the attic wouldn't have a patch on how lonely I could feel whilst surrounded by people.

Shaking myself, I pull the rack closer to familiarize myself with the contents. The powerful smell coming from the tube on the left tells me that's the hydrochloric acid and the odorless tube on the right must be the hydrogen peroxide. Following the instructions provided, I head to the equipment cabinet for a beaker, small bottle of distilled water and an iron nail. The other students give me a wide berth as I round the room back to Clay's old table.

Donning my latex gloves and plastic glasses, I begin the experiment Peterson called 'Bleeding Iron,' in which dissolving the outer coat of iron makes it appear as if the nail is bleeding. I'm happy for the distraction, playing around with chemicals as if I'm back at Aunt Marg's with the science kit she bought me on our first Christmas together.

Soon enough, I'm sitting back in satisfaction, the red swirling inside the beaker. My eyes slowly drag across the room, seeing five pairs of lab partners working together and sharing inside jokes. They're more concerned with something on their phones, a new meme no doubt. I couldn't care less, but find joy in the fact that the gif is becoming old news. Let the world move on whilst I fade into the background. It's like I'm seeing the room from Clay's perspective, and it's depressingly detached from reality.

Peeling the gloves off, I lean on the table and lower my face into my hands. I know I had no part in Clay's departure, but it doesn't stop me from feeling guilty. I should have done more, tried harder to make him listen to me. And it's times like this, when I can't distract myself by reading or even studying, I can't deny the simple truth any longer. I miss him.

A drop of water lands on my palm, a tear escaping my eye. Dammit, I need to get a grip on myself. I try to shift my mood to one of anger at the asshole that has essentially stood me up, but even then a small voice in the back of my mind whispers 'I really thought he would come.'

Peterson touching my shoulder makes me flinch, a sharp prod of his finger to tell me the class has ended. Once the beakers are washed and the table is wiped clean, I shoulder my backpack and head towards the quad, hoping to become another body lost to the crowd. Although, it seems I never get the reception I want. Side glances single me out, students shifting far away as if I've got a virus.

Ignoring them, I make a beeline for the library for a brief study session before Hargreaves' next lecture. I'm going to have to bust my ass, squeezing every drop out of the days if I don't want to have my head in a book over the entire Christmas break. Outside, the reactions are even worse.

Sophomores jump out of my way like I'm on fire, whilst students sitting on the lawns try to hide their faces before I see the expressions of awe or confusion. The cheerleaders lining the wall by the library turn away dramatically. All except for Klara. Her eyes are burning a hole straight through my skull and her lips are pursed like she's chewing on a wasp.

Jumping down from the wall, she storms toward me, intent on a screaming match until an arm links with mine and drags me away. For a brief, stupid second I mistake the tattooed forearm for someone else until I notice the candy-pink skater dress floating around her thighs. Addy doesn't care about the dip in temperature like I do, wrapped in black jeans and two underlayers beneath my leather jacket.

She drags me into the cafeteria, the grin on her face stretching at her dermal dimples. Her brown eyes are filled with mirth. Releasing me, she grabs a plastic tray and proceeds to add two paninis and coffees.

I walk ahead, tapping my college ID on the payment terminal before she has a chance, and turn to find her already scanning the room with mirth shining in her brown eyes.

Every seat is occupied, every face turned my way. A creeping sensation slithers up my spine, one I can no longer ignore. There's something going on, and I want no part of it. Hunting down some takeaway cups, ready to take this spontaneous lunch over to the library as planned, Addy strides into the center of the room. I follow behind, cautious like we're entering a lion's den. There's not a single seat available, yet Addy's steps don't slow as she approaches a table of five jocks. I can't hear the complaints, but as she shifts her shoulder to the side to reveal me standing there, they all jump up and scurry away in a rush of movement. I'm left gawping, confused, and lowering into a rather warm seat.

"Okay, start talking," I sign, leaving my receivers in my backpack. *"What the hell is going on?"* Addy's smile is huge and beaming, her eyes alight with mischief.

"You're a genius, that's what!" I raise a brow over my coffee mug as I take a sip. Instead of signing back, Addy pulls out her phone and shows me a public post pinned to the student newsfeed.

Harper Addams belongs to me. Anyone who disrespects, threatens, or even looks at her the wrong way, will answer to me. No fucking exceptions.
RW.

My mouth drops in time with my stomach, my hand barely able to place the coffee mug down before I've shot out of my seat. What the actual fuck?! Backpack in hand, I abandon my brunch, marching out of the building with my boots stomping against the icy ground. How *dare* he!

Every step I take across campus feeds the anger growing inside of me. I don't *belong* to anyone. Least of all the man who begged me to reprimand him and then didn't bother to show up. As usual, Rhys has taken the easy way out, using his reputation to do the work for him. It's as if he's forgotten who I am.

A winter wind whips through my hair, curling around my hands as I aggressively snap my receivers in place. I want to hear his bullshit excuse to justify me battering him with my textbook. Lost to my own grumbling, I barely register stepping out in front of a car that swerves to avoid me. The blare of a horn seeps a headache straight into my skull but I don't flinch. My eyes are rooted on the oddly quiet house at the end of the street. There are no lights on inside, but I'm not fooled. I can sense he's in there, a monster lying in wait of a worthy adversary.

Throwing the front door open without the courtesy of knocking, I search the bottom level, much to the surprise of some guy I've never seen before with a cleaning caddy in hand, before jogging up the stairs. The only door closed is the one to his bedroom. My hands shake as I push down the handle, then kick the door open with my biker boot like a true badass. Damn, I've always wanted to do that.

However, I was not prepared to come eye to eye with a recently showered Rhys stepping out of the bathroom, towel wrapped around his waist and water droplets sliding down his skin. Registering me in the doorway with fury seeping from my eyes, his chest falls on a sigh and he drops onto the edge of his bed. Defeated and slumped, just like he was in my room the other night.

I don't know what I expected to find. His usual cocky self, guarded by a designer tracksuit and reassured smile. The stunt he pulled on the app is something the old Rhys would have done, leading me to believe the scene I found in my bedroom was just that. An act from the oh so wonderfully talented master of masks. Well, if this is still part of the performance, he isn't going to fool me.

"Belong to you, really?!" I ask, dropping my bag and folding my arms. Rhys' tattooed shoulders slump further, a finger drawing the figure of eight on his bare thigh absentmindedly.

"You said they were tormenting you," he mumbles back. "They won't torment you now." Scoffing, I storm over and shove his shoulder, forcing him to look up at me beneath the artificial light.

"So instead of showing up in person, like I asked you to, you thought you'd hide away behind a screen. How are you any better than the sad lowlife that made that gif?" The words leave my mouth before I can catch them, the instant impact evident in Rhys' cold eyes. That was a low blow, no matter how annoyed I am. Taking a moment to catch my breath, I stare at the curtains blocking out the sun. "Where were you today?"

Rhys doesn't answer, his head turning away in my peripheral. I can't help but yearn for the fight, for him to push back so we can hash this out at last. In the many scenarios I conjured on my way over here, he retaliated in all of them. I would scratch his face, shove his chest, kick his shins and the victory would have been so much sweeter.

But this...this isn't going to work. I can't attack him like a rabid animal when he looks so defenseless. Still, I grab his chin and force him to look at me.

"Why beg for a punishment if you weren't going to see it through?" I start with, trying to navigate our conversation in a singular direction.

"I didn't want that kind of—" Rhys starts until I press my knee in between his legs, the grip I had on his chin moving to his throat. Other than the grunt vibrating beneath my palm, he still doesn't react. Those pools of blue entirely focused on me, his lips parting on a low exhale.

"That's the point. You didn't want it, and that's why I decided to give it. I can't keep going in circles with you. You hurt me, and I hurt you. Can we just...start again?" Lowering my hand, I find my body slumping into Rhys', the fight rushing out of me. I'm so tired of being this girl. The only one who needs to keep the campus bully in check, the only one trying to protect others from his wrapped wrath when they'd turn on me in an instant. I'm tired of trying to be so strong, when all I really want is a hug.

I want a reaction, whether it be a harsh retort, or his arms wrapping around me. Lord help me, I want the old Rhys back. That man was vibrant with life, he knew who he was and what he stood for. That's the man I was falling for.

Call it desperation or foolishness, but the next minute my mouth is on his. The cool metal of his piercing contrasts with the softness of his lips, a warm caress that seeps through my entire being. I only exist where he touches, and his fingers push my jacket to the floor and wrap around the tops of my arms. Gripping the wet strands of his hair, I yank his head back further and use the movement to push my tongue into his mouth. If he's not going to give me the answers I'm looking for, I'll take them by force.

His taste hits me like a drug I swore I'd never touch again. Familiar, addictively dangerous, and impossible to stop once it's on my tongue. Every ounce of fury I've been carrying melts into something fiercer, and I can't tell if I'm devouring him or if he's the one unraveling me piece by piece. There's no pulling back this storm I've started, our teeth and tongues clashing. Our hands searching and grabbing. Rhys' touch brands itself on my arms, shoulders and neck, feeling too much like punishment and salvation all tangled into one.

Heat pulses under my skin as his grip tightens, fingertips digging into my arms like he's anchoring me to him. My back collides with the mattress, the plush sheets inviting my shoulder blades to sink deeper. I arch into him, chasing the way his tongue tangles with mine. Every ounce of anger he's been holding back bleeds into me, feeding the fire already tearing through my chest. Skating my fingertips over the dips of his ribs and the multiple circular scars hidden beneath his ink, I want to whimper for the pain Rhys has endured, but he doesn't want my sympathy. He wants my appreciation for the power thrumming in his veins, for what he's crafted himself into.

"Stay with me," he murmurs near my ear. "We can stay here, just like this. Nothing else matters." His lips are greedy, dragging over my face and neck. A low burning ignites in my core, chasing away the bitter coldness I'd not realized had settled there. Like a moth to the flame, my body is pulled against his of its own accord. Nothing makes sense when it comes to Rhys, every action having an opposite effect. I can hate and hurt him, and his desire only grows.

"I can't," I sigh as his mouth dips lower. A rough growl leaves him.

"Yes, you can. I have everything you need." Peeling my layered shirts up, the heat of his palms almost burns my stomach and ribs. He's burning with passion, ready to scorch me alive, but I can't do this. It's not right for us to hide away when people I care about are out there, some struggling more than others.

With serious effort, I dislodge Rhys and raise to my feet, putting space between us. He doesn't lunge for me, but rather leans over his mattress with his hair falling into his eyes and his chest heaving.

"Staying in here won't solve anything." My head is shaking as I walk backwards, dipping to pick up my backpack. "People are hurting because of us. We might not have been directly involved, but we were used. Don't you want to put it right?"

Rhys twists his head to peer over, his eyes ice cold. I hold my ground as he rises to stand, the veins coiled in his neck.

"Put it right?" He scoffs. "No one was there to put it right when I was young and bloodied on the floor of my father's office. No one came when I was locked in this damn house for weeks, going out of my mind with desperation for you."

Raking his hands through his hair, Rhys prowls closer, his jaw impossibly tight. I take a hesitant step back, my back knocking into the wall. This is a new side of Rhys I'm not familiar with, one I doubt he even knows himself.

"I don't owe this world a single fuck, because I'm a selfish, reckless bastard who's beyond saving. But you. You," Rhys sighs, wagging an inked finger in my face. "You're just so freaking stubborn. You don't succumb to the hatred you should have for what you've lost. For what has been taken from you," Rhys cups my jaw, his thumb brushing over my ear. I shiver at the contact, holding his cloudy gaze.

"I refuse to live in the past, Rhys. I left my pain behind in my aunt's attic so I can start living the life I was supposed to have."

"You're lucky you can compartmentalize. My pain is like a cloak always hanging on my shoulders and choking me with its cord. One of these days, I think it will pull too tight and finish the job." His fingers toy with the ends of my hair, distracting himself from the ache building between us. "I'm wavering, Babygirl, and the only thing that feels real anymore is you."

Catching me mid-gasp, Rhys steps into my body to pin me against the wall. His expensive toiletries encompass us, the soft tackiness of his clean skin shifts between my palms as I attempt to keep him at a distance.

"Stay," he says again. I shake my head, continuing to fight against whatever principles I was trying to uphold as his hands smooth over my hips. Rhys lifts my thigh, curling my leg around his waist. His groin pushes against my jeans, the towel doing nothing to hide his growing erection underneath while his fingers brush the hair behind my ear. The contrast between desire and nurture is too much. My head spins, the heat becoming impossible to resist anymore. Kissing the thrumming pulse in my neck, he drags his lips up to my receiver.

"Give me today, and I'll walk out of here with you tomorrow. I'll follow wherever you go. I'll be whatever you want me to be."

My mouth pops open, words tumbling out with the truth I can no longer deny.

"I want you to be Rhys Waversea, in all of his fuck-up glory."

CHAPTER FIVE

The growl that leaves my chest is nothing short of feral. All my life I've heard, *why can't you be someone else? Why do you have to be such an asshole? What the hell is wrong with you?*

But not Harper. She's just given me a long lost validation I didn't know I was chasing. She wants me. Just me, in whatever form I am. Nothing has ever made me so hard, so fast. I grab her other thigh and carry her over to the bed, not leaving an inch of space as we drop onto our sides. My towel is forgotten, peeled open to reveal my need for her. It's gone beyond desire. This visceral craving must be fulfilled or I'll explode. I can't take not being near her any longer.

Her breath catches against my jaw as I shift, her thighs still caged in my grip. She's trembling, but she's not pulling away. When I drag my knuckles up the inside of her leg, the little sound she makes nearly undoes me. I press my forehead to hers, our noses brushing, our breaths colliding, trying to get a grip on myself.

"Look at me," I rasp. My voice is rough, a growl scraped from somewhere deeper than I've ever let anyone hear. Her eyes flutter open, wide and glassy.

I kiss her mouth like it's the only thing keeping me alive, slow at first, then hungrier when she tilts her head to deepen it. Her fingers tangle in my hair and pull, a gasp breaking between us. I answer with a low, satisfied noise, dragging my lips down her throat, biting gently at the spot that makes her shiver.

"Tell me you want this," I murmur against her skin. My thumb strokes circles over her hip, coaxing, teasing, feeling her arch into my touch.

"I want you, Rhys," she whispers my name, gifting me her complete submission. The dark side of me thrums to life as if being stroked by her pleasure. We've needed this for weeks, this reconnection of what was served.

I know Harper regrets what she said about me that day, as if it's not the least I deserve. There's no better person to give me a reality check, because I don't give a shit what anyone else says or thinks about me. But still, I don't want or need her apology. Harper can show me how she feels through her soft touches and gentle moans. She can praise me with her tongue, licking my wounds clean and start healing me in a way only she can. Yeah, I've got it real bad for this one.

I move my mouth back up to hers, swallowing her next breath with a kiss that's half-devotion, half-threat. My hand slips beneath the hem of her shirt to palm the soft curve of her waist, not rushing, but not gentle either. She shivers, clutching my shoulders as I press her down into the mattress, our bodies aligning until there's no space left.

"Harper..." It comes out like a prayer I didn't mean to say. Her skin is warm under my palms as I hook her knee higher and draw her closer until she's flush against me. The heat of her body sears straight through me, making it impossible to think. "I don't want to stop." Her nails rake lightly across my back, driving me closer to the point of no return.

"Then don't," she whispers. For a heartbeat I hover there, breathing hard, watching her lips part in anticipation, the pulse at her throat hammering beneath my mouth. My fingers slide into her waistband, inch by inch, the tension between us coiling tighter. I don't have the time to question why this feels so raw, why I feel so exposed. We've fucked before, but this...this isn't fucking. This is something else entirely.

The teeter I've been clinging to snaps. My mouth crashes onto hers, intent on devouring her whole whilst stripping her free of her clothes. Her receivers go too, because I can't trust what is going to come out of my mouth. At least if only one of us hears it, I can pretend Harper doesn't have me choking on the figurative leash she holds. Ever since the first time I had her in here, chained and bound to her every whim, the collar hasn't really come off. It's only gotten tighter.

She's all heat and soft skin beneath me, arching into my touch like she's been waiting for this. Waiting for me to show her how lonely I've been, trapped in a prison of my own making. My palm covers her breast through the lace of her bra, my thumb sweeping over the peak until she gasps against my lips.

"You drive me fucking insane," I growl, kissing her harder, tasting her moan as her legs hook around my waist. I grind against her, rough and needy, and she answers by pulling me tighter, forcing my erection to press harder against her soaked panties. I can smell her lust, and it drives me freaking insane.

Dragging the fabric aside, I can't help myself, can't hold back anymore. Thrusting inside her, Harper cries out and writhes within the cage I create around her. Fuck, she feels incredible. Her pussy grips my cock, dragging against my piercings in the most delicious way. It takes concentrated effort to stop myself from exploding then and there, a shudder rolling through my spine. Burying my face against her neck, her nails imbed themselves into my back.

"*Christ*, Babygirl." My hips jerk forward involuntarily, chasing her desperate cries. I can't get enough, rolling the head of my cock against her g-spot, drawing strangled cries from the both of us. Afraid to put any space between us, I don't withdraw from her searing hot cunt. I'm in heaven, seethed tightly whilst my hips roll and drive us both closer to the abyss. Everything else disappears. The academy, Clayton's memory lurking like a shadow, the world outside of this room. It's just Harper and me, tangled together in reckless devotion, burning for something neither of us can control.

My grip on her panties becomes bruising, the stitching ripping free. Desperate to have her bare beneath me, I fumble with the clasp of her bra, pulling back just long enough to drink her in. We're both panting and flushed, but she's breath-taking. She's looking at me from beneath hooded eyes, like I'm not just a decay rotting everything I touch. Right here in this moment, I'm the man she *chooses*.

Pulling out an inch, I sink back into her, a guttural sound ripping from my throat. Spots pepper my vision, blinding me with the notion that we can stay like this forever. Slamming into her deeper than I thought possible, Harper surprises me, as she always does, by raising her hips to meet my every thrust. Pressing my forehead against hers, I breathe her in, hunting for the anchor that stops me from spiraling completely.

I can't fuck her the way I'm used to, using the tactics I've perfected. Harper deserves to have my desire curve around her and bend to her will. Every deep thrust is in tune with the pinch of her features, the whimpers escaping her lips. She's beautiful to watch, panting beneath me as her nails carve patterns into my skin that I want inked there. I want to wear the evidence of this for everyone to see, because this is the day she's truly broken me. This is the moment I've become truly hers.

HARPER

CHAPTER SIX

True to his word, Rhys walked out of his house beside me this morning, dressed in his jersey and ready for the morning basketball practice alongside his team. This also means I'm up at the crack of dawn, my eyes sore and inner thighs feeling especially tender. Sitting on the bleachers, I track the players back and forth, starting to feel my head droop when a coffee cup appears before my face. I blink, fairly certain I'm imagining it, until the stream wafts into my face and I inhale the caffeine.

Accepting the cup from one of the lackeys who used to stay at Rhys' place, he digs a hand into his pocket and tugs out a small box. My eyes blow wide at the sight of the Plan B, which I quickly snatch and hide beneath the hem of my sweater.

"It isn't...we didn't," I stutter but thankfully, the lackey leaves before I blurt *'he didn't cum inside me'* across the basketball court. Things did get very heated, very quickly yesterday, and it wasn't just the once. Rhys took full advantage of his time hiding from the world with me.

Whilst the coach whistles for the next set of drills to start, I sneakily take the pill with a huge swig of coffee whilst simultaneously searching for a health clinic on my phone. Not that I don't trust Rhys to keep himself clean, but he has been with many, many women, and I don't particularly trust *them*. Screw it, I'll get us both booked in for peace of mind.

On the court, Rhys isn't exactly blending in. He's mouthing off at the coach, dragging his sneakers instead of sprinting, and throwing the ball with unnecessary force at his teammates. But he's here, taking the first step of integrating back into society. When the whistle finally blows to end practice, I can't help but laugh at the sight of him stomping toward me, just as pissed off as when we arrived. Sweat has plastered his jersey to his back, his hair falling out of place from the slicked style he'd started with.

"This is torture," he groans, collapsing onto the bleacher beside me. "Pure, state-sanctioned torture."

"You lasted an hour," I sip the bitter coffee smugly. "I'm impressed." He mumbles in response, snatching my cup and drinking the rest without asking. I suppose he did pay for it, in his obnoxious, entitled way. It is kinda nice to have a hint of the old Rhys back.

Leaning close enough for his damp shoulder to brush mine, I rear back in disgust. "Ew, go shower. I can't go to breakfast with you smelling like that."

"Are you offering to come and wash me down?" Rhys lifts a hopeful brow. Despite the flutter between my legs, I keep them firmly shut.

"Ask the others to wash your back. That's part of a normal team bonding, right?" Rhys doesn't dignify that with more than a snort, but he rises and heads for the locker room anyway. Smiling to myself, I close my eyes and stretch my neck, wondering if I have long enough for a quick nap.

Today is a cozy kind of day, as my sweatshirt states. *'Comfort first, fucks given later.'* The teal material reaches mid-thigh so I feel comfortable in black leggings without giving everyone an eyeful of my bubble butt. Although, they shouldn't be looking anyway. Women's rights motherfuckers.

A shoulder nudges mine, the stench of body odor intensified, and I give a small shake of my head.

"I thought I told you—", I start, coming up short when I see Kenneth's red hair bursting free of the black hood. "Oh, hey Kenneth. What are you doing here? It's not even seven in the morning."

"Early shift at the Caffeinated Toad," he grins and gestures to the empty cup beside me. "Some guy said he was getting a coffee for Harper, so I figured I'd come check if you were okay. Haven't seen you around in a few days." A pang of guilt rises within. I'd forgotten to let Kenneth know I wouldn't be around for our nightly study/reading session.

"I'm fine, but God, Kenneth, you need to stop wearing his clothes." There's no need to specify who, when he's been wrapped in Clayton's hoodies for weeks. "Have you even washed these?"

"I didn't want them to lose his smell," he replies bashfully. My nose wrinkles and I fight a gag.

"Trust me, you've lost his smell. Meet me outside the launderette after dinner today, with *all* of Clay's stuff you've been wearing. We're going to wash and send them all back to him."

Not that I've been searching for one, but this gives me the perfect guise to reach out to Clay. All I need to do is convince Rhys to use his connections to find me a forwarding address. Kenneth's eyes are watery, his arms wrapping around the hoodie tightly.

"Even his boxers?" he whines and a shudder rolls down my back. I'm certain Clay would prefer they were incinerated rather than touch them again.

"No, you can keep the boxers. But you still need to wash them," I swallow thickly. Luckily, Kenneth perks up and switches the conversation to idle chat, discussing the assignment Hargreaves has recently set. A yawn pulls at my lips, my body settling with the weight of missed sleep. I try to focus on what Kenneth is saying, but I find I'm just nodding my head absentmindedly. Thankfully, Rhys appears before I nod off.

"Fuck off Dickerson. Go crawl back into whatever hole you belong in." he growls, not looking any better than how I feel. His eyes aren't as sharp as they usually are as he reaches for my hand.

"It's Dockerson," Kenneth hisses with more venom than I thought him capable of. I give him a backwards wave, all too happy for Rhys to pull me through a side door on the court.

"Rhys," I mumble, a strange warmth tingling in my limbs. "I don't feel too good."

"We're just tired," Rhys agrees, keeping his arm locked in mine. I can't tell if he's just using my fatigue against me, hunting for any excuse to return to his empty frat house, but I'm not complaining. Taking a few shortcuts, we somehow manage to make it back, although I'm certain Rhys is leaning on me just as much. My foot catches on the stone steps, my balance all over the place. We crash through the front door together, slumping onto the floor. My breathing turns shallow, the weight in my limbs crippling.

"Rh..." I stretch out a hand to his sleeping form. His eyes are closed, chest rising and falling steadily. Army crawling, I close the distance between us and lower my head onto his shoulder just before the darkness takes over.

I jolt awake with a strangled gasp, my body jerking as if I've just surfaced from underwater. My tongue scrapes like sandpaper, my head stuffed with cotton. The floor beneath me is different, the hardwood replaced by something softer and scratchier. My lashes flutter open and then slam shut against the sting of light. What the hell happened?

My throat burns as I swallow, the metallic tang of stale coffee clinging stubbornly to the back of my tongue. The rush of sneakers and bodies, the plan B and coffee...it all blurs together until the shifting of my hair drags me back to the present.

"Harp, can you hear me?" Rhys asks, brushing my hair back. I peek up through cracked eyelids, forcing the world into focus as I search for him. He's hunched over me, his jersey discarded and hair damp from sweat, flicking over his temples in straight points. Somewhat ungracefully, I roll onto my back, groaning at the dead weight still wearing me down. Rhys exhales and sits back, his elbows digging into his knees. "Thank fuck. Your receivers were over there on the fireplace. I didn't really know how they...I mean, I just held them close and they just snapped in."

Reaching up, I adjust the plastic around my ear and wave off his concern.

"You managed just fine. They can be fiddly." I roll my head to the side, taking in the room we're in. It's not Rhys' bedroom, but one of the others. A dust sheet-covered bed sits beside me, yet I'm laying on the carpet. Rhys scrubs a hand over his jaw, his eyes darting to the curtained window as if he's checking for shadows. "What the hell happened?"

"I was in the shower when the drowsiness hit. I'm not even sure how we managed to make it back here before collapsing." My stomach drops, dread creeping in. Had it just been me, I might have been able to convince myself I was just *that* tired. But for Rhys to pass out too?

"It must have been the coffee. There's no other explanation," I frown, managing to push up onto my elbows. Each movement is sluggish, like I've been in a coma for months. Clearly having longer to come around, Rhys leans forward far more smoothly.

"The coffee? Who gave it to you?"

"You did." I accuse, and Rhys' brows shoot up. Blinking through the fog clouding my mind, I search for clarity. "I mean, you set it up, right? The coffee and the plan B."

Even before I've finished, I can tell by the dark shadow falling over Rhys' face that he didn't orchestrate anything. That I took a drug and drank a coffee without knowing where it came from. And more than that, someone knows what Rhys and I did yesterday without a condom. Suddenly, every window and open door leers over me, the shadows sneaking in. Someone was here last night, listening, potentially watching. The same sense of alarm washes over Rhys' face.

"*Fuck.*" He hisses, pushing himself up onto an armchair. "You need to show me who handed them to you, then get as far away as you can." A flash of murder lights his features, his blue eyes turning glacial and his fingers curling into a fist. "I made it clear to everyone that you're mine, and harming something that's mine won't end well."

"Rhys," I breathe, a tremble in my voice. Whilst he leans on rage, it's fear that's crumbling my resolve. Someone got to us, or rather, someone planned to drug just me. In all these weeks of radio silence, I thought the person messing with us had grown bored, or that Clayton was their intended target. Rhys and I were simply collateral damage. But I can't deny what has happened this morning. This was a direct attack.

Cold shivers along my spine as the pieces slam together. I can't remain here, listless on the floor. What if there's still someone in the house? Gradually pushing myself to sit upright, Rhys drops back to his knees to help me, despite the clear struggle he is also having in navigating his limbs. Together, we exit the guest bedroom and pull and drag each other down the staircase.

Rhys steadies himself on the wall, muttering something foul under his breath. My tongue still tastes like metal, the memory of steam curling harmlessly from the takeaway cup has my stomach in knots. I don't know who to trust anymore.

By the time we make it downstairs, some feeling has returned to my legs and Rhys' hand on the small of my back is all that's needed to keep us both steady. We round into the kitchen, chasing the promise of water. Dim light filters through the blinds, the setting sun striped over the basin. Damn, we were out for *hours*.

I reach for a glass from the cupboard when my gaze snags on something spread across the counter. Laid out in a neat little line, some overlapping at the edges, the glossy surfaces of polaroids catch the light. My heart plummets, the breath locked in my lungs as I step closer. Rhys is slower to notice until he follows my eyeline, and the harsh hiss he releases cuts the air in half.

The first photo shows me slumped sideways on the couch, mouth slightly open, head tilted against the cushions. Vulnerable and lifeless. In the next, Rhys on the floor, arm stretched out toward me, his tattooed chest bare and expression eerily peaceful. Another shows me curled against him, our fingers nearly touching. Posed, orchestrated. Bile rises in my throat instantly.

"Oh my God." My voice breaks, and I clap a hand to my mouth. The sound is muffled, strangled as my pulse hammers at the base of my throat.

Rhys grabs the edge of the counter so hard that his knuckles whiten, veins bulging along his arms. He doesn't say anything, just stares at the images like he could burn holes through them with his rage alone. It's all too much. Backtracking, my spine hits the refrigerator, the cool metal doing nothing to ground me. Every inch of my skin crawls, goosebumps prickling sharp enough to sting. As if the drugging wasn't enough, someone was standing over us while we were unconscious, arranging our bodies like dolls for their amusement. The realization hits me in jagged pieces. There was nothing spontaneous about this plan.

Rhys finally growls, the sound guttural and terrifying, and swipes an arm across the counter, sending the polaroids scattering across the floor. A few land face-up, staring back at us with grotesque familiarity.

"*Motherfucker.*" He spits the word like poison, pacing back and forth, dragging his hands through his damp hair until it sticks out at wild angles. His chest heaves as if he's spiraling into a panic attack. I can't bring myself to comfort him because that would require moving, and I've found myself paralysed in place. "I swear, I'll kill whoever did this. I'll fucking skin them alive."

My stomach twists at his fury, but the sick part is, I want the same. This has gone too far past the point of mere pranking. Someone wants to humiliate us, and the lengths they're willing to go to have crossed the line. My nails dig crescents into my palms.

"We should call the cops," I whisper.

"Forget it," Rhys pinches the bridge of his nose. "No one is going to believe I didn't do this myself. I'm afraid my reputation precedes me. And there's so much weed hidden in this house, they'd arrest me on sight regardless." Rhys' eyes slice to mine, blazing with a hint of regret. I nod once, a tiny movement, but it feels like the ground is being pulled out from beneath me.

"Rhys, I can't stay here. I'm scared." It occurs to me that I have no idea how Rhys would react to seeing me so uncertain. Our entire relationship is based on my iron backbone and his desire to hammer kinks into my armor. Vulnerability isn't Rhys' forte, but I didn't need to have any reservations. Kicking the polaroids beneath the counter as if we can erase them from our reality, he closes the distance between us and wraps me in his arms.

"This is my fault. I wasn't around. I let the bastard grow too confident. I..." Rhys turns his face away. "I didn't protect you." I don't realize I'm trembling until Rhys' arms tighten, his chest solid against mine. Finding it easier to mimic the steady rise and fall of it, I force my lungs to intake air, eventually dropping my head into the crook of his neck. Somewhere within the stifling silence, Rhys seems to come up with a plan. "It's winter break next week. We can dip out early, I'll make the excuses. Let's just get far away from here until we can figure out what's going on."

A thousand reasons we shouldn't die on my tongue. I should refuse to be forced out, or stubbornly decide to stay for that last precious week of lectures. Addy and Kenneth will wonder where I've gone, Aunt Marg will burst a vein if I ran off with a menace covered in ink, and those who have been willing me to fail will temporarily win. But none of that tops the one reason I can think of to leave.

"We should check on Clayton," I announce. The arms around me stiffen, the jaw beside my temple ticking as Rhys' face hardens to granite.

"He's fine," Rhys drops a few octaves. He pulls away from me, putting the distance between us to lean against the counter. My heart beats at double time.

"How do you know?" I hold Rhys' stare, wondering if maybe he does care. Deep, deep, *deep* down. But I should have known better.

"Okay, I'll admit I don't know how he is and I don't give two shits. He isn't here, and he isn't the one who's going to protect you anymore. You've got me now." A challenge ignites in his blue eyes, a dare to deny him. Chewing on my bottom lip, I crack first, angling my head downwards.

"You promised to get his scholarship reinstated. Have you even looked into it yet?"

"Jesus Christ," Rhys scoffs, striding across the kitchen to kick a bar stool by the island. "Give me a few days at least. It's not easy, you know. I didn't realize you were so desperate—"

"I'm not desperate," I glare, my voice gaining strength. "It's the right thing to do."

"So what? Clayton can swoop in and play the hero while I stand here useless?"

"This isn't about you!" My shout cracks, raw from the dryness of my throat. Tears blur my vision, but I force them back, shaking my head. "It's not about your pride or my stubbornness. Someone drugged us, Rhys. Someone touched us while we were unconscious. Someone is in this house. We need help, and Clay...Clay is the only other person I trust."

Rhys' breath rattles, hot and uneven, like he's fighting not to explode. For a moment, I think he'll walk out, leave me here shaking in the kitchen with the polaroids staring up at me from where they poke out beneath the counter. Then his shoulders slump, just barely but enough to show he's hearing me. Rhys curses under his breath, dragging a hand down his face.

"I hate this," he mutters. His eyes burn into mine, fury and misery seeping through his features. "I fucking hate this. But...a second pair of eyes might not be the worst thing. If Clayton is what it takes to keep you safe, then fine. We'll go find him, together."

Relief surges through me, a crash of elation and giddiness and relief all at once. I don't know what to do with it, but I'm careful to keep the solemn mask over my face.

"Thank you."

"Don't thank me," Rhys huffs, reaching for my hand and dragging me out onto the back porch. "Just don't ask me to like it."

The promise of a sunny day has passed, leaving us with the bitter chill of a winter night. Pulling a pack of cigarettes out from beneath a chair cushion, I don't comment as Rhys sparks up. It's been a stressful day all round. I curl my arms around his naked torso, amazed by how warm he is.

The silence that follows is thick, the air heavy with fear and frustration and something else I can't quite name. The scattered photos in the kitchen are burned into my memory, and I have no idea how I'll be able to settle anytime soon. One second at a time I suppose, and attached to Rhys' side for the foreseeable future. The man in question is also struggling to relax, his chest rising and falling unevenly, his hands flexing at his sides like he's itching for violence he can't yet deliver. Between dragging on his cancer stick, his eyes catch mine, softening for just a fraction of a second, before the hardness returns.

"I'm not going to replace you with him, you know," I murmur, placing my cheek on his back. An expanse of angels and demons stare back at me, all twisting and contorting, reaching up towards Rhys' nape. His sigh rocks through me, his response almost lost to the night.

"In every aspect of my life," he takes another long drag and expels the smoke, "I've never been enough." I tighten my arms around his torso, pressing my cheek harder against the ink covering his back.

"That's not true," I say softly, not lifting my head. Rhys gives a humorless huff.

"You don't have to—"

"I'm not saying it because I have to," I cut in, lifting my face enough for the words to brush the base of his neck. "I'm saying it because it's true. You've been enough for me, Rhys. Even when you were making a mess of everything, even when you were trying to scare me off, and even when you tried to push me away, you came back, and you didn't have to."

Rhys stills, the cigarette frozen between his fingers. The ember glows faintly, then dims as the ash drops to the porch. Good, I've got his attention. Sliding one hand up to the back of his neck, my fingers brushing the short hair there.

"I'm scared out of my mind right now, but I'm not scared of you. I'm scared of what's out there, what's creeping back in. And you're here, by my side." Twisting his head to the side, Rhys' lips twitch, not quite a smile but it's something.

"You're either insane or lying."

"Maybe a little insane," I admit, tugging lightly at his arm until he faces me fully. "But definitely not lying." Rhys drops the cigarette and grinds it out with his heel, the smell of smoke hanging between us. His hands hover like he doesn't know where to put them, then settle on my hips. It's tentative, like he's not sure if he's allowed.

"You're not a replacement," I insist. "You're Rhys, and you're mine."

For a long moment he just looks at me, his eyes searching cautiously. I know how difficult it is for Rhys to open up, how he wraps himself in a tattooed cage to keep the rejection out. But when he looks at me like this, I know he's baring a piece of his soul. He exhales slowly, his forehead dipping until it touches mine.

"I thought claiming people like objects went against your high morals," he whispers. I chuckle softly, tracing his abdomen with my finger.

"Only when you announce it to the world before you tell me." Rhys lets out a low sound, almost like a laugh but rougher, and pulls me in until I'm completely wrapped against him. His chin rests on top of my head, and for the first time all day, he doesn't feel like he's about to break something or someone. He's finally at ease. I bathe it in while it lasts, because I know this isn't the last time we'll have this conversation. Once we leave to find Clay, it might become an hourly necessity.

CLAYTON

CHAPTER SEVEN

Itching the dissolvable stitches under my military jacket, I stare at the care home until the truck radio dies mid-song and leaves the world oddly quiet. Perfume hangs heavy in the passenger seat, the yellow roses giving off that sweet, fake smell. I've driven up this driveway more times than I can count over the past few weeks, unable to make it any further than the parking lot. Today I figured spending money I don't have on flowers would be what gets me to cross the threshold. So far, it's not working.

The building looks softer than I expected, mismatched bricks like somebody tried to stitch something decent together out of scraps. Strings of white lights trail the roofline and wrap around the green canopies hanging over balconies. Frost rims the grass on either side of the path, the flowerbeds bare except for wired reindeers sporadically spaced amongst the soil. A plastic wreath sits crooked above the entrance, its red bow sagging, but the sentiment is there. Christmas is coming, even if some of us have no reason to celebrate.

Drumming my fingers on the steering wheel, I watch family members enter and exit through the double doors ahead. I should be amongst them. I should stop tapping my foot and get out of this damn cab, but what am I supposed to tell her? I'm not the son she's expecting, the one she'd prefer. I'm the criminal turned college dropout. Usually people do those things in the opposite way, so props to me I guess.

Fuck it. There's no use leaving just to come back and sit here again tomorrow. I'll still be the same me. Swallowing whatever is left of my pride, I grab the bouquet a little too roughly and climb out of the truck. My boots hit the pavement with a solid beat until I reach the reception desk, my heart pounding in my chest. The woman behind the monitor is engrossed in her screen, so I ring the bell with a sharp ding.

"Sign the visitor book," she grumbles without looking up, and I instantly recognize the voice as the same woman who snaps at me whenever I call. She's exactly how I presumed she would look, all scowl lines and bitter vibes. I pull the book toward me and snag a pen, scrawling my name in the visitor column until my eyes snag on another name on the opposite page. I flip back through the book and find the same name repeated several times in the last few months, all under my mom's name.

"'Cuse me?" I ask, lifting the book high so the receptionist has to stop what she's doing and focus. "Who is this?" I point to Dekken H. Cornstone's name written in unnecessarily fancy cursive. Her brow lifts, a suspicious glint passing through her features.

"And you are?"

I snort, slamming the book down. The frustration I feel isn't solely directed at her, it's at myself. I've been a ghost in my mom's life, only dropping in a call when I have the strength to deal with the fall out. I've been a part-time son, and now I'm here throwing my weight around like I deserve answers.

"I'm Clayton Michaels. My mother is a permanent resident here. Please just...can you tell me who this is?" The receptionist twists her mouth, considering whether to humor me or not.

"Well, it's nice you're paying her a visit. I'm sure Anya will be very happy to see you," she says in a syrupy, sarcastic tone. "Surely you recognize your own cousin's name."

"My cousin?" I frown, the heat rising beneath my collar and causing those stitches to burn. She nods slowly as if explaining a grammar rule to a child.

"The child of your aunt is your cousin. He's rather popular around here. Always stopping by for a chat, bringing cookies for the staff. A very nice young man." The corner of her mouth softens whilst mine sharpens. He must be a very nice young man indeed, considering he's charming enough to convince everyone that my mother isn't an only child. I don't have any fucking cousins. I don't have anyone except the woman somewhere in this building who doesn't have a clue who I am.

"Where's her room?" I bark harshly. I'm offered a reluctant point of a finger by the shit receptionist who apparently never checks ID. Forgetting about the flowers, I storm away before I do something rash, such as launch the damn computer through the window. I'm already fighting one mission, but as soon as I leave here, I'll be contacting whoever is responsible for not installing surveillance cameras in a building filled with vulnerable people.

It takes everything in me to quell that anger before I burst through my mom's door. That wouldn't be the entrance I've spent weeks psyching myself up to. I lean against the wall, taking a few steady breaths. I do not know what I will find inside, and I still don't know how I'm going to handle being myself. I planned to go into that room as Jeremy, the golden boy, but I can't. It would be an injustice to his memory, and to my mom. Regardless of my self-esteem being in the gutter, she doesn't deserve to be lied to. For today at least, I'll let her see me. Not the ghost of Jeremy, not some stranger she's forced to invent. Just me.

I knock softly, and step inside with the faintest of smiles. My chest tightens at the sight of her in the chair by the window, hunched over a cross-stitch as the sun catches her hair and makes it look like it has a halo. The woman who dressed me, fed me, and kept me warm when everything else fell apart is reduced to a fragile frame and a ball of wool. I shut the door behind me, the tear I cannot hold back slipping past my defenses. Her dark eyes swivel to me and she lets out a delighted shriek as she throws the stitching to the floor.

"Jelly Bean!" she calls, arms raised. Sucking in a painful breath, despite the slice carving through my chest, I shake my head.

"No, Mom. It's me." I pull my beanie off and force my voice to be steady. "It's Clayton." The words taste like an apology, like I am saying sorry for not being the son she remembers.

"Clayton," she breathes, her reach becoming hesitant. I close the distance, allowing her hand to smooth up my arm, and as I lower, to cup my face. For a moment, I see her searching, her dark eyes flickering with panic, confusion, and then something worse. Emptiness. She looks past me, scanning the corners of the room like I've slipped out of view, like I've become one of the ghosts her mind conjures to keep her company. My chest caves as her fingers falter, dropping back to her lap, and she starts humming to herself, rocking just slightly in her chair.

"Mom..." I whisper, crouching down so we're level. But she's somewhere else, years back or in a place I can't follow. My throat burns as I press my palms together, begging silently for her to see me. Then her gaze catches mine again with a sharpness so sudden, it's as if I can see the clouds parting.

"My baby boy," she says, a smile breaking across her face. My mom leans forward, kissing both my cheeks as if she hasn't missed a beat, as if the last few minutes didn't happen. "You've gotten so big."

The relief hits me like a gut punch. I swallow hard, fighting the sting in my eyes, because I know it won't last. The clarity will come and go like flickers of light on the water, never enough to hold on to. I grip her hand, anchoring us both in a moment that shatters in the next second.

"Is your brother with you?"

My throat tightens. I don't want to lie, as much as I cannot bear causing her heartache for what she has already lost.

"No, Mom. Just me." I force a smile that feels weak and lead her toward the bed, my arm banded around her brittle body. She's a shadow of the vibrant, confident woman I remember. The one who tried her best to shield us from the debt collectors banging on the door, and the gangs on the streets adamant on recruiting young boys. I don't blame her for wanting to forget the past, even if it all seems worlds away from where we are now.

The room is small but clean, a double bed, two chests of drawers, an armchair by the window and a framed photo of the three of us beside an empty mug. I'm beyond grateful that she is somewhere safe and warm to stay, even if I had to resign to using Wavershit's money to keep her here.

Once settled in bed, I sit beside her, filling the silence with mindless chatter. I tell her of my new job as a night porter, of the tiny room I rent, even of the girl who almost held my heart.

"It's her loss," she hums, stroking the back of my hand through habit. I rest my chin on her head, the stuttering of her breath surrounding us. I can almost hear her clarity slipping, the way she slumps and phases in and out of conversation. Forcing the tears back, my eye catches something out of place on the dresser and whatever fragile calm I had found suddenly collapses.

Slowly, I rest my mom back against the headboard, tucked in by cushions, and move across the space to pick up the light gray beanie. It's a shade lighter than the one in my other hand, the one that's still warm from my own head. A wash of cold dread runs through me.

"Mom? Where did this beanie come from?" Her gaze flicks toward me, pupils trying to catch focus, but I can already see the veil slipping back down.

"Jelly Bean! You found Clay's hat. You know how much he likes to dress up like you," she beams cheerily. Just another dagger to my damaged soul. I move back to her side, resting on the edge of the mattress.

"Stay with me, Mom," I whisper, brushing my thumb over the

back of her hand, willing her attention to hold on. For a heartbeat, her eyes shine with fleeting recognition, then soften again as confusion seeps in. She hums under her breath, the same little tune she always hums when she's drifting, and I feel her slipping through my fingers despite I'm holding on. "Who's hat is this?"

"It's Clay's hat," she mumbles. My jaw clenches because she's not wrong. It *is* my hat, and that's the problem. The cheapened fabric and foreign care label are part of a bundle I ordered online from a dodgy website.

"Mom, I need you to think. Who else has been visiting you?" The bright onyx in her eyes has dimmed, yet she smiles the way she always would when reminiscing.

"Do you remember that winter? The boiler broke and you spent all of your paper route money on hats and scarves from the corner stall. Clayton threw a tantrum over the color and you had to swap with him just to convince him to go to school." She smiles fondly, but I don't feel any fondness at the memory. Only dull acceptance that Jeremy always made things okay, and I wish he was here now more than ever. And no, I wouldn't be seen dead in a Garfield orange hat.

"Mom, please. Who came here? Who wore this?"

"You boys know my door is always open," she says and lowers her head into the cushions, humming that same tune. I'm sure it was a toothbrush commercial when I was little, but it makes her smile as her eyes blur out. There's no use pushing her any further. Leaning over, I kiss her forehead and leave with both beanies in hand.

Rolling my neck, wincing at the settling scar forming on my collarbone, I head straight for the front desk with anger licking underneath my skin. I thought I'd left all of this shit behind, the games and the mindfucks. I took it when only I was involved, used to being bullied. People always try to break me into submission, finding I'm a worthy target because I'm immovable. I don't have the emotional range to give a shit. But bringing my mother into this was a mistake. Someone has crossed a line, sending a message loud and clear. They won't let me run away, I need to deal with this head on.

Almost crashing into the desk, I slam my hand on the counter. The receptionist only briefly peers away from her screen, seeming used to agitated family members.

"You need to tell me who has been visiting my mom before I get the police involved," I seethe, voice laced with venom. Rolling her eyes, she sighs as if I'm a menace she wants rid of. I'm not going anywhere without some answers. "I don't have any cousins and since you don't seem to have any CCTV, you'd better start painting me a vivid fucking picture."

"He looks like you, but skinnier." Her lip curls back as clicks aggressively on her computer, insinuating that I'm wasting her time. Reaching over, I rip the cables out of the back.

"You need to try harder than that," I growl. A man in blue scrubs appears from the backroom asking what the problem is but she waves him off, snatching the cable back from my hand.

"It's time you left before I ban you from returning." There's a stare off between the two of us, pure stubbornness clashing in the middle. Grabbing the pen, I write my number beside my name in the visitor's book.

"The next time he comes, you call me," I order. The receptionist opens her mouth, no doubt with some sarcastic retort but I hold up my hand. "Regardless of your opinion, I'm her next of kin. I have full legal capacity. You will call me or there will be an investigation into your lack of security." At her pursed scowl, I toss the pen aside and turn away. If I hang around any longer, I'm likely to end up back in jail before nightfall. Throwing the glass door wide, I stomp back toward my truck when my eyes fall on the person I never wanted to see again. What the fuck is he doing here? Of all the places in the world...unless...

"You," I rasp, my slowed steps ramping back up. From his position leaning against the Audi, Rhys lifts a brow, taking his attention off his cuticles to notice the man running at him full speed. I don't stop, slamming my injured shoulder into his chest and chucking him over the bonnet like a sack of shit. "It's you, isn't it?! You fucker!" Grabbing Rhys from where he ungracefully landed, I lift him by the lapels and pummel my fist into his gut. A figure jumps out of the driver's seat, her pink-tinted hair whipping across her flawless face.

"Clayton, wait!" Harper cries out, her presence adding to my confusion but my fist is already swinging whilst my mind races. They're in this together. Even though they got what they wanted, they're still messing with me. Here, at my mom's nursing home. The fresh gut of betrayal almost buckles my knees but my focus is on breaking Wavershit's nose, blurring the red on my fists with the shade coating my vision.

"You followed me here," I seethe through harsh breaths. "You want to destroy me. You're succeeding." Grappling against my hold, Rhys opens his mouth to spew some bullshit I don't want to hear. I quickly whip the beanie from my back pocket and shove it into his mouth.

"That's enough!" Harper pulls on my bicep uselessly. My fist raises again as a stupid smile curves around the beanie. For fuck's sake, he's loving this. I rear back, shoving Harper off me and head straight to my truck. Harper tries to call for me but I ignore her, slamming my door and peeling away as soon as the engine turns over. A screech fills the parking lot, the smell of burnt rubber trailing me as I fight to get images of Harper and Rhys out of my head.

Apparently they haven't done enough damage. They want to flaunt their relationship in my face, to prove that I'll never escape their taunting. And to bring my mother into this? Bile rises to my throat, the world collapsing around me. I manage to make it back to my drab room before keeling over, the breath wheezing in my chest. I need to be free of them for good.

Surrounded by the quiet, shrouded in the dark, I claw back at recesses of my mind. Reclaiming the traces of logic I hang onto. Next time they inevitably appear, I'll be more prepared. If Wavershit wants a war so much that he brings it to my front yard, I'll happily give it to him, and if Harper is affected in the fall out, then so be it.

CHAPTER EIGHT

"Well, that went... even worse than I thought it would." I roll my eyes, striding toward my Audi as Rhys spits out the last strand of cotton and pops a stick of gum in his mouth like nothing happened. We slide inside, and I throw my head back with a sigh. Rhys casually stretches his arms above his head, as if he isn't sporting yet another split lip and bruised cheek by Clay's hand. I toss him a tissue and start the engine.

"What exactly were you expecting?" Rhys asks through the mic clipped to his collar which is thankfully unscathed. "A hug? The guy thinks you sold him out." His voice is muffled as he wipes his lip clean, but his sarcasm grates me all the same. Spearing him with a side-glance glare, I throw a fist towards his crotch in a downward arc. Rhys easily catches my wrist with a laugh, and then he snags the other too, twisting me at an angle I can't escape. Instead, I snap my teeth at his neck.

"Only because you *let* him think that, you motherfu—" My elbow slams the horn, blaring loud enough to grab the attention of those in reception. A security guard has joined the nurses gathered there, staring out curiously. Drawing a crowd won't help, so I go limp, groaning in frustration until Rhys releases me. I don't comment on his easy grin, or how relaxed he was the entire drive here. Considering the lengths Rhys went to in order to evict Clayton from my life, I figured he'd be more on edge with the prospect of seeing him again. I'd like to think that's down to the security of our relationship growing stronger, but I don't dare ask. I'll ride the wave and see where we end up.

Placing my hands on the wheel, I turn out of the parking lot, following Clay's general direction. I have his address but heading straight there seemed too personal. I now realise this was a terrible plan B. Rhys' hand slides onto my thigh as I drive, his thumb stroking back and forth over my leggings. It's far too comfortable, all things considered, and I won't admit how much I like it.

I shift my focus away from him and back to driving. Aunt Marg once swore I'd never set foot in another car after the accident, let alone get behind the wheel. But freedom has always been the one thing I craved more than proving people wrong. Nothing feels freer than this. The windows down, wind tangling through my hair, pedal pressed to the floor. For a while, it feels like I could just keep going and never stop, but the road always has to end somewhere and the return drive is always hell. Just like life, I suppose. The further you go, the harder it is to turn back.

Rhys's fingers creep higher along my thigh, testing boundaries he already knows too well. He's been doing it since we left Waversea. Twenty-five straight hours of flicking my hair, jabbing my ribs, whispering into my mic just to make me flinch.

Normally, I'd write it off as his usual need to be an attention whore, but he's been in an unshakably good mood ever since he vanished for half a day while I was packing up my dorm. Turns out, he tracked down the kid who handed me that coffee.

I didn't ask what he did, mostly because I don't want to know, but he came back with bruised knuckles and a menacing smile. The kind of smile that says *problem solved*.

Deciding it's too peaceful in the car, Rhys angles his head downwards and pops a gum bubble right by the microphone, causing me to jolt and swerve the car. I backhand his chest with an irritable groan.

"I swear I'm going to kill you before we make it back to the academy. Then I'm going to get a tattoo of your face on the bottom of my foot so I can stomp on you every day for the rest of my life," I seethe despite the humor trickling through. Rhys might be an annoying asshole as the best of times, but I would take this over the mopey recluse he was any day. His laughter rings through my mic, forcing a grin through my pursed lips.

"Firstly, watching you kill me might ironically be the highlight of my life, and secondly, a tattoo of my face can be arranged. I know a guy—"

"Obviously, I was joking. There's no version of this world where you'd be permanently marked on my body," I shake my head, keeping my eyes focused on the road after. Rhys leans over, his hand on my thigh squeezing hard.

"You weren't complaining when my teeth marks were embedded into your ass," I see him toying with his lip ring in my peripheral, knowing all too well of the vivid image that just slammed into my mind. Rhys' head between my legs, my body slick from his shower as he drags his tongue from my clit to my ass before biting hard enough to make me see stars. Heat floods my cheeks and my core clenches. Damn him and his ability to turn me on so easily. All too aware of my reaction, Rhys chuckles and pushes himself back into his own seat. "Come on then. If you wouldn't get any ink for me, what would you get?"

Continuing over the intersection, I tilt my head in thought. Many ideas filter through my mind as I dismiss them as too cliché or generic. I would want something strong, yet soft. Powerful, but with a hint of vulnerability.

"I think I would go for a bat." I half-shrug, ignoring the noise that bursts from his throat. It was somewhere between a choke and a jeer.

"A bat? Like a baseball bat? That's pretty hardcore."

"No, like the animal," I say defensively. Rhys leans forward, his expression doubtful.

"You're serious?" He raises a brow and I nod. "Who the hell chooses a bat as their spirit animal?"

"Deaf girls who wish they could hear from over forty feet away, I suppose." I quickly glance over, just long enough to catch the solemn expression that takes over Rhys' face. He sits back, out of view, to mull it over for a few moments. I let the radio take over, filling the cab with something other than my vulnerability.

"Bats live in huge colonies," Rhys says after a pause that could be considered too long to continue this conversation. "You're not a huge colony kind of girl. More of a select few type."

"Well, aren't you lucky to be sitting here beside me then?" I snort. Keeping to the straight road, I spot a sign for a diner up ahead. One that happens to have a beat-up, orange truck parked alongside the dirt patch it calls a parking lot. Pulling over, I peer through the building's murky windows and spot a grey beanie hat sitting alone in a booth near the back. Unbuckling my belt, I grab my phone and start to exit, until I notice Rhys doing the same.

"Um...maybe you should wait here?" I suggest, my hand curled around the door handle. Rhys' blue eyes flash with disgust, whether at being asked to hang back or at the loss of a round two, I'm not sure. He insisted on being the first one to speak to Clay last time, and that wasn't exactly a successful encounter. Finally conceding, Rhys leans back in his seat with a dramatic huff. His boots slam onto the dash as he pulls out his phone and dismisses me with a lazy flick of his hand.

The corner of my mouth quirks despite the knot in my stomach. Reaching over, I ruffle his hair up and say, "Good boy," before jumping out of the car. I carry the smirk with me all the way to the diner, but it dies the moment I step inside.

The diner is all scuffed linoleum floors and the sharp tang of coffee burned hours ago. The hum of a neon sign outside bleeds through the window, casting the place in tired, red light. Booths stretch along the left wall, leather cracked with age, and a curved wooden bar gleams dully on the right. Behind the bar, a smudged mirror reflects the back of the waitress. Her tight curls shake as she looks up from wiping the bar, a small red beret balanced on top to match the red checkers of her uniform.

Noticing me, she reaches for the notepad and pen in her breast pocket until I hold my hand up, my eyes landing on the one I was looking for. Apparently, the only patron in this whole place. Clay has his back to me as I approach the furthest booth away, the top of his beanie appearing over the leather cushioning.

Before I make myself known, I notice the glass of tap water he's clutching and a soft sigh escapes me. Whether through habit or stubbornness, it seems Rhys' money hasn't impacted Clay's lifestyle. I'd hoped he would have got something out of the situation we've been thrown into.

"Can we talk?" I ask softly, lowering myself into the seat opposite. Clay doesn't move, as if he expected me to follow. All of the fight has escaped him, misery swirling in his black eyes. His arms tense in his muddy green military jacket and a white t-shirt. Blond stubble shadows his jaw, causing my fingers to itch with the desire to reach across and cup his cheek. It's been weeks since we last properly saw each other, and he still won't even look at me.

The waitress appears, her notepad primed in hand, so I slide my phone onto the table with the transmission app live. Ordering two large chocolate shakes and burger combos, a glint of excitement flares in her eyes at the prospect of a paying customer that doesn't simply sit and stare into his water.

"I don't accept charity," Clay murmurs as she moves away, still refusing to look up. His black eyes are trained on the table, his shoulders hunched over his glass. I quirk a brow, leaning my forearms onto the table and finding it's as sticky as it looks.

"Who said they were for you? I'm starving." Finally, a kink breaks through his armor, the quiet snort he makes seeming like the smallest of victories. We sit in a stilted quiet, interrupted by the blender behind the bar that most likely needs replacing. Instead of giving me any sort of acknowledgment, his gaze slides to the window. In particular, to where Rhys appears to have turned up the radio in my car. I can't hear it, but I presume he's not excessively head banging and playing an air guitar just for the fun of it. I'm too late in hiding my smirk, and Clay notices.

"Why are you here?" he asks, those black orbs suddenly latching onto me as if I'm caught in a vice. "Are you back for another round because I'm not gonna lie Harper," he sighs with the weight of the world pressing down on his shoulders and forcing them to curl in further, "I can't take it." The misery is back, all-consuming and hollow. I can practically taste it, and it takes everything in my power to keep my hands tucked into my arms. I've ached alongside this man. His pain is my pain, his grief is embedded with mine.

"Do you honestly think I could hurt you?" I frown, wanting to shout my innocence from the rooftops but willing myself to stay calm. "After everything we shared, you think I could use your past against you?" I lean further forward and implore Clayton to see the truth in my expression. Desperate for him to hear me.

"I was so mad when you left. I couldn't understand how you could twist what we had and turn me into some villain. You didn't even give me the chance to defend myself. You took Rhys' word over mine, as if he didn't have an agenda?!"

"You don't seem to have a problem trusting him. It looks like he got exactly what he wanted." I pause, refusing to be baited. This isn't a pissing contest, this is about Clay knowing the truth. What he does with it is up to him.

"Neither Rhys nor I had anything to do with what happened to your locker. We thought it was just a sick prank, but there have been... recent developments," I clear my throat. "Someone else is targeting all three of us. We-, well I just wanted to make sure you were okay. It's been...difficult not having you around."

The chocolate shakes are placed in front of us and I lean back, biting down on my lower lip. My intention was to make him aware of the threat we're facing, but now that I'm sitting here, I find I just want him to know he's been missed. To see how much I need him back in my life. His kind-hearted, tortured soul resonates with my own. Swiping a hand over his face, Clay crosses his arms and sets his jaw.

"Well, it's too late now. Time has moved on, and I'm sure you won't have much trouble doing that either." Clay cuts another glance to the car and my jaw hardens.

"Don't belittle my feelings. You have no idea what it's been like. How I've missed you every second you've been gone. My days without you don't get easier, they're becoming unbearable. Rhys can fill a room with bravado and distraction, but he doesn't fill the hollow space you left in me."

My voice cracks, betraying me. Clay's gaze locks on mine, searching for something, but after an endless stretch of silence, he looks away. It breaks my heart to see him so guarded, so cautious to let me in. I clear my throat, sighing out all of my frustration and pull my milkshake closer. Neither of us make a move to actually drink them though.

"Look, Rhys has pulled some strings. If you want it, your scholarship has been reinstated following winter break. You don't have to speak to or even look at me ever again, but you deserve to have your chance at a future back." I rest my head against the leather to let Clay process my words, a thousand pleas dying on my tongue. A soft chuckle sounds in my head and for a moment, I thought I'd imagined it. Then, I see Clay's bitter smile.

"You're as bad as him, you know that?" My mouth pops open and my brows knit together. "You think you can play God with my life, moving me around like a chess piece. I'm expected to drop everything I've started to build here because you'd deemed it so."

"Are you not hearing me? We weren't the ones who forced you out. Someone else is playing us like puppets, and the Clayton I know would have wanted to find out who. He would have stuck around and endured the fight."

"That man is gone." Clay stands as our food is delivered, the clang of plates loud against my phone's mic. I wince, shuffling around the waitress to reach for Clay's arm before he can put any more distance between us. However, it's not me who manages to stop him. Rhys blocks the exit, leaning on the doorframe as he flicks a coin into the air and catches it. Peering around Clay's shoulders, I squint to read the words curling around Rhys' lip ring.

"-you feel about me. Someone drugged Harper. Fuck knows what could have happened. You're supposed to be her loyal protector, but all I see now is a pussy who won't seek the revenge he's owed." My breath freezes as I watch the pair stare at each other, their hatred tangible. Another punch up is imminent, even though Rhys' cheek is already bloodshot red from earlier. After a moment, Clay roughly shoves his way through the door and leaves without looking back.

The sting of that rejection cuts deep, leaving me numb as Rhys winds his arm around my shoulders and guides me back to the table. Dropping into Clay's seat, Rhys dives into the food and drinks the shake without a care in the world, whilst I watch the orange truck outside drive away, taking my heart with it.

He's never coming back to Waversea. An ache fills my chest, the dream of easing his pain and bringing the rare smile back to his chiselled face drifting away. Rhys seems to notice my expression mid-bite of his burger, and lowers it with a lopsided grin.

"He'll come around." Rhys wipes his hand on a checkered napkin and reaches over to curl his fingers around mine. Rolling my eyes, I lean my cheek on my other fist.

"I don't know what part of him storming out you saw as positive, but I assure you, he's not going to come around. We might as well leave for my Aunt Marg's now. If there's not too much traffic, we should be there by nightfall tomorrow."

My aunt and every one of her twenty-seven cats will have a heart attack when I walk Rhys through the front door, but we're running out of options. Hanging around here seems like a bust, Rhys is adamant we can't go to his family home, and Waversea is about to close for the holidays. Thankfully, that means the perverted fuck who's harassing us will be taking a two week hiatus and we can stop looking over our shoulders for a short while.

"Do you want him back?" Rhys tilts his head, popping a french fry into his mouth. At my confusion, he rolls his eyes. "The giant brain-dead asshole who just walked out on you, *again*. Do you want him back?" I sense a trap, but nod anyway. "Then I'll get him for you. Leave it to me." My brows raise, a sense of foreboding trickling along my spine. Sensing my caution, Rhys grins wider. "I promise."

I can only imagine Rhys has plans to abduct Clay, a bag over his head and ropes around his body, but the more pressing question is, why? Why would he promise to bring back the person he fought so hard to remove from our atmosphere? And more than that, why is Rhys so relaxed in general, eating his way through the plate of food like we're a regular couple on a regular date?

Since the second we left campus, Rhys has been a different version of himself. As if the shadows have peeled back and the weight has lifted, as if I'm the first person to see who Rhys is without the strain of his father's legacy hanging over him. I try to feign calmness as my heart jackhammers in my chest at the prospect of trusting Rhys to handle this his way.

"Okay," I agree quietly. Rhys' resulting beam is enough to melt away the rest of my reservations, although I can't help but feel sorry for whatever he has in store for Clayton. Let the record state, I did try the gentle approach first. Rhys pushes my plate towards me, encouraging me to eat until we're done.

Grabbing my phone for me, he throws a few hundred-dollar bills on the bar and leads me out of the diner as the waitress collapses in the background. I turn my head to check she's okay, finding her hugging the notes and kicking her legs excitedly like a child. A genuine smile curves my lips, my hand sliding into Rhys' warm one.

Instead of heading for my car as expected, Rhys tugs me around the corner and hoists me against the building. His mouth is on mine before I've barely had the chance to brace my hands on his shoulders. His kiss scorches me from the inside, the press of his lips hot and demanding. He grinds against me, the sound of passing whooping and honking reaching my phone. I pay it no attention, lost to the rhythm Rhys creates as he rolls his hips.

"What's got into you all of a sudden?" I breathe heavily. Tucking my phone into my bra strap, the mic end poking out of my shirt, Rhys's thumb strokes my neck both tenderly and possessively.

"I just hate to see you so sad," he breathes. A different kind of gut-punch hits me, one I didn't know I needed until Rhys offered me his nurturing on a platter. Clawing a hand in his hair, I push my tongue into his mouth, taking more of his offerings. I never thought Rhys would be the person who would make me feel seen. His hands roam my body in powerful strokes, squeezing my thighs and gripping my curves desperately. Only once I'm panting does he pull back, his blue stare filling my vision.

"We're not going back to your Aunt's. I managed to find a decent hotel not too far from here with a casino attached. We can stay there whilst I work on his royal Broodiness." His wicked grin grows, poisoning my own. Not ready for the loss of contact when he places me down, I instinctively reach out to link our fingers together once again. Infectious, that's what he is. The panty-melting smolder I receive in return has a tremor running through my body, my focus wavering when he speaks again.

"Let's go blow all my dad's money!"

RHYS

CHAPTER NINE

Pushing the key card into the lock, I slip into the hotel room on silent feet. The lights are on, highlighting the accents of silver in the bedframe and desk chair. The walls are powdered blue like the spongy carpet, a large mirror over the desk which I stop to check myself out in. Behind a closed door in my reflection, the shower thunders, steam billowing out as Harper hums to herself. *Perfect.*

I'd left her here with the direct order to relax and pamper herself, before heading back to the mall I saw down the road. The stores were limited but once I flashed my father's gold card, the staff were more than accommodating.

Tossing down a handful of designer bags on the desk, I rifle through the clothes I can't wait to see Harper in. Although *clothes* might be a stretch for the strappy pieces of fabric that cost more than most people's monthly wages. I nudge them all aside for now, grabbing a navy bra and thong set to place artfully on the bed. In the center of the bra cups, a satin bow is held in place by a sparkling jewel. Her receivers are on the bedside table, so I pocket those before moving toward the balcony.

A floor-to-ceiling curtain separates the room from the sliding glass doors that lead outside, the fabric heavy enough to hide behind. I slip behind, tucking myself into the narrow gap where the curtain meets the glass. The sliding door to the balcony is cracked open, letting in a faint breeze that shifts the curtain every so often. Pulling out my phone, I type out a message to the bastard I once vowed never to speak to again.

> Me: Tick tock. Time is running out.

The reply bubbles appear and disappear a few times, his hesitation bringing a bigger smile to my face. I'm practically giddy as I hear the shower water shut off. Slowly, I ease the sliding door open a little wider behind me and slip out onto the balcony. My phone buzzes in my hand.

> Shitface: You're bluffing.

> Me: Let's test that theory, shall we?

Hitting the video call button, I balance my phone on the small hanging plant just outside the open door, its camera angled toward the view so he can see the hotel's name glowing on the building across the street. Despite himself, Clayton accepts the video call, his background confirming he's here. I chuckle under my breath, throwing up both middle fingers toward the screen. He can pretend he doesn't care, but we both knew he would show. He can't resist his own damn morals.

A shadow crosses the other side of the curtain as Harper makes an appreciative sound at my choice of underwear. I step closer to the fabric, my pulse kicking up. *Showtime.* Excitement courses through me, a snigger threatening to escape my throat. Not that Harper would hear it, but I bite back the noise regardless. I haven't felt this alive in...well, possibly ever. I've made my girl a promise, and I'm about to cash in. She's going to be so wet for me after this.

I slide a sliver of the heavy fabric aside just enough to watch her dress like a creep. The delicate curve of her spine as she pulls on the thong, the clasp of the bra, the way her damp hair has already started to curl at the ends. She's the most beautiful thing I've ever seen. Harper shifts, hunting for her receivers and starting to turn as I shift back onto the balcony. The curtain billows perfectly, luring her in, baiting her curiosity.

The second she steps close enough, I strike, pulling her through the curtain and twisting her by the hips. Her scream pierces my skull, but it's nothing compared to the sound she makes as I lift her waist and back her up to the railing. An evil grin has grown across my face, my soul soothed by the control powering its way through my core. Placing her on the edge, I bathe in the moment as she tries to claw my eyes out. She thrashes, her fear painting her eyes bright and wild. Beautiful. Exactly how I pictured it. I cage her in and lean close, letting my lips scrape her cheek.

"Rhys! Put me down! What are you - let go of me!" She writhes frantically. Every muscle in my body is alive with the kind of anticipation that makes my teeth ache. I humor her, despite her not being about to hear me.

"It's okay, Babygirl. Your golden retriever hero will save you." Planting a kiss against her temple, I shove her backwards. Her screech tears the night in two as I lurch over the railing to watch it all unfold. The fall is exhilarating, my heart barely contained in my chest. This high is better than any drug.

Just before Harper hits the pool below, a silhouette dives forward from the ledge and catches her. It's poetic really. They crash into the water, the splash drenching the sides of the pool. Scooped up in the safety of Clayton's arms, Harper bobs to the surface, cursing my name into the sky. Laughter rushes through me, my hands shaking with adrenaline. I knew she'd be wet for me.

Returning to the bags, I dig out my celebratory cigar and lighter. The air is fresh tonight, the sky clear enough for the moon to shine proudly. Settling in a wicker chair on the balcony, I puff thick circles of smoke into existence and praise myself for a job well done. I knew Clayton wouldn't be able to stop himself from being her savior. It's as engraved in his bones as tormenting is in mine. Leopards can't change their spots, no matter how far they try to run away from them.

The door behind me slams open, an employee asking Harper if she's sure they don't need the cops called. Considering she can't hear, Clayton responds with a gruff no, vowing to kill me himself. Bring it on. Two sets of footsteps stomp through the hotel room, a very soggy Harper appearing to slap the cigar from my hand.

"What were you thinking?! I could have died!" she screams, snatching the offered towel from Clayton. I get a good look at her in the lingerie set first, wondering what Clay's scowl is about. I literally packaged her up with a bow and threw her into his arms. It doesn't get more romantic than that.

Digging her receivers out of my pocket, I hand them over, despite the intensified rage that contorts her features. Once she's clicked them in place, I stand and retrieve my phone from the hanging plant pot.

"I knew the pool was there, obviously. I had every faith you would be fine."

"Every faith? Every. Fucking. Faith?!" Harper flies into a rant, cursing me in ways I've never heard, as she storms back into the bedroom. I follow, leaning against the door, appreciating once again how beautiful she is. Especially when she's mad. Her lip peels back in a snarl, her hand fisted around a brush while she takes her fury out on her hair. Even the red flush that's covering her heaving chest. Fucking exquisite.

Clay stands around, glaring a hole into the side of my head. I pointedly ignore him and his assumptions of what I'm thinking. I texted him two hours ago and told him I was going to throw Harper over, and no one can say I'm not a man of my word. As if I would actually put Harper's life in danger. She's too precious to me. The only thing that's worth preserving in my life, and if that means throwing her into another man's arms, if that's what will make her happy, then so be it.

After a beat of watching Harper attempt to make herself go bald, Clayton groans and walks over to grab her wrist in midair. He wheels her around, planting the two of them in a desk chair and pries the hairbrush from her grip. Her ass is pressed against his dick, her arms crossed like a tantruming child as he brushes the tangles from her pink hair and then reaches for the hair dryer. I laugh and roll my eyes, heading for the shower myself.

"Play nice you two, and stop dripping all over the carpet. There are clothes in those bags for everyone and dinner is booked for eight." Closing the door between us, I lean over the basin and give myself a high five in the mirror. Plan 'get Clayton back in Harper's life' was a huge success, and the feisty, angry sex I'll get later will be an added bonus. Ahh, who am I kidding? It was my entire incentive.

Two neat stacks of casino chips slide across the polished counter toward me. I wink at the tanned dealer, then pull the chips toward Harper, wrapping my arm around her waist when she tries to back off. With my free hand, I flick open her clutch and hold it up with my intentions clear. She can have every other night, tonight I'm in charge. She drops the chips inside, her lips pressed in that little line that makes me want to ruin her lipstick just to see it smudged.

"Where first?" I murmur into the mic clipped to my mauve shirt. The fabric clings tight across my chest, my jeans pressed and dark, my loafers shining under the casino lights. The ink of my tattoos gleam from the oil I rubbed into them, my cologne sharp in my nose. I've turned myself into walking temptation, and fuck, it's even working on me.

Harper also looks like a prize worth stealing. Gold dress hugging her body, mesh sleeves sparkling as the lights dance off them, ponytail bouncing with every step. The back dips low, bare skin daring my hands to stray lower, and her legs look like they go on forever in those heels. The dress stops short of revealing her ass, and every inch concealed beneath belongs to my imagination.

The casino drinks her in like I do. Heads turn as we pass, men openly staring, women whispering, and I'm content to let them look. She's on my arm, not theirs. Clayton trails behind us, a shadow moving just far enough back to look like he's minding his own business, but I know he's watching. He won't let me and Harper out of sight, as if I'm going to chuck her in the nearest trash can or down the nearest stairwell.

Harper steers us to the roulette table, the crowd parting for us automatically. It's commonplace when you're filthy rich. People can sense the unentitled privilege like they can smell it on my extortionately priced cologne.

"Place your bets," the croupier calls. He's a burly man, in his forties maybe, with flecks of fiery red showing beneath his silver-streaked hair. When Harper doesn't make a move, I take a handful of chips from her clutch bag and hand them over to be exchanged for roulette chips. Harper's eyes widen, a small intake passing through her parted lips.

"Rhys," she breathes my name, looking at the black and silver striped chips in her hand. "That's seven-thousand dollars." I nod, deciding not to remind her how much she has resting at her hip if this is freaking her out. Closing her hand in mine, I hold the focus of her sea-green eyes while guiding her to release them randomly over the table's grid. Our blind guess has landed us on red eighteen, the croupier spinning the wheel before waving his hands to signal no more bets.

There are loads of chips on the table, many smaller amounts spread across multiple numbers around our tall stack near the centre. The crowd starts to buzz excitedly as the ball bounces across the wheel, slowing to drop into black thirty-one. A man at the other end who needs to lay off fast food hollers, his dismal pile of chips being doubled. Aware that lightning doesn't strike in the same place twice, I urge Harper to cash in some more chips and place on black thirty-one.

Her confused expression flicks to me, but she complies, grinding her ass against me deliciously as she reaches over the table. I slide my thumb under her hem, dragging it against the heat between her thighs. She gasps and shoves my hand away, but not before Clayton notices and gruffs harshly. The wheel is spun again, red seven taking the win and I blow out a low chuckle.

"You're trying to lose, aren't you?" Harper turns her head to me, her back to my front and my hand splayed across her hip.

"Am I though? If my father is losing, technically I'm winning." The grin that splits across my face aces with its smugness. Turning fully, Harper raises her eyebrow and my cock twitches with her sassiness.

"You could donate the money to charity, you know. There's so many kids that could use—"

"Ugh," I groan loudly, gaining the attention of those around us. "Why'd you have to spoil my fun like that?" Cock well and truly sunk, I take Harper's hand and lead her back towards the bar.

I don't care when others disapprove of my lifestyle choices, but something about Harper doing it makes me crave for a strong drink. Like the casino, the bar's surface is polished and black. Bottles ranging from fermented piss to high society champagne and everything in between line the shelves behind several bartenders, all dressed in fully black uniforms. A guy about our age is the only one who steps forward to serve me.

"Single-barrel Jack Daniels on the rocks and a strawberry rosé spritzer," I demand with a rough edge to my voice. Harper's hand trails the length of my back and eases the tension from between my shoulders.

"Make that two whiskies," she adds before the waiter leaves, pointing to Clayton who has taken a seat further down the bar. For now at least, Harper remains at my side, concern in her gaze. I soften, kissing her shoulder and inhaling the floral scent of the hotel's shampoo in her hair.

"What's wrong?" she asks as our drinks are placed before us. I down mine, immediately clicking my fingers for another.

"Nothing," I murmur weakly. There's no point trying to hide it when she can see through me, but I try anyway. Flicking her clutch open, I pull out one of the ten-thousand-dollar chips hidden in there and hand it to the bartender as he returns with my second drink. His face pales amongst the mess of brown curls framing it, stuttering his appreciation and something about paying off tuition as I turn to face Harper.

"Keep the rest of those," I jerk my chin at the still open bag. "Cash them in and donate to whoever you want."

"Rhys, I didn't mean to spoil your fun." She pouts, thawing out any parts of me that were disappointed. Chuckling softly, I pull her into the stool beside me and tug it so close, she's practically on my lap.

"It's fine. You're right, as per usual." The bar top gleams under the soft amber lights, Harper's hand resting on the polished wood next to mine. A few stools down, Clayton watches us over the rim of his glass. He's like a sentry, waiting for the moment the switch flips in my head and I lash out. Tracing the hair trailing over Harper's shoulder, I have an intense urge to sink my teeth into her neck and drink her blood, just to see what he'd do. Following my eyeline, Harper peers over to our not-so-welcome guest and tilts her head.

"Hey Rhys," she leans into me, her scent washing through my senses. "Are there any private rooms around here?" My lip ring tugs as I smirk, my brow raised and eager. Now we're talking.

"What are you thinking?" I nudge her jaw with my nose, gaining me access to the patch behind her ear. My lips press over the implant hidden beneath her skin and she shudders against me.

"Perhaps we could gamble with something other than chips." Harper's lashes lower, her mouth curving. Heat floods my system, making a beeline for my cock. Harper knows how to reduce me to nothing but a horny dog and I have my bone ready for her.

"You mean...we could bet with our clothes?" I wriggle my brows, seconds away from panting. Harper's laugh cuts through the bar, her palm pushing against my shoulder to put some space between us.

"No, you idiot. We can bet with our secrets." Harper smiles sweetly and my head slams forward on the bar. I'm certain this girl hates me.

HARPER

CHAPTER TEN

"This is a stupid idea," Rhys grumbles, even though he's gone to the trouble of hiring out a private room. I disagree, this is a brilliant idea. Better than throwing me over the balcony by far. Air out our bullshit, see if there's anything worth saving underneath.

As annoyed and shaken as I am for the stunt earlier this evening, there is something magnetic about the way Rhys moves like he owns every building he steps into. The cut of his suit, the confidence in his strides. His palm finds my lower back without thinking, keeping me close by at all times. That might have something to do with Clayton following close behind, his presence on high alert. Even without peering back, I can sense the rigidness to his spine in the shirt and jacket Rhys gifted him. All of this is playing havoc with the rub of my thighs beneath the tiny dress.

My heels click against the polished marble, cutting through the electronic buzz of slot machines and the low hum of chatter filtering through Rhys' mic. The pink liquid in my cocktail glass ripples as I carry it towards a closed door on the far side. A bald security guard stands beside it, his hands crossed in front of him, a black coil leading to his earpiece. Rhys hands him his ID, confirming the name that gains him access to these luxuries, and the three of us are escorted inside.

Once inside, the noise cuts off as if someone hit a mute button. The room is dim and cool, lit by strips of LED lights tracing the ceiling. A green felt table sits at the center, the surface pristine and waiting. A vent hums quietly overhead, directly above a pack of cigarettes, a lighter, and a bottle of whiskey set neatly in front of the first chair. Apparently, Rhys made specific requests when briefly meeting with the casino's owner, whilst I shimmied closer to Clayton at the bar and convinced him to humor me. For tonight at least.

Next to it, a chilled bottle of rosé sweats in an ice bucket, condensation dripping down the glass. By the last seat, a small army of beer bottles waits for Clayton. It seems none of us are getting through a night in each other's company without being shitfaced. In the middle of the table, a fresh deck of cards.

"Classy," I murmur, sliding into my chair. The leather creaks softly under me. I cross my legs and take a slow sip of my drink, letting my eyes travel between the two of them. Rhys leans back in his seat, fingers drumming once against the whiskey bottle before pouring himself a heavy shot. Meanwhile, Clayton stays standing for a beat longer, eyes sweeping the corners of the room before he finally sits. Tension hangs heavy over us all, the chill in the air raising goosebumps all over my arms. Okay, this might not have been the brilliant idea I thought.

"So how's this going to work?" Clay asks, his voice laced with that familiar edge of suspicion. It's the most he's said in hours. Back in the hotel room, after he'd brushed my hair free of tangles and pushed me from his lap, he'd muttered, "What the fuck am I doing here, Harper?" And I didn't have an answer for him. Hopefully I can conjure up the answers now.

"Blackjack," I say, reaching for the newly sealed deck. Unwrapping the plastic, I shuffle the way I would whilst trying to fill the time in my aunt's attic. "The dealer acts as the house. The winner of each round takes a drink whilst the loser must reveal a truth. Something you want the rest of us to hear."

"I can't believe we've come all this way for you to trick me into a therapy circle." Rhys tips his head back with a groan. I smile sweetly, despite not being overly confident on how this little experiment will go, and deal out the first round of cards.

Clayton studies his hand, his expression a perfectly stoic mask. Rhys downs his shot and flips his first card with a snap of his wrist, a smirk already forming. I look between them, shivering beneath the weight of tension colliding against my sides and I flip the house cards. Clay sticks straight away, whilst Rhys cockily smacks his hand on the table asking for another card, then another. I raise my brow, sliding it over, anticipating the moment he growls and throws his cards across the green felt.

"Twenty-one my ass."

Beneath his breath, Clay chuckles, sipping on his victory beer. I lean on my elbow, facing Rhys' direction, resting my chin on my hand.

"Truth time."

He glares at me for a long moment, jaw ticking, before tossing back another shot of his whiskey anyway. "Fine. I—" He breaks off, glances at Clayton, then back at me. "I binged Pretty Little Liars one summer, and now I have a crush on Lucy Hale. I watch everything she's in."

Blinking slowly, I try to withhold the grin that tries to break through. It's not exactly the kind of truth I had in mind but it's a start. Rolling my eyes, I pass the deck over, declaring it as Rhys' turn to deal. Using incredibly skilled fingers, he splits the deck multiple times and reshuffles multiple times, showing he's done this before.

Steady breathing vibrates softly through the microphone on Rhys' shirt, reminding me that I can only hear one side of the conversation. Not that Clayton has much to say, but I switch over to my phone's Bluetooth and place it in the center of the table instead. I keep throwing him side glances, wanting to say so many things but settling for the fact he's here and staying. I can't believe Rhys' plan to get him here worked, and that's the only reason I haven't scratched his eyes out.

Two cards are dealt in front of us, and a sneak peek reveals that I'm happy to stick. However, Clay's jaw tics fiercely.

"Hit," he grinds out. Rhys leans back in his chair, swirling his whiskey around the glass.

"Change of rules. You've got to pay with a truth if you want another card."

"I hate your fucking guts. How's that for the truth?" Clay bites back instantly. Laughing loudly, like a crack slicing through the air, Rhys slides a card across the table before revealing the cards laid out before him. His face splits into a wide grin, his posture far too comfortable for someone who will be back in the game next round.

"House wins. What else you got to tell me, Scum?" Rhys chuckles, collecting the cards back in. I sink into my seat, taking my glass of rosé with me. The fruity taste is a good anchor whilst my mind is screaming, *mission abort.*

"Just before I left campus, I received a certain gif on my phone," Clay says with a hidden smile. My stomach drops. "I replay it every night before bed to help me sleep." Rhys shoots to his feet and I react, grabbing whatever I can reach to get him to stand down. Evidently, it's his waistband, as he allows me to tug him back into his seat.

Clay's lip curls, but he doesn't rise to the challenge in Rhys' glare. That's the thing with him. His anger doesn't explode, it simmers beneath the surface. Sometimes, his silence is louder than Rhys' shouting, and it sets my nerves on edge.

"Clay, it's your turn to deal," I announce, pushing the deck of cards his way. Twirling the stem of my glass between my fingers, I try to remain an impartial barrier between them, until Rhys drags my chair closer and places his hands on me. Over my bare thigh, across my back, around my nape. He possesses everywhere he touches, hitting Clayton in a place that fists can't reach. I bat Rhys off and scoot my chair back, reaching for the bottle. It's going to be a long night.

Two cards land in front of me. A decent hand, but not brilliant. I sip my rosé like a continuous stream, weighing whether to risk another hit, while Rhys leans back in his chair, his arms spread like a king daring someone to unseat him. I narrow my eyes.

"Hit me," I say quietly. Clay pauses, the faintest flicker of disapproval in his eyes before he slides a card toward me. *Bust.* I groan, letting my head drop into my palm.

"Truth," Rhys drawls, smug as sin. I peek at him through my fingers. His grin is lazy yet curious, waiting to see what I'll give. My pulse skitters but I force myself upright, refusing to let him see nerves.

"When I was sixteen, I thought about running away with someone I barely knew. The mechanic's son. Packed a bag, had a bus ticket and everything. Aunt Marg stopped me at the door and smacked me with a hand towel all the way back to my room." Rhys' grin falters for half a second, then he shoots a look at Clay and snorts.

"So you've always had shit judgment." I huff, and slap his bicep.

"Evidently. I'm sitting here next to you." Clay's eyes flick between us, unsure about the dynamic Rhys and I have fallen into. His jaw flexes, but he says nothing as he passes the deck over to me.

This round goes quicker. Rhys busts almost immediately, tossing his cards across the felt with a curse. "I hate the frat house being empty," he states without needing to be forced. He takes a long pull of whiskey and sets the empty glass down with a soft thunk, whilst a small smile grows on my face. Now we're getting somewhere.

Alcohol warms my limbs, my body easing into a relaxed state which is unaffected by the tension in the room. Perhaps the tension has washed away entirely, along with the sensations in my fingers. The cards slip and tumble across the table, an unladylike snort escaping me. It's even worse to hear it reflected back through my phone's mic, like something that belongs in a farmyard. Rhys comes to my rescue, collecting and taking ownership of them. I'm not even playing anymore, simply watching cards being passed back and forth, truths coming out much easier now.

"I hate that you joined the basketball team," Clay glares at Rhys over my head, trapping me between them. I hiccup and slide further down until my head leans against the chair. "You couldn't let me have one thing, one outlet without you stepping in to ruin it. And for that alone, I'm going to beat you beyond repair one day. I'm going to break all of your bones and bruise your flesh so bad, not even your tattoos will be recognizable."

Woah, some of us are angry drunks. My eyes widen, not sure of where to look. But when my eyes do stray to Rhys's face, I find him biting his lip ring and rubbing his dick through his jeans.

"Keep going, Big Boy. All this fighting-talk is making me super hard." That snort comes from me again and I cover my mouth with my hand. I really need to stop doing that. The game is forgotten at this point, both Rhys and I too far gone to care while Clay remains sitting ramrod straight. I sigh, wondering what it would take to remove the burdens he carries. To help cut him loose, even if just for a little while. Reaching out a hand, I place it on Clay's forearm to offer up a truth for free.

"I've missed you," I admit in barely more than a whisper. He doesn't respond, but something flickers in his pitch black eyes. A flash of light so brief, I might be able to convince myself I made it up. It's a pretty little dream though, to think my Clay is still in there somewhere. If he was ever mine to start with.

Rhys takes a coin from his pocket, gaining both of our attention to watch him flip it high in the air. He reckons he can flip a heads every time, some party trick apparently. I smile lazily, wrapped in the warm, clumsy blanket of inebriation. The coin spirals through the air, taking my gaze on a journey I can't quite keep up with. Each time Rhys flicks it high, his catch becomes less effective until I'm sure he's seeing double. I know I am.

"You're both so...stupid," I murmur to myself. The conversation I intended to have out loud continues in my head. A string of moans about all of the energy they waste on hating each other when they could aim it literally anywhere else. Like starting a magic act with Rhys' impressive coin trick. Several scenarios pass over my glazed eyes, most with Rhys in a smart jacket and wand, Clay dressed as a white rabbit complete with tall, fluffy ears. Laughter is bubbling from me in a constant stream as the door opens at our backs.

"Master Waversea. You have a phone call," the security guard raises a cell phone in our direction. "It's your father. Your tab has been cut off for the night." Rhys' eyes blow wide, the pin being pulled from his grenade. I stand too quickly, a rush of dizziness threatening to take my heels out from beneath me, but I manage to place a hand on Rhys' heaving chest before he lifts the phone to his ear.

"Don't lose your temper. Just listen to what he has to say, and we can continue this back in your room." I force a weak smile, lifting my rosé bottle. It might not have been a perfect night, but this is the first time Rhys and Clay have willingly been in a room together. I want it to last just a little longer. Except Rhys can't resist showing off when he has the upper hand.

"Our room," Rhys grabs my ass and hauls me into him, his cocky glare antagonizing Clayton. A sweep of cold air hits my back as Clay exits, the reprieve we'd found thoroughly broken. I rush after him, shoving the bottle into the security guard's hand as I pass.

I'm by no means graceful as I follow Clay's large frame through the casino, oblivious to the shrill of slot machines and amused patrons around me. My phone is back on the poker table, overhearing trickles of Rhys' conversation with his father. The disjointed sound is jarring against my surroundings, closely pressed bodies trying to prevent me from passing. I'm not as wide and forceful as Clayton, carving a path through the lobby.

Pushing against a robust gold handle, I step out into the night, a crescent moon hanging overhead in the midnight sky. Clay pauses when he notices I've burst into the street, my dress doing little to bar me from the icy chill. I shiver, longing to step into Clay's arms. Aching to earn his trust back so he doesn't feel like a stranger once again. Jerking his chin to indicate I should go back inside, Clay begins to walk away, and I storm after him.

"That's it?!" I call, unaware of how loud I'm speaking. "After all of the ground we've covered tonight, you're going to walk away?" He turns slowly, his features falling into shadow. The unevenness of his blond waves are unnatural to me, peeling away from the gel he tried to smooth it down with. Clay visually searches for my phone or a mini microphone, and when he comes up empty, he pulls his own from his pocket.

'What do you want from me?' Clay types on his notes and turns the screen to face me. I wince at the sudden bright light, my head starting to throb. I step closer, lowering his phone from view. My heels put me at a six-inch advantage, but Clay still towers over me.

"I'm trying to be patient, Clay. I know you've been hurt, but I had no part in it. I just want...I want..." Clay's head tilts, his face illuminated from the casino's light leaking through the glass door.

"*What?*" he mouths.

"You." Closing the rest of the gap, I press my body against his. Bolstered by too much rosé and too little food, my mouth lands on his. He tries to resist, to step away on instinct, but I won't let him. We're too far adrift for words to pull us back to shore. He needs to taste my apology, to feel my need for him to stay close. The savior I never asked for, but can no longer be without. Finally, after an eternity of awkwardness, Clay's lips respond to mine.

My hands fist his shirt, our mouths uniting in a heated struggle to portray emotion. Unlike the raw power Rhys' kisses provide, Clay's lips are soft and tender. He doesn't rush, he savors. He doesn't fight for control, but willingly lets me have it. I slip my tongue into his mouth, urging his to dance with mine. Butterflies fill my stomach as his large hands take residence on my nape and lower back. His muscles squeeze around me like a cocoon of safety.

My fuzzy mind runs away with me, tapdancing on cloud nine somewhere in the distance, but words echo within my damaged ears. *This feels like home. This is home. Safe, reliable home.*

All too soon, Clayton pulls away, although not far enough to release me. I rest my head against his shoulder, breathing in the woodsy scent I had begun to forget, despite how hard I tried to cling onto it. His stubble scratches my temple as we stand rooted in place, as if the moment we break apart, everything will be shattered again.

"Please come back to Waversea." I beg, winding my arms around his waist, talking into his chest. "Not for me. Do it for yourself. You started something, you have to see it through. Jeremy wanted this for you." I know the moment I've gone too far when Clay's chest tenses, his arms going stiff. Dammit. Clamping my lips shut, we remain still for at least another full minute, not ready to let go. At least, I know I'm not. As soon as I step away, I have the distinct feeling I may never see Clay again. There's only so many times I can lose him, lose the hope of what we could have been.

His hand trails the length of my sleeve, running a smooth path to my wrist. This is it. This is where he pries me away and leaves me standing in the street. I want to be strong enough to accept the inevitable, to hold my head high and say, 'his loss'. But instead, I cling tighter to his body. Gently curling his hand around jaw, Clay forces me to look upwards, his mouth right in front of my eyes.

"I'll think about it."

CLAYTON

CHAPTER ELEVEN

I left Harper at the casino door, telling her to go inside while I made the long walk back to my place. The night air was bitter, slicing through my shirt and straight to my bones, but I welcomed it. The cold let me think, let me scrape some clarity out of the mess in my head.

But whatever conclusion I came to, whatever optimism I convinced myself I felt, vanished the moment I approached my studio door. Two policemen were waiting to escort me down to the station, where I was held until now. Turns out Dr. Hollister had been running a state-of-the-art CCTV system with integrated audio recording. Brilliant on his part, catastrophic for me. They had me on video, laying out the plan, stabbing myself with the scalpel, so I confessed to the whole thing.

Two days later and I'm reusing the smart gray trousers and shirt Rhys bought, sighing with the weight of stress I almost escaped. The courthouse waiting room smells of stale coffee and old carpet cleaner, its retro pattern swirling beneath my shoes. Rows of wooden chairs line the walls, their armrests too narrow for someone my size. The scar under my shirt itches like hell, but I don't scratch. I let it fester, since it's the reason I'm sitting here in the first place.

I check my phone for the millionth time since the casino, both glad and annoyed I haven't heard from Harper. She's giving me space, but all that does is give me time to overthink. To wonder what the pair of them are doing, where they're going, if they've even left the hotel room at all.

When I was a kid, jealousy meant hiding in the school bathroom after Christmas break so I wouldn't have to see the other kids' new gadgets and sneakers. It meant watching people stroll by with shopping bags I couldn't afford, salivating over their lives from a distance. Eventually I learned, if you look hard enough, there's always someone worse off. Someone who'd probably envy me for the family I had and the scraps of love I was given.

This jealousy is different. The image of Wavershit's hands on Harper's skin, the thought of his mouth on her. It eats me alive. I keep my hands clamped in my lap, resisting the urge to fidget. My hair falls into my face, shielding me from the fluorescent lights, the posters about rehabilitation, and the low murmur of felons and thugs scattered across the room. Not that I'm any better, I'm a convicted criminal too.

"Mr. Michaels?" the receptionist calls.

I stand, keeping my spine rigid as I cross the hall to the door her bony finger points to. My heart is hammering, but my face is a mask of calm. I promised myself I'd never set foot in a courthouse again. At least my mother isn't sitting in the back row whilst her heart is breaking this time.

The district courthouse is smaller than I expected, empty wooden benches spanning either side of the dreaded walkway. I step through the gate in the center and take my seat at the left desk, utterly alone. I was offered a state attorney but I have no defense. I'm guilty, as my future is once again in the hands of the judge at the front of the room. A man with thinning black hair, a wide nose under thin glasses, and a black robe draped over his shoulders, holding my file.

To my right sits Dr. Hollister, his own attorney at his side. Neither of them look my way, their faces resolute as they listen to what the judge has to say.

"You're an extremely lucky young man, Mr. Michaels," he announces. I almost laugh out loud. I don't think of myself as lucky in any sense of the word, but I keep my hands folded in front of me and my expression neutral. "Against the advice of his counsel, Dr. Hollister has taken into consideration a new piece of evidence which was presented to us this morning. Your state scholarship to Waversea Academy has been reinstated, and as such, the plaintiff decided to drop the charges against you."

For a second, the air locks in my lungs. My head whips toward Hollister and his lawyer, but neither spares me a glance. I'd been prepared to take the jail time they were sure to give me, finding the small blessings in a place to stay and meals provided. I'm bigger now, more capable of holding my own in the prison yard.

"However," the judge continues, "there is the cost of the medication taken and the damage to the building's exterior to be considered. Since your accomplice could not be found, who by your own admission is a minor, we think it's only fair you cover Dr. Hollister's losses."

I nod, relief loosening a knot I hadn't realized was sitting in my chest. At least the kid got away, and maybe his mom can breathe easier for a while. Still, the guilt lingers. For the second time, Hollister has shown me kindness unlike I've ever known. A stranger who has offered me a future, even after I deceived him.

With a flourish of his pen, the judge signs the paperwork and hands it to a security guard, who promptly ushers me out so the next case can begin. I hear murmurs behind me as I leave, but I keep walking, a fire under my ass to not hang around long enough for anyone to change their minds. The receptionist at the front desk holds me up whilst she prepares the paperwork, outlining what has been decided here today and the fine I must pay. Shifting my weight from foot to foot, I notice Dr. Hollister by the door, shaking hands with his lawyer and pulling on his coat. I tell myself to keep away, but my feet ignore me.

"Dr Hollister," I say quietly, my head dipped. Pausing with his fingers over his coat button, he turns slowly, agreeing to hear what I have to say. "For what it's worth, I am sorry I let you down." Noting the sincerity in my gaze, the doc nods, finishing the buttoning with the deft fingers of a medical professional.

"I grew up in a similar neighborhood to you, and I know all too well the desire to help everyone. But you simply can't. There will always be suffering and heartache. We can only do so much before it consumes us, and we deserve to live too. It's not selfish, it's necessary," he pauses, his expression softening. "You're not a bad person, Clayton. Get your education, gain some life experience, and one day you'll be in a position to help others."

The next inhale I take comes a little easier. The doc's tone is even, lacking all traces of the disdain I'm owed. It's been a long time since I've had someone I can look up to, an example of what a decent man looks like. He may not know it, but Dr Hollister just became that example for me. Pulling his collar higher, he braces himself for the wind howling against the doors.

"Come pay me a visit sometime. I want to see the man you become." Pushing the door open, he disappears as the ache in my chest eases. My name is called, the paperwork ready, and I'm soon slipping outside too, tugging a beanie over my hair. It's out of place with the rest of my outfit but I instantly feel better, like a piece of home comfort is with me.

Heading for my truck, the cold air is biting but no longer cutting quite as deep. Somehow, I've walked out of here without cuffs or community service. I'm starting to think my luck has turned around, until I see the tattooed cocky bastard leaning against my driver side door. His smile grows wide, as if he's greeting an old pal.

"Well, did it work?!" he holds out his arms, the brand new parka jacket on his torso stretching wide. I slam the papers into his chest, moving past to unlock my trunk.

"Let me guess, you submitted the new evidence?" Peering over my shoulder, Rhys chuckles, reading the conditions of my release.

"Six thousand dollars," he whistles, invested in the papers as if they're the evening news. Ignoring him, I hop into the driver's seat and almost flinch when Rhys pops the passenger door and climbs in. "I've got to say, I'm impressed, Scum. Robbery and property damage. I didn't know you had it in you."

"I don't. I helped a kid steal meds for his dying mom," I grumble, turning over the engine. Rhys goes still, his hands dropping into his lap. Thankfully, for one merciless moment, the stupid smile is wiped clean off his face.

"Why do you have to suck the fun out of everything? The next time I have to bail you out, there had better be at least one guy on a ventilator because you bashed his head in with a pipe." He folds the paper and shoves it into his parka pocket, seemingly resolving the next dilemma I needed to face. How to pay the fine. I don't argue, I just drive since Rhys seems intent on tagging along.

"There won't be a next time," I grit through my teeth. His laughter is low but I hear it over the roar of my exhaust, the billowing black smoke trailing behind suggesting I've got other problems to fix. Clenching my jaw, I focus on my hatred for the asshole daring to reach forward and mess about with my radio stations. This is the last time I'll accept his money. Being indebted to Wavershit is a prison sentence in its own right.

Pulling up outside the apartment building, I head inside, stopping short when a pair of footsteps follow. Rhys crashes into my back and I whirl around to glare at him.

"What are you doing? Where is Harper?" He shrugs like the question barely grazes him.

"She's fine. Her time of the month arrived so I left her in the hotel room to mope around." I grind my teeth.

"You didn't think to stay and comfort her?"

"What do I look like, her gay best friend? She's got a wide screen TV and room service, I assure you she's quite happy tucked up in bed watching sappy movies." To prove his point, Rhys brings up some camera footage on his phone of Harper beneath the covers, a wooden tray of several desserts poised over her lap. I don't get the chance to ask why the fuck he's keeping surveillance on her, because he barges past and takes the stairs two at a time. I suppose at least we know she is safe, even if it is creepy as hell.

"Besides," Rhys calls back. "I'm here under her strict orders anyway." That has me groaning. Since when did Rhys follow orders, and what exactly has Harper put him up to? Climbing the staircase, I shoulder past him, the smell of damp and burnt toast following me to the third floor. My key jams in the lock, like even the door knows I shouldn't be here anymore.

Inside, the studio looks worse than I remember. Or maybe it's just me seeing it clearly for the first time. The cracked linoleum, the wire bedframe shoved against the wall, the half-eaten takeout containers lined up like trophies of failure. The radiator clicks once and dies, leaving the air stale and cold.

"Wow," Rhys says from the doorway, his tone dripping with disgust. "This place screams *serial killer starter pack.*"

"Leave me alone," I reply flatly, crossing to the corner where my duffel sits. I start throwing clothes inside. Hoodies, shirts, the few pairs of jeans that don't have holes in them. There's no system to it. Just the need to get my stuff packed before someone from the court decides to do it for me.

Rhys doesn't step inside, but he doesn't leave either. He lingers in the doorway like a bad smell, his designer jeans and expensive jacket looking almost obscene against the backdrop of mold-stained walls and the faint scratch of rats inside them. His hair is styled in that *I-woke-up-like-this* way that takes at least an hour, and his tattoos catch the thin light from the hallway, wrapping around his throat like the armor he never takes off.

I can feel his shrewd gaze on me as I crouch to drag out the last box from under the bed. It's filled with books, sketchpads, and a few old photos I can't bring myself to throw away. Lifting Jeremy's guitar from the corner, I close the duffel with one harsh tug and swing it over my shoulder, the strap biting into my palm.

The walls are starting to close in, misery stitched into the cracks. Nights staring at the ceiling, wondering how I'd fucked up my life this badly. Days where the silence was so thick I thought I might choke on it.

"Enjoy the show?" I glare at Rhys, who still hasn't moved from his spot. "You can head back to your luxury suite now and laugh about my suffering."

"Do you always have to be so *mundane*?" Rhys sighs, rolling his eyes. He reaches into his jacket and pulls out a small white card, the kind that smells faintly of money and arrogance. I glance at the printed address but make no move to take it.

"No need to be shy," he says, waving it closer. "Meet us here, if your rust bucket of a truck can actually make the trip." Curiosity gets the better of me. I snatch the card from his hand and glance down at the address. Before I can ask, Rhys leaves, that trademark swagger already back in his stride.

"I'm not staying anywhere with you," I call after him. Rhys pauses, slowly turns back with one brow arched in mock amusement.

"Oh no? What's your plan then? Shack up with your parole officer? Pitch a tent behind the courthouse?" He chuckles, dragging his thumb across his lip ring. Then his phone buzzes in his pocket, bringing him back to reality. His expression sobers, just barely. "Running won't fix shit, Scum. It just makes you harder to find." I open my mouth to bite back a retort, but he cuts me off with a knowing look.

"You know she won't stop looking," he adds. "The place I've rented is big enough that we don't even have to see each other. Just... humor her by being there." My throat constricts, the grip around the guitar tightening.

"Why are you doing this?" I frown. Rhys is a bully, born of privilege and bred by entitlement. He doesn't care for anyone other than himself. Yet his gaze softens as he assesses the wall beside my head.

"I'm trying this new thing where I only care about making Harper happy. It's a nice reprieve from antagonizing my father for a while, plus it's real easy. All Harper wants is good food, some nice clothes, and endless sex. I mean, the orgasms that girl can have are just—"

The sound that escapes me is low, the kind that promises violence and broken legs. Rhys's grin widens, proud of himself for getting the reaction he wanted. He flicks invisible dust from his jacket, smug as ever.

"But for some reason," he continues, "she also wants *you*. And like the obedient little lap dog I am, I'm here to collect. You probably thought you had that golden retriever thing going on, all sappy eyes and bleeding heart. Turns out I'm more of a mastiff. Loyal, sure, but I tug the leash when I'm bored." He bobs his brows, conceited as ever.

The duffel digs into my shoulder, the urge to leave this studio apartment far behind, but I can't bring myself to move. Because for one split second, I see something different behind his grin. The man standing before me isn't the one who harassed scholarship students, or the one who wore his anger as easily as he slipped into a fine suit. No longer the arrogant bastard who's made my life hell, but someone who is trying far too hard to sound like he still enjoys this game.

"You've changed," I mutter.

Rhys tips an invisible hat, grin returning just enough to look like himself again. Then he finally leaves, footsteps fading down the corridor until it's just me, the hum of the dying light, and the echo of everything I thought I knew.

CHAPTER TWELVE

Snowflakes the size of feathers drift past the windshield, catching in the headlights before dissolving into nothing. The world outside is muted to me, the kind of silence that holds its breath as we drive deeper into the unknown. Rhys taps the steering wheel to the rhythm of a song I can't hear, his eyes fixed ahead through my Audi's windscreen. Neither of us have said much since leaving the city, and if he's feeling the same trepidation as I am, he doesn't show it.

The phone call with his dad the other night had temporarily drained away all of his cocky remarks to let me see the man beneath. Raw and stripped back to a boy craving affection, a motherless child who wasn't taught how to love. We were blind drunk and could have easily turned reckless, but instead Rhys wanted to be held all night. Much like when he broke into my dorm, the physical contact of my fingers stroking his back was enough. Then my period arrived and he's been treating me like I'm made of glass, as if this isn't a monthly occurrence I have learned to endure.

The car turns onto a narrow country lane, and I shift in my seat and glance out the window. The forest breaks into a clearing, revealing a house set so far back from the road, you wouldn't know it was even there. My eyes widen, the serenity of it nothing like what I expected. I'd imagined something sleek and modern, a show of Rhys's wealth. But the place before us looks like it's been plucked from a winter postcard.

A two-story cabin stands, wrapped in strings of soft golden lights that trace the eaves and windows. A wreath hangs on the red front door, the kind made from pinecones and ribbon, while a pair of lanterns glow faintly on the porch steps. Snow coats the roof, gathering thickly along the rails of the wooden deck that circles the front.

"Woah, Rhys. It's... beautiful," I murmur, content to simply stare at it. Rhys throws the car into park and stretches his arms behind his head, pretending nonchalance but watching my reaction from the corner of his eye. Is that nervousness I sense? Tilting my head in his direction, the warmth of my smile ignites his own. "You have good taste."

His laughter falls on my deaf ears before we open the car doors and step out into the cold. The air bites at my cheeks, my boots crunching beneath my feet as I tilt my head back, taking it all in. The lights, the quiet, the faint smell of wood smoke in the distance. Shouldering our bags, Rhys trudges toward the door and punches a code into the lockbox beside it.

Inside, warmth greets us immediately. The living room glows in shades of amber and gold, a fire already crackling in the stone hearth. Someone, probably the rental staff, has gone all out. A Christmas tree stands in the corner, tall and full, its branches dusted with faux snow and trimmed with glass ornaments that glint in the flickering flames. Red stockings hang above the fireplace, white fur trim around each one.

Digging my receivers out of my pocket, where they were stowed for when I inevitably fell asleep during the drive, I click them in place. I want to experience this with all of my senses. There's music playing softly from somewhere in the house, a slow instrumental version of a Christmas song. It's like walking into a memory I've long since stored away, of a little girl giddy to spend the holidays with loved ones. I feel like her again, so much so tears gather in my eyes.

Rhys sets the bags down with a grunt, his boots thudding against the floorboards.

"Too much?"

"It's perfect," I say, hiding my face by kneeling in front of the fire to warm my hands. Then, a thought strikes and I twist back to see Rhys watching me. "Do you have any pleasant Christmas memories?" A harsh laugh echoes around the large room as Rhys drops heavily to his knees at my side.

"I got everything I ever wanted," he replies bitterly, knowing full well that's not what I'd asked. I decide then and there that I'm going to relive some of my favourite festive traditions this holiday, and I'm not talking about the costumes Aunt Marg would force me to dress her cats in for their annual photoshoot. I mean the ones I used to share with my parents. Rhys deserves to know what family is supposed to feel like.

Once warmed through, I hang up my coat and wander through the open archway into the kitchen. It's huge, with marble countertops, copper pans, and a long farmhouse table that could seat ten. A garland of evergreen stretches across the cabinets, and there's a bowl of oranges on the counter beside a handwritten note welcoming us to the property. Rhys eventually joins me, leaning against the counter with his arms folded. His gaze sweeps over the room, but I know he's only half-seeing it. He's distracted today, and I reckon I know why.

"Do you think he'll come?" I ask, not needing to specify who I'm talking about. Rhys glances out of the window, his body remaining just as tense.

"I don't know." I walk toward him, watching the way the firelight from the living room casts lines across his face. Placing my hands on his arms, I dislodge him and step into his hold.

"Whether he does or doesn't, it means a lot to me that you asked him. Thank you." I lean up on my tiptoes and brush my lips over his. Rhys groans softly, his palms slipping under my t-shirt to cover my back.

"I can't seem to resist you."

"Good," I smile, pulling his bottom lip between my teeth. Rocking his hips against me, that groan comes again, and Rhys' fingers dig into my hips. Then, he pushes me a step back and hangs his head.

"Stop teasing me. You're out of action for at least another few days." Rearranging his dick in his jeans, Rhys turns to lean on the counter. A mischievous smile crosses my face as I drape myself over his back and whisper into his ear.

"My mouth isn't."

"Fucking hell," Rhys chokes, spinning so fast I shriek. Lifting me, he plants my ass on the countertop and buries his face into my neck. "Such a naughty little minx. I'm trying so hard to be respectful for the first time in my damn life." I reach between us and grab his shaft through his jeans.

"Mmmm, so, *so* hard Rhys." Shoving himself away from the counter, Rhys grabs the bags and storms up the stairs, shouting for the entire world to hear.

"You're going to be the death of me, Harper Addams!"

Outside, the snow keeps falling, blanketing the world in white. I peer out of the windows often, as if I can materialize Clay out of pure longing. The worse the weather gets, the more my hope diminishes. Even if he isn't coming, I hope he's somewhere safe. Worry gnaws in my gut as I go about the house, unpacking our bags and checking the pantry. Rhys and I bought out most of Target on the way over. Extra clothes, junk food, a bunch of things I just thought were cute. The house owner offers a grocery delivery service, although the refrigerator is fully stocked to see us through the rest of the week. We have mostly everything we need.

I've lit all of the candles lining the mantelpiece by the time Rhys appears with two steaming mugs of cocoa. Streams of chocolate drip over the rim, a smudge of powder on his cheek. I conceal my reaction, both amazed that Rhys has evidently never made himself a hot drink before and humbled that he put the effort in for me. We settle down on the sofa, a thick blanket pulled over our legs. The fire cracks, the tree glows, and the mounted TV is playing a cheesy movie.

It's a picturesque evening, even if my gaze wanders to the front door more times than I can count. Sighing gently, I lean my head against Rhys's shoulder, the heat of him seeping through my sweater. He doesn't say anything, just tilts his head until it rests lightly atop mine. If this is what it's like when Rhys isn't trying to get into my pants, I might pretend to be on my period three weeks out of the month.

We remain like that for hours. The fire burns low, soft embers glowing like the last heartbeat of the day. White flakes swirl against the windows in steady waves, the whistle of the wind sounding over the TV. Rhys' head grows heavier and I know soon, we'll have to lock up and head upstairs.

"Rhys," I mumble, nudging my shoulder against his chest. He jerks upright, momentarily disorientated.

"Huh?" he blinks sleepily, noticing the credits of the movie are rolling. I pry the empty mug from his hand and set it aside.

"If I ask you a question, will you tell me the truth?"

"Probably," he yawns behind his hand. I push myself upright and fold my legs beneath me.

"You did invite Clayton, right?" A knowing huff leaves him as he scrubs a hand over his eyes. He was waiting for my doubt to creep in.

"Regretfully, yes I did."

"And you gave him the correct address?" I press on. If this has been one big trick on both of our parts, I'd rather know now. Rhys raises a brow, his face unimpressed. I lick my lips, glancing towards the window again. "It's just...he should have been here by now. He had a head start."

I knew the hotel wasn't a permanent situation, but when Rhys' father put an end to our stay, we scrambled for a solution. One that would be far enough away from the creep back at Waversea, and one that could accommodate all three of us, should Clayton need a place to stay. Catching me chewing on my bottom lip, Rhys pries it free with his thumb.

"Maybe he's not coming, Babygirl. If that's the choice he made, then you have your answer. You've done more than enough." Rhys' voice is firm but not unkind. Still, it lands somewhere deep in my chest, where the last fragile hope I've been holding onto starts to splinter. My throat tightens and I stand, walking toward the window. The warm light spilling out from the lounge makes everything blurred and golden. My reflection stares back. Tired eyes, messy hair, a faint frown etched between my brows.

The truth is, I miss Clayton with every aching part of me. I miss the way his voice softened when he said my name, the way his gaze lingered, always on high alert for the next threat. But I can't keep waiting around. Rhys is right, I've done enough. I've groveled for a prank I had no part in, begged for forgiveness that wasn't mine to seek. I've put my heart on the line for Clayton to cherish or crush. I suppose I have my answer. He's not here now. He didn't come.

Arms wrap around my waist, fingers brushing my hips. Leaning back into Rhys' chest, the reflection changes. No longer alone, I'm now being held by a man who has chosen me time and again. Even when he did have reason to cut me off, Rhys couldn't stay away. He's the opposite of Clayton. Selfish, entitled, vain, and devoted to me. Rhys's hand comes up to my jaw, twisting my face to look up at him.

"Let's go to bed." There's no mistaking the way he's looking at me, practically famished. Turning in his hold, I flutter my lashes innocently.

"Even though I'm out of action?" I smirk. A flare of lust bursts within Rhys' blue eyes. He lowers his head and laughs deeply beside my ear.

“Your mouth isn’t.”

HARPER

CHAPTER THIRTEEN

Morning seeps in with the promise of another silvery day, even in the first rays of dawn. From the comfort of the king-size bed, I peer at the network of pinks and reds bleeding across a cloudless sky. Rhys is pressed against the length of me, our backs aligned as we face outwards. His ribs rattle slightly as he breathes deep, hinting to him snoring. Luckily, I have the option of leaving my receivers behind as I slip out from beneath the thick cover, the floorboards unforgiving beneath my toes. Pulling on an oversized sweatshirt and socks, rubbing warmth into my arms, I pad downstairs.

The living room is still, absent of light and life. Cinnamon candles sit melted on the mantel, our mugs forgotten on the table. I collect them up, haphazardly folding the blanket and putting it back in place before heading into the kitchen. Filling the kettle, deciding I need a hot drink before I can tackle making breakfast with icy limbs, my gaze snags on something beyond the back door. The porch light is on, blinking as if it's due a replacement.

Frowning, I step closer to the frosted window, rubbing at the glass to peer through. The back yard is blanketed in white, the edges of my vision blurred. The trees bordering this piece of land are pale and void of life. The light continues to flicker so I unlatch the door, stepping out on tiptoes. Maybe there's a switch to turn it off until we can inform the owner. But as I slip into the icy morning, my breath fogging before me, a dark bundle catches my attention. Huddled on the decking, clumps of snow coat a military jacket and beanie hat. My heart stutters.

"Clayton!" The name tears out of me, half-choked. Cold forgotten, I drop to my knees, lifting his head in my hands. His skin is deathly pale, his lips tinged blue. "Hey. Hey, can you hear me?" My fingers shake as I tap his cheek. Clay's head lolls slightly toward me, eyes barely open. He tries to mutter something, but I can't hear him, so I start screaming for Rhys instead.

Trying to shift Clayton, he's dead weight, his muscles refusing to cooperate. I manage to lift his head uneven to drag his duffle bag beneath him, but his attempts to help are jerky and uncoordinated. Classic hypothermia.

"What the hell, Harp?!" Rhys' voice suddenly explodes inside my head. I flinch, jolting Clayton and now hearing his resulting groan.

"Help me get him inside," I order without looking behind me. There's a sigh and a grumble, but Rhys leans down and grabs Clay beneath the arms. I'm not much help, using the stiff material of his jacket to drag him over the threshold, like pulling a sandbag through water. We manage to get him halfway across the kitchen before my trembling arms give out.

"Damn heavy bastard," Rhys complains, heaving Clay the rest of the way to lie him before the fireplace. I run on shaky legs, collecting up the blankets that are dotted around, mostly for decoration.

"You need to strip off his clothes," I demand. Rhys makes a guttural sound, suddenly dropping Clayton where he is.

"I will be doing no such thing," Rhys scoffs. I swivel around to glare at him, now noticing the rush in which he got dressed. His vest is inside out, his sweatpants tugged in awkward angles and hair sticking up. It looks like he came running to my aid, until realising I'm not the one in trouble.

"We need to get him out of his wet clothes and bring his temperature up *slowly*. If we do it too fast, his body will go into shock. His heart's already under stress."

"Well, your screaming won't help with that. Sing him a lullaby or something." Rhys pressed his lips together, not moving. My face fills with rage, all of the curses and threats I could possibly think of filling my head. Just before I lose my absolute shit, Rhys rolls his eyes. "Fine. You undress him. I'll do the fire."

Clay is freezing to the touch, his core temperature easily below ninety-five. "Jesus, what the hell were you doing out there?" I hiss, carefully removing the clothes from his body. I peel off his beanie hat first, before tackling his jacket and t-shirt. Rhys conveniently becomes invested in picking the right pieces of firewood, not responding to any of my grunts or sounds of struggle. Wrapping blankets around Clay's torso and arms, I start removing Clay's shoes, socks and sweatpants. They're like cardboard, rigid and awkward to drag off Clay's motionless legs but I succeed, falling back on my ass. Now for the next challenge.

"I need you to lift him so I can get his boxers off," I state. Rhys drops the wood into the fire and pinches the bridge of his nose. His hesitation is infuriating, and I use Clay's soggy sock to smack the back of his legs. "Rhys Maximus Waversea. You will lift him right now or so help me, I will tell any reporter who will listen that you have syphilis."

Finally, Rhys growls and lifts Clay's hips so I can peel off his boxers, both of us looking in opposite directions. Covering Clay's dignity, I wrap his legs and drop down by his head. He collapses against me with a low groan, his body convulsing with uneven shivers as I cradle him in my arms. Rhys returns to the fireplace, appreciating the flickering flames he's conjured.

"I don't have a middle name, by the way," he mumbles into the mic. I stroke Clay's hair with the edge of a blanket, drying it strand by strand.

"I know, but it felt like a full naming moment." The fire crackles back to life, casting orange light across Clay's face. His skin's blotchy, patches of red and white rising as if his body's fighting to circulate blood again. Dropping my voice, I move in closer to cradling his head in my lap. "You stupid fool. You could have died."

"Would have served him right," Rhys replies. I glare at his back, and I know he senses it. "He should have been here yesterday. Or maybe he shouldn't have run off like a pussy in the first place."

"You paid him to leave," I narrow my eyes, jaw tight with frustration. Rhys shrugs without a care in the world.

"Pussies run."

"And jackasses stay, evidently," I snip back. I can imagine Addy's cheering in my head, her signing *cum stain* over and over like a cheerleader's chant. Rhys mutters something under his breath and storms toward the kitchen, knowing full well I can still hear him as he apparently opens every cupboard and drawer possible, before slamming them shut one after the other. It's like gunfire bursting within my skull, but I leave him to his tantrum, focusing on Clayton instead.

"Stay with me," I whisper, rubbing his arm. "Come on. You're okay. You're going to be okay." Clay's hand twitches beneath the blankets. I catch it before it falls away, wrapping my fingers around his cold ones. His skin is rough and clammy, his pulse a weak flutter beneath my thumb.

I don't know how long we remain there, the cold seeping from his bones and into mine. I'm shivering, until a thick parka jacket is wrapped around my shoulders. Rhys drops to his knees, pressing hot water bottles to the outside of the blankets rather roughly. Now the mic is back in the vicinity, I can hear Clay's mumbling through lips that are developing in colour.

"Door..." he croaks, barely audible. "Locked."

"That's what happens after midnight, you moron. Keeps the burglars out," Rhys replies. Leaning his back against the sofa, he flicks on the TV and channel surfs as if we're not in the middle of a crisis. The screen's light flickers over Clay's face, highlighting the deep lines of his exhaustion. The tremors in his jaw are easing, the faintest pink returning to his cheeks. I reach down to press the hot water bottle against his abdomen, the heat seeping slowly through the layers of fabric.

Clay is stabilizing, his breathing evening out as sleep takes over. His body has suffered a trauma, fighting against itself to keep his organs functioning. Holding him close, I let him drift off, now that I'm not scared he won't wake back up. Although, it will be a long while yet before my heart will stop racing, because I know just how close it came.

One more hour in that cold, and he could've gone into severe hypothermia, unconscious, heart arrhythmias, cardiac arrest. My stomach twists painfully at the thought so I just keep brushing my thumb over his knuckles, letting him know I'm still here.

CLAYTON

CHAPTER FOURTEEN

Sirens wail somewhere far off, their pitch climbing and falling, red and blue strobes dancing across the slick brick walls. They flash over my hands, my face, and the alleyway, before plunging us into darkness again. The stench of old oil and garbage clings to my nostrils. I press my back to the damp metal of the dumpster, peering around its edge.

"Where are they?" I ask for what seems like the millionth time. A shiver of déjà vu races along my spine. Antonio shifts behind me, his sneakers squeaking on the wet pavement. Another kid like me, a high school drop out who's only made it to seventeen because a local gang has been conditioning us to join their ranks.

However, this being our first real job, his nerves are showing. His breath comes too fast, clouding in the air with white puffs like smoke signals. I tamper down my own reservations, forcing myself to keep a level head. I can freak out later.

My brother, Jeremy, has been the man of the house for too long. Tonight, I pull my weight. I can help to pay off the gambling debts our bastard father left us drowning in and give Mom a better life. More than that, once I've passed initiation, the GDK gang will protect us. They take on one man from each family, and it's my time to step up.

The walls closing in on us are coated in graffiti, names and tags of our rival gang sprayed over one another until nothing is legible. It doesn't need to be clear who's tag is more prominent, since we're deep in rival turf anyway. Other than the dumpster, metal door opposite and a random black cat, we are alone in the dead end.

I spin just as two figures step into view. Khan is a huge fucker dressed head to toe in black. Beneath his balaclava, I know there's a thick scar running from his temple to his chin and hundreds of theories on how he got it. Vince beside him isn't as large, but the lack of emotion in his dead eyes is the same. These men are brutal. One small slip up and they won't hesitate to tie up the loose ends. I refuse to be a loose end.

Smooth as butter, Vince crouches by the door to pick the lock, whilst Khan presses objects into mine and Antonio's hands. I frown at the heavy weight, squinting and turning it over to make out the glint of a gun. Holy shit, a gun! I swallow through the dryness coating my throat, my forehead sweating beneath one of Jeremy's beanie hats. I thought it would be a good disguise.

My surroundings blur and alter to the inside of a vault, fragments of time slipping through my fingers. Floor to ceiling drawers line each wall, like tiny deposit boxes. I don't know how I expected a jeweler to store his stock, but being here now makes it too real. This is serious shit I'm getting into, and something tells me it's only the beginning.

I picture my mom, shivering beneath a tattered blanket as she tries to sleep. Her teeth chattering whilst hunger rips her apart from the inside. Then there's Jeremy, his hands faltering as he packs to go off to some elite academy he's been accepted into. He keeps arguing that he should stay here, but there's no life for him here, and we don't need him anymore. I'm going to be the man of the house now.

"Don't just stand there, empty them out!" a bark shouts from behind. I shove the gun into my pocket, tearing open drawers and emptying the contents into my duffle as quickly as possible.

Suddenly, an alarm blares. I drop my bag in favor of slamming my hands over my ears. Shoulders shove me aside, hard enough for me to stumble into the wall, as they take the loot and prepare to leave me behind. The alarm is hammering a nail into my head, making it painful to even open my eyes. So I just start running. The hallways stretch, my feet barely touching the ground as I race through the maze I don't remember being here.

The door to outside is ahead, a green exit sign lighting the way. I stretch out my hand for the handle, but someone wrenches it open from the other side. Dragged out by the scruff of my neck and thrown to the ground, agony explodes in my side. The impact of a boot breaks my ribs, blood clogging my throat. I roll to the side, spluttering and gagging as I bump into something solid. Something cold. My head rises, the image of Antonio's open, glazed eyes etching themselves into my memories. Blood pools from a bullet hole in his jacket, the click of a semi-automatic being cocked.

"Sorry kid, one of you triggered the alarm. Someone's got to take the fall and your fingerprints are all over the lockboxes." Dread takes over, but whereas some may falter beneath the weight of it, I seem to flourish. Unaware of my actions, the gun is out of my pocket, the safety flicked off and my hand raises towards the man pointing a barrel at me. I can barely see in the darkness of the alley, but the sirens are growing louder and time is running out. I don't have a choice. It's me or him, and I can't let my mom lose a son.

Closing my eyes, I hear a scuffle as my finger squeezes the trigger. Wheels skid, sirens blare, shouts and screams follow gunfire. Then it all stops. Complete silence rings in my ears, my hand still raised in the air. Officers close in, the holler of one telling me to put down the weapon sounding faint. I drop it, and crack an eyelid, temporarily blinded by the brightness I find there. Pain seizes me as they descend, forcing me onto my front and grabbing my arms. My ribs scream for attention, bound by the awkward angle my hands are cuffed in. At least it's over now. I can give my statement, I'll cooperate and be home soon enough. The gravity of what I nearly got involved in hits me like a freight train. I almost died.

With my face smushed against the concrete, I peer at the reflection of myself in a window and frown. My nose is slightly crooked, though I don't remember it being so, and the stubble on my jaw has somehow grown in the last hour. But it's my eyes. They are wide, lifeless. Too similar to the way Antonio was staring endlessly at the night's sky. Somewhere within, a dull thud cracks through the confusion and just before the police haul me to my feet, I realize the truth. There's no window in this alley, and that's not my reflection. That's Jeremy.

I lurch upright with a gasp, the sound that rips from my throat somewhere between a broken snarl and general panic. My lungs seize, my hands clawing at nothing as I search for the gun, for the door, for *something* to stop the spinning. The world is blindingly bright, visions left in the recesses of my mind flashing before me. The white walls of the interrogation room fade, bleeding into cream tones and the faint scent of gingerbread and cinnamon. My heart's still pounding like I'm being chased, my body shaking uncontrollably with a tremor deep in my bones that is a combination of fear and the cold.

"Stop it!"

My head jerks toward the voice, but the room doubles. Everything lags half a second behind, like my eyes can't keep up. I blink hard until my vision steadies enough to make out a soft throw blanket sliding from my chest, the couch beneath me too plush and warm. Where the hell am I?

Reaching down to pick it up, agony stabs my entire body. My hands are like ice, my fingers aching when I move them, the joints swollen and red. My skin feels tight, stretched thin over bone. I blink again, forcing the fog from my mind. I'm not in an alleyway. I'm not bleeding. I'm not seventeen. I'm sprawled on a sofa in a house I don't recognize, muscles seizing from the cold.

There's a Christmas movie playing above a roaring fireplace, and the smell of baking sugar is thick in the air, tugging me somewhere I don't belong. Laughter trickles through from the next room, a familiar sound that doesn't quite fit in my nightmare.

"Rhys, you can't just eat the decorations!" The bastard chuckles, doing something that causes Harper to squeal, and as a result, pierce my skull. I close my eyes, pressing the heels of my palms against my temples. Trying and failing to rise, I immediately regret it as the room tilts and a groan escapes me, followed by a clatter from the kitchen.

"Clayton!" Harper rounds the corner, flour dusting her cheek. "Perfect timing! We need a judge for our gingerbread houses before Rhys eats all of the adornments off mine." She pauses, assessing me properly and her brows knit together. "Are you okay? Do you feel any better?"

"Better?" I repeat hollowly, my voice not sounding like my own. Then, like a jigsaw gathering all of its pieces, I start to remember. The cold, the porch, the locked door. My truck is buried in snow where I abandoned it a few miles back. The gnawing in my bones until everything went dark.

I can tell, even without Harper's evident concern, that was a close call. So close, that my life started flashing before my eyes and I despised every bit of it. If that's the life and legacy I'll leave behind, then there's no use even giving me a headstone. It's a waste, but it's not over just yet.

As the confusion seeps away, a new emotion takes hold. One so strong, it overpowers the dull ache in all of my limbs. Harper blinks up at me, hesitant to lay her powdered hands on my chest, her green eyes filled with concern. She's wearing pale blue pajamas with tiny snowflakes. Her hair's a mess, tied up in a knot that doesn't quite hold. There's a smudge of icing on her wrist, and her socks don't match.

I've never seen anything so innocently beautiful, so far removed from the nightmare that plagues me. I'm carrying around baggage of bloodshed and a misfired gun I had no business using. My criminal record is like a noose that never quite loosens, but Harper? She's a survivor. A phoenix born from the ashes of her grief, who looks upon my tainted soul as if I'm worthy of her affection.

Before I can stop myself, I reach out and drag her into my lap, crushing her into my arms. She gasps against my chest, and after a second, locks her own arms around my waist. After the endless hours of being cold, of feeling my pulse slow and my breath frost in the air, her heat is a shock to my system. I tremble from the force of withholding everything I want to say, the realizations I've come to after fighting them for so long.

For a heartbeat, the house disappears. No kitchen, no gingerbread houses, no rival standing three feet away. Just the girl I've been running from and running toward at the same time. She smells like buttercream and woodsmoke, and she feels like home.

Shifting slightly, Harper places her palms against my ribs. "Clay," she says softly. "You're shaking. Let's get you upstairs." I loosen my hold just enough to see her face. Her cheeks are flushed pink, her eyes bright with something I can't name.

Swallowing past the lump lodged in my throat, I nod and try to stand again. Harper shifts aside, her steady gaze keeping me centered. Her hands linger at my elbows, gently easing me upright.

It's in that moment, as my feet find some stability and the multitude of blankets fall away from my lap, I discover I am completely naked. Jerking to grab the last blanket to fall, I cover myself just in time, a simmer of heat returning to my cheeks. Harper snorts in that cute way she doesn't realize, helping me to tuck the edges of the blanket around my waist before leading the way to the staircase.

Rhys stays two steps behind, his scowl a permanent feature on his face. The cocky asshole I'm used to isn't present, leading me to believe I've interrupted something. I can't help but grin a little at that.

Breaching the landing, I pause to take in my new surroundings. The air is cleaner somehow, carrying that faint pine scent that clings to every corner of this place. Sunlight spills through the wide hallway windows, turning the wooden floors honey-gold, and for a second, I forget that I arrived half-dead on the doorstep.

Harper's steps are light, her socked feet making no sound on the boards as she leads me past half-open doors, one to a guest room with crumpled sheets, another that is a study. The whole house feels lived-in already, in that effortless way she has of softening a space just by being in it. There's a garland trailing the banister, little fairy lights twined through it, blinking in slow rhythm.

We reach the master suite, and I stop so suddenly, Rhys' shoulder crashes into mine. Have they left this room for me? It's bigger than the entire studio apartment I've left behind. The wood theme continues, pine furniture blending into the cladding and floors. A bed sits dead center, its headboard carved from dark oak and piled high with cushions in neutral tones. At the far side of the room, the bathroom is visible through a glass divider. Harper crosses the threshold and points her finger in a bossy way I kinda like.

"Sit on the edge of the tub. I'll get the water running."

The freestanding bathtub faces the panoramic windows that stretch from floor to ceiling, revealing a landscape painted in frost and gold. The dense tree line breaks, revealing rolling fields speckled with white, and in the distance, the faint shimmer of a frozen lake catching the morning sun.

Steam starts to curl up from the tub as Harper tests the water with her wrist. She adjusts the faucet slightly, her concentration meticulous. I catch myself staring, not just because she's beautiful, but because she's *real*. She's warmth and movement and light, while everything inside me still feels numb and heavy.

I sink down on the tiled ledge beside the bath, the porcelain cold beneath my skin, and stare out the window. For the first time in what feels like years, I allow myself to just *look*. The snow falls softly now, in lazy spirals that melt the moment they hit the glass. There's peace here, something I haven't known since I was a kid.

My thoughts drift back to the alleyway, the gun in my hand, Antonio's blank eyes. Even now, the image clings to the edges of my mind like smoke. The kind of memory that follows you no matter how far you try to run. I rub at my wrists, trying to scrub the sensation of cold metal from my palms. Harper glances over her shoulder, brow furrowed slightly.

"You're still trembling," she frowns. "You need to get in before your body temperature drops again." I allow myself to smile, just slightly. I'll never know what I've done to deserve Harper's concern, but I'm not as quick to brush it off anymore.

"I'm sorry I was late," I say, rubbing a hand over my nape. It feels exposed without a beanie pulled down low. "I went to visit my mom and got swept into a festive bingo session." It's mostly the truth.

I can't say the receptionist was happy to see me again, and upon seeing my mom in the main hall, I welcomed myself to join her game. I'd hoped this mystery cousin I don't have would show up, or my mom might have a moment of clarity slip through. But neither happened, as she was having a bad day. I might as well have not bothered, but my conscience knows I went. That I saw her closer to Christmas than I have in years.

Harper turns back to the tub, shutting off the faucet. The water swirls, a perfect balance of steam and calm. "It's ready," she says gently. "Jump in. I'll grab some dry clothes in a minute." I hesitate, clutching the blanket around my waist. The room's quiet except for the soft hiss of cooling pipes and the faint creak of Rhys pacing the hallway. I glance toward the door, watching him turn and stride back, scowling at me. I'm taking Harper away from him, and I'm not mad about it.

So I let the blanket fall and step into the water. It's hot enough to sting at first, but I sink down anyway, groaning as the warmth seeps into my frozen bones. My fingers twitch as blood starts to flow properly again, my heartbeat finally finding rhythm in my chest. Harper kneels beside the tub, her reflection blurred in the glass behind.

"Better?" she asks. I nod, eyes half-closed, watching the condensation bead and slide down the windowpane.

"Feels like my body's remembering what it means to be alive." She lets out a small laugh.

"Good. Let's try to keep it that way."

I study her profile as she sits back on her heels, the light catching the faint sheen of icing still dusted on her face. There's something achingly human about her, how she carries both exhaustion and grace, worry and affection, all at once. Reaching for a towel, she folds it neatly over the side of the tub, busying herself.

"You should stay in there for fifteen minutes. Any longer and your blood pressure might drop too fast. You're still recovering."

"Yes, doctor." I smirk faintly. Her lips twitch, fighting a smile.

"Don't test me. I know exactly how to monitor a pulse." Comfort settles in my chest and I sink lower, resting my head on the rim. Harper stays, and I reckon she's timing me in her head. Having her so close is doing frenzied things to my mind, especially when there's another man beyond the door also aching for her attention. Yet there's no rushing her, as she brushes imaginary creases out of the towel.

Before I can stop myself, I reach out, water dripping from my fingers as I catch her wrist lightly. She blinks up at me startled, but doesn't pull away.

"Thank you," I murmur. "For taking care of me." Harper's green eyes soften, the corners crinkling slightly.

"I'm just glad you're here." For a long moment, we just stare at each other, me half-submerged and her kneeling at my side, the world beyond the window nothing but white and quiet. And for the first time in years, the silence doesn't feel like punishment. It feels like peace.

HARPER

CHAPTER FIFTEEN

The front door bursts open, letting in a gust of wind and a spray of snow that scatters across the wooden floorboards. We waited a few days, hoping the weather would improve but it's only getting worse. Clay decided we couldn't leave his truck and belongings out there any longer, and since the ski clothes provided in the wardrobes were men's, I got to stay back.

Clay stumbles in first, shaking his head like a drenched golden retriever, snowflakes clinging to his eyelashes and collar. Rhys follows behind him, slamming the door shut with more force than necessary, his jaw set in that way that means *don't ask.*

Both of them are covered in white, their hair, shoulders, and boots walking a blizzard into the living room that melts into small puddles. Dropping the bags, they turn to me in comical unison, their matching scowls damping the festive atmosphere and causing my mass of cinnamon-scented candles to flicker.

From my position on the sofa, ankles crossed on the table, cradling a mug of hot chocolate in one hand and a book in the other, I wonder who is going to break the silence first. I should have put money on it being Rhys.

"I literally gave you a check for more than most people's houses are worth, and you couldn't put some aside to get that shitheap truck fixed?" Cutting him with a sharp side eye, Clay throws his coat onto the back of the armchair.

"I put all of it towards my mom's care."

"Such a fucking martyr," Rhys groans, tugging off his gloves with his teeth. His cheeks are pink from the cold, and a snowflake is melting on the bridge of his nose. I hide my smile behind the rim of my mug. The fire crackles merrily in the stone pit, throwing warmth into the cabin's wooden walls and thawing out the tension the boys carried in with them.

"Would it kill you two to pretend you like each other for just one day?" I ask, leaning forward to set down the mug and book. My tone's teasing, but my gaze lingers between them, curious to see if there's been a change in dynamic. As if it would be that easy.

Rhys tosses his gloves onto the hearth and proceeds to strip down to his boxers, leaving his wet clothes in a heap on the floor. Lifting the blanket from my legs, he sinks into the sofa beside me, tucking us both beneath the thick layer of fluff.

"Pretending would imply effort," he mutters. Leaning into my side, Rhys' head finds the hollow of my shoulder, sighing with the entire weight of his chest. I can't expect too much, I did manage to convince him to accompany Clay for a small hike in the impending blizzard. There's a Christmas miracle in itself.

"Did you play nice?" I nudge Rhys playfully.

"I always play nice," he replies instantly, although Clay scoffs as brushes off his jeans and heads toward the kitchen.

"He spent the whole time throwing snowballs at the back of my head!" I feel the twitch of Rhys' lips against my shoulder.

"I thought he'd learn to duck out of the way."

"I can't duck out of the way of you stuffing snow down my collar," Clay hisses, audibly shifting around as he undresses. Rhys chuckles to himself softly.

"Semantics," he drawls. Clay comes back around, now free of

clothes aside from the boxers he's covering with his hands. Unlike Rhys, who is naturally entitled and at ease being naked, Clay is more reserved. I smile, both appreciating his pronounced muscle and finding his shyness endearing. The reddened line marring his collar bone stands out like it did in the bath last night, but I avoid looking at it. If Clay wants to tell me what happened, he will.

"I'm going to shower off, then I'm cooking dinner for everyone," he announces with a decisive nod. My brow raises.

"You can cook?" I ask, cringing at the way it comes out all squeaky with surprise. Clay ducks his head slightly, as if he's struggling under the scrutiny of my gaze.

"I can when I've got the ingredients to work with." A faint pink twinge highlights his cheeks. My heart melts and my smile doubles.

"Well then, consider us your sous chefs."

"Yeah fucking right," Rhys huffs, settling down as if he's about to take a nap. I stroke my fingers through his damp hair, teasing the knots out of the longer strands on top. Clay takes the stairs two at a time, disappearing from view. The fire crackles softly, Rhys' head growing heavy on my shoulder as I stare into the flames.

Unknown to the guys, I've placed microphone clips in each room, giving me surround sound hearing of the house directly into my inner ear. If they start a scrap, I'll know about it quickly enough to break it up. The last thing I want is for Rhys to come up with a new bribery technique or for Clay to be pushed out by thinly veiled threats. I know Rhys isn't perfect, and I don't need him to be. I just hope the three of us can find some kind of truce whilst staying here, locked away from the world's expectations and judgemental stares.

A faint static hum builds in my left ear, the pulsing sound of water hitting tile. I can picture the moment Clay steps beneath the spray with the way the sound changes, no longer smacking the ground but curving around his broad frame. I can imagine it all too well.

Continuing to stroke Rhys' damp hair against my collarbone, his breathing has gone steady, but my mind isn't nearly as still. It wanders, flitting restlessly across the quiet cabin. With nothing to distract me but the storm beating against the windows and the glow of the embers before me, every sound feels more intrusive, more alive.

After a few minutes, the shower's downpour has lulled me into a sense of serenity. Like white noise, I dip my head back against the sofa and simply enjoy it, until a grunt brings me back to the room around it. I startle, eyes wide at the ceiling as the sound comes again. I'm about to fly from the seat and run to check if Clayton is okay, if he's hurt elsewhere, but then he hisses a broken word.

"Fuck," he groans. My heart rate kicks up a beat. Diving deeper into the water's spray, audibly hunting for sounds beneath the noise, I hear it. A rhythmic thrusting, slickened and wet. Holy hell. Clay's breathing becomes ragged, enticing mine to do the same. My fingers are still in Rhys' hair, caught halfway through a stroke. The room becomes warm, the heat creeping under my skin having nothing to do with the fire.

I shift, tugging the blanket lower over my chest. The result is a brush of my nipples and a rush of chill causing them to tighten. My teeth sink into my bottom lip, the slippery pumping prevalent in my mind. My core tightens as I imagine in all too vivid detail how it would feel for Clay to be pushing inside of me with those recurring thrusts. How he'd dominate my every thought, drawing me towards the orgasm I've been yearning for him to give me.

The groans become longer, more insistent. The intimacy of sound is almost too private to hear. I should stop listening, but the human mind is cruel in its curiosities. The faint hitch of Clay's breath draws me in like a thread, wrapping tight around my pulse until my own body forgets how to stay still. Beside me, Rhys stirs. His lashes flutter open, a sliver of awareness cutting through the dim glow of the room.

"What's going on?" he asks, but it's obvious. There's no denying the heavy shift of my chest, pushing my nipples further into the air. A flicker of lust passes through his blue eyes, and thankfully, he doesn't question the how or why. Reading my body language, Rhys smooths a hand over my thigh, feeling how tense I am, and chuckles. "Whatever it is, seems like you need some help, Babygirl."

I don't argue. Beneath the blanket, Rhys peels my leggings down the length of my legs. They're tossed to the floor, those inked fingers skating back up my thighs. It's slow and teasing, his eyes locked on mine as my pupils dilate. Hovering just over my panties, I ache for contact, and as my body betrays me, I shift my hips up to meet his touch. The soft scrape of his knuckles against the fabric has us both moaning.

"Fuck, you're so wet."

The quickening tempo echoes faintly through my implants, blurred beneath the patter of water but unmistakable. It's smooth then rough, soft then harsh. Each punctuated by a sharp inhale and grunted exhale. I bite the inside of my cheek, forcing my expression to stay neutral, though my lungs can't seem to find their usual pattern.

Rhys is mesmerized by my face, his gaze drinking me in as he shifts my panties aside. Brushing his thumb over my clit, I throw my head back, already seeing stars. Thanks to the imagery Clay's noises are providing, I'm strung tighter than an archer's bow. Enjoying my suffering, Rhys mimics the action. Slow, tentative brushes that set my blood on fire, his tongue trailing along my throat.

Each quiet gasp from the bathroom tugs me further away from the moment I'm in and into the one I'm not supposed to witness. The sounds are soft, unguarded, *raw.* The kind of sound someone makes when they finally give into their desire.

Being kept on the precipice of pleasure, I grope my own breasts, teasing my nipples shamelessly while my hips roll, desperate to urge Rhys closer. To coax him into taking me with the same brutality I know him to have. I need it more than I need my next breath. Clay mutters words beneath his breath, my name on his lips as he ramps up his movements. The sound is obscene in its desire, like listening to porn on loud speaker in my skull.

"I don't know where you are right now," Rhys grabs my chin and brings my eyes level with his, "but I want you here with me." Suddenly, two fingers push inside me whilst his mouth claims mine, swallowing my groan. My teeth sink into his lip, my nails clawing in his hair. I can't see through the lights spotting my vision, sinking me into a dirty fantasy I didn't want to admit. It's like they're both here with me, driving me towards the point of no return.

Even without knowing it, Rhys' tempo mimics Clayton's. The speed increases, the moans intensifying. My legs drop wide open, Rhys shuffling aside and dragging me to lie flat. He grips my nape as he claims me in all ways, his tongue battling with mine whilst his fingers pump at rocket speed and cause my back to bow.

The room shrinks around us, growing smaller and warmer until only the sofa beneath me exists. My thoughts blur between what I'm hearing, what I'm feeling, and what I can't admit out loud. Three hearts in the same house, all beating for different reasons, and yet, in this suspended moment, everything feels like it's happening at once.

For once, it's not about choosing. It's about *feeling*. And God help me, I feel *everything*. Finally allowing me to breathe, Rhys drops his head to my chest, pulling my nipple into his mouth straight through my T-shirt. The heat and wetness of it is intoxicating, pushing me over that final ledge. I'm certain I explode at the same time Clayton does, the groaning in my head and the rawness of my throat blurring into one messy, delicious moment.

Rhys doesn't move away as I fall apart for him, for them both. His eyes lift to my face, slicing blue through darkness around us, close enough to share ragged breath. Clay's sounds taper, a low sigh swallowed by the rush of water. I exhale with him, my chest falling as I shudder through the aftereffects of my orgasm. It ends as quickly as it started, my mind left dizzy. It continues to spin as the water shuts off, leaving a hollow ache behind.

The fire pops sharply, drawing me back to the present. The smell of pine smoke, the flicker of light against the log walls, the soft hum of Rhys' breathing, it all wraps around me like a secret I can't untangle.

Somewhere in this cabin, another secret drips down tile through the steam. I lie there, caught between three heartbeats.

A few minutes later, once I've discarded my soaking panties and tugged my leggings back on, Clay appears at the base of the stairs. His damp hair curls against his forehead, his T-shirt clinging to him, darkened in places as if he didn't dry off properly. His skin is red raw, the temperature of water no doubt punishingly hot. Dropping my gaze to his hand, there's a deep imprint of teeth marks surrounding his knuckles. Clay promptly tucks his hand into his lounge pants pocket.

"Shall we get started on dinner?" Clay asks, a roughened croak to his voice. I lick my lips, wincing at the matching bite marks I've embedded there.

"Yes, food. Let's sort food," I reply almost robotically. Standing and closing the distance between us, Clay stares at me closely. I know my cheeks are pink and my neck is flushed, but neither of us comments on it. Realising Rhys hasn't joined us, I clear my throat theatrically. "You coming with us?" I choose my words wrongly, causing Rhys to laugh. My entire face sets on fire.

"Nah," he throws his feet onto the coffee table and lifts two glistening fingers into the air. "I'm all good here." Pushing his fingers into his mouth, my own jaw drops at the way he blatantly sucks, moaning softly into the microphone on the fireplace. If the atmosphere in the room wasn't awkward before, it sure is now. Thankfully, Clayton is too much of a gentleman to comment on it.

Gesturing toward the kitchen, already heading that way, his damp footprints mark the polished wood floor. I toss a glare back to Rhys, the firelight dancing across Rhys' face and casting him half in gold, half in shadow.

"Smug bastard," I hiss at him. His blue eyes glisten with arrogance as he spins my panties around his inked index finger, his laughter following behind me. Goddamn, these men will be the death of me.

RHYS

CHAPTER SIXTEEN

Opening my eyes, I lie in bed, waiting for the excitement to set in. It never does, but I've heard people are supposed to be excited on Christmas Day. Every year, I follow this ritual, my own tradition if you will, hoping that for one day a year, a giddy thrill might bubble in my blackened soul. Even demons should get a day off from torment, right?

Usually, I spend Christmas morning in a cold mansion where the walls are too white and there are furnished rooms just for show, pretending not to notice that my father's already gone to some resort or meeting that apparently couldn't wait for his son. It's always been that way, as if he's ran from any situation that might require some nurturing.

Even with the customary feeling of emptiness, I know this year is going to be different. There's warmth here, a lazy kind of peace that creeps beneath my skin. The air smells faintly of cinnamon and burnt wood from the fireplace downstairs. There's a faint murmur of voices, Harper's soft laugh and Clay's deeper one blending together. Any other day, the sound would have grated on my last nerve, but I suppose that's the magic of today. For the first time in years, I'm not surrounded by empty gestures or silver platters. I'm surrounded by people who have experienced life.

I roll onto my back, staring up at the timber ceiling, its panels uneven and imperfect. My father would've sent builders to replace them immediately. My chest tightens in a way I don't like, an ache that isn't anger or jealousy, just something softer I haven't named yet. I hate that Harper's probably responsible for it.

Dragging myself out of bed, I pull on a shirt and wander down the hall, the scent of coffee and something sweet hitting me halfway down the stairs. Harper's in the kitchen wearing a pair of fluffy socks with one of my hoodies, the sleeves pushed up to her elbows as she flips pancakes on an ancient stovetop. Clay's beside her, arguing over whether syrup counts as a food group. The sight is so absurdly domestic, it makes me freeze at the bottom step, unsure if I belong in the frame or if I'm just intruding on something perfect.

"Morning, Scrooge," Harper teases when she finally notices me, her smile curving her perfect lips. Clay doesn't look up, but I catch the smirk tugging at his lips. "You hungry?" she adds, and I shrug, wandering closer just for an excuse to be near her warmth. She doesn't realize how effortlessly she exudes the humble gratification that some people spend lifetimes chasing.

Uncaring of the bodyguard looming beside her, I step in behind and wrap my arms around Harper's body. She leans back into me as I steal a hug and move on just as quickly. The pair must have been awake for a while, considering how the table is pre-laid with plates, cutlery, and a little stack of mismatched mugs that look like they came straight from someone's grandmother's attic. There's even a candle flickering in the middle, red and white striped and shaped like a candy cane.

At Harper's instruction, Clayton carries over a mug and plants it in front of me. Whipped cream floats over the hot cocoa, and when I sip the rim, I get a straight shot of spirit. I almost choke, the taste catching me off guard until Harper winks and giggles. Hot cocoa and whiskey. I'm going to marry this girl.

Stacking the pancakes high on a plate, the pair of them join me with their own drinks, a peaceful calm falling over the table. It's strange, but I endure it, listening to a quiet Christmas playlist in the background. Maybe this is what's normal. We eat, drink and settle until the stack is gone and the mugs are empty.

"What's Merry Christmas in sign language?" Clayton asks, wiping his mouth on a napkin with gold trim. Harper beams as if he's just given her some incredible gift, brushing her flattened palm twice against her chest and making an arched C shape with her hand. Clayton copies it back, much to Harper's delight and I roll my eyes. *Suck up.* Harper stands to clear up but Clayton rushes to stop her.

"You go relax. We'll handle this," he gestures from himself to me.

"Will we?" I ask, my voice loaded with a challenge. This asshole is becoming far too comfortable in my company these days. Harper's already shrugged and walked away, her fingers stroking the line of my shoulders as she goes. Huffing, I collect up the plates, making sure to clatter them noisily the entire time. Dumping them on the side, I go to turn away when Clayton slaps a hand towel against my chest.

"I'll wash, you dry," he grunts, pushing his hands into the soapy water filling the basin. He's lucky I don't shove his head in it. Call it the Christmas spirit but I stand there, drying fucking dishes like the maid. As Harper puts on a cheesy festive movie, Clayton leans in.

"You've got her a present, I presume." I freeze in place, water dripping from the plate in my hand.

"A present?" I parrot back, my brows pulled tightly together. Clayton looks at me like I'm some kind of idiot.

"Yeah...like a gift. Where do you think Christmas presents come from?"

"Personal assistants," I answer honestly. Clayton's expression grows concerned, but I shrug off his unease. When I was young, my father's personal assistant would pick up and wrap presents, leaving them at the end of my bed like a prim version of Santa in heels. A few years later, I walked in on him screwing her in a Santa Claus suit and any innocence I had left quickly died. Clayton groans, fighting with himself to keep his voice low and level.

"You need to give Harper something."

"Like what?" I ask, annoyed with myself for needing the bastard's help with something so simple. I've never given a present in my life. I wouldn't even know where to start. Wiping the towel out of my hands, where it's been held in suspension, Clayton finishes the drying himself.

"You're supposed to put thought into a gift and consider who you're gifting it to. What they will like, something they've been wanting and won't get for themselves." Finishing the chore, Clayton pulls open a drawer and retrieves a rectangular package, wrapped in greaseproof paper or similar. He's far too self-assured, his shoulders pulled back as he approaches Harper. I stalk after him on silent feet, watching the display with keen interest.

Clearing his throat, Clayton lowers onto the rug to where Harper has slunk down to be closer to the fire. Redirecting her eyes from craning her neck to see the TV, her hair catches the glow like spun copper and candy floss. She blinks at Clayton, a smile already forming. I hate how easily she gives it to him. How he doesn't even have to work for it. He holds out the small parcel, suddenly awkward in the way he shifts and angles his head away from her direct stare. Harper takes it gently, her brows lifting as she peels away the paper to reveal an old, leather-bound notebook, the edges frayed and the corners softened by time.

"I found it on the bookshelf," Clay mutters, scratching the back of his neck. "Figured you could fill it with all those thoughts you keep to yourself." I snort to myself. What a fucking loser, she won't care for that.

Except I'm eating my words as Harper's mouth parts, her hands cradling the notebook as if it's a precious piece of treasure. Then her hands fly up to her mouth, and I swear her eyes glimmer brighter than the goddamn Christmas tree behind her. She whispers something I can't catch before throwing her arms around Clay's shoulders, the notebook pressed between them as she giggles into his chest. He stiffens at first, then melts, actually freaking melts like his limbs have liquefied, his hand hovering uncertainly before landing at her back. A punch slams into me, right in the center of my ribs.

I've never seen her look like that. Not even with me. The sound she makes, a soft, breathless, and unguarded noise, rips through me worse than any fight we've ever had. Clayton doesn't even notice I'm watching, too wrapped up in her quiet joy, and for a split second I envy him. I've never envied anyone in my life, but then again, no one has ever had something I wanted. I want her to look at me like that. To see something I've done, something I've given, and think it's enough. My fists clench at my sides before I can stop them, nails biting into my palms. When Harper finally pulls back, she's still smiling, thumb tracing the notebook's cover.

"It's perfect," she signs and speaks. Clay's answering grin is small but genuine, the kind of smile that makes him seem years younger, erasing years of trauma in a flash. I hate that it suits him. I hate that it works, this stupid gift giving sentiment. Harper looks down at her notebook again, clutching it to her chest, and I can't take my eyes off her. I should be happy that she's happy, but all I can think about is how badly I want to be the one who makes her light up like that.

I storm back upstairs, two steps at a time, muttering every curse I know under my breath. The door slams behind me, the echo bouncing off the wooden beams like a reprimand, but I don't care. My jaw aches from clenching it too long, my pulse caught somewhere between anger and desperation. An old notebook is all it took. I can do better than that.

I tear through drawers, rifling through half-empty cupboards and shelves of useless trinkets, refusing to admit that the real problem isn't that I don't have anything to give her, it's that I don't know what she likes. Aside from my dick, but I can't even find a ribbon to tie around that.

My frustration hits a wall of despair as I backhand a row of miniature bottles across the bathroom counter and onto the floor. My reflection in the mirror looks deranged, driven mad with the need to impress the girl downstairs and improve the man staring back at me. The bottles roll, one tapping my foot. Slowly looking down at the offensive object, a lightbulb pings to life in my head.

Retrieving the complimentary toiletries, I hold the lotion, moisturiser, and body oil in my hands, the cogs in my mind turning and a smile carving across my face. I've got it.

When I call her name, Harper's answering laugh floats up the stairs. She climbs them silently with her socked feet, appearing in the doorway a moment later. Her green eyes sweep across the bedroom, her brow quirking with suspicion and dropping to the weighted pillowcase twisted around my hand.

"What's that?" Harper jerks her chin outward, refusing to step any further into the room. Her shoulders are tight beneath the fabric of my hoodie, her stance guarded. For once, her bodyguard isn't trailing behind her, so I understand the suspicion crossing her features.

"Your Christmas gift," I say, holding out the pillowcase-wrapped masterpiece. Her brows lift skeptically, but she humors me anyway, striding closer. Staying at arm's length, Harper's nose wrinkles as she gives it a cautious shake. Anyone would think there's a live cobra inside.

"Again, what's this?" she asks, tugging at the edge of the fabric until the jar rolls into her palm, glass catching the low light. She studies it, her head tilted, a few strands of hair falling from her messy bun to brush her cheek.

"A face mask," I answer, unable to stop the grin creeping up one corner of my mouth. "I'm going to pamper you." I shuffle over on the bed, patting the space beside me in invitation, but she doesn't move.

Instead, Harper's expression shifts, something softer unfurling behind her guarded stare, and just like that, she drops into my lap. Her warmth seeps through the thin fabric of my sweatpants, her laughter humming low in her chest.

Holy shit, gift giving is amazing.

"You didn't have to do anything for me," Harper says, her eyes flicking up to mine. "Just being away from campus, being able to stop looking over our shoulders and just... settle. I think this trip will do all of us the world of good." Her lips twitch. "And you being nice to Clayton wouldn't go amiss either."

"Now you're asking for too much." My grin is crooked as I reach to brush a smudge of flour from her jaw, my thumb lingering longer than it should. Forcing myself to pull back, I tug at the fabric of the hoodie. "Take this off and lie back. I'm going to look after you today, so you can have a day off from looking after us." Her brows arch, distrust glinting in her eyes.

"Is this a trick to stick your dick in me?" I twist my lips, almost going back on my own decision. No, I must be strong. For once in my damn life, I will be selfless.

"Not this time."

"You promise?"

"I promise," I say solemnly, even as my smirk betrays me. "Even when you eventually beg me for it, my cock is remaining firmly in my pants. That's the second part of your Christmas present, since I know you take great joy in giving me blue balls."

Harper's laughter bursts out in that untamed way, and it hits me right in the chest. Like a moth, I'm drawn to her light, a genuine smile stretching across my face that's so different from the casual smirk I usually hide behind.

Eyeing me for a long moment, Harper huffs a sound of submission that stirs the monster in me. Reaching for the hem of the hoodie, I help her peel it off, just barely withholding a groan at the strappy tank top underneath. She's braless again, her nipples pebbling against the fabric.

I mentally chastise myself for deciding today of all days to be celibate as she climbs across the bed like a sexy minx. She knows exactly what she's doing, her hair tumbling from its bun in that just-fucked look. Laying on her back, Harper crosses her hands over her stomach as if she's being prepped for surgery.

"Relax," I demand, instantly realizing that's probably not the best tactic. Instead, I move to her side, kneading the tension from her shoulders. It takes a couple of rotations but Harper seems to beat the urge to both tense up and giggle insistently. "See? That wasn't so hard."

Her lips twitch, but she keeps them sealed, eyes fluttering closed in feigned patience. Rolling the jar between my palms to warm it, I open it to dip my fingers into the smooth mixture. The faint scent of coconut rises from the surface as I brush the first stroke across her cheek. Harper shivers, a sound caught somewhere between a sigh and a giggle, before melting into the pillows.

"It's your turn to be worshipped," I hum quietly. The twitch of her smile messing with the even layer I was painting onto her face.

"You're worshipping me now?" she murmurs, half-mocking as I spread another careful streak along her jaw.

"That's what you want. Otherwise you'd only have one man in this house desperate for your attention." Harper's lashes flutter open just enough to glare at me, though the creamy white face mask makes her expression adorably unthreatening. I set the jar aside and reach for the plate I'd stashed on the bedside table. Pressing two cucumber slices over her eyes, I press play on a calming playlist on my phone. It's meant to free her chakra or some shit like that. I didn't really pay attention, otherwise distracted by the creation process of her face mask.

Falling quiet, Harper's breathing evens out, and I shift down the bed, my fingers tracing over the curve of her ankle. She twitches instantly, jerking her leg back with a squeal of laughter. I reprimand her, catching her foot and pulling her sock off. Planting it on my thigh, I push my lotioned thumbs along the curved edge, rolling small circles across the pad of her foot. I've had enough pedicures to know how the motions should go. I'm practically certified. Relenting to me, Harper sighs, her body relaxing once more. Her toes flex against my palm, a pleased moan escapes her.

"God, that feels good," she admits softly. I find myself smiling again, a strange warmth blossoming in my chest. It's chased by a fluttering sensation, the thought revolving around my mind that I'm finally doing something right. I'm really getting a hang of this Christmas thing. "And this mask smells amazing," Harper inhales deeply through her nose. "What's in it?"

I grin to myself, working my thumbs south towards her heel. "Well, I didn't have much to work with other than the complimentary toiletries. A bit of lotion, some cocoa butter, a spoon of honey. It's mostly made up of its base ingredient, which is semen." Harper jerks up onto your elbows, scraping the cucumber slices aside. An irritated sound leaves my throat. She's supposed to be relaxing.

"Tell me you're joking," she demands. My brows hitch, a look of seriousness on my face. Releasing her foot, I wipe my hands clean on a towel, raking my brain for the right thing to say.

"I was just following Clayton's instructions. Give you something you'll like and wouldn't gift yourself."

"And you thought I wanted your cum *rubbed into my face*," Harper's voice turns all high pitched and squeaky. She leans forward to snatch the towel from me, wiping her face clean.

"No," I shake my head slowly. "I thought you'd want romance. What's more romantic than cleansed pores?" Harper pulls the towel away from her face, a smile growing across her face. A face that is glowing, by the way. She's very welcome, that was some of my best masturbation material.

"You're right, Rhys," Harper flutters her lashes, all seductive-like. I shudder at those words. I know I'm right, it's just nice to hear those words come from her full lips. Crawling her way towards me, I'm distracted by the valley of her cleavage, too slow to react to her gripping my hair, dragging my head back and straddling my thighs. The next second, the open jar is in her hands.

"There's nothing more romantic than cleansed pores," Harper murmurs, just before she slaps a handful of the face mask across my cheek. It hits me in the eye, seeping into my nose and mouth. I can confirm, it definitely does not taste as good as it smells.

CLAYTON

CHAPTER SEVENTEEN

Sirens wail again, like they always do. They bend through my skull like ghosts of a night that never ends, red and blue lights stuttering over wet brick, over my hands, over her. Harper stands where Jeremy used to. The same alley, same slick walls, but her hair glows gold under the flash. Her lips move, but no sound comes out. All I hear is the rain, pounding onto my head and streaming down my back, slapping the concrete where I kneel like a man praying for redemption. Beneath it, the crack of a gun that hasn't been fired in years.

I reach for her, just like I reached for him, my fingers slick with guilt I'll never wash off. She takes a step back, her green eyes haunting and filled with pity, that same look she gives me when I promise her things I can't keep. I'll protect you. I'll fix this. I'll save you. Lies that rot the air. Behind her, the door to the vault creaks open, spilling light so bright it burns.

"Clay," she whispers finally, her voice breaking like glass shattering all around me. "You can't be my savior. You can't even save yourself."

Suddenly, she's standing amongst blood-soaked snow instead of that alley. Her breath clouds the cold air as her knees hit the ground. Once again, I'm on the outside looking in. Too far away, too slow to act. The gun in my hand morphs into the trembling fist I once used to knock on

145

her dorm door, to check if she wanted me to walk her to class. Sirens morph into the sound of her laughter echoing down the lodge hallway. Both end the same way. Suffocating silence.

"I c-can help. I...want to try," I rasp, but the words fall apart before they reach her. My lungs ache like they did when the cops dragged me from the ground, like I'm still gasping on concrete. I want to say she deserves someone better, someone who isn't stitched together with regret, but my throat won't form the words. When I blink, she's gone, leaving only the echo of my promise and the resounding certainty that I was never meant to be anyone's savior. Not then. Not now.

I jolt awake, a sound I don't recognize coming out of me. A strangled, broken gasp that scrapes my throat raw. My chest heaves like I've been running for miles, the air too thick to breathe. For a second, I don't know where I am. The walls are wrong, the light is wrong, the silence is *wrong.* My mind's still in the alley, in the snow, sirens flashing, blood slicking the ground, Jeremy's lifeless eyes and Harper's unresponsive body alternating with each blink.

"Clayton," a soft voice gasps, small hands shaking my shoulders. Strands of loose hair trickle onto my cheeks, concealing eyes that bore straight into my soul. The room starts to form around me, the lodge coming back from the brink of my mind. A digital clock beside the bed shows its ten minutes until midnight. I drag my hands over my face, pressing the heel of my palms to my eyes until black spots bloom behind them. It's still Christmas, and I'm still bleeding from places no one can see. Harper's hand slips to my jaw, her grip tight and trembling. "Hey, you're okay. It was just a dream."

I take her wrist in mine, peeling her hand away. My head's still spinning, my heart not believing it's her. She looks too perfect to be real, too *alive* for me to trust it. I watched her fall. I felt the judder of her last breath as if it was my own. Yet as I lie there, the truth seeps through the icy chill claiming my bones.

Harper's skin feels warm against my palm, too warm to be a ghost. I trace the shape of her wrist like I'm memorizing proof of life, the faint pulse thudding beneath my thumb. Harper doesn't pull away. She watches me explore, waiting for me to realize she's here, and she's not going anywhere. A shudder escapes my chest, half a sob, half a prayer, and before I can stop myself, I'm dragging her closer. My hand slides up the back of her neck, tangling in her hair as I press my forehead to hers.

Her breath catches, our noses brush, and then her lips find mine. She means for the kiss to be gentle, careful not to jar me too quickly, but that's not what I need. Pulling her flush against the length of my body, every ounce of fear I've swallowed for months is poured into where our mouths connect. Every sleepless night, every moment I thought I'd lost her for good. My fingers twist in the fabric of her nightshirt, clutching like I'm afraid she'll disappear once again.

The world blurs to nothing but the slide of her mouth and the soft sounds she makes when she exhales. I kiss her like she's the only thing that's ever tethered me to this planet, like if I stop, I'll fall straight back into the nightmare. She murmurs my name against my lips, and it's the sweetest, most agonizing sound I've ever heard. It doesn't matter that my heart's still racing or that the tears haven't stopped, she's here. She's here, and I can finally breathe again.

When we break apart, our foreheads still touch. Harper's thumb drags over my cheek, catching a tear before it falls. I can't look away from her, not even as I fall apart in a way I'd never want her to see. The air between us changes, hanging on a thread of fragility. Whatever this is, it's a twisted combination of heartache and relief, enough to silence every ghost that's ever haunted me.

"I need to have you," I whisper, hoping she has her receivers on. Whether Harper hears my words or senses the stirring of my body, her breath trembles against my mouth. I can taste that she wants me in the same way, but she's hesitant. Maybe she's worried the way my body responds to her is a desperate distraction for the images in my head, but that couldn't be further from the truth. I'm laser focused on what matters, what I've been holding myself back from for too long.

Trailing her fingers down my jaw, Harper's hold settles over my chest, feeling the pounding of my heartbeat against her palm. I'm alive, and she's the one who's pulled me back from the edge. Closing the distance between our lips, Harper kisses me with a tenderness I'm not used to as her hand drifts lower, tracing the rise and fall of my ribs. The contact burns in the most delicious way.

Every part of me comes alive beneath her touch. Our legs become tangled as I slide an arm around her waist, unable to face any reality where she's not pinned against me. Her hand continues its journey, the very tips of her fingers grazing the waistband of my boxers. I stifle a sound against her mouth, tilting my hips upwards. Harper doesn't hesitate, peeling the material down my thighs as if she's been waiting for this just as long.

Somewhere across the room, a shuffling pricks at my ears. That's when I know Harper can't hear, because she continues to kiss and tease me with her nails, oblivious to the small square foil being tossed onto the pillow beside my head.

"Impregnate my girl and I'll cut your dick off," Rhys grumbles, stalking away as quickly as he arrived, slamming the door behind him. I reach up to retrieve the condom packet, confusion quickly slipping away as Harper wraps a hand around my dick. I gasp against her skin, my mouth falling to her jaw. Her touch feels so much better than my own. She strokes me leisurely, my shaft feeling like silk against her small palm.

I wish I could hold off, to adore Harper the way she deserves, but I've been waiting too long for this. Pushing the condom into her other hand, the ghost of her laughter fluttering across my stubble, I reach between us. My hands feel gigantic against Harper's thigh, her breath hitching as I stroke upwards to find her without underwear. She was asking for trouble running in here to console me like that.

Sitting upright, Harper straddles my hips, her legs primed open for me. Gliding my fingers across her center, I tease her wetness towards her clit, rolling the bud in achingly slow circles. Her hand returns to my cock, my shaft solid and pulsating now, as we stoke each other's desire higher. Her soft groans blend into mine, her thighs quivering. My fingers run the length of her slit, teasing her opening before gliding upwards again.

Every time I almost push inside, Harper's entire body tenses in preparation. She grows frustrated before I do, sheathing my dick with the latex and positioning herself over me. I wish she could hear the words that linger on my tongue, how I'd encourage her to go gentle. I don't know what Rhys is packing, but I know my own girth. Instead, I grip her hips, slowing her descent as she tries to take all of me at once.

Lifting her in short bursts, I ease into her, inch by inch, giving her time to stretch to accommodate me. She doesn't reach the base but it's enough, our desire taking over. Slamming her hands onto my chest, Harper takes over, bouncing her ass into the air. I grip the nightshirt, ripping it over her head. This is our first time together, I want her bared to me, even in the dark. My hands feel calloused against her skin, her ribs shifting and breasts bouncing. I cup them, kneading and brushing my thumbs over her nipples, discovering one of them is pierced.

In the shadows, I watch the outline of her head tilting back, her hair tickling my thighs. She's a goddess. A woman who has walked through the ashes of hell and come back fighting. A soul so pure, I'm in awe of her. The palms on my chest shift to either side of my head, Harper's mouth coming back to me. God, I hope she always comes back to me. The storm inside my chest rages against the tempest she creates around us. Her pussy is so tight, so blissfully sweet, I know there's no way I'll last for her the way I'd like.

Smoothing my hands down her back and over her ass, I hold tight and roll Harper onto her back, not breaking our connection. As her legs part wider, her pussy takes me deeper, so does her mouth. I push my tongue inside, dancing with hers as I thrust harder, claiming her deeper. Arching her back, Harper takes all of me at last, and we groan in unison at the perfection of it.

For once, I don't try to control everything. I just let it happen, the natural rhythm of my body harmonizing with hers. Our heartbeats sync, our mouths dragging over patches of skin and jaw, teeth nipping lightly. It's not about hunger or possession. It's about the ache beneath my ribs that matches hers. About needing to feel alive after too many nights of detachment. When she sighs my name, it's quiet, like a plea in the dark. A promise I can't deny.

"I'm here, Beautiful," I mutter the vow to myself. "I'm here, and I'm not going anywhere. I'm all yours."

HARPER

CHAPTER EIGHTEEN

Smirking to myself, I open my new, leatherbound notebook. New year, new notebook. It's incredibly naïve and nerdy of me to believe that will resolve the world's problems, but I smile anyway. Give this girl a fresh page and a sweet coffee, and she feels unbeatable.

Not to mention, both Clay and Rhys are beside me, ready to see our first day back in true student fashion. Well, ready might be a stretch for Rhys, who is slumped back in his seat. I've read the words, *fuck my life*, on his lips at least six times this morning, but he forces a sarcastic smile and thumbs up every time I glance over. It's ready enough.

Then there's Clay. His shoulders are pushed back, as is his hair. Blond waves tamed away from his face without the need of a beanie. I can't hide my smile, pride swelling in my chest. Both at the progress he's made, but also at myself. Yay for a strong female who can shoulder burdens until her man's ready to take them back. If he is my man, but after Christmas night, I can't help but believe he is.

Between Clay's passionate, slow thrusts and the scrape of his stubble on my cheek, something cracked wide open between us. His kisses worshipped me, his hands admiring my body with a need for me to do the same in return. I still don't know what the extent of Clay's nightmare was, but it has awakened an urgency for affection I've never seen from him before.

Now he sits at my side, almost a new man. His muscles aren't tightly coiled, he's not glaring around in suspicion. In fact, there's a hint of a smile gracing his lips. Someone sought to rid this campus of Clayton, and he's back. Unbeaten and undeterred.

Christmas feels like it was months ago, not just two weeks. The morning after the night I spent cradled in Clay's arms, his cock buried inside of me, Rhys not so subtly found a way to put me on a private jet so I could spend some time with my Aunt, deciding to drive my Audi back to campus himself.

Although it was nice to be back amongst the cat hair and my dusty paperbacks, I can't say my Aunts interrogations were particularly enjoyable. Where have you been, why haven't you called, where's your car, is that a hickey?! I love my Aunt, but within a few days I was longing to be back at Waversea. Now I am, thanks to a limo and chauffeur at Rhys' request, filled with the optimism that this year will be better.

At the front of the hall, Peterson walks in, straightening his lab coat with the small microphone clipped to his lapel. Rhys has been a busy boy in his time back. Each of my tutors now have brand new mic clips that they are expected to wear, to save me running back and forth with my own. Peterson briefly glances across the room, not missing a beat before getting straight to business.

"Welcome back everyone. I hope you had a refreshing break and all that. As a part of our new topic this term, you will be expected to complete a project of your choosing. Make full use of the labs and equipment to back up your findings with evidence. You may work alone or with others, but you must produce individual essays on your findings." That last statement was spoken closer to the mic on his lab coat and was clearly meant for me. I roll my eyes, fighting the urge to bite back that it was one time.

A few rows ahead, Kenneth's head whips back so fast, I worry he might snap his own neck. Initially I thought the plea in his eyes was to partner up with me, but if I move my head ever so slightly, I can see his intended target is Clay. The desperation spreads to a wobble in his lip, the extent of how much he's missed his roommate evident for everyone to see. Sniggers are passed around, hidden behind hands and textbooks so I can't decipher where they came from.

Shifting uncomfortably, Clayton drops an arm over the back of my chair, sealing some decision I wasn't a part of. Kenneth runs from the room with his face in his hands, whilst my hearing is focused on Peterson reading through the criteria on the whiteboard. I'm not getting involved.

"The topic of this project is open to personal choice but must correlate to the human body. If I have to read about asthmatic pigs or diabetic rats anymore, I'm going to quit in favor of becoming a marine biologist instead. Sea life can't complain about the deadlines they were aware of or moan about the grades they deserve."

I share a confused look with Rhys. Despite turning away, I can still hear Peterson muttering under his breath, my microphone picking up on a rant about fish being the only schools that should exist. I'm going to hazard a guess that the winter break wasn't kind to our professor.

His lecture drones on, a humdrum sound I try to follow but can't seem to hold onto. My thoughts slip, drawn back to Christmas break, specifically that afternoon when I listened to Clay whilst Rhys's hands were on me. It's become a recurring fantasy I'd never dare say aloud. But now, with Clay's arm draped around me and Rhys's thigh pressed against mine, the air between us feels charged enough to make the idea almost seem possible. A forbidden daydream, the kind that tempts you just by existing.

The thought alone sends a shiver through me, my pulse fluttering in its cage, my skin prickling at the ghost of their touch. It's stupid, really. A fantasy best kept for the dark quiet of my room, where no one can see the way my mind wanders. In reality, the two of them together would be like a lion and a wolf fighting over a carcass, blood and dismembering included. Yeah, no thanks. I'll settle for them sitting in the same room. At the same table no less, which makes me feel all kinds of giddy.

Peterson's voice cuts off suddenly, his attention distracted by the phone he drags out of his pocket. I seem to be the only one who notices the change in his posture as he faces the class, assessing each of us in turn with shadowed eyes before glancing at his watch.

"I'll leave the slides on the board. Last person out switches off the lights," he huffs loudly in my head and gathers up his belongings. The sound in my head cuts out with the switching off of his mic, the professor exiting classes ten minutes after it has started.

After a moment of passing around glances, students jump up and rush out to make the most of the extra time they've been gifted. I stay long enough to take notes of the assignment, before packing up both mine and Rhys' books and pens. Clay catches my attention, confusion bleeding into his onyx eyes.

"You're carrying his shit around?"

"Oh," I blink down at my bag. "It's not like that. We have a deal. Rhys has to write his own notes, but I know for a fact he will have no issues using said-notes as rolling paper for smokes or unnecessary midnight bonfires. So, I keep them safe in my possession between classes."

I see Rhys chuckling to himself, placing a cigarette behind his ear as he walks past empty-handed. Only when he gets to the door does he pause, looking back to check I'm following. Such a good boy, I muse to myself. Turning back to Clay, the uncertain expression is still present.

"Seems like I missed out on a lot while I was away." I take his hand in mine with half a smile, not sure how this tag-team dynamic is going to work. But I've learnt to enjoy what I have and not worry about the future until it slaps you in the face. Once we've caught up with him, Rhys walks on as if he's leading the way, although his frequent glances back suggest otherwise. He doesn't have a clue what our next class is.

Ignoring the looks from other students as we step into the hallway, more than a few lifting their hands to hide non-discreet comments, I tell myself to keep walking, to pretend I don't feel the eyes that trail me and sense the whispers of my name. Although a pang of longing wishes we were still in the rental, just the three of us, as unrealistic as that is. The world doesn't stop turning and I'm not going to graduate by hiding away.

Further down the row of lockers, a vibrant pink head of hair whips back and forth. I raise a brow, closing the distance between myself and Addy. There's no need for her to be in the science block, but the panic in her brown eyes is reason enough. Spotting me, she stops fidgeting with the strap of her backpack and rushes forward.

'Harper, something's happened,' she signs, blocking everyone else out of our conversation. My gut flips, the optimism I started the day with fleeing. Addy glances at Rhys and Clay behind me, then back down to her hand, where she's clutching something small and pink. *'This was slipped under our door. It's got your name on it.'*

I take it from her, my pulse already spiking. The paper is heart-shaped, cut unevenly, edges frayed, as if whoever made it used dull scissors. It smells faintly of marker ink and something chemical, paint thinner maybe. The handwriting inside is bold and jagged, pressed so hard the paper has nearly torn.

You shouldn't have brought him back.

The words curl in on themselves, black ink bleeding into the paper like veins. There's a small smear where someone's thumb must have dragged across the wet letters, a print left behind in a faint reddish tint. My mind snags on it, the methodical side of my brain cataloguing details before the rest of me can process the meaning. The pressure points in the loops of the letters. The slight tremor in the downstrokes. Whoever wrote this was angry, but deliberate.

My breath snags as Clay's shadow falls over me, his fingers plucking the paper from my grip. Addy shifts uneasily, the bright smile she had this morning a distant memory. We were so excited to be back, spending last night catching unpacking our duffles and sorting out our backpacks for a fresh, new semester. Now, we're straight back in the midst of someone else's game.

Peering over my shoulder, I watch Clay's expression darken as he scans the message. His fingers twitch slightly, crumpling the paper without meaning to. Rhys moves closer to read it too, his jaw ticking once before his gaze flicks to mine. We've spent long enough together to know what the other is thinking, and Rhys is contemplating murder. He just doesn't know who's.

The same gossipers from before have huddled nearby, pretending to shuffle books into their bags, their ears pricked and eyes wide. I scan their faces one by one, looking for a flicker of guilt, a curl of a smile, anything that gives them away, but they're all too practiced in feigning innocence. Phones are already out, ready to capture a new post for the student forum, giving the person who sent a front row seat to my reaction. I'll be damned if I give them the satisfaction.

Slowly, I inhale, forcing a calm I don't feel to take over. Then, deliberately, I place myself between the two gorgeous men either side of me, Clay on my right and Rhys on my left, before plastering on a nonchalant smile.

"I don't know about you two," I say lightly, plucking the note from Clay's hand and tossing it aside like the trash it is, "but I'm ready for my third coffee of the morning." They both eye me curiously, but don't question my behavior. Addy stares as if I've grown another head, but I sign that I'll catch her later. Together, we walk through the crowd without a care in the world, or at least that's what I want everyone around us to think.

Inside, though, my pulse thrums like a warning siren. Because if that note was hand-delivered, someone knows exactly where I sleep, what I've been up to and when I would have been out. Approaching the exit, I reluctantly click my receivers into place. Another benefit to the winter break was the silence, giving me a reprieve from the loud hustle and bustle of campus life. There's nothing quite like a thinly-veiled threat to bring me back down to reality.

"I hope you haven't unpacked. We're getting your shit and you're staying with me from now on." The authority in his tone makes my head jerk up. I gape at him, looking to Clay for backup, but finding none. He watches on silently, his arms crossed.

"I can't leave Addy to fend for herself," I protest. "They were *at the dorm*, Rhys." Not humoring this conversation any further, I move in the direction of the cafeteria. Rhys grabs my forearm and drags me into the shadow of the building. Clay is by his side, glaring at me as if they are actually in agreement for once.

"This isn't up for negotiation," Rhys growls. The tic in his jaw is all aggression, but the flicker of worry in his eyes gives him away. I lift a brow, standing my ground.

"And what about Clay? He's also the focus of these taunts. You planning to offer *him* a cozy spot in your bed too?" The mental image of the two of them arguing over who gets to be the big spoon spreads a grin across my face. They both make the same strangled sound of disgust perfectly in sync, suddenly jerking away from each other.

Patting Rhys' bicep, I brush off his concern as if I can manifest the same within myself. Someone is playing pranks that are, admittedly, going too far, but I can only put it down to jealousy. We just need to see it through, show we won't be bullied and they will grow bored. Eventually.

"Look, I appreciate it, but I'll be fine." Rhys' face contorts, his rage rising to the surface.

"For once in your goddamn life, Harper, do as you fu—" Clay halts Rhys's words by shoving his shoulder aside and stepping closer to me. His hand cradles my cheek, forcing my eyes up to his.

"We just want to make sure you're safe. If something were to happen to you because of me, I would never be able to forgive myself." The fight drains from me at his gentle words, my hackles lowering as logic overtakes defiance. I guess I hoped if I kept denying the truth, I could diminish the seriousness of it all.

"Okay, fine. I'll agree to an escort when moving around campus, but I'm staying in my own dorm and continuing my routine like normal. I came here for freedom and independence. I won't be stopped from going to classes and studying in the library on weekdays."

"No fucking way!" Rhys barges his way in between us once more. His hands close around my shoulders and his chest brushes mine, halfway between a hug and a cage. "The library's a goddamn maze, too many dark corners for creeps to hide. You can study at my place. I'll get pizzas, go down on you as you type, whatever the fuck you want but there's negotiation on this."

I can see he's trying, and a tiny part of me is swooning for it, but keeping me from a library is like cutting off a limb. The smell of pages and the millions of words waiting to be devoured sooth my soul. It's the only place I can silence my thoughts and truly escape.

"Rhys," I breathe, pleading with him to see it from my perspective. He wouldn't be told where to go and what to do, and I'm equally as stubborn. "I'm not going to hide away, and I need access to all of our source material that's in there. I doubt you have books on the clinical correlations of biochemistry stashed beneath your bed."

Clay reaches for my hand, brushing my knuckles reassuringly. I've missed his presence, the feeling that someone always has my back.

"Clay will look out for me during our study sessions and I promise I won't wander off."

I take Rhys's huff as acceptance, leaning up to place my lips on his cheek but he steps away. I blink at him in confusion, seeing none of the worry he couldn't hide a moment ago.

"I see how it is," he nods, distancing himself from our quiet conversation. Spreading his arms wide, he walks back into the cold like a lone soldier fighting a solitary battle. "You have your loyal protector back now, so what the fuck do you need me for?" He levels Clay with a stare that could melt iron, the rigid edge to his jaw back like an old friend.

"Rhys, wait," I call after him, but he's gone, his retreating footsteps like nails piercing my heart. I stand there for a moment, suspended in the silence he leaves behind, doing all I can to resist leaning on Clay for support. The last thing I want is to create a situation where one is always stepping in when the other can't, but Clay doesn't have the same inclination.

His arms wind around me, his chest supporting my cheek as a bitter chuckle escapes me. The first day back, a day that started with such optimism, has fallen flat on its face. Not the best omen going forward, but even without the note, it wasn't going to be easy going. Nothing ever is when Rhys and Clay are close to one another.

CHAPTER NINETEEN

A strange sense of satisfaction hums within at seeing the frat house full again. I didn't care for the drunken squabbles and revolving door of jocks until they didn't exist anymore. That's when I discovered what I'd been doing all this time was filling the silence so the doubts in my head didn't have to. I don't like my own company, and after this, I won't have to endure again for a long, long time.

Sneakers thump against the hardwood, arms filled with bulky textbooks and paperbacks. I've got the entire football and basketball team at my disposal, the promise of extra credit looming over their heads. Ferrying books from the library to my living room, each one tips their head to me on the way in. I'm leaning against the staircase, a lollipop in my mouth, feeling far too smug for a man who's whipped enough to swap out his usual cigarette for candy.

Harper refuses to stop visiting the library, so I'm relocating it to where I can keep a close eye on her. And should I become distracted, as is a regular occurrence in her presence, the newly installed surveillance system I've set up will catch any suspicious behavior. The week I spent here alone after Christmas was not wasted.

The scent of paper and graphite soon seep into the walls. Stacks upon stacks of hardcovers, paperbacks and journals with cracked spines build up around the sofa and cover the coffee table. It's taken all afternoon, and I'm not sure how long we've got before the librarian returns from the vets.

For the record, I did not run over her cat. I just told her I did. She was an obstacle that needed to be temporarily removed whilst I effectively stole the entire science section, from Organic Chemistry to Molecular Biology, and everything in between. And just so Harper can't insist there's something missing, I've got Joey clearing out the dark romance aisles and taking them straight up to my bedroom.

"Ahh, Rhys," a guy with short hair and tattoos of spiders over his huge biceps shoves his hands into his pockets, "We're about to bring in the last batch, but there's no room left unless you want to block the walkways or take over the sofa."

Pushing upright, I follow the jock back into the living area. He's right, something is going to have to be sacrificed. We can't put any of the books on the kitchen island, because Harper's new coffee machine is there. Call it a late Christmas present, now that I understand the meaning of *practical gifts*. I'd thought my present in the cabin was extremely thoughtful, but Harper has made sure to have a talk with me about boundaries since.

Twisting my lips, I look back and forth across the room and nod, deciding there's only one thing for it.

"Cover the sofa, and restack those books in the corner to create a throne."

"A throne?" Jockey Boy questions and I hit him with a hard stare.

"Yes, a throne. Every King deserves one, does he not?" The others nearby pause, exchanging looks but they obey. Keeping watch over the rearranging of physics books Harper is likely to not need, adrenaline prickles beneath my skin. It comes together quickly, which is lucky. Harper's nightly study session is due to start soon.

Dropping onto the throne, I marvel at its sturdiness. The base is built from hardcover tomes, the armrests from stacked binders of lab notes, and the seat is a thick slab of texts covered by a single sofa cushion. Said sofa has been lost beneath the towers of anatomy manuals, the coffee table lost beneath molecular models and open notebooks. I catch myself smiling as the jocks all line up before me, eager for my approval.

"Good job gentleman. I'll speak to Coach in the morning." Dismissing them with a flick of my wrist, I lean back, smug as fuck. Harper can fight me all she likes, but when it comes to her safety, I'm not taking any chances. If she won't stop visiting the library, then she'll have to come and find it here.

Ten minutes past seven, my legs are crossed and I have a celebratory whiskey in hand as my front door flies open. I hear her pass through the lower level, her stomping hard enough to rattle the windowpanes, before she rounds the stacks, her eyes alight with rage. Haloed by the light from the hall, her hair is flustered from the wind, cheeks flushed pink. She seems to be alone but I know better than to think Clay isn't hanging back on the porch.

"What the actual *hell* did you do?" Her voice slices through me like a siren, high and furious and, God, so fucking alive. Resting my glass on the cover of *Cellular Metabolism and Human Function,* I crack my neck side to side.

"Improved your access to study material," I say smoothly, gesturing around us. "Welcome to your new library."Her eyes flick from the piles of books to the throne I'm sitting on. Her mouth opens, then shuts again, and for a long moment, she just stares, caught somewhere between fury and utter disbelief.

"You *stole* them?" she accuses, eyes narrowing.

"*Borrowed,*" I correct smoothly, straightening my collar. "I checked the library policy. Turns out there's no actual limit on how many books you can borrow within a two-week period. So, unless I decide to extend my lease, you've got exactly fourteen days to cram and crank out Peterson's new assignment." I flash her a slow grin. "You can thank me by writing my essay too."

Her laugh is harsh and humourless, her hands slapping against her legging-clad thighs. Muttering curses beneath her breath, I watch

Harper catalogue the texts, presumably checking for damage. When she can't find anything, she folds her arms and taps her foot.

"They're not alphabetized," she pouts. I grin, unable to ignore how cute that pout is, and reach my hand out for her.

"I'm only human, Babygirl. A simple thank you would suffice." Those green eyes swing to me, incredulous beneath pinched brows.

"For being so overbearing, you've cut off everyone else from the material they're going to need as well? It's not all about me, you know." I snort. She's wrong there.

"I don't give a fuck about anyone else. Now, sit in my lap and praise me the way a King deserves."

Her sigh is long and exasperated, but her shoulders loosen just enough for me to catch a flicker of amusement beneath the irritation. I know, I'm irresistible. Taking two steps towards me, Harper whips her phone out of her jacket pocket and taps out a quick message before relenting. As expected, Clayton's silhouette passes beyond the window as he strides down my pathway, effectively being dismissed. I smile with all the arrogance of a man who's just gained the upper hand.

Curling my arms around her, I breathe in the vanilla scent of her shampoo and nudge my nose against her receiver. If someone had told me a year ago that this would be the girl that turned my world upside down, I would have laughed in their face. But back then, I didn't know someone like Harper existed. That someone who's known pain, grief and misery can still be so spirited, bold and pragmatic. I thought the only way to deal with trauma was to bury it, not to own it.

Indulging in my cuddle for a few minutes, Harper pats my head like a puppy and slides free from my lap. She retrieves her backpack from where it must have been tossed by the front and raises a brow at me expectantly. I stare blanky, not quite sure what to do now. I'd kind of anticipated that she'd be on her knees in front of me, overwhelmed by gratitude as my cock sinks into her mouth. Instead, she's rolling her eyes and tilting her head to the side.

"Come on then. It's study time." Using the pathway provided,

Harper walks to the dining table and pulls out her highlighters and sticky notes. "Pick up a book, Rhys. We need to settle on a topic for the essay that you're going to write yourself." I gaze after her, my mouth parted.

"I'm sitting here on a throne, ready to have the soul sucked out of me, and you want to study?!"

"Actually, it's *you* who wants me to study. Isn't that why you've done all of this, to become my new revision partner?"

My mouth slams shut, my thoughts stuttering to a halt. Looking over the stacks with new eyes, the smugness falls away as I realize what I've effectively done. I've cockblocked myself by giving Harper two thousand reasons to ignore me. Pinching the bridge of my nose, I'm preparing to set the entire room on fire as the doorbell rings. A murmur of voices bleeds through the walls, and when I peer through the window, I find my front lawn covered with figures.

"Oh, I hope you don't mind," Harper pitches in, unable to hide her smile, "I know how you like to make outlandish statements on the student forum, I thought I'd give it a try. Ooo, is that a coffee machine?" She distracts herself, wandering off. A tic beats in my jaw as I march across the room, tearing my phone out of my pocket. Just as I reach the front door, I see Harper's public message and almost lose my shit.

RHYS' LIBRARY - OPEN NIGHTLY TO SCIENCE STUDENTS BETWEEN THE HOURS OF 7-10PM

Ripping the door open, ready to snarl at them to get the fuck off my property, Clayton leads the parade, barging past me with a stack of pizzas in his arms. There's no hiding his smirk, the bastard. Streams of nerds shove their way into my house, marveling at the height of the ceilings and size of the room as they scuff the floorboards with their muddy shoes. Through the shitshow that has become my evening,

Harper catches my eye and blows a kiss. I storm upstairs and throw a spoiled tantrum in my room.

Once I've calmed down, and the growling in my stomach will no longer be denied, I leave the smashed lamp on my bedroom floor behind and slump back into the hallways, each step hollow like my damn soul. *I hate this academy. I hate these people. I hate my plans backfiring.*

The chatter below is louder, and none of it is interesting. Clayton climbs the stairs, pretending I'm not lurking around like a hostile shadow as he enters the bathroom. I wait outside like some crazed stalker until he reappears.

"You're walking on thin ice, Scum," I growl. I expect his shoulders to tense in his white t-shirt, but instead he looks amused. With his blonde waves free from the god-awful beanies he usually wears, he almost looks like a regular college jock. Not the convict scraping by on the last of his luck I know him to be.

"What did I do?" he chuckles. *Chuckles.* The audacity is treading on my last nerve. Without breaking eye contact, I gesture over the banister to the room below where the mumbling and giggling is emanating from. His eyebrow cocks over black eyes that are enjoying my distress far too much. "You know as much as I do, Harper won't be bossed around. Besides, have you seen her?"

After a moment, I follow his eye line and spot Harper. Not that I've been looking at much else, but now I see how wide her smile is. She's crossing the lounge, handing out steaming mugs and leaning over to answer a question. Her ass looks fantastically plump, but then her laughter rings out. She's interacting with people. Students that have judged and scorned her for months are finally smiling, shifting books aside to make room for her beside them. She's actually making friends.

"Harper needs this," Clayton says from behind me, moving toward the staircase. I stalk after him, fisting my hands by my side.

"She doesn't need anyone except me," I glower. I'm not sure where that comes from, but I won't deny it either. The way she tames my beast, pushes me beyond boundaries I didn't know where holding me back. I sure know all I need is her, so why can't it work both ways? Why can't I be the center of her world too?

"Then what am I doing here?" Clayton mutters with the hint of a smirk, not stopping his descent. I slap a hand on his shoulder, forcing him to face me on the bottom step.

"Harper and I connected whilst you were having your shit-life crisis. She belongs to me and any kindness she's showing you is out of pity." My fingers twitch for the fight he isn't going to give me. If I can't get a rise out of Clayton, I've either lost my touch or I'm not hitting the right nerves. Prying my hand away, he dusts his shoulder off before shrugging.

"I don't really give a shit about your *connection*. You wanna know why?" I want to shout *fuck no* and punch his face inside out, but curiosity gets the better of me, so I remain standing there and grit my teeth. "Because I'm biding my time, waiting for you fuck up or grow bored. Everyone knows nothing you do is long term, especially her." Clayton walks away, returning to his borrowed laptop on the kitchen island whilst I stand there seething. I'm losing my fucking touch.

Harper spots me lingering and rises to make her way to me, but I hold up my hand. With every fiber of my being, I hate that Clayton's right. She needs the chance to make friends, to realize what a waste of time and energy they are. But when it comes to her sex life and the focus of her affections, I'll take the baton. Like a fragile, little bird I need to capture and hold close until she sees that being with me is the best option. The only option.

Unlike Clayton, I do not have the love and nurturing of a mother to fall back on. No experience to pull from. Despite all that, Harper wants me the way I am, a notion that's never happened before and may not again. I can't lose that, no matter the cost.

I hover at the base of the stairs, feeling out of place as nerds litter every available space. Three girls are sitting on my cashmere blanket *on the floor,* another pair are sharing a pizza on my throne and the four at the kitchen island with their laptops each have a perfectly brewed coffee. It's anarchy. To make matters worse, Dickerson has his head stuck in my fridge, fingering every fucking beer bottle before picking one from the back. He beams at me, far too comfortably for a little buttmunch I've spent all year bullying.

"Hey Rhys, do you have a coaster?" he asks from behind his freckles. His cheery tone offends me so much, I punch the bottle clear out of his hand. It flies toward the window, smashing against the glass and falling into the basin.

"Do I look like I own *fucking coasters*?!" I bellow, raising my fist until he's running anywhere I am not. He doesn't leave though, but instead takes refuge behind Harper who is now offering out the last slice of pepperoni pizza in the box. I snatch it from her with a glare. Her smile doesn't slip, clearly self-satisfied with her handy work. That smile threatens to melt away the anger I'm clinging to.

I consume my pizza, turning away before she sees my expression soften and ask me to do something ludicrous, like study alongside her again. I don't need to study. I had only the best private tutors my whole damn life, sat my SAT test at fourteen and was considered a mathematic prodigy at one point. A fact that Harper will never know.

Being book smart doesn't count for anything when your dad can unleash an attack on you for no good reason. Knowledge didn't attend to my wounds or hold me close at night. I picked forensic science purely because it's an area my father knows nothing about and hence, can't take an interest in my education. Not that I ever planned on actually attending a lesson.

Shooing the couple out of my throne, I drop down and lace my fingers over my stomach. The surrounding conversation dies suddenly at my arrival. A guy with dark hair I've seen on the front row of every class hides behind his book to avoid my narrowed stare. Dickerson drops his pen between the stacks and as he crawls by on his hands and knees, I lift my legs and cross my ankles across his back. Harper instantly barks at me and I sigh, letting the little fucker scurry away. It grates on me to be seen as weak, but when it comes to her, I can't help it.

At least the people in this house are probably the closest to Harper and therefore, key suspects of whoever is fucking with her. With all of us. So, I've resorted to waiting and watching. Watching every person who interacts with her with such scrutiny, they'll have nightmares about my eyes fixated on them. It's all I can do, since I'm no longer in charge of what happens under this roof.

Before Harper arrived on campus, life was predictable in its irregularity. No two days were the same. Students I didn't know were crashing on my sofas, fights were erupting in the front yard. Girls would get so drunk, they'd start sucking cocks while the guys chugged on beer kegs. Pure academy insanity I became so accustomed with, that nothing shocked me anymore.

Then a pair of green eyes and deaf ears walked into my life, flipping my world on its axis. She sees me in a way no else has cared to, and calls me out on my shit when no one else would dare. Her mind intrigues me as much as her body. Even now, in her leggings and baggy sweat-shirt, all I want to do is feel her skin against mine.

The sound of chairs scraping and increased movement drag my eyes across the room once more. Banding together, the nerds help Harper to clear away. Bottles clink as they're dropped in the trash, my cashmere blanket folded and put back neatly, pizza boxes disposed of. Grouping together, they each take a stack of textbooks, but instead of scurrying away to return them to the library like I'd expected, they create a neat stack beneath the window.

I watch the spectacle curiously, so unused to the civilized nature. Mutual respect fills the air, laughter fighting against the animosity that lingers here. Something is changing. In the house, in me, and I'm not sure I like it. Harper takes a sweeping glance at my brooding posture, and her resulting smile knocks me off kilter.

"Same time tomorrow night?" asks a blonde I believe to be called Felicia, or at least she looks like one. My body jolts into action, propelling me from the throne to where people are starting to filter out of the front door.

"No, no, no, *no!*"

"Yeah sure," Harper replies cheerily, guiding them out. "See you back here from seven." I plant myself at her side, glaring furiously.

"My house, my rules. No freaking way are we doing this again."

"Great, see you then," the group wave back to Harper before heading out. Clay hangs back long enough to stroke the back of Harper's hair.

"I'll wait at the footpath to walk you home. Don't be long." He places a kiss on her temple, though his eyes are locked on me. Taunting me. Once he's finally left, I sigh dramatically and slump against the wall.

"What the fuck is happening right now?! Am I invisible?"

Harper turns, her head angled upwards with a glazed look to her eyes, whilst reaching up to smush my face in her hands.

"Who's there? Uncle Henry, is that you?" I can't help but laugh, all the angst of the evening washing away in an instant.

"Why don't you feel lower and find out?" I drag her hands down my body until she lurches back on a giggle.

"Ew, Uncle Henry never would have said that." Her nose scrunches up but she's smiling. Dragging her closer, I pull her arms around my waist like I've been wanting to all night. My chin rests upon her head, the breath sawing out of me.

"Thank you for tonight," Harper says against my chest. I snort, since I didn't have a choice in anything that's happened here, but I'm happy to take credit for it. Especially if Harper expresses her gratitude through sexual favors. "I've never had friends before Rhys. And I don't think you have either, not really. This could be good for both of us."

My chest warms at the way she says *us,* but she's wrong. Friends are distractions, and distractions are never good news. They complicate matters with their whining and drama, expecting you to care and perform selfless tasks to keep their meaningless friendship. *Exhausting.*

But if that's what Harper thinks she needs, I can humor her. It won't be long before they become a drain on the precious little time she has.

"Fine, you can have your little geek sessions here. As long as you'll stay with me tonight?" I hate the desperation in my voice, hoping her receivers don't pick up on it. Breaking away, she shoulders her backpack instead of answering. With a brief kiss to my neck, she saunters out of the door and leaves. *Fucking leaves.* After everything I've done and put up with tonight, I'm not even going to get my dick wet.

There's never been anything in this world I've ever wanted so badly, it physically aches. Harper is the exception. Every time she turns away from me, another piece out of my chest is carved free, hollowing me out one heartbeat at a time. I know it's irrational, obsessive even, but logic ceases to exist when she's near. I'd lock every door and bar every window if it meant keeping her here. She can hate me, despise me, punish me if that's what she decides. All I know is, I don't want to be alone anymore.

HARPER

CHAPTER TWENTY

Clayton sees me all the way to my door and remains until I shut myself safely inside, much to Addy's amusement. I grin and roll my eyes, ignoring the butterflies that flutter through my abdomen. Any other night, the stubborn side of me might have had something to say about being a strong, independent woman, but not right now. I'm too busy swooning that Rhys created a library just for me, kind of, and that Clay's fingers slipped into mine as we strolled across campus. I am fully having my cake and eating it.

"You going to join me or are you just going to lean against the door?" Addy both says and signs. Seeing the room properly for the first time, I notice how the beds are pushed together, facing a TV upon the dresser. A yellow sticker on the side labels it as property of the media department. The bedspread is littered with snacks and pampering products, and suddenly I remember.

"Girl's night," I nod slowly, recalling the plan we made. If Addy can read the revelation all over my face, she doesn't make it obvious whilst patting the bedspread beside her. Unshouldering my backpack and kicking off my boots, I sink into the mass of cushions, thinking how lucky it is I didn't surrender to Rhys' advances the way I wanted to.

Addy presses play on a romcom, and then proceeds to tell me all about a casual fling she's had with her childhood neighbor during the Winter break. It's a good thing I wasn't in the mindset to watch the movie, as I curl up on my side and soak up every sordid detail she wants to tell. How her flexibility came in handy, how she convinced him to dress up like Ghostface and used rubber weapons for multiple uses. I'm as impressed as I am mortified.

"What about you?" Addy beams when she's finished. I blink slowly, trying to fight off the sleep that wants to creep me.

"What about me, what?"

"Your Christmas," Addy laughs and nudges my arm so hard, I have to stop myself from rolling onto my back. "Did anything saucy happen? You left campus with Rhys and arrived back with Clayton. There's definitely a story there."

"That was purely coincidental. I asked the limousine to drop me off around the corner, and Clay's bus happened to just be rolling in. Then he insisted on taking my bag so...yeah I can see how it looked."

"The limousine?!" Addy's eyes bulge and I realize my mistake. Okay, now there's no denying that stuff happened with Rhys during the break, but I smile coyly and keep it to myself. Enough of my life is plastered on the forum or gossiped about, and although Addy is my closest friend, I just want to keep some things private. Where Rhys, Clayton and I are concerned, I don't know how to put our connections into words, so I'd rather not try. Thankfully, Addy doesn't push.

"Well, if you're okay riding in an *Uber*," Addy scrunches up her face with disgust and I smack her arm, "a couple of the dance girls are going shopping on Friday. Wanna come with?" I glance at the wall, wondering why Friday seems to be ringing some sort of internal bell and then I remember.

"The boys have a basketball game Friday afternoon. I said I'd show my support."

Addy lifts a shoulder, not fazed by my declining her invitation. I can handle girl's time in our room, but I'm not one for big crowds of squeals and air kisses. The chaos of the mall will be a quickfire way to give me a migraine, and I don't care for dressing room sagas.

"And who are you supporting exactly?" she quirks a brow. I roll my eyes again, too tired to come up with a witty answer. I see the stares people give when they think I'm not looking, how everyone is waiting for me to break Rhys' or Clayton's heart. The notion of choosing doesn't sit right with me when they each speak to very different parts of my soul. Although one day, that decision might be taken out of my hands.

Addy's fuchsia hair tickles me as she snuggles down into my shoulder, the fleece of her pajamas reminding me of a giant teddy bear. I yawn widely, laying my cheek on Addy's head. Discomfort presses against my ears, and I shift my head several times to find a comfortable spot. I hate wearing my receivers at the best of times, but I'm in no frame of mind to read sign or subtitles so I've left them on. My eyelids droop, until the sound of popcorn crunching jolts me awake. I cringe, shoving Addy aside with a groan.

"Am I disturbing you?" she grins knowingly, starting the next chick flick I'll barely focus on. She clearly isn't planning on sleeping tonight. "Oh hey, I was going to ask you if one of your boys might consider auditioning for the Spring Talent Show. Millie pulled out so I've been promoted to chief organizer, and we're seriously missing some eye candy." The laugh that leaves me is packed with sarcasm.

"Real funny."

"I'm serious. Word on the street is, Rhys will do anything for you. This would be one more step in the Rhys Renewal Program." My brows knit together and Addy shrugs, tossing another piece of popcorn into her mouth. "Not my label. It's a trending hashtag on the app." Pulling out my phone, I scroll through recent posts and discover that she's right. Students from all departments are commenting how Rhys has gone soft, how he's pussy-whipped and changed for the better.

"But...I don't want him to change," I mutter.

"Yeah right," Addy giggles as if I've just made some huge joke. "You want him to be the bullying asshole who dared the jocks to see who could throw a math's geek the furthest across the football pitch? Or who set a girl's backpack on fire? How about the rumor he's fiddling with the scholarship funds?"

"Well...no, but—" A knock sounds at the door, a shadow seeping beneath the frame. Both Addy and I freeze, staring at it without moving. It's past midnight, and we haven't yet processed the whole note under the door thing yet. The knock sounds again and I finger-sign for Addy to switch on her phone's video cam before tiptoeing across the room. Look at me being a big, brave girl.

Swinging the door wide open, I find the hellion himself leaning against the door jamb with a smirk that could melt my panties off. Rhys leisurely undresses me with his eyes, despite my clothes being the same grey sweater and patterned leggings I was wearing at his house earlier. I shiver under his scrutiny.

"Can I help you with something? Or did you just come to look?" I question, popping my hip to the side. His smile widens, drawing my attention to his lip ring.

"You left something at my place."

"Oh," I frown, looking at his empty hands. "What is it?"

"This." Before I can respond, Rhys grips my chin and claims my mouth in a kiss so fierce, it knocks the breath from my lungs. His lips crash against mine, rough and needy, tasting heavily of whiskey. My surprise melts the instant his tongue sweeps across mine, coaxing a helpless sound from the back of my throat.

The room spins. My fingers clutch at his shirt, searching for balance as his hands frame my face, thumbs pressing lightly at my jaw to keep me exactly where he wants me. There's no urgency, only the intent that has my pulse thundering in my ears and every coherent thought burning away in the fire he's ignited.

When he finally pulls back, it's only far enough to let me breathe. His mouth hovers inches from mine, a slow, wicked smile curving his lips as if he can still sense my surrender. My own lips are swollen and tingling, a tremor threatening to buckle my knees as he turns casually and walks further into the room, leaving me standing there with heat pooling between my legs.

Spinning on my heels, I notice Addy tucking her phone away, a menacing grin on her face. Oh god, don't tell me she filmed that whole thing?! She catches my eye and signs, *that was so hot*, whilst Rhys removes his jacket. I blink hard, pulling myself together and closing the door with my back.

"Um, it's girl's night," I say weakly. Rhys wobbles slightly as he drops onto my side of the bed, reaching for the popcorn. He's wasted.

"Sounds good. What are we watching?" he asks, indulging himself in our snacks. Heat creeps up my neck and lands in my cheeks. He's sinfully gorgeous in the low lighting, shadows accentuating his sharp jaw and seeping into his inked skin. Finally shifting my gaze back to the TV, I can't even remember the name of the film, but Addy saves me from answering anyway.

"Actually, we were about to paint our toenails. What color do you want, Master Waversea, strawberry margarita or cranberry flame?" She places the choices in Rhys' lap as he chokes on his salted snack. I use his distraction to quickly sign.

"What are you doing?"

"Proving a point," she bobs her brows. A tremor of disdain rattles through me. Rhys isn't perfect, and his boredom creates havoc for anyone nearby, but he's not some test subject. Maybe he has changed, as the hashtag suggests, but not because he was a problem that needed fixing. It's because the version of him who he was supposed to be was beaten down and withered by his father, where it waited for the right person to set it free. Oblivious to the rage that's stirring within me, Rhys downs my water to clear his throat.

"There's no fucking way you're painting my toenails," he croaks. I catch Addy's mischievous expression as she raises her shoulders in a nonchalant shrug.

"I'm sure Clayton would—"

"Give me the fucking cranberry," Rhys spits. My jaw drops, whilst Addy makes a high pitched noise I grimace at. I'm getting far too tired for all this noise. Rhys removes his socks and jeans, reclining in just black tank top and boxers with yellow cordoned stripes around a sign in the center that reads, 'Caution: May contain nuts.'

"You really don't have to," I tell Rhys but he's already reclining against the headboard, his limbs growing limp.

"Have your girl's night, do your girly things. I'll just...lie here," he mumbles, his eyelids lowering. Five bucks says he'll pass out before she's even done. Humming a little tune to herself, Addy paints Rhys' toenails at lightning speed, pushing the brush back into the pot with a satisfied nod of her head.

"All done princess," she teases to his sleeping form, and I give her a glare. Excusing herself to the bathroom, I catch up with her in the hallway by dragging her arm backwards.

"That wasn't cool," I sign, in case of eavesdroppers. A frown forms on Addy's face.

"I didn't mean to cause offence," she shakes her head slightly. *"I'm sorry, I thought we were having fun."*

"Well next time, don't do it at his expense. He's not some lab rat to be tested for the amusement of others." My hands are a flurry of movement, shaking slightly, and I head back to the dorm.

"Harper," Addy calls after me out loud. "Harper, wait." I don't wait. I slip inside and nudge Rhys to wake up.

"Hey, you can't stay here," I push against his arm until his blue eyes flicker back open. Staring at the ceiling, Rhys takes a minute to revive himself enough to realize where he is. "Let's get you back home."

"Home," Rhys mutters, dragging himself upright by pure will. He leans against the wall whilst I grab some necessities and shove my feet into my biker boots. Dressing Rhys is a damn sight harder, but he rouses enough to do up his jeans button and throw on his jacket. "Is everything okay?" he asks, the thickness of his voice returning.

"All fine," I smile weakly, shouldering my bag and leading him out into the hallway. He hisses at the harsh lights. Addy lingers by the bathroom, watching us leave, her face the picture of confusion. A stab of guilt bursts in my chest, wondering if I've made a mistake, if my gut feeling to protect Rhys has caused me to misinterrupt Addy's intentions.

Either way, we step out into the cold, heading back to the house I was adamant I wasn't going to stay in whilst Clay was on campus. I didn't want to be seen choosing a side, or inadvertently cut ties I'm not ready to cut. Rhys keeps his arm around me, only stumbling a few times whilst trying to get a glimpse of my face in the streetlamps.

"When we get back, will you tell me what's upset you?" he asks. I huff a cloud of white in front of my face, although my cheeks are on fire.

"Maybe," I settle down, looking both ways as we cross the road to his pathway. "Depends how much whiskey you've got left."

CLAYTON

CHAPTER TWENTY ONE

The ball smacks into my palms, and instinct takes over. I tear down the court, sneakers squealing against the polished floor, the familiar rhythm of the dribble echoing through the gym. A few bodies dart into my path, teammates and opponents alike, but I weave through them, muscles burning in the best possible way.

We're all Waversea players out here today. After the disaster that was our last big game, Coach decided we'd have a monthly *'friendly'* scrimmage to sharpen up. There's ten of us on the court, spilt evenly with four more watching from the side benches beside the cheer squad. Huxley and Garret are here too, leaning back in the bleachers amongst small groups of students littered throughout. Harper is front and center.

Her eyes meet mine, and I can't help but grin, right up until Waver-shit comes flying out of nowhere to slap the ball clean from my hand. I spin, trying to recover, but he's already bouncing away and sinking the basket I'd been gunning for.

"Same team, asshole," I grunt. There's no doubt Rhys has been getting the practice in. His movements are smoother than before, and he's working better with the others, but apparently that courtesy doesn't extend to me. He shoulders past like I'm invisible, his focus already on Scott who's caught the rebound.

His eyes widen in panic, quickly passing to Richie before jumping out of Rhys's way. I hang back, watching as the tattooed predator stalks his prey with calculated movements. It's laughable how the players scatter and duck out of his way, while he moves with deliberate slowness. Having that kind of power must be exhilarating, but I would rather be respected through loyalty than fear.

With the rest of the players staying too far back, Richie is left on his own inside the arc with the ball firmly gripped between his white knuckles. I have to give him credit, he doesn't balk and toss the ball over to my waiting hands like I'd expected, but lines himself up with the net. Waiting for the exact moment Richie is about to shoot, Rhys vaults himself high enough to pluck the ball straight out of the air.

Interestingly, the rest of the opposing team have banded together to form a four-man wall to block Rhys's return. I raise my eyebrows that they managed to find their balls in the last ten seconds of the match, internally commending them for at least trying.

On our team, Max and Lennox are waving their arms for a pass we all know Wavershit won't give. Instead, he eyes the basket and braces for a shot from the arc despite the line of players in front of him. As expected, they all jump the same time he does, and I lose sight of Rhys in the commotion. Suddenly, the ball bounces under Dazza's legs and flies straight into my hands. I don't hesitate, leaping to dunk the ball through the net as the claxon sounds.

Looking back, everyone is clasping hands and praising each other for a good game. Wavershit is nowhere to be seen, and I'm left replaying what just happened. Did he fake a shot in favor of passing to me? That can't be right. Forcing my feet to move forwards, I join the team, pushing myself to make a real go of making friends this time round. There's a beat of awkwardness, me standing on the outside of their camaraderie until several hands pat my shoulders and back.

The sophomores and Coach join us, pointing out areas which need improvement before we can take on another school. Instinctively, I radiate toward Huxley, who clasps my hand and pulls me into half a hug to speak low in my ear.

"It's good to have you back." Even after he's released me, I don't move away from beside him. I know he's not Jeremy. Hell I barely know the guy, but his blonde wavy hair, calm demeanor and silent confidence briefly soothe the grief I've struggled with for years. More than that, there's a haunted edge to his brown eyes I know all too well.

The students in the bleachers head out to continue the rest of their afternoons as Coach dismisses us. Most of the team hang around to chat, the adrenaline still coursing through our veins. Huxley ruffles a hand through my hair before leaving, sending me into a flashback that makes my heart squeeze until Garrett slaps my ass and knocks me back out of it.

"Good hustle, Bro!" he hollers. I shake my head, regaining the conversations happening around me. I don't really fit into any of them, so I loiter, half invested in each one until a high-pitched squeal sounds from across the court. Klara storms out with the cheer squad at her back, and that's when I see him. Rhys is cupping Harper's face, his mouth attached to hers. They're sitting so close, she's almost in his lap and a round of low laughter trickles through the players. My name is muttered in the same sentence as blue balls and short leashes.

I angle my head down and shift my feet, waiting for Rhys to release Harper without making a scene. Adding fuel to the flames won't do any good, and it'll make me look petty.

I've had plenty of time to think about the circumstances I've found myself back in whilst lying in bed at night. Sometimes I don't even sleep, I just lie still contemplating my feelings on everything I've seen and heard.

Especially since the morning I went to collect Harper from her dorm, only to be told she hadn't stayed there. She snuck back to *his* house after I'd dropped her off. I could have demanded answers then and there, but I've taken a back seat. I'm lying in wait. Watching from a distance during every study session we've had at Rhys' this week. He'll grow bored soon, he'll royally fuck up, and that'll be my cue to swoop in. I just have to wait for Harper to get him out of her system.

That's my plan. I returned to Waversea with a new perception, deciding to do things differently this time. I'm not making choices based on what Jeremy would want, but rather who I want to be. How to live a life I'm proud of and who I want by my side. That's why I'm not worried about Harper's faze with Rhys. He's in it for a good time, whereas I'm in it for the long haul.

Breaking free from the mindless chatter, Richie grows bold, his voice echoing across the court. "Yo, Rhys! Friday night party back at yours, right?" Scott steps forward, pretending to ponder deeply, clearly playing his part in this pre-rehearsed little performance.

"Dude, haven't you heard? The only parties Rhys throws these days involve books and bores." He snorts, and laughter ripples through the team. Harper smiles too, though there's no humor in it. More like the kind of smile to keep her from baring her teeth.

Rhys moves like a bull at the sight of red, rounding the railing in three heavy strides. Harper's quicker, ducking beneath the same railing to block him and press her hand flat against his chest. This adds to the team's delight, causing them to howl. A few make kissy faces, smacking their lips in exaggerated taunts. I slowly lick my lips and take a measured step back, foreseeing how this is going to end. Harper turns slowly, each step measured as she closes in on Scott.

"You know," she purrs, her voice velvet and venom, "we *bores* prefer the term intellectually superior." Before anyone can process the words, her fist snaps up into his throat, followed by her knee slamming into his groin. Scott crumples like a puppet whose strings have been cut, gasping soundlessly as he hits the floor. For a heartbeat, there's a pure, stunned silence before the gym explodes with laughter.

Harper flinches at the noise, not from fear, but because it must've jarred her hearing aids. I stroll around the back of her to reach up, brushing my fingers into her hair and pressing the button on her receivers to mute them. She blinks up at me, confused for half a second, then sighs contentedly. Her green eyes warm, the way they always do when I shield her from harm. She can stand up for herself, as just demonstrated, but she loves being taken care of anyway. I'm coming to learn that everyone craves a little protection once in a while.

A few of the guys rush to help Scott limp off toward the locker room. The others linger like vultures, waiting to see what Harper will do next. If it's round two they're after, they will be sorely disappointed. I wind my arms around the fierce little creature in front of me and jerk my chin toward the exit.

"Think we can get some privacy in here?" My voice goes unheard, no one moving a muscle until Wavershit joins in.

"You heard Scum. Get the fuck out." he bellows, his shoulders and spine rigid. The rest scatter instantly, skittering for the locker room like ants beneath a boot. Rhys stays, predictably, leaning against the railing, although his eyes are downcast. A frown pinches his features but I'm not concentrating on him.

I slide my hand into Harper's jacket pocket, finding her phone. A flick of my thumb activates the mic before I rest it on the railing beside us.

"Are you okay?" I ask, lifting her hand to examine her knuckles. Other than being slightly red, there's no damage done. I can't resist pulling her hand up to my mouth and pressing a kiss there. Harper hums softly.

"Just another day," she tries to laugh off. I'm not laughing though.

"He's big and ugly enough to fight his own battles, you know. You shouldn't be putting yourself in harm's way." Rhys grunts but doesn't deny it. Harper is a firecracker in her own right, but only for worthy causes.

"I would do the same for you," she declares. I shouldn't approve, but I can't help my small smile from seeping through. "And I would hope that out of respect for me, you two should stand up for each other from now on."

"Keep dreaming, Babygirl." A bitter laugh leaks from Wavershit as he pushes off the railing and strolls away, effectively ending the conversation. Harper watches me carefully, hunting for a promise I'm not able to give her. There is zero chance of that happening.

I can't defend a man who always puts himself before others and doesn't care who he hurts, as long as he gets his own way.

"Clayton," Harper breathes, bracing her hands on my thighs. "I think Rhys has some difficulties coming his way soon, and I know you guys don't see eye to eye, but he really does care for me. In his own way." She smiles weakly. "I'm not asking for you to wave a flag around with his face on it, but if you hear or see anyone mocking him, can you shut it down? It'll be safer for the whole academy if you help me with this."

I feel myself sag, my shoulder becoming heavy. How that weasely shit has managed to get Harper to see the good in him, I will never know. But she is right. In the interest of everyone in a five mile radius, it would be best to keep Rhys' precious ego intact.

"I suppose I am your loyal protector," I nod, and Harper flies into my lap to kiss me. Splaying my hand across her back, I keep her there, allowing her warmth to banish the rest of my doubts. It should bother me that Rhys' mouth was so recently here, but instead, it spurs me on to replace him with my own brand of kiss. To eradicate him from her existence piece by piece.

Rhys is my opposite, my rival, but I plan on using that to my full advantage. I can give her everything Rhys can't. Patience and understanding. I can see his faults, observe what he does wrong and then do it better. My protective nature is back in full force, but this time it's not just from physical threats. I'll protect her heart, even if I'm not the one who will ultimately hold it.

HARPER

CHAPTER TWENTY TWO

I force myself to sit straight, look dead ahead. I will not lean into Clay, no matter how warm his thigh is pressed up against mine. Students from our science classes fill the living room, and there's more in the kitchen. Considering Rhys is lording over us all from his throne, they've managed to make themselves quite at home.

Even without my receivers on, I can tell every time someone dares to use the coffee machine, because Rhys throws down his tablet and marches over to check it's being used, *and cleaned,* correctly. Chuckling to myself, I force my nose back into the heavy textbook in my lap.

Today's study session began early, as Peterson gave us the afternoon off for 'open learning'. I reckon that's a ruse for him to simply take a day off, but I'm not complaining. Anything to give us more time to do this vague assignment he's set and I'm all game. Clay and I have decided to work together, finding a series of case files from the eighties amongst Rhys' hoard. Fuck knows what the proclaimed King is doing hunched over his screen but I hope it's productive.

Every once in a while, Clay leans over to stick a post-it note under my nose, adding the stream of them I have building up. All interesting finds about one of four patients we've discovered, who seem to have no relation but all suffered from the same symptoms. With the advancements in medicine and technology, we're analyzing the data, hoping it proves not to be a total bore to write an essay about.

Leaning forward, I pull an aged, brown folder from the table just as Rhys places down a steaming mug, and then retreats to this throne. I peer at him from beneath the curtain on my pink-twinged hair, concealing a smirk. He's up to something, and I think I know what it is.

Clay catches on quickly too. A prickle creeps up my spine as his presence moves into my personal space. Fingers grasp my chin gently, twisting my face to the side where he places a kiss on my cheek. The peck was soft, but flames burst to life through my being and result in a searing blush. I feel the heat of Rhys' glare and as others nearby flinch, I can assume he's made some sort of guttural sound.

Less than a minute later, my phone vibrates with a message. I'm already rolling my eyes as I drag it out from underneath my thigh.

> Your New Master: Hope you're enjoying yourself.

I sigh, sensing the macho bullshit seeping across the room.

> Me: Jealousy isn't a good look for you.

I tease, trying to lighten the atmosphere that is quickly growing tense. Rhys laughs, an animated motion that causes his Adam's apple to bob and all the students to shuffle out of his vicinity.

> Your New Master: Babygirl, there's nothing that man can do to you that will make me jealous. If you want a kiss, you'd better open wide for my tongue to fuck your mouth.

I choke on the air, spluttering and reaching for my coffee. Clay's laptop is dislodged from his lap, whatever progress we were making ceasing. He places it on the table, leaving it open just in case we find it in ourselves to return to the spreadsheet we were working on. I seriously doubt it but the intention is there.

I'm not surprised when people start to pack up and leave early, Rhys' scowl chasing them out the door without so much as a second glance. I sigh, setting aside the files and books I have spread out over the table, making sure they're packed away with care. If I were to leave it up to Rhys, he'd scatter them all over the floor.

Once I'm satisfied the books are safe, I look up, surprised to find Rhys is nowhere to be seen. Clay has stayed behind, which is no great shock, his hands digging into his pocket to pass over my receivers. I'd given them to him when the murmuring in the room became too distracting but I couldn't be bothered to move.

We move through the rooms cautiously, like a pair of zookeepers hunting for a lion, until I spot the flare of a cherry on the back porch. As far as I know, Rhys hasn't smoked since we came back after Christmas break, not that I asked him to stop. I simply didn't hide my aversion to the smell and taste. Turning to suggest that Clay should hang back, he's already moved across the kitchen to wash up the mass of dirty mugs and empty snack bowls.

The porch is cold beneath my socks, shadows looming over Rhys' silhouette. Two steps out of the house and I can smell that he's not actually smoking a cigarette, but a joint. Walking around to his front, whatever relief he's chasing, he is yet to find. His eyes drag over my face, his jaw twitching. He is not impressed.

"What's with you today?" I ask, winding my arms around his middle. I already know the answer, but I wanted to give some sort of signal that my hearing has been activated, like a superhero I suppose. Winding his hand around my wrist, I suspect he was on the way to holding my hand but doesn't quite get there.

"I can't have you in my house a second longer and not have you in the way my body needs." There's a desperate edge to his voice and a tight pinch to his grasp. Toking on his joint, he puffs a cloud over my head and then sets it aside on the railing. Tugging me inside, Rhys grips my hips and plants me on the kitchen island. "I'd tell him to leave if I were you," he jerks his jaw towards Clayton, not taking his hungry stare from my body.

I peer over my shoulder, gauging Clay's stance. Legs wide, arms cross, he leans against the counter by the basin. His face is passive, not revealing the flare of stubbornness within. He's not going anywhere, and I wouldn't ask him to anyway. Rhys' fingers trail my arms, bringing my attention back to him.

"I don't know when you're going to learn that I don't tell either of you to do anything," I say as his hands land on my thighs, warmth seeping through my jeans. "You're grown men, make your own choices." Rhys' nostrils flare, his pupils blowing wide. I don't hear Clay closing in until another set of hands curls around my shoulders. An instant bolt of lust shoots between my thighs.

This is dangerous territory. To be touched by them both, desired by them both. To open myself up to something that can't last. I can't pick one without losing the other.

Nibbling on my bottom lip, a hand cups my jaw to turn my head back. It's Clay who is commanding my attention, and Rhys is allowing him.

"If you want to be with him, then I won't stop you, but I'm not leaving either. I don't trust his mood right now. I won't be able to forgive myself if he hurts you."

My heart flutters but the tightening in my core takes over. The thought of Clay watching me with Rhys is something I've only thought about in my deepest refuges in my mind. Something I didn't dare try to bring into any version of my reality. But here we are, and I would hate myself if I let an opportunity go to waste.

"What if I like it when he hurts me?"

"Don't push me Harper," Clay growls. His protective side ripples with the promise of violence, and fuck if my thighs don't clench tighter. I'm sick, twisted, and I'm not sorry about it.

Not needing any more encouragement, Rhys pries my face from Clay's hold, his fingers either side of my mouth as he drags me forward. His lips seize mine, an explosion of desire barreling into my chest. Hands push into my hair, though I'm not sure who's, removing my receivers in a clear indication that no more talking is needed.

At first I don't return his kiss, still unsure about how far this is going to go. I know where I want it to go in theory, but now it's happening, I hesitate. I'm not shy about my body, but I've never tiptoed into exhibitionism before. When Rhys does release my mouth to trail kisses down my neck, I catch sight of Clay on the other side of the kitchen. He's pushed himself up onto the counter with a beer in his hand, his body rigid and eyes watching intently.

My doubts vanish as Rhys drags the t-shirt over my head, unhooking my bra and planting his mouth on me. Heat envelopes my pierced nipple, his tongue swirling around the ends of the metal bar. He palms my other breast, massaging firmly as I claw my hands into his scalp.

My hair tickles my lower back as I allow my head to drop to the side, lost to the sensations of Rhys' tongue and the pulsing between my legs. Wetness seeps through my panties already, my hips rolling in my jeans. His mouth switches to my other nipple which he instantly bites down on. I gasp loudly, dragging my nails across his shoulders.

I glimpse at Clay, wondering if he would step in if things got too rough. He takes a long swig of his beer, moving jerkily as if he's barely restraining from launching himself across the room. Rhys pulls back, his hand grabbing me by the roots of my hair and angling my face toward him.

"When I'm pleasuring you, you focus on me," I watch his lips move and feel the rumble vibrate through his chest. Refusing to be dominated, unable to let go of my stubborn pride, I snarl and shove him back a step.

"If you don't want my attention to wander, you'll need to do a better job at pleasuring me." Rhys' blue eyes burst with approval, his hand wrapping around my throat and roughly shoving me to lie back onto the island. I arch, hissing. The marble counter is cold against my skin, not that I have time to gasp as Rhys rips my jeans and panties off in one smooth, practiced move. Dragging me closer to the edge, he throws my legs over his shoulders. I don't have time to be embarrassed as his fingers dive into my slick heat, my core clenching around him instantly.

I can't hear Rhys' praise, but I can sense it. Hummed against my thigh, muttered between hot, wet kisses. My hands fist by my sides with nothing close by to grab onto, all of my willpower going into not giving Rhys the satisfaction of bringing me to orgasm so quickly. Pumping his fingers leisurely, the pad of his tongue scrapes over my clit before he takes it into his mouth. I moan, writhing against the onslaught of pleasure consuming my body.

Distracted by the colors bursting behind my closed eyelids, I flinch at the touch of a mouth covering mine. Not believing my own mind, my eyes fly open to find Clay leaning over me. His blond waves tickle my neck, a deprivation to his black eyes I didn't expect. Rhys quickens his pace, thrusting his fingers into me while his mouth devours my clit and draws strangled cries from me. Well there's no acting coy now. Throwing away all inhibitions, I grab Clay by the neck and drag him down to clash my mouth against his.

His lips are fuller than Rhys', soft and tentative. I don't let him withdraw now, my chest heaving and noises muffled by his mouth. On my next gasp, his tongue darts into my mouth almost hesitantly, which I take full advantage of. Clay might want to take baby steps, but my body is balancing on a tightrope above an abyss. There's no time for hesitancy.

Delving my tongue into his mouth, my hands fist in his hair and shirt desperately. I need him to follow me into the fire. Within seconds, his tongue is battling against mine, my moans swallowed whole. I bite his bottom lip, nibbling along his stubbled jawline before returning to his mouth that's waiting to devour me. Needing more, I search for his hand and cover my breast with it, squeezing hard in encouragement.

This is a fluke, one I'm sure will not happen again, so I might as well see how far we can go. I'm past the point of return now, my head spinning and my core tightening. Rhys is relentless, sucking and licking my clit like his favorite lollypop. He adds another finger into me, pumping more vigorously and dragging me closer to sweet release. I want to give it to him, but I also don't want this to end.

As his confidence grows, Clay breaks our kiss to latch onto my hardened nipple, taunted insistently by his hand. His tongue is like a caress after the bite mark Rhys left there, the clash of aggressive and gentle on different parts of my body causing me to spiral. Nothing exists beyond the building orgasm that's threatening to be my ruin, and the two men staking a united claim over me.

With a hand embedded in both of their hair, I grind shamelessly against Rhys' mouth and pull Clay as close as possible to chase my release. It answers my call immediately, the dam breaking in a rush of ecstasy. My back arches, my pussy crushing Rhys' ever moving fingers. Strangled moans I'm glad I can't hear escape my throat, which Clay kisses and nibbles his way across. I shudder at the throbbing of my clit, at the throes of rapture overriding my limbs. Rhys finally stops his tormenting, his breath fanning my center as he watches the display with rapt interest.

Withdrawing his fingers, Rhys stands and nudges Clay aside. Even after we've just proven they don't always have to butt heads, there's a battle of shoulders before Rhys leans down and captures my lips in a kiss coated with my own arousal. It's chaste, purely intended for the reason to claim. His eyes are wild, a smirk dancing across his lips. I can't see Clay, but his fingers are trailing a pattern up and down my arm to let me know he's still here. I blow out a laugh, the realization of what we just did settling in. Holy crap, we've crossed a line, and I don't want to go back. I want more. There has to be more.

My head lolls to the side as my body enters the blissfully numb aftermath stage. That is, until a tiny flash of red from the living area catches my attention. My eyes narrow, a wash of cold settling over my naked body. I reach up gripping Rhys' shoulder as I make a pointless event to cover myself, twisting away from the open laptop set on the living room coffee table. I know I can't hear their answers, but I need to ask the question burning my tongue anyway.

"Um...guys? How long has the light on Clay's camera been on?"

CHAPTER TWENTY THREE

"What the fuck, Rhys?!" Harper's cry wakes me and a sudden headache tears through my skull. Pulling myself upright on the sofa, I frown and instantly regret it. Pain explodes in my head, the daylight burning my retinas. What the hell happened?

I remember Harper's fingers clawing through my hair. Her taste on my tongue, her sweet cries as her cunt clenched around my tattooed fingers. The sight will forever be imprinted in my mind. Then, like a beckon of dread, a tiny red light flashes through the image.

That's when it all comes rushing back. How I'd barely contained my rage long enough to demand Clayton get Harper out of here. How she kicked and screamed as he crowded her upstairs, while my white-knuckled grip trembled on the counter. How I let the monster within take over, a living entity crawling beneath my skin that begged for blood and promised pain.

Someone took invading Harper's privacy to a whole new level. No one gets to see her in the throes of pleasure, flushed and dazed with desire. Well, except Clayton in this one scenario, but I wasn't focused on him. I was being driven by my need to possess and indulge. By the primal need to mark and own her. Her body is mine. Her soft moans, clawing nails and flushed skin belong to *me*.

Slowly easing upright, I hold the sides of my head together as if they might crack open. Various points of my body ache as I tense, the whole motion of sitting up like I'm being dragged through tar. At some point last night I'd lost my t-shirt, but my jeans are still in place. Dark spots have stained the blue material, my brows pinching together as I check myself for injuries.

"It's your nose," Clayton states. Striding into view, he hands me a wet cloth. Accepting it tentatively, I press it to my face and jerk back as blinding pain shoots through my already pounding head. The throbbing is unbearable, a string of harsh hisses escaping me. The bone is going to need to be reset.

"Can you find my phone? I've got a physician on speed dial." Harper looks around the room, lowering to her knees to peer beneath the sofa I'm sitting on. She's wearing one of my t-shirts, the white material drooping forward as she bends and pushes her peachy ass into the air, also clad in my boxers. Finding the device, she hands it over and crawls into my side, nuzzling softly. I wish I could smell the scent of my laundry powder mixed with her vanilla shampoo, the way our scents compliment each other.

Pulling Harper closer, I wrap one arm around her body and stroke her back, my phone in my other hand as I shoot off a message to the doc. He responds instantly that he's on his way, as the doorbell sounds as McClean arrives for his morning shift. Clayton lets him in, muttering a low apology about the mess. My arm tightens around Harper, the throbbing in my face resonating with one spasming in my chest. Why the fuck is Scum apologizing for me, for the mess I made, for the monster I am? It doesn't sit right. Neither does the way Harper strokes my abdomen with her fingers, pretending I'm not some asshole who can't contain his rage.

That's when it all comes rushing back. How I'd mercilessly owned her body, worked her sweet pussy into a frenzy with my fingers and tongue. She tasted divine. She screamed my name. Only to have the moment ruined by someone pathetic bastard who decided they deserved a front row seat through the webcam. No one gets to see Harper like that except me, and apparently Clayton for however long Harper takes pity on him.

Last night wasn't my first time sharing or being watched, but it's the first time I was controlled by pure possessiveness. When it comes to Harper, I can't fight the primal need to mark and own her. Her body is mine. Her soft moans, clawing nails and flushed skin belong to *me*.

Sweeping a gaze around the house, I see my reason for not having expensive décor or personal belongings has finally come to fruition. Honestly, I'm surprised it took this long. The staircase banister is hanging uselessly to one side, there are holes in various walls. Behind me, the kitchen floor is covered with smashed plates and glass. A baseball bat lies on the central island, a vision of me playing crockery cricket flashing to mind. But there's something else. An arm winding around my neck and hoisting me off my feet. A figure and a fist, just before it all goes dark.

"You broke my freaking nose," I rasp nasally as Clayton rounds the sofa and drops into my book throne. His arms are crossed, microscopic smirk pulling at his mouth. For some reason I try to sniff, sending white hot agony splintering through my face. "Jesus Christ!" Clayton chuckles deeply, the noise more like a rumble infiltrating the air. Not a trace of regret passes through his face.

"I found myself in the rare position of being able to land a punch without you getting hard over it. And you're welcome. You wouldn't have had any furniture left if I hadn't."

I can't deny I would have done the same in his position, but glare at him regardless. Needing painkillers, I gently ease out of Harper's hold and make my way into the kitchen. The cabinet where I keep the Xanax is missing its door, a lone mug left in the cupboard beside it. I turn to the basin, finding the faucet torn clean off and laying uselessly on the counter. Someone had the good sense to turn off the water, and I reckon it's the same person who's stepping into my personal space now.

"You need to sort your shit out. You can't be losing it like that with her in the house," he warns as I swallow the tablets raw. Shoving past him, I pick up a bar stool to perch on, glass crunching beneath my bare feet.

"If you're so concerned, why don't you take the hint and fuck off already? She's only being dragged into this bullshit because of you." I spit back, refusing to acknowledge that he's right. I can't be blacking out with fury when Harper is under the same roof. My head hangs heavy as I've got a hangover without the sweet oblivion of the night before.

"I'm not the sole target of these taunts," Clayton grits through clenched teeth, his eyes on the floor. Bending, he picks at the edge of a polaroid that's peeking out from beneath the counter and returns to his full height, the tic in his jaw beating. A darkness has fallen over his face, his black eyes blazing with an emotion I know all too well.

I turn away, not ever wanting to see those photos again. Any images of Harper and I will be far more graphic and better yet, *consensual.*

"Someone has to be there to pick up the pieces when you toss her aside. That's what you do to women when you're finished with them," Clayton jabs. He's hurt me physically, now he's hunting for my vulnerabilities. Luckily for me, I know what I bring to Harper's life. I know how she looks at me, how she aches for me. It's something I don't need to explain to anyone.

"Maybe I want her as much as you do." I challenge.

"Impossible." Clayton's eyes flash, the depth of his feelings starting to show at last. Before I can so much as smirk, never mind rib him the way I want to, a shoe slams into the side of my head. Spots burst behind my eyes on a groan as my other high-top hits Clayton's back.

"If you're both finished talking about me as if I'm not here," she swans over, batting her lashes in that sugary sweet, I'm-about-to-fuck-you-up, kind of way. During our quarreling, she pulled her leather jacket over the T-shirt I'm apparently not getting back and tugged on her jeans. "I've had a text from Addy, we have some things to discuss.

And before you get all macho," Harper holds up a hand to silence Clayton, "she's waiting outside and I will not be without an escort. Play nice you two. I'll be back by seven."

I groan, leaning my forehead on my palm. Harper is fully planning to go ahead with tonight's study session, regardless of the looming aspect of being recorded. A kiss is placed on my cheek and she leaves. I spin, demanding to know what she thinks I'm going to do with Scum, but the rush of blood to my face floors me with another wave of agony. Where is that fucking doctor?

Pushing upright anyway, I stagger towards the window, checking Harper is in fact with company. The pink-haired imp who desecrated my toenails doesn't seem as bubbly today. I still need to figure out how to get the offensive color off. Regardless, I track the pair until they are out of view. The house suddenly goes cold, or maybe that's just my chest as I watch Harper leave. Clayton huffs, dropping onto the sofa as if he's actually going to stick around.

"At least she didn't take the laptop," he grumbles, drumming his fingers on his thigh, staring at the coffee table. It's a wonder I didn't smash it alongside everything else. "Do you know anyone who can do anything with it? Get it scanned or wire tapped or some shit?" Resting against the windowsill, I run a hand through my hair.

"I tried a hacker last time but he couldn't get a trace. Maybe if there's new leads, he might find something to latch onto. I'll hit him up again."

"Could you, ah...can I ask a favor?" Clayton rubs the back of his neck, his eyes dropping to the floor. I wait for him to look back at my face and read the bored expression there. If he wants something, he'd better bloody say it. "Someone has been visiting my mom with a fake name, pretending to be related to me. Dekken H. Cornerstone. His name was in the visitor's book and I found a beanie hat in her room. I think he's...impersonating me?" Clay mutters. A bubble of fury rises within but I just about manage to keep it contained. Why the fuck didn't he tell us this earlier?

Plucking the laptop from the coffee table, I head back to the kitchen island. The very same surface I had Harper laid across like a buffet and ate out like a man famished. I still am, and my appetite is only for her.

Taking a few photos of the model numbers, or whatever shit the hacker might want, I'm so invested in my phone screen that I didn't notice Clayton let the doctor in. He might as well put on an outfit and become my official bellhop. I'm distracted by messages while my nose is reset, more so by the extortionate sum the hacker is demanding. I'm sure this is just some kid who lives in his bedroom, but he came recommended.

In the background, McClean is tackling the dry wall scattered all over the floor. I'm curious to see what he does with the broken railings before telling him I'll call in a repair crew. My nose is taped in place, the deep ache of bruising seeping towards my eyes. It won't be pretty, but I have bigger problems to deal with. One of which is throwing his weight around, huffing and pacing without any sense of direction. Waiting for the Doc to leave, Clayton leans his arms on the counter.

"We can't keep sitting around, waiting for these threats to get worse." I shudder at his use of the term, we. There is no we. There's no, the boyfriend of my girl is also my boyfriend, type shit going on here. We're enemies trapped in some ridiculous paradox where Clayton Michaels is in my kitchen, looking for some kind of camaraderie. "What about a private investigator?"

"I can't risk hiring anyone officially and my father finding out. He'll intervene, and trust me, you don't want Harper in his sights." The thought makes me shudder. We've got enough problems without adding my father into the mix. "Anyway, stop your fretting. I've been working on it," I grunt, tensing my features to test out the extent of pain in the center of my face.

"You have?" Clayton frowns. "When?" Rolling my eyes, I nudge my stool over to put space between us.

"You don't think I've actually been studying every evening, do you?

I've been cataloguing." Opening a locked folder on my phone, I bring up my spreadsheet and flash it at him. A smile grows across Clayton's stupid face and I snatch my phone back with a grimace.

"You've made an actual spreadsheet? With an attendance list?" He's almost laughing now and my fingers form into a fist.

"Stalkers always return to the scene of the crime," I mutter bitterly. I don't know why he's mocking me, he's the one that said we need to do something. Well, I'm doing something. He should be thankful I'm not twiddling my thumbs, only considering how to next pleasure Harper. I'm covering all bases here. "Whatever happens, we can't let that recording get out." This suddenly sobers him, the scowl I'm accustomed to returning in a flash.

"Worried about your reputation?" Clayton scoffs. I'm used to the accusation that my interests are only surface level, and up to a few months ago, they would have been right.

"I don't give a shit about my reputation. I won't let any harm come to Harper." Rising from the stool, I wander to the far end of the island, needing the space to think this all through in the clear light of a new day. "There's nothing we can do to take back the recording now. If it's going to be leaked, then we will just have to own it. Unless..." I stop mid-stride, my left eye beginning to twitch. "It's intended to be used for blackmail."

"Blackmail for what?" Clayton cocks his head to the side. I throw my arms in the air.

"Oh, I don't fucking know. I smashed my crystal ball last night," I bite back sarcastically. "But blackmail is the best outcome. We can bend to demands, I can pay the fucker off, whatever it takes." The atmosphere in the kitchen thickens, falling heavily between my declaration and Clayton's scrutiny. His dark eyes are fixated on my face, hunting for the deceit he's accustomed to.

"So what, we're making some kind of truce?" he asks. If my head wasn't already throbbing, I'd have thrown it back in disgust.

"No truce, just a basic understanding. Harper's wellbeing is paramount. What we are to each other is insignificant. Agreed?" Being the voice of reason isn't a skill in my wheelhouse, in fact, it tastes like acid on my tongue, but Clayton nods, dropping into my vacated stool. As far as making a pact, that's as deep as I'm willing to go.

I stare at him for a few moments, watching this brain tick over as he makes absolutely no move to leave. Ugh, I don't have the energy for this. I'm going back to bed. Passing McClean in the hallway, I tell him to call in a repairman and plumber. He gives me a solid thumbs up in response and I decide I might actually like him.

I make it halfway up the stairs before Clayton speaks again, following my ascent.

"Do you really care for Harper?" I stall, slowly turning back to glower at him. Clayton doesn't falter or shrink back, and that's how I know I'm losing my touch. "Do you really care for her safety, her hobbies and interests, her wellbeing and her happiness?"

"What does it matter to you?" I spit, my heckles rising. Since when did anyone dare to scrutinize me in my own house?

"It matters because if I'm going to compete for her affections, it had better be against someone worthy of them. If being with her is just another way to get at me," his knuckles crack, "if you build her up just to toss her aside when you're done, I will come after you. I'll show you what true pain feels like."

My scowl falls away for a menacing smile to break free. Clayton has no idea what true pain feels like. He has suffered loss, but he had that love to lose. I was raised by hired staff who feared my father's rule. I was beaten into submission before I stood a chance to rebel. Well I'm rebelling now, and no one is going to take Harper away from me. Not whilst I have breath left in my lungs.

Shaking myself, I continue up the stairs. Why I even tried to come up for an answer for Scum is beyond me. I don't owe him shit. Slamming my door shut, streaks of sunlight bleed through the curtains, illuminating the twisted covers on my bed. Two head prints are indented in my pillows, the smell of musk and sleep perfuming the air. My teeth clench hard enough to crack.

Of all the spare rooms down the hallway, they came here. Violating my space. Clayton spooned Harper in *my* bed, and that better be all he did. I should storm back out and kick his ass, but I'm exhausted. I'm tired of always being angry. My limbs are heavy from the constant fight I have with my own being.

If I had controlled my temper, it could have been me here with her last night instead. Clayton wouldn't have had the chance to swoop in and cradle her as she sleeps. Wouldn't have felt the curve of her ass pressing against him, the silky ends of her hair tickling his chest. I drove her toward him, and it won't happen again. I flop onto the mattress, dragging the covers over my head. This is no longer working for me. This lone wolf, me against the world attitude.

Do I really care for Harper? The question echoes around my head, but I don't have the tools to fully understand the answer. I have no comparison to what this feeling actually is, but it's something. It's real and alive, pulsating in my chest everything I think about her. Yet, admitting it out loud sets me up for everything I try to avoid. Rejection. Humiliation. It opens up a void in which others can witness my demise, should Harper eventually tire of me.

She bends my steadfast morals, she's the voice of reason in my head. I feel her burying herself into my soul, the weight of her burdens causing my own to seem irrelevant. She's my weakness and my strength, my power and my flaw. It's not so much do I care for her but that I *need* her. I need her to bring the light to my darkness. A dull, bitter laugh trickles from between my lips as I realize, I am completely and utterly fucked.

"Yeah," I whisper the answer for my ears only. "I really do care for her."

HARPER

CHAPTER TWENTY FOUR

The quad is busier than I expected, buzzing with that pre-lunch energy of students rushing to beat the food lines. Addy walks beside me, a dampened down version of herself. Wearing soft tones of beige and cream, her skirt sways limply over thick tights and her guilt is visible like an accessory on her fluffy long-sleeved sweater. Even her hair doesn't appear as vibrant in the winter sun, which struggles to break through clouds of gray.

"*Hey,*" I sign, redirecting her attention from the concrete at our feet to my face. "*You look tired.*" It's true, the bags under her eyes are more present today. I can make an educated guess that Addy hasn't been sleeping, given that I've stayed at Rhys' since our disagreement and made sure to sneak back for clean clothes when she's not around. Although, that isn't a necessity now that Rhys has told his cleaner to include my items in his laundry.

Addy smiles sadly, her lips pressed tightly together. A sharp pang of guilt hits me in the gut and we both start signing apologies at the same time.

"*I'm sorry about the way I left.*"
"*I'm sorry I upset you, I was just messing around.*"

"And I missed your shopping trip."

"I still think he's a cum stain but he's your cum stain."

I laugh, tucking my hair behind my ear. My receivers are tucked safely in my pocket, the possibility of a hearing-free lunch too enticing to pass up. We pass the library and the Dean's offices, joining on the back of the line to the cafeteria.

If I were in a rush, I'd suggest we head to one of the other cafes on campus. As it stands though, I'm happy to waste as much time as possible, interested to see if the boys come to some sort of truce after last night. I'm negating the laptop light issue from my mind. For all we know, it was a technical fault, or the camera could have been accidentally activated when we were packing up. And if it wasn't, then we'll deal with it, but I won't regret what happened.

Catching Addy fidgeting with the hem of her sweater, I nudge her shoulder and smile.

"It's fine, water under the bridge. You didn't mean anything by it."

Addy winces, guilt consuming her face again.

"I kind of did." She shrugs, twisting her lips. *"I just worry. You know how he gets."*

"He's different with me," I insist, the truth of that statement shining in my eyes. Addy doesn't look convinced.

"That's what Ed Gein's girlfriend said, and he made people into skin suits."

"Addy!" I smack her arm. The line shuffles forward and I shake my head at the sky. I suppose she wouldn't be a true friend if she didn't care for me. I understand people have their reservations about Rhys, and they likely always will. He is who his father made him into, there's no changing bad habits now. When we finally reach the cafeteria doors, I nudge her gently with my elbow. *"No one's perfect."*

"Clayton is pretty perfect," she counteracts, much to my surprise.

"Should I be worried?" We both laugh, the tension easing at last. Linking my arm in hers, I let Addy guide us along the booths

displaying drinks and packaged food items. My attention is on the room, the students laughing, bodies jostling, chairs scraping. I feel the vibrations under my feet and I find that it's comforting in a strange way. A pulse of normalcy.

We grab trays and make our way down the line. Addy loads hers with salad and fries, while I go for a grilled cheese and tomato soup. Comfort food at its finest. After both opting for water and paying, we find a table near the window. The midday light falls over Addy's face, her freckles a pattern across her nose and cheeks. She signs quickly once we're seated.

"I really am sorry, Harper. I don't want to make you feel like I'm judging you."

"I know you're just looking out for me," I sign back, and ready to put this behind us. Not that it hasn't been eventful staying at Rhys', but I want to go back to my dorm. I want to curl up with a book, to be a vegetable in my pajamas without a horny hound breathing down my neck. Dipping my spoon into my soup, I watch the steam curl into the air. Addy nods, popping two fries into her mouth and brushing off her hands.

"Besides, it's not you I'm worried about. If you keep dangling Clayton in front of him, Rhys might snap and do some real damage."

"Or," I finger spell, unable to hide a cunning smile behind my spoon. Addy's brow raises, her eyes shifting between mine. *"They might find some common ground. AKA, me."* There's no denying the meaning behind my grin. My cheeks heat as Addy's mouth drops open. Her fries are forgotten, and she covers her mouth to stop a laugh.

"No way," she signs, leaning closer. *"You mean, both of them? At once?"* I shrug one shoulder, suddenly invested in my grilled cheese. Reaching across the table, she smacks my arm. *"Harper! You little slut,"* she throws her head back and laughs. I witness the sound rather than hear it, her throat working above the colorful ink that spans her collarbones. My own humor rises to the surface, a hysterical bubble of

laughter escaping me. Anyone nearby will think we've lost our damn minds, and I couldn't care less.

I've missed this. Just girls being girls, sharing secrets and laughter and the kind of teasing that only happens when you know someone has your best interest at heart. This is what normality feels like, the kind of peace no amount of polaroid's, messages or cowardly threats can take from me. I won't be controlled by fear, I will live with stubborn pride. I have the right to be here. I deserve to love and be loved, to laugh and be free.

Returning to eating, Addy waves her hand in my face. *"Well, come on then. I want all the juicy details."* Shaking my head, I mimic zipping my lips just as a shadow falls across the table. I peer up, and my stomach drops, just as I was starting to enjoy myself.

Klara stands there, hands on hips, her blonde hair flawlessly pulled back in a high ponytail. She must be taking a day off from cheerleading practice, her legs cased in extra tight jeans. A low V-neck jumper hangs off one of her shoulders and exposes one side of her leopard print bra. Flanked by two of her cheer squad members, the three of them wear matching sneers.

"Wow," she says slowly, exaggerating every syllable so I can read her lips. "Didn't expect to see you here." I don't need sound to know her tone is sugar-laced with venom, I can see it in the pinch of her features. Addy rolls her eyes, lifting her bottle of water to her mouth, whilst I stretch out my arms wide.

"It's a public cafeteria Klara, welcome to all. Why don't you pull up a chair and we can swap notes on how Rhys likes to have his cock sucked?" Addy spits out her water, spraying half the table including my grilled cheese. It's fine, my appetite has soured anyway. Klara has turned an unhealthy shade of beetroot red, which was my intention. "Not interested? Then maybe you should move on and we can go back to pretending we don't exist to each other."

Leaning back in my chair, I purse my lips, refusing to be goaded whilst I'm having lunch. Klara has been on my back since I arrived on campus, before Rhys even meant anything to me. Stomping her foot in frustration, she flusters over her response.

"Well you sure seemed cozy with him last night." I sober in an instant, rising to my feet. Klara smirks at my reaction, her chest sticking out impossibly further.

"What do you know about last night?" Addy joins my side, her solidarity for the wrong reasons but I appreciate the gesture. Addy is supporting the fact she thinks I've had a threesome, but Klara regains her composure as if she knows otherwise. Could it be that Klara has something to do with the webcam light flashing?

"He was meant to be at dinner with my family. A car waited outside for an hour, but I bet you know all about that. You're the reason he didn't come." Her lip twitches as she fights aside a snarl.

So that's why he was so reckless after kicking everyone out last night. Rhys ignored a summons, and I'm sure there will be some type of repercussion for it. My heartbeat spikes, thumping against my ribs. I shouldn't relish the thought of Klara and her family sitting with Rhys' father, pissed off and tapping their fingers against the dinner table, but I do. Rhys missed their dinner to feast on me instead. Poetic.

"If you think I control Rhys, you clearly don't know him as well as you think you do," I chuckle softly. We're going in circles and I'm quickly growing bored of it. Klara folds her arms, shifting her weight onto one hip and narrowing her eyes.

"You really think you're special?" she scoffs. "You're just a play-thing. Something for him to screw until he gets bored and comes back to me."

My god. She's delusional. Maybe not about the Rhys growing bored part, but I know for a fact he'll never go back to her. Even if their parents get their way and the pair end up married, there's no future of Rhys accepting her as his wife. I almost feel bad for her, that female pride coming around to bite me in the ass. I don't want to be the bitch she's trying to make me into.

Addy, however, has no such reservations. She lunges forward, and I rush to put myself between her and Klara before shooting her a warning look.

"She's not worth it," I sign quickly. Klara watches my hands, her upper lip curling in mock amusement.

"Oh, how cute," she teases, tilting her head to the side. "Do you do that because you're scared to talk?" Her friends giggle, whispering something to each other before bursting into actual laughter. We're gaining more attention from the tables around us, smart phones appearing in my peripheral vision. Nothing is ever sacred in this place. I take a deep breath, trying to remind myself that losing control is exactly what she wants.

"Actually," I say, loud and steady, "I do it because I can. You should try learning something new instead of spreading your legs for half the football team."

I feel the silence that follows, its sharpness cutting through my jacket and Rhys' T-shirt. Even Addy freezes, blinking at me like I've just slapped someone, a slow psychotic smile spreading across her face. Klara's features drain of color before flooding red again, the kind of red that is usually accompanied with a shriek or a slap.

"You bitch," she mouths. Her hand twitches at her side, but she doesn't follow through. Picking up my backpack, I sling it over my shoulder, refusing to let her see my hands shake. Addy hurries to do the same.

"Run along, Klara," Addy says. "Your claws are showing." Tilting her chin upwards, she stands tall alongside me, daring Klara to make her move. It's not like we're practiced fighters or anything, but I reckon I could land a punch if I really needed to. I kick and hit Rhys enough.

The cheerleader trio exchange glances, then sharply turn and stalk away, their ponytails swinging as if they're synchronized. Klara glances back once before disappearing out the door, her glare promising that this isn't over.

When they're gone, the tension leaks out of me so fast it leaves me dizzy. Bodies suddenly shift, students at the tables cheering and clapping enthusiastically. The movements are too fast, the cracking of palms blurring my vision as if I can see the sound waves. Tugging Addy outside a few moments later, we head in the opposite direction of the cheerleaders. We head for the library, in particular the quiet zone. Dropping onto the beanbags, Addy is still beaming whilst my anxiety sets in.

"She's jealous," Addy signs once she has my attention. *"Don't let her under your skin."*

"Too late," I reply, managing a weak smile. I just showed a side of myself I don't like in front of so many witnesses, and those who weren't there have probably seen the livestream on our student forum. I don't want to be that bitch. The new girl who waltzes in to steal boyfriends and brings their exes down. The narrative they're going to spin is all wrong, and as much as I pretend I don't, I care. I'm just starting to make real friends here.

Resting my elbows on my knees, I press my palms to my eyes. The darkness is a small relief, but I can still see Klara's face burned against the inside of my mind, smug and knowing.

Addy reaches across, gently pulling my hands down. *"Look at me."* When I do, she gives me that kind of smile that feels like sunlight filtering through the rain. *"She's just proven she's all bark, no bite. Rhys made his choice, remember?"* I nod, though there's a flicker of unease I can't shake.

"She mentioned last night, I sign. *How would she even know?"*

Addy frowns, her eyes lifting in thought. *"She's probably bluffing. Gossip spreads fast around here, especially with your name attached."* Her lips soften into a small smile. *"Don't let her make you doubt yourself."*

Flopping back in the beanbag, I inhale slowly through my nose. She's right. Klara thrives on attention and on getting reactions. It's what gets her through each day. I know that what I have with Rhys is real, whether the rest of the world wants to accept it or not.

The tension in my shoulders finally starts to fade. I watch the sunlight spilling through the library's domed skylight, realizing how much I've missed coming here. The smell of paper draws out memories of safety and comfort. Addy nudges my foot, her smile patient as if she's waiting for something.

"You still owe me the juicy details," she signs. I groan, rolling my eyes, but the laughter that bubbles up feels lighter this time.

"You're relentless," I say out loud, shaking my head. Going back to signing, I keep the conversation to ourselves. You never know who is listening in around here. *"Clay is a private person. He won't want his business shared all over campus."*

"It's hardly all over campus. It's just me," Addy pouts. I grin, but make no move to fill in the gaps she's asking for. Addy is the closest friend I have, but she has more influence than she thinks. She's popular amongst certain crowds, and not that best at keeping secrets. The small voice in my mind is warning me against oversharing. I just want to keep this for myself.

"Okay fine," Addy holds up her hands in defeat. *"Can I at least ask how Clayton is doing? After the whole locker thing, then leaving and then coming back. I'm kind of Team Clay over here."*

"Really? I hadn't noticed," I narrow my eyes, my expression dripping with sarcasm. Relenting, I sit upright and twist my lips. *"He's okay. He makes slight headway and then reverts back into himself. Sometimes it feels like it's two steps forward, five steps back with him. But he's here, and he's not letting Rhys push him around."*

Catching Addy's frown, I lick my lips, worrying that I've said too much. Guilt slithers along my spine, cold enough to make me wrap my arms around myself. So much for Clay's privacy. It must be impossible for him to work on himself when Rhys is always around, ready to put him down again. I'm the reason Clay is in Rhys' orbit, and vice versa. I should make more effort to smooth out their differences. Waving my hand through the air, I reset the conversation.

"We're all works in progress. No matter what I've gotten myself into, it'll work itself out in the end."

Still, Addy doesn't look convinced. She nudges herself forward, balancing on the edge of her beanbag to reach across and squeeze my arm. Like a light has turned on behind her eyes, her face brightens and the smile she gives me in nothing short of manic.

"Leave it with me. I have an idea."

CLAYTON

CHAPTER TWENTY FIVE

I pull up outside Rhys' house in my truck, the orange paint reflecting the sun's rays. It's supposed to be clear skies and somewhat warmer today, or in the very least, not snowing. At least, that's what Addy told me, after thumping on my door with a picnic basket in hand and strict orders.

I don't know much about Harper's roommate, especially her feelings towards me or her intentions. Perhaps she's enjoying watching the sitcom that is Harper's life, but I won't say no to having Harper to myself. In fact, it couldn't have come at a better time.

Right on cue, Harper appears, leaving Rhys' house with a bounce in her step. A lilac dress skims her thighs beneath her black leather jacket. Her hair is braided over her shoulder for a change, the pink ends bouncing with each step in her biker boots. Noticing me, her green eyes narrow as her smile grows, curious but happy to play along as she nears the truck.

"Hop in, Beautiful. We're going on a date." She reads my lips as they move, her head tilting.

"I thought I was meeting Addy for a girl's afternoon?" she queries, leaning against my open window on her forearms. I lean down to kiss her temple with a shrug.

"You've been set up, but I'll try my best to talk about boys and compare breast sizes." A laugh bubble of laughter bursts from her and she bops me on the nose.

"Oh Clay. Luckily for you, I'm not that kind of girl." Rounding the truck, she hops into the passenger seat and dives into her bag for her receivers. I watch her click them into place with a small snap, marveling in her quiet resilience for the hundredth time. Even in the midst of a faceless threat, she still manages to find a smile for me. Just before I press on the accelerator, a figure leans in the house doorway, Rhys silently delivering threats across the distance with his eyes. I make sure to throw up a middle finger as we speed away.

"What is this place?" Harper blinks up, eyes wide with wonder at the scene before us. Greenery bursts through rocky outcrops on either side of a roaring waterfall. A wide stream rushes by, broken by giant stones that act as stepping paths toward the manmade woodlands on the far side. Overhead, a glass dome encloses the lush foliage, shielding it from the winter chill. Along the far wall of the dome, a massive image has been pasted against the glass, a seamless illusion of endless fields and forests stretching to the horizon.

"They're calling it the Terra Nova Project," I say with a grin, impressing myself. "It's an education center for environmental sustainability."

Reaching for her hand, I pull her onto the first rock and help her hop across the stream. With the picnic basket hooked in my arm, I drop from stone to stone, steadying her waist every chance I get. She doesn't complain. Not even when I use both hands to pull her close, any excuse to touch her after what I saw the other night. Rhys claims Harper as if he has every right to, so why shouldn't I?

"This is awesome, Clay," Harper says, keeping her hand in mine even when she doesn't need to anymore.

"I can't take the credit. Addy planned the whole thing."

We follow a marked trail through the trees, no words needed. Birds sign overhead in the thick canopy, the shade breaking up the soft, filtered sunlight. The air smells green and alive, unlike anything from my old neighborhood, where even weeds didn't bother fighting the concrete. Even the raccoons knew better than to dig through our trash. They'd starve before finding anything worth stealing.

The trail climbs upward, each step providing me with a dangerously good view of Harper's creamy thighs. It's a form of torture. I grab a water bottle from the basket and hand it to her, trying to play it cool. Her responding smile is everything. My gaze lingers long enough to follow the path of water as it slides down her throat, leaving me torn between pushing her against the nearest tree and reminding myself not to screw this up by moving too fast. Wavershit is the one who's going to burn out quick. I'm the one who's going to stay the course.

Reaching the top of a slope, we find ourselves above the waterfall we'd seen upon entering. Couples are scattered across the grassy overlook, picnicking on blankets just like we're planning to do. I steer Harper toward a quiet patch, away from curious eyes.

"You hungry?" she asks, pulling the checked blanket from the basket and giving it a little shake.

"Famished," I reply, watching her bend over to spread it out. Her dress rides up, and every ounce of decency I have wrestles to keep my eyes elsewhere. I'm not Rhys. I don't take what isn't freely given. But as soon as Harper gives me permission, I'll have her beneath me, panting my name and clawing at my shoulders.

"Clayton," Harper says, giving my bicep a playful shove. I blink, realizing I'd completely zoned out. "The basket?" She gestures to where it's nestled in the crook of my arm.

"Oh right," I give myself a little shake. Come on Clayton, keep your head. Lowering to sit at the edge of the blanket, I leave space for the basket between us. My cargos can take a little dirt, they've been through worse.

Harper unpacks everything, each item more of a surprise than the last. Two mini bottles of rosé, a spread of cheeses and crackers, and chocolate-dipped strawberries. Addy seriously outdid herself.

"What is all this in aid of?" I finally ask, the question burning in my mind. "Is Addy advocating for us?" It's a mischievous question, and Harper knows it. Giving me a sly smirk, she half shrugs.

"She's groveling, not that she has any need to. I'm the one who was out of line." My brows raise at this. I was under the impression that the two had grown really close.

"Dare I ask what happened?"

Harper shakes her head and I drop the subject. Either way, I owe Addy big time. Truth is, I couldn't have pulled this off alone. I barely had enough gas money this week, and I've been living out of Rhys' refrigerator rather than face the red light of doom on the cafeteria scanner. Just the thought of being back in this position and living day to day stings, but I shove it away. My mom is in the clear. That's all that matters.

And besides, Harper's not the kind of girl who cares about price tags. She blushes at the smallest compliments, lights up when I call her beautiful, and leans into me like my presence is her go-to comfort. I rest back on my forearms, pretending to admire the view whereas I'm stealing glances at her. The vibrancy of our natural surroundings emphasizes the green of her eyes, the pink in her hair glowing warmer under the dome's light. Strands slip forward as reaches for the rosé and carefully lifts the miniature bottle to her mouth.

She's at ease here, because it's quiet. It's peaceful and so far removed from the academy we've come to know. Her bare knees brushing the blanket, her dress fluttering in the artificial breeze. A soundless kind of joy radiates off her, one that I could watch forever. A smear of liquid glosses her lower lip, and all I can think about is how easy it would be to lean in and taste it. Noticing I'm not eating, Harper leans over to lift a strawberry to my mouth.

"Try one," she insists, watching me closely. I take a slow bite, my lips brushing her fingers on purpose. A blush instantly coats her cheeks. Attempting to sit back on her patch of the blanket, I grip Harper's hips and pull her closer, tucking her into my side. She lies back on the arm I tuck behind my head, our gazes caught on the dome ceiling without really seeing it. Nudging Harper, I open my mouth for another strawberry, and she complies with a giggle. Music to my fucking ears.

For the first time, possibly in my entire life, I relax. Whole bodily and mentally. I release myself of the thoughts that plague me, the guilt I carry like a dead weight on my shoulders. Here in this dome, I'm just a jock who's acing his classes, part of the basketball team, and with an incredible girl feeding him strawberries. I've paid my dues, I've suffered for long enough. For once, I get to be that guy.

"Can I ask you a question?" Harper's voice breaks through my thoughts. I smirk, resting my jaw against her temple.

"Technically you just did." She smacks my chest playfully, her hand lingering to stroke the cotton of my t-shirt nervously. I sober instantly. "Ask me anything."

"I, um, I get the impression that you weren't very social before I came along. Like, with the ladies." Harper turns her head to the side, pretending to study the landscape, and I get the impression that her cheeks are on fire. I'm glad she's not watching for my reaction, because my eyes are wide and my brows are pinched.

"What are you asking me exactly?"

"Well, I was curious if you... had you... been with a girl...before me?" Harper's voice goes all high-pitched at the end, whilst I lay there mortified. It's as if someone has taken a vacuum to my dick and attempted to shrivel it into dust.

"Was I that bad at it?!" I choke, dislodging Harper's head. She sits upright as I do, placing her hand on my chest. I was right, she's flushed red like a beetroot.

"No! No, no. Oh god, forget I said anything," Harper ducks her head, nuzzling it in my shoulder. I can't forget it now, my poor dick is all sad and droopy. "I just wanted to find out how many girls you've been with, that's all. It was incredible, I promise."

Slowly, I come back to myself. Being with Harper was incredible. The way she clung to me, panting and shaking. How her body reacted. I don't need to be told that she enjoyed it with words, I felt her satisfaction. Wrapping my arms around her, my hand strokes her upper back.

"Maybe next time, just ask for a ballpark figure," I murmur by her receiver. Harper chuckles a shrill laugh that's bordering on hysterical, and I decide to save her from any more embarrassment.

"When I left the JDC, I lost my way. Like most guys would after being locked up with other dudes, I reckon. I met young women online or at bars, all the hazardous stuff you should avoid doing. But it got old real fast and instead of making me feel better, I just felt more hollow inside. So, I promised myself that the next time I took a woman to bed, it'd mean something. That there'd be actual feelings involved."

Reaching up, I cradle her jaw and coax her to look at me. Her green eyes dart everywhere but mine until I finally catch them.

"And have you? Had actual feelings for anyone since?" she whispers.

"Not until you." Her lips part slightly, her breath brushing across my face until it's swallowed by my kiss. I take her mouth leisurely, my tongue teasing hers in lazy, unhurried strokes that have her melting into me. I don't rush, not when she deserves someone who will devote every second to pleasing her. Reaching up to free her braid, I let the pink curls tumble loose between my fingers. Her vanilla shampoo mixes with the crisp sweetness of rosé still lingering on her tongue, and it's intoxicating.

I push the basket aside, the motion careful yet charged. Lowering her onto the blanket, I brace my forearms on either side of her head.

Her chest rises and falls in quick, shallow breaths, her green eyes darkened to a stormy jade. She's stunning. Wild and soft all at once, hair fanned out like a halo, her mouth kiss-swollen and glistening. I kiss along her jaw, down the graceful curve of her neck, feeling her shiver under my lips. Her fingers slide into my hair, tugging lightly as she exhales my name like a secret.

"What about you?" I ask, a crooked grin finding its way back. It's a pretense for the jealousy I'm about to feel. "I'm guessing there's an army of exes I should be on the lookout for?"

"Nope." She swallows, her eyes flicking away. "I've never had an official boyfriend." My eyebrows rise before I can stop them. In one sense, her declaration fills me with some internal hope. Firstly, because her and Wavershit clearly haven't decided anything officially, which means I am still in with a chance. But it also hits me with a huge amount of pressure to get this right, to not fuck this up and give Harper some jagged sense of what a relationship should be.

"I'll never rush you, Harper," I say quietly. "But I want you. I want to hold you when you sleep, help you study, watch you succeed and fail, and still get up again. I want to be your everything." I feel the shift between us before I see it. Her desire and her fear. Her eyes glisten, and I realize I'm leaning too close. The last thing I want is to make Harper feel cornered. So I shift, rolling us onto our sides, giving her space while keeping my arm beneath her head and my other hand resting lightly on her hip.

"What about..." Her voice trails off, barely a whisper.

"Rhys?" I supply for her. It's no wonder that's where her mind goes. He's overwhelming and all-consuming, even when he's not here. Harper nods hesitantly and I withhold my sigh, even if his name does taste bitter on my tongue.

I know she's conflicted, but if I'm honest, I don't think I'm built for sharing.

"I do get it." I say, even though it kills me. Even though I know I'm not built for sharing and our current circumstances won't last much longer. Still, I force myself to be the bigger man for her. "With him, it's fast and fierce. And although I'm more reserved, I want to make it clear I'm just as invested in winning you. He may be fire, but I'm ice. I'll soothe away the burns he creates and pull you back from the flames when they grow too wild. I'm your loyal protector after all."

Harper's eyes begin to swim with unshed tears, indecision shattering her expression. It breaks me. I never want to be the reason for her sadness, so I cup her jaw and pull her into me. Hovering just close enough for her chest to brush mine with each breath, my gaze seeks permission before I find her lips again.

This time, Harper takes control, kissing me back hungrily, her hands curling around the fabric of my shirt. I let her roll me onto my back, let her take control of her emotions whilst moving to straddle me. I won't take it any further since there are people in the vicinity, but my hands do land on Harper's bare thighs and I find myself being tested in ways a lesser man would fail. In a way that Wavershit would fail miserably.

I'm better than that, and him. I just need to hold on long enough for Harper to see that too.

HARPER

CHAPTER TWENTY SIX

The last few weeks have passed in a blur since that perfect day. The ideal landscape, the lovely picnic, and Clay's kisses. I keep myself in that blissful bubble, being as productive as I can be before it all goes to shit once again.

The science students actually smile as I enter the lab, Millie reaching over the aisle to hand back the textbook she borrowed from Rhys' place for some late night cramming. I've told him this week is the last he can keep the books, no more extensions. They belong back in the library where everyone can assess them, and I'm done hiding. I want to be back amongst the shelves and the civilization. I didn't trade my aunt's attic for another gilded cage.

Clay stays close to my side, attentive as ever. Helping to lift the bag from my back, he waits for me to unpack before leaning to place it by the leg of my stool. Rhys drops down on my other side, holding his hand out for a pen with a blank expression on his face. He's bored. Bored of attending classes, bored of the study groups. Bored of the consideration Clay gives to every aspect of my day without any effort. It doesn't matter that Rhys convinces me to stay over at his more nights in the week than not, he always wants more.

Peterson decides to grace us with his presence today, if only to oversee an assessment. Handing out the thick booklets to the front row and asking them to be passed back, he eyes Clay with a scowl until he shuffles his stool away from me. We have two hours to complete the stapled worksheets, which means Peterson has two hours to sit and to dutifully grade our recent assignments. I'm rather proud of the work Clay and I came up with. Rhys did not hand one in.

Quiet falls over the room as we are told to begin, and I immediately yank my receivers off. I'm growing more used to wearing them, but they'll never feel natural. Flipping over the first page, I force myself to ignore the heat pulsing from either side of me and focus.

Clay has stuck by what he said. He's been giving me the freedom to get Rhys out of my system, if it's even possible. Every time I have Rhys to myself in the dead of night, I get a new side of him. A new vulnerability or depraved need comes to light. Rhys is more complex that even he realizes, like a Rubik cube that's only just learnt it has different colors, never mind how they twist and shift into a uniform pattern.

But we're always separate. It's me and Rhys, or me and Clay. Whenever I'm with one, the other tries to steer my attention back. The almost threesome we had on Rhys' kitchen island is a distant memory now, the rift between them starting to splinter once again. I don't know how to stop it, and I haven't been actively trying. I never signed up to be their rivalry counsellor.

Currently, Rhys is tapping his pen on the page, much to the annoyance of those nearby. Luckily, I can't hear it. Clay is racing through his paper, scrawling out lengthy answers in cursive handwriting. For me, the words on the page begin to jumble, my eyes feeling itchy as I rub them. I try to answer as many questions as possible, lying to myself that I'll go back for the ones I've skipped. Come on Harper, focus. It shouldn't be this difficult to separate my education and personal life, but they seep into each other too often.

Clay nudges me all too soon, signaling that the timer has finished. I reluctantly clip my receivers back on with a huff. There's nothing like an assessment to prove to yourself that you've retained absolutely nothing of relevance. Glancing over to Rhys, I see that he was productive in the last twenty minutes, doodling a tattoo design on the back of his paper. He slides it over to me, the pen sketch of an upside down bat staring out of the page with large eyes. A smile grows across my face.

"Why didn't you become an art major? You have a skill for it," I ask. Rhys makes a strangled noise, waving me off as if I didn't see the slight twinge of pink touching his cheeks.

"Yeah right," he stands and strides off. I shove the drawing into my backpack, before heading up front to hand in my test paper. Rhys hovers outside the door, leaning against a locker that one of our classmates is trying to gain access to. I link our arms and walk him further down the hallway.

"Are you guys free later? I said we'd help Addy set up the gymnasium for her talent show."

"Why the fuck would you do that?" Rhys scrunches up his nose in disgust. I shrug, keeping him close to my side. When I'm asking for help, he's the biggest flight risk.

"Because it's nice to help our friends. Her team has been slacking and she's worried it won't be ready by the weekend." The whole college has been buzzing about the talent contest for weeks. Posters have been plastered on every available surface, an air of excitement bringing a pleasant change from the mundane day to day.

"She's no friend of mine," Rhys grumbles so I turn to face Clay instead. Running a hand over his beanie, he looks everywhere I'm not.

"I won't be able to today, I'm afraid. I've got...something else on." Clay shuffles from foot to foot. I raise an eyebrow suspiciously.

"What have you 'got on'?" I air quote with my free hand, bringing a shy smile to his full lips.

"A counselling session with one of the sophomores. I made him a deal a while back," he says cryptically. Shrugging, I pat his forearm and withdraw my arm from Rhys'. Counselling would be great for Clay, but I didn't miss the fondness that shone in his eyes when he spoke about this mysterious sophomore. Clay has a friend, which is even better.

"No problem. It's just setting up and Addy will be there. I'll manage being on my own for an afternoon."

"Like fuck you will," Rhys' gruff voice penetrates the air, severe and sudden. I flinch, as do the students surrounding us. My widened eyes flick to him, assessing the clench of his jaw and the flare of nostrils.

"Jesus, don't do that," I chastise. "There's no need to be in defense mode all the time. It's one afternoon. I'll be fine. It's just some painting and set arranging." Rhys' eyes do not waver, his protectiveness radiating in dark, rolling waves. He's the one who didn't want to come, now he's acting like I was trying to get away from him.

"I'll watch over you until Clayton returns." He states matter-of-factly. My mouth pops open.

"You'll watch over me but you won't help out?" I question and Rhys nods, not a hint of regret in his discussion. Sometimes I forget, just because Rhys has warmed up to me, that he's still an asshole to everyone else around him. Shaking my head, I adjust the strap of my backpack. "I'd rather just see you later. I don't need you standing watch at my back, like some kind of guard dog who won't wear a muzzle."

A ripple of silence falls between us, the back of my neck prickling with instant regret. Rhys raises a solitary brow, his pierced lip turning downwards. Clay lingers, unsure whether to stay or go.

"Shit, Rhys, I didn't mean—"

"Is that what you think I am?" Using his tongue to toy with his lip ring, Rhys nods and strides past me. I share a quick pitying glance with Clay, who salutes me and mouths, *good luck*. Great, thanks for that.

Catching up to Rhys' side, I try to get him to slow down and look at me, but he's a man on a mission. Said mission apparently brings us to the café in the veterinary building. I'm not overly surprised, since Toadfully Caffeinated is Rhys' favorite coffee spot and it is lunchtime. I've got an hour before I told Addy I'd be at her disposal. One hour to bring Rhys back from whatever dangerous mood I've put him in.

Rhys stops short, opening the door and waiting for me to enter first. I blink, forcing my feet to move as he stalks in behind, his heavy boots thudding against the polished floor. The faint smell of disinfectant and freshly ground coffee mingle in the air, the low chatter of students studying over lattes dipping into an uneasy silence as we pass. They can feel Rhys' mood like I can. It's practically a black raincloud hanging overhead, each step brewing a storm beneath his skin.

Despite the wariness of those seated at tables, I straighten my shoulders and slip my hand into his. As Rhys clamps his fingers between mine, electricity burns in my veins, a heady power swimming through me. It must be intoxicating, being the most feared man in the room, and I'm his woman. I'm the barrier between him and those who fear him.

The hiss of the espresso machine fills the space, stream polluting the air behind the counter. With fogged glasses, Kenneth blinks up at me and grins.

"Hey Harper!" he calls out, oblivious to the way Rhys tenses. Or perhaps Kenneth doesn't really care. "What are you doing here? Oh that's right, Clayton has his therapy thing with the sophomores. They've challenged him to add more color to his wardrobe. Did you notice his green socks today?" Kenneth's smile is so broad, his muddy eyes are alight with glee.

"He told you all of that?" I raise my brows. It's not that I don't expect Clay to talk to his roommate, but I only just heard of this counselling thing ten minutes ago. Kenneth tilts his head back and forth, his vibrant orange hair flopping around.

"He talks in his sleep. So what can I get you? We have a new frog-themed menu," Kenneth points to the chalkboard overhead and talks me through each item. Rhys is vibrating with impatience but I grip his hand tighter and make him wait it out. Kenneth is just being good at his job, and there's nothing wrong with that. Grinning at his lengthy explanations, I cut in to order before Rhys wrings Kenneth's neck.

"I'll have a maple leap latte, and a caramel swamp macchiato for

Rhys." Kenneth looks at the tattooed man beside me for the first time, and dismisses him just as quickly. The lack of trepidation in Kenneth's face is interesting, but perhaps Clay has shared more in his sleep than he's aware of. Kenneth is being a good friend in having roommate's back.

"Grab a seat and I'll bring them over to you."

Turning me away swiftly, Rhys' jaw ticks as his gaze sweeps the room, searching for the table he'd like. I know in Rhys' mind, that isn't limited to vacant tables. When someone brushes past him reaching for a stirrer, he growls.

"Watch where you're going." The student freezes, stammers an apology, and retreats like he's just brushed against a live wire. I roll my eyes, dragging him over to an *empty* table in the window.

"Can you not?" I whisper, keeping my tone low as I switch my hearing over to a microphone that Rhys clips onto the neck of his T-shirt. This way, it's more streamlined to the person I'm having a conversation with, rather than flooding my skull with background noise. "You're scaring people."

"They should be scared," he mutters, eyes narrowing at the group in the booth we sat in last time. "Someone knows more than they should. I'm just waiting for them to slip up." Kenneth carries over a tray and sets down our coffees, along with a pecan pond pie on the house. I smile as he retreats, waiting to be alone before speaking.

"Anything come back from the hacker this time?" I try to sound nonchalant. Inside, I'm burning for answers as strongly as I'm fearing what those answers might be. The bubble around me is growing thin, but I will live in it until I'm forced to do otherwise. I want to be as normal as any girl who has two almost-boyfriends and trying to get the degree that might just kill her off before someone else gets the chance.

"He ran a trace on the guy that gave you the coffee before winter break," Rhys says cryptically for anyone eavesdropping. What he wants to say is, the guy who drugged and photographed us whilst unconscious, who he then proceeded to beat the shit out of without digging any deeper. "The demand came from a burner phone and he was wire-transferred a good sum of money from an off-shore account. Another dead end that leads nowhere."

"Who on campus would have an off-shore account and that kind of money lying around? Other than you, of course." I scrunch up my nose as I stir my latte. In my peripheral vision, Rhys goes still. His icy blue eyes flicker with annoyance before he exhales through his nose.

"That's the second accusation you've made of me. What am I, an unmuzzled dog or a psycho stalker?" The urge to roll my eyes is strong.

"What you are is on your man-period," I reply. Rhys leans back in his chair, the wooden legs creaking under his tension. I sip my drink, watching him over the rim as he tries to get himself under control. The micro expressions are twitching, the crease between his brows is contracting. After a couple of minutes, Rhys exhales over the microphone and although it's like a leaf blower going off in my head, I smile and reach for his hand. I know he's frustrated, but anger isn't going to help. It's just going to suffocate both of us.

"Look, Addy has asked for my help. I want to be a good friend. You can support me in that, or you can let me go alone. Those are the two options." I hold his stare, refusing to back down. I know it's naïve to become comfortable, that the weeks of silence from this creep shouldn't be taken lightly, but I can't live on edge all of the time. I can't look over my shoulder forever, or as Rhys would prefer, hide in his frat house. I need to live. "So...are you coming with me or not?"

RHYS

CHAPTER TWENTY SEVEN

I hang back near the gymnasium door, keeping my promise to watch over Harper while mentally cataloguing every idiot who so much as looks her way. I tell myself that staying close to the exit means I can leave whenever I want, but that's a lie. I couldn't walk away from Harper any more than I could leave my balls nailed to the railing I'm leaning on.

After leaving the cafe, she insisted on going back to her dorm to change into 'more appropriate clothing'. But now, as I stare at her bent over a sheet of MDF in leopard-print lycra, I wish I'd dragged her out in the baggy sweatpants she'd had on before. Her curves are on full display for anyone who dares to look, her stunning face is frozen with concentration. Then there's her tongue poking out from the corner of her mouth. A tongue that's good for so much more than simply dragging along the underside of my cock. Said-cock jolts in my boxers and I have to sneakily rearrange myself.

How can she still be affecting me this way? Harper is pure sin wrapped in a silent strength others don't have the right to see. I no longer crave her insults like whips, slicing through whatever soul I have left. I crave her compliments. The hidden smiles and light touches.

How she's building me up, brick by brick, showing me a path I never thought possible.

One that's led me here, watching the set up of a farce. The talent show is in two days, and somehow, I'm supposed to believe the anarchy before me will turn into a performance worth watching. Contestants are scattered across the basketball court, practicing their acts while art students frantically paint props and backdrops. A guy on a unicycle juggles between two ladders while students hang glittering stars from the basketball hoops. A wannabe opera singer goes off key when the unicycle juggler bumps into a passer-by and the paint they're carrying splatters all over her dress. The whole thing's a disaster in motion, and this is just the rehearsal.

Harper's in the middle of it all, on all fours, bobbing her head to music only she can hear. A paintbrush in her hand, another tucked behind her ear, she's working on a night-sky skyline backdrop. Every so often, she glances my way, probably to check if I'm still here, and grins with satisfaction. I raise my brow as if to say, *Babygirl, I'm not going anywhere.*

"If you're going to stand there glaring like a gargoyle, you might as well make yourself useful," Addy calls out as she strides over, attitude dripping from her. Her tiny shorts and gym vest show off her tattooed arms and legs, the colorful ink a complete contrast to the black and gray that cover mine. There's a streak of blue paint on her forehead that ruins her attempt at a glare.

I don't need a sign to display Addy's dislike for me, and the feeling is mutual. Ever since she violated my toenails. I picked the polish off in the end, but the pink twinge lingered so I colored over them in black sharpie. It seems to have held up and Harper is yet to say anything.

Planting herself in front of me, Addy tries to push a giant, metallic star into my chest. I make no move to accept it.

"I don't trust you," I growl, pinning her with a deadly glare. Addy rolls her eyes, unaffected and perhaps a little amused.

"And I don't care. But since it's *your* name we're working our asses off to promote, you can at least hang some stars." I follow her pointing finger just in time to see a large, slobbery dog in a pink, ruffled dress plow into a ladder on stage, the student who was at the top now dangling from the basketball hoop. Yeah, no. Not happening.

Ignoring the imp in front of me, I head straight for Harper. Plucking the paintbrush from behind her ear, I kneel beside her, dipping it into the white paint tub nestled between her thighs. She grins but doesn't say a word, which is fine by me. Talking would only make the descent from my throne so much worse. Focusing on the backdrop, I help Harper paint the hundreds of tiny windows on the skyscraper already outlined by someone else. Essentially, it's one giant paint-by-numbers.

Harper is in her element, humming her tune, lightly bobbing her head. Pulling my wireless headphones from my sweatpants pocket, I lift Harper's phone from in front of her and pair them. For the millionth time, I'm about to demand she adds a passcode to her phone when the music bleeds into my ears. Of everything I would have guessed she'd listen to, it never would have been this. It's cheesy and old school, a boy-band's concoction of electric guitars and drums.

"What the fuck is this?" I ask, more to myself. Checking her Spotify, the album cover shows five sets of overgrown fringes and juvenile faces. Turning my headphones off, preferring to sit with the chaotic background noise in the gym, Harper gives me a tiny shrug.

"If you don't like it, then don't be here." Her smile widens, although she tries to conceal it behind her hair. With her phone still in hand, I switch her implants from the music to the microphone app and hold it close to my mouth.

"Let's ditch this. They're doing just fine here," I say just as a loud crash and scream sounds behind us. Harper flinches, the white paint of her window smearing out of the lines. I ignore the cries for help, focusing on making the timber of my voice as husky as possible. "My place isn't far. We can sneak out and be back before they've gotten this mess under control. I'll be quick," I lie. I'm never quick, but she doesn't complain once we've started. It's getting her away from Scum and the other meaningless things she distracts herself with that's the real trick.

Harper tries to make a noise of annoyance but it comes out weak.

"How are you still horny? A gigolo gets less sex than you." Dumping the paintbrush into the pot, I sit back on my hunches, bringing the phone to my lips.

"I don't think you understand that you're on my mind constantly. Your eyes and your perfect tits and your curves. The smell of your shampoo, the birthmark on the bottom of your right foot. How beautifully you take every inch of my cock, how you ride me until you collapse. I think about fucking you every minute of every day, and at night, I dream of more ways I could defile you. It's a visceral need Harper. There's never a moment that I'm not hard and throbbing for you."

"Rhys," Harper turns her head to scowl pathetically, a tremble in her words and a searing hot flush in her cheeks. "There are people around."

"I don't give a fuck. I need you naked and in my lap in the next ten minutes or I'm going to cause a scene." Switching off her phone, I hand it back and stand to leave. The outside air is a blessing, but it does nothing for the erection becoming obvious through my sweats. I wrap my hand around myself, leaning against the building wall, trying to relieve whatever pressure I can.

Harper has no idea how hard it is to be near her and not touch her. Literally hard and aching. The fact that I even try shows that she has me well and truly whipped.

I enjoy pain, revel in punishments, and actively seek retribution against the world, but I hate this. This is a torture unlike any I've ever known. She makes me bleed from the inside out, reopens old wounds that used to crave for affection and shows me a future I never believed possible, only to hold it just out of reach. I'm a monster. I've been pushing her away since before I even knew she existed, carving a path of destruction that would make me forever unlovable.

Unable to take the burning inside my chest any longer, I figure she isn't coming. Striding down the hillside, I head back to my house, longing to hear her footsteps following. It dawns on me that I just fucking *left* her alone and vulnerable, which I specifically told Clayton I wouldn't. Well, fuck him. If he wants to be her watch dog, then he's welcome to it. I can't be near her another second and not claim her brutally the way my soul desires.

Now faced with my empty living room, I don't know what to do. The book throne is intact, although the rest of the texts have moved to make room for the nerds that occupy my pad every evening. It's tempting to use my frustration to undo all of their hard work, tossing the hardbacks into the hot tub and using the paperbacks as fire fuel, but I don't have the energy. Neither do I want the fleeting satisfaction of aggressively jerking myself off. I don't even want a smoke.

I just stand here, arms by my side. I don't often think about my way of life, since I'm stuck in an endless cycle of self-sabotage and vengeance, but I don't think I can go on like this for much longer. The yearning, the intention to drop all of my anger and become Harper's loyal simp, and then the hatred that settles in after. Since when did I care who I was and who I hurt? Since when did I feel like I have no place in the world without her.

The door slams closed behind me, pulling me from my thoughts. I turn just as a fist connects with my cheek. My head wheels to the side, my smile growing in an instant. All trepidation that I'm losing my touch vanishes as I gaze upon Harper, her green eyes feral and her fury palpable. I don't need to change or be fixed. Not when my little minx is just as twisted as I am. Not when her hunger stems from a violence that's dying to break free.

"That's for leaving me behind. This is for pulling me away from helping my friend," she shoves my shoulders and I allow myself to be forced back a step. "And this is for making me so flustered, I could barely stumble here whilst feeling my thong soak through." She kicks my shin and I groan with pleasure. I fucking love it when she's feisty.

"You're wearing a thong today?" I bite my lip ring, not meaning to look smug as shit but I know I do. Harper narrows her eyes.

"You know I am. You broke into my dorm, replaced all of my underwear and burned my comfortable panties." A chuckle radiates from my chest. Yeah, I did do that whilst she was out on a date with Clayton. It seemed like a reasonable response.

"What color?" I ask, slowly licking my lips. Harper tracks the response, her anger lessening. I can't have that. "Because anything other than black won't look very slimming—" Her hand grabs my throat and I narrowly dodge her kneeing me in the balls. Given how painfully hard I am, that would have put me down for days.

Harper moves the same time I do, our mouths colliding with enough force to bruise. There's no hesitation, only lust burning through our veins. The hand around my throat is a command that strips me of every ounce of control I've ever clung to. Her tongue slides into my mouth, fierce and demanding, and I meet her head-on. She shoves at my jacket, nails scraping down my arms, while I grip her hair like it's the only thing keeping me tethered to reality.

God, I need this. More than any amount of money or air, I need Harper straddling me. Dominating me. I let her push me back toward the stairs. Every step feels like surrender. My jacket hits the floor, her t-shirt joins next. We stumble upward, devouring each other, breath and sanity burning out between us. My pulse thrashes as Harper pushes me again, and I tighten my hold until our bodies crash together. I'm the one who usually cages, but right now, she's keeping me contained. She's holding me back because my wildness belongs to her.

By the time we reach my room, the sexual tension is blinding. My clothes are too heavy, too uncomfortable, my cock straining to be released. I pause by the dresser, tearing open the top drawer. Forcefully twisting Harper, I dare her to look at it. All of it. Leather, steel, restraints. All of the new tools I bought just for her, for us, laid bare for her use on me however she sees fit.

"Choose whatever you want," I say beside her ear. Nudging her head with my nose, I realise she doesn't have her receivers on. Tilting my head back, I make sure she can see my lips before repeating myself. It's not just an offer, it's a plea. I'm not asking for pain. I'm asking for her to decide what I deserve.

She looks down at the drawer, and for a second, I am almost giddy for what she might pick. Even if she can't hear me, the intention is clear. I submit. An ache works its way through my being, one that leaves me utterly exposed. I close my eyes, lower my mouth into the curve of her neck, palming her breasts through her bra. I'm drunk on the anticipation, grinding against her ass as if I might die without the contact.

"No." My eyes fly open. Harper turns to watch me like she's seeing the rot beneath my skin, and she doesn't fear it. The breath hitches in my lungs. Is this it? Her final rejection where she walks away and never looks back? "I don't want you like this."

I can't breathe. My hands clamp around her arms, desperate to hold her here by sheer will. Could she be so cruel, to dig so deep into my soul and hurt me in a way no else can? A way I've allowed her to? Harper doesn't flinch. Instead, she steps into me and rests her head over my heart. I hold her there, because if I let go, I'll come apart. Then Harper whispers, her lips directly over the blackened heart she manages to crack wide open.

"I want you like this." A physical pain strikes me, so intense that gasp passes my lips. Her words bounce around my mind, hope and self-loathing drowning them out. Shifting my hands from her arms to her head, I pin her against me, a thousand words on my tongue, but I can't put any of them into a coherent sentence. Luckily, I don't have to.

Tugging herself free, Harper drags me towards the bed, her steps careful and precise. Lying us down, our heads are on the pillow, facing one another. Harper is beauty personified, like the calmest of seas bathed in the glow of the most perfect sunset. From her hair framing her heart-shaped face to the creamy cleavage exposed in a black bra. I feel unworthy just looking at her.

"I don't know what...tell me what to do." I beg like a virgin. *A freaking virgin.* I'm stripped bare, tears prickling the backs of my eyes, but I won't let them fall. No matter what, I'll never be that vulnerable little boy again.

"Hold me Rhys," her voice cracks slightly. "Show me we can be more than everyone says." And in that moment, I decide nothing will hold me back from doing just that. Pushing the sweats down my legs in smooth, unhurried movements, I maintain her gaze. Her leggings go next, then her underwear and my boxers. Piece by piece until we're fully naked and scarcely touching.

This time when I kiss her, I worship her. I give her every broken piece of me, offering it up like a sacrifice. Her lips caress mine slowly, each one like a balm to my being. I cup her cheek, brushing my index finger against the metal disc beneath the skin behind her ear. Harper has more strength than I ever have or will. I'm weak in comparison to her.

Every part of our bodies comes together, our legs tangled and hands exploring. Harper's mouth trails across my jaw and neck, and I simply hold her as she asked. Each hidden scar she discovers beneath my tattoos, she bends to press a kiss against it as if banishing it from existence. I tremble, fighting the urge to be rough, allowing her to investigate my body and soul with her lips and desire.

It would be laughable to think such gentle touches could have my cock pulsing, but here I am, hard as stone. Harper scores her nails across my thighs, forcing a hiss from my lips. She ducks lower but I stop her. This isn't about just my pleasure, or just hers either. This is about us standing in the eye of a hurricane together, the winds of uncertainty and misconceptions whipping around us.

Hooking her leg over my hip, I catch myself this time, pulling a condom from my bedside table and rolling it on before fully sheathing myself inside her. She's so tight, I can't fight a groan. Her hands flatten on my chest, her own moans filling the air as I roll my hips against her. I repeat the motion over and over until my skin is lined with a sheen of sweat.

It's almost painful to take her this slowly, to savor her cries every time the metal of my piercing smooths over her G-spot. Harper tucks her face into my neck but I drag her back, forcing her to watch how she's undoing me. How she's destroying me.

With my arm beneath her head, her breasts crushed against my chest, our hearts thump wildly against one another. I wind her leg further round my waist and roll her onto her back. Harper's eyes roll back in her head with the new position deepening how far my cock can sink into her. Slow and steady, primal yet profound. I hold her on the edge of the climax fluttering within her perfect cunt, denying us both.

I thought Harper was beautiful before, but now. Holy shit. Her lips are parted in bliss. Her neck is flushed, her hair untamed. Rocking my hips in time with hers, together we fall into the abyss. There's no start and end, there's just the building pressure between us. I already know I'll never be the same after this. Pulling me down, Harper pleads for the release she needs against my lips. I shake my head, the tips of our noses brushing.

This is too incredible to let it end. With how tightly her pussy is gripping my cock, her orgasm would set off my own, and I'm not ready for it. Her nails dig into my back, her thighs squeezing my waist as her ankles lock around me. This connection is unbreakable.

Harper's heat seeps through me, sparking the wick to my internal dynamite. When it reaches the end of the fuse, everything I previously was will explode and I can start to rebuild with her by my side.

"Rhys, please," Harper begs, her teeth sinking into my neck like a damn vampire. Her nails scratch deeper, seeking a pain reaction from me, and she gets it. Slamming into her harder, Harper's back arches and she screams out. I do it again, hitching her hips higher, thrusting into her deeper. My balls slap against her ass, my muscles tightening and starting to shake. Her moans grow louder, my name a constant on her lips. Those nails scratch my back to shreds, those blunt little teeth drawing blood.

There's no stopping now, I will chase this girl into oblivion and happily lose myself in the process. Picking up my movements, I finally give her what she's begging for. My movements become jerky and rash, sweat pebbling my ink skin as I fuck her senseless.

"Break for me now, Babygirl," I mutter against her ear, fully aware she can't hear me. "Break for me like I have broken for you."

HARPER

CHAPTER TWENTY EIGHT

Considering how far behind Addy's team was the other day, I'm genuinely shocked they managed to pull this off. Beams of light slice through the night sky above the gymnasium, and a red carpet winds up the hill like something straight out of a movie premiere. A line of students stretches ahead of us, one that Rhys tried to skip to the front of until I held him back. *Barely.*

His arm is linked with mine, that telltale smirk finally back in place after too long. I'd insisted we dress up a little tonight, which led to dark jeans, an unbuttoned shirt halfway down his tattooed chest, and slicked-back hair for him. The result is a dangerous combination that should probably come with a warning label.

I went for an off-the-shoulder navy sweater that falls to my thighs, cinched with a belt at the waist, and knee-high boots. Clay looms just over my right shoulder, all quiet storm and watchful eyes. He wasn't exactly thrilled that me and Rhys snuck off to make love – because that's exactly what it was - during his counseling session, but true to his word, he hasn't made an issue of it either. In a red flannel and tan cargos, he's giving serious *hot-lumberjack-in-a-beanie* energy.

The line inches forward at a snail's pace, and every irritated shuffle Rhys makes has me giggling. I left my receivers back at the dorm, figuring tonight would be too loud for my implants to handle. Both guys are wearing microphone clips, so I'll still catch background noise, but their voices will cut through.

By the time we make it inside, the bleachers are already packed. I'd bet half the student body is here. Kenneth sits around halfway back and waves like a maniac when he spots Clay and me, until Rhys scowls in his direction and Kenneth promptly drops out of sight behind the crowd.

The gym is unrecognizable. Fabric drapes in soft folds across the ceiling, the wooden stage covering the court lines, and a section near the locker room has been roped off. Contestants are clustered on the bleachers behind the stage, too focused on their last-minute prep to watch the show.

Volunteers with yellow lanyards guide people to their seats. A mousy-haired boy with a young face turns as we approach, and I instantly recognize him as the guy that gave me the drugged coffee. I never asked Rhys what he did to him outright, but the way his eyes go wide at the sight of the man on my arm, I can make an educated guess.

"M-M-Master Waversea," he stammers formally. "We've reserved a space on the front row for you and your... friends." His gaze flicks nervously between us before darting toward three empty seats front and center.

Rhys strides ahead, barking at people to move their legs while I awkwardly shimmy past knees and handbags to follow. I slump into my seat, ignoring the waves of judgment burning into my back. I may have made a few friends within the science students, but none of those are present now. Thankfully, the lights dim almost instantly, and a spotlight cuts across the stage. Addy steps into the glow looking absolutely stunning in a pink and cream jumpsuit, sky-high heels, and lipstick as bold as her hair.

"Welcome, students of Waversea and members of the faculty!" she shouts into the mic. Cheers and whoops erupt behind us, and both guys beside me quickly cover their mic clips so the noise doesn't blast through. Leaning forward, I spot the staff section down the aisle. Peterson and Hargreaves are a few rows back, whispering to each other in a way that looks *a little too cozy.*

Addy launches into the pre-rehearsed speech I've had to sit through every evening this week in our dorm, thanking everyone who helped, including the cheer squad for fundraising by washing cars half-naked. A particular section in the crowd roars with whoops, a group of jocks punching their fists into the air. No doubt they are the ones who have sparkling clean cars out in the parking lot. I keep my attention on Addy, marveling at how she can be such a natural up there, her usual bright and magnetic self.

"Well, let's get on with it, shall we?" she grins. "First up tonight, Katrina Keys and her amazing contortionist act!"

The applause swells as a petite blonde steps onto the stage in a gem-studded leotard, her hair twisted into a tight bun. Classical music swells through the speakers, and Katrina bends backward into a bridge before crawling through her own legs. Then she props her chin in her hands and casually folds her feet over her head like it's the most normal thing in the world. As impressive as it is, the act starts off slow after several impossible handstands and twists, a mumble passing through the audience.

That's before two muscled male assistants appear, just as sparkly and scarcely dressed, each one holding a flaming ring. Every female in the bleachers suddenly sits upright, myself included. I hear Rhys' grumbling response but I smack his thigh, engrossed as Katrina curves into a C-shape and holds still while the men carefully pass the fire around her body. Gasps ripple through the crowd, equally as entranced. It's like that game where you can't touch the wire or get buzzed, only this time, if she slips, she'll get *burned.*

Flipping into a handstand, her legs split open in a perfect line. The assistants hold out metal rods, and she grips them with her toes before they balance the lit rings onto the bars. The crowd leaps to their feet, cheers echoing through the gym as the music crescendos and her act ends in a blaze of applause.

"Wow," I breathe, grinning at Clay as I settle back into my seat. "That was awesome!" The corner of his mouth twitches in a reluctant smile, not seeming half as impressed as the rest of us. I lace my fingers through his and arch a brow. "What? You think you could do better?"

"She was never in any real danger. It's all part of the theatrics," Clay rolls his eyes.

"Ahh, so you're a cynic. That tracks," I give him a sly smile. "Maybe you can try fire play with me sometime." A vendor carrying a tray passes with refreshments as the acts change over, and I reach for a plastic cup of soda. Rhys slaps my hand away and takes a bottle of water instead, planting it in my grasp while Clay mumbles directly into his mic for my hearing only.

"If that's a kink of yours, I'm game."

I fumble with the water, spilling it onto my knees. Whilst Rhys huffs and pats me down with some tissues, clearly jealous of not receiving any attention, I throw my head back and laugh. I enjoy seeing the playful side to Clayton far more than any act that will grace the stage. Resting back in my seat, I settle in for the next act with Rhys' hand settling on my thigh.

I wish I could say the talent show just got better and better, but unfortunately, I think Katrina set the bar too high. There are more than a few pitchy singers, a couple of dancers who can't seem to find the beat, and one poor magician whose dove escaped right out of his jacket pocket. When Rhys offers me a swig from the hip flask he smuggled in, I take it without hesitation. The whiskey burns down my throat, but it's a welcome distraction from the ass-numbing plastic seat beneath me.

"Next up is Sheila Newton, ready to impress you with some stand-up comedy." Addy's eyes dart around nervously, her laughter fake and high-pitched before she hops off the stage. Oh god, she's panicking. I take my cue to be the support my best friend, preparing to stand.

"I'll be right back," I whisper to the guys, but both of them clamp their hands on my thighs to keep me rooted in place. I fight the urge to roll my eyes, understanding they're protective but also that we're in the most public of places. I've refused to live in fear up to now, so this would be a terrible time to start. "Stop it both of you. Addy needs a friend, and I need to pee. I'll be back in ten minutes."

I aim my plea at Rhys since he's the one most likely to argue. When I flutter my lashes and pout, he finally sighs.

"Ten minutes," he grits through his teeth, eyes sharpened like daggers. "Then I'm coming to find you." I grin, needing to take care of the background noise first. There's nothing worse than peeing while listening to private conversations, especially when they're threatening to kill one another in my honor. Switching off Rhys' mic and kissing his cheek, I slip out of my seat. Bending to turn off Clay's too, I attempt to give him a chaste kiss also, but Rhys's hand lands on my ass with a sharp sting. I glare at him as he mouths, "Get moving. I'm counting."

These men will be the death of me, of that there's no doubt. I'm not even mad about it. There are far worse ways to go. Snorting to myself, I shuffle along the row and edge around the side of the court. There's a black tent concealing the locker room entrance, and I slip inside, thankful for the momentary escape from the crowded sports arena.

Addy's easy to spot. She's pacing in small circles, wringing her fingers together as commotion swirls around her. Students drag props, others shout instructions, a dog is barking for their owner's attention, and Addy is oblivious to it all. When she sees me, she barrels into my arms so hard I stumble back a step. Her breath fans across my neck, but I can't make out her words, so I step back and sign that my receivers are at home.

'It's terrible. The acts weren't this bad in practice. What am I going to do?' she signs in a panic. I still her fretting fingers and force her to mimic a deep breath with me.

'*No, it's not terrible. Just... not great,*' I sign back with a wince. '*Why don't you get up there and dance? You're an incredible dancer.*'

Addy's shoulders sag, her smile barely flickering before the dog in its ruffled collar bounds between us, dragging its owner behind a tangle of leashes.

'*I can't compete. I'm the organizer,*' she signs once the chaos has passed. Her bottom lip wobbles, and tears shine in her eyes. Addy doesn't do "less than perfect." To her, anything short of excellence is failure.

'*Okay, breathe*', I sign, resting a hand on her arm. '*Everyone's having fun, and no one's going to hold you responsible for a few off-key performances. Just save your best act for last, so everyone goes home smiling, okay?*'

Addy exhales shakily, then leans in to hug me, her arms looping around my neck. I rub her back until she steadies.

'*You're right,*' she signs finally, a real smile breaking through. '*I do have a huge surprise planned for after the show. I can't wait for you to see it!*' I raise a curious brow, but I don't ask for more information. I'm just glad to see her spark returning.

'*Sounds good,*' I sign with a wink. "*Now I have to hit the bathroom before Rhys comes hunting for me.*"

Heading deeper into the locker room, my gaze catches on Clay's locker. It's spotless now, but I can still see what it used to look like burned into my memory. I still can't believe Rhys' hacker hasn't been able to dig up anything. Still, with each day that passes, I think Rhys was right to not go to the police. I don't want to run the risk of having our business splashed on the front covers of every paper. So much for laying low and staying visible.

I know there's a small private bathroom past the showers, so I continue on in that direction. The door's closed, and when I test it, it feels locked. I lean against the wall, giving it a minute. I know Rhys. If I take too long, he'll probably insist on *supervising*. He hasn't crossed that line yet, but the man's getting close.

I smile, remembering our afternoon together. Making progress with the king of self-destruction is like scaling a mountain barefoot. It takes patience and blood, but standing at the top with him, finally getting through to him, that's a high no substance could ever match.

The door opens suddenly, and I find myself staring into a pair of cold blue eyes. Klara. Her over-foundationed face twists in disgust, her fake lashes fluttering like they might fly off. She blocks the doorway, refusing to move. We've already danced this dance before. I know she hits like a toddler and hates losing. So she sticks to glaring, her stare sharp enough to cut glass.

"*He was mine first, you know,*" she mouths. I roll my eyes. Not this again. Her gaze drifts down me and back up with that '*what do you have that I don't?*' look, and I can't help but pity her.

"Green's not a good color on you," I say flatly, attempting to step around her, but she mirrors me like a bratty twin. Her perfectly manicured brows pinch together.

"I'm not wearing green," she replies, utterly confused. I shouldn't burst out laughing in her face, but I can't help it. I'm all for girls standing together and raising each other up, but she can't be that dimwitted, surely? Pushing past her, not taking no for an answer, I slam the door before Klara can say anything else. She needs to move on. In an ideal world, she could find someone who can show her her worth, but I understand that Mr. Kavanagh and Mr. Waversea have other plans for their children. Ones that will see them both trapped in misery for the rest of their lives.

One problem at a time. I move further into the small bathroom, eyeing the oval mirror hanging above the basin and small window of frosted glass above it. Quickly taking care of business, I wash my hands and study my reflection in the mirror above the sink.

What do I have that she doesn't?

Sure, Klara has the looks and the confidence many men would die for, but she's also got the warmth of a viper. I'm not exactly a catch either. I got my dark hair and green eyes from Dad, my hermit tendencies from Mom. Hardly the kind of girl who winds up with not one, but two dangerously protective, model-tier men orbiting her.

I smile at myself, ever-so-slightly, at that thought. Mom would probably high-five me. She's the one who filled her bookshelf with paperbacks covered in shirtless men, after all. She's also the reason I love stories, the kind that remind you passion and pandemonium can coexist. Running my hands over my hair, I adjust my sweater, and head to the door.

Unlocking the latch, I twist the handle, but it doesn't budge. Frowning, I try several more times before banging my fist on the wood.

"Hey! This isn't funny!" I yell, figuring Klara's standing on the other side, laughing her ass off. Yes, ha ha good one. I can appreciate a good joke too, but I don't want to miss Addy's big surprise. Shoving my shoulder against the door, I lock and unlock it just in case the bolt got stuck. The door isn't shifting at all, so I stop wasting my efforts. It's fine. Rhys knows where I am, and he'll be here soon anyway.

Standing back, I cross my arms. Seconds turn into minutes, my patience wearing thin enough for me to braid my hair over my shoulder, unravel it and do the same over the other side. Silence wraps around me, strangely thick and heavy for a change. Once the boys realize I'm stuck, they'll activate their mics and we can at least have a conversation through the door. For now though, there's just a stillness I'm usually comfortable with, but right now is making me twitchy.

What the hell is taking him so long?

CLAYTON

CHAPTER TWENTY NINE

"That's it," Wavershit huffs, slapping his jean-covered thighs. "I'm going to get her." I'm quick to slap a hand against his chest, and his eyes fly wide. There's a ripple of unease from all of those sitting around us, figuring I should know better than to hit Rhys in public. I do, but I don't really give a shit.

"Don't be a dick your entire life," I roll my eyes, my leg twitching irritably. I used to refuse to be in the same room as him, now I'm two seats down and desperately clinging onto any thread of patience I have left. "Drink your whiskey and give her five more minutes. She doesn't get enough time with Addy because you keep kidnapping her." Sitting back, I shuffle to try and get comfortable in the tiny plastic seat whilst Rhys exhales through his nose.

"She walks to my bed willingly, thank you very much." Pulling out his hip flask, he takes aggressive shots, his scowl deeply engrained. The pair of us fall back into the uncomfortable silence we've had to endure since Harper left, although we should be used to it by now. We're both too stubborn to walk away, so these instances will only become more frequent.

The next performer takes the stage, a magician with too much gel in his hair and a nervous smile, but my focus drifts. Shadows flicker against the back wall, warped by the moving lights above. I glance toward the exit doors, tracing the outline of the gym and then settle on Addy's form off to the side of the stage. She's speaking into her earpiece, her body rigid with stress, no sign of Harper anywhere. Something feels...off.

Rhys leans forward, his jaw tight, scanning the crowd like he senses it too. I can't name it yet, this pulse beneath the music, this wrongness threading through the cheers, but it's there, crawling up my spine with icy fingers. The mocking laughter around me starts to blur, replaced by a low hum of unease in the pit of my stomach.

This time when Rhys stands tall, I don't stop him, or the little show he's putting on for anyone who might be watching. He stretches with that infuriating smugness of his, arms overhead, spine flexing, completely unbothered by the whispers behind him. He's about to saunter off when, without warning, the lights cut out.

A chorus of screams pierces the dark. Panicked movement ripples through the bleachers, sneakers scraping against the polished floor. A hand grips the shoulder of my shirt, my instincts about to come out in full force before I realise it's Rhys, pinning me in place and making sure I'm still there. Suddenly, a harsh glow slices through the blackness as the projector comes to life, casting a warped light across the stage. The magician stands frozen mid-trick, blinking as the projection covers his face in white letters. Ducking out of the way, he reveals the words in full.

What do you call a man who isn't able to pleasure a woman by himself?

Muttering breaks out, everyone's curiosity piqued. I can't see Addy anymore, the rest of the gym still hidden in shadow as the words shift and morph into two words that steal the breath from my lungs.

Clayton Michaels.

The pit of dread opens before I even see it happen. Then, like a knife twisting into the wound, a video starts to play. Harper's body floods the screen in devastating detail, Rhys' face buried between her thighs. Her breathy moans echo through the speakers, the sound so intimate it feels like a violation just to hear it. Then there's me, my tongue swirling around her pierced nipple, her hand gripping my hair, her body arching with pleasure that was supposed to be ours alone.

Nothing is censored, and nothing is sacred anymore.

A ripple of horrified silence sweeps the room. Every pair of eyes burns into my back. Shame, fury and disbelief all hits at once. I shoot to my feet, the blood roaring in my ears. This was our private moment, stolen and shared to the masses. I'm just glad Harper isn't here to witness it. Wait, where is Harper?

The video switches off, thankfully cutting out the high-pitched moans Harper was reaching just before her orgasm hit. Rhys is dragging me to my feet, although I was already trying to force my frozen limbs to move. Half twisting towards the crowd , a sickening amount of raised smart phones glint in the projection's light as it shifts back to text.

I heard she likes fire play. Let's find out if that's true, shall we?

I've barely finished reading the message when a blaring sound pierces the air. The fire alarm doesn't even resonate over the roaring in my skull. My heart is hammering against my rib cage, my lungs no longer working. Wavershit shoves at my shoulder, snapping me back to reality. Bedlam breaks out all around, students clambering out of the bleachers and running for the exits, all sense of order abandoned.

Without wasting another second, I vault over the railing, boots landing heavily on the wood floor. A wave of panicked bodies surges toward me, a blur of faces and flailing arms, but I push back against them, forcing my way through. My sole focus is on getting to the black tent at the edge of the court. Through the blur of movement, I catch sight of Rhys cutting through a mob that is parting for him like the red sea. His face is murderous, the projector lift catching on the hardness of his glare. The siren keeps wailing, a relentless scream drilling straight into my skull.

It takes far too long to reach the tent, and the flap is about to close when I grab it. Inside, Rhys is already there, stalking through the shadows like a caged animal, scanning every corner for our girl. No, my girl. Fuck, there's no time for possessiveness.

I'm right behind him, the air thick with heat and smoke. Until now, I prayed it was all a hoax, a cruel trick to evacuate the gym and ruin the show. But the scent of burning hits my chest, and that hope dies an instant death. Breaking into a run, Rhys and I round the corner beyond the showers at the same time, the sight ahead stops us in our tracks.

Flames. Flicking orange and red, crackling around a pile of what looks like books burning in a heap outside the bathroom door. Lighter fluid coats the floor, the stench stinging my nose as smoke curls across the ceiling and seeps beneath the closed door.

Movement beyond the fire catches my eye, a shadowed figure lingering in the open doorway to watch the scene unfold. Definitely a man, judging by his height and stance. He's calm, collected even, leaning against the door jam, a beanie pulled low over his head. My blood turns to ice. It's him. The person who's been visiting my mom, he's here.

"Save Harper!" I yell, already moving. "This fucker is mine!" Before Rhys can argue, I launch myself forward, leaping through the fire like it's nothing but a hurdle. The flames lick my arms, heat biting my skin, but I make it through. The bastard flinches back, clearly not expecting me to take chase. Sprinting away, the door slams in my face as I reach it. I shove against the metal bar, tumbling into the car park at the rear of the gymnasium.

The night hits me like a cold punch to the chest, reeking faintly of rain and smoke. Streetlamps cast long, eerie shadows over rows of empty cars. My breath comes out in ragged bursts as I scan the lot frantically, finding no sign of him. There's no sound either, aside from the distant alarm and pounding of my own heartbeat in my ears. He was right here, he can't have just disappeared.

I stalk the length of the car park, my knuckles cracking as I waste precious time. Dropping to my knees, I peer beneath the nearest row of cars, moving fast, scanning the ground. Still nothing. Frustration spikes hot in my chest until I finally straighten and a shape catches my eye. Leaning casually against a streetlamp, like he's been waiting for me, he suddenly bolts down the hill.

My muscles snap tight, my boots hardly touching the ground as I take chase once again, my clenched fists pump by my sides. The incline of the slope forces me to slow before I go head over ass and roll to the bottom. Mud slips beneath my soles but my eyes don't waver from the back of his beanie-covered head. The rest of him is covered in black, from his hoodie and trousers, to his gloves and boots. Whoever he is, he knows the layout of the campus.

Veering right, I follow him beyond the arts building into an expanse of trees. I burst through the tree line, my shoulders tense enough to cramp but nothing will stop me from catching this asshole once and for all. A flicker of a shadow catches my attention to my side, forcing me to quickly alter course before I slam into a tree trunk. The night consumes me, the fire alarm barely audible in the distance. I slow now, stalking closer, squinting to make out the moon-illuminated woodland around me.

A twig snaps behind me, and I turn in confusion. Drawing me back the way I came, I spot the shadow darting across an opening amongst the trunks. I close in on him, jumping over a fallen log and rushing forward on hurried feet. I lose and spot him repeatedly, barreling forward with one clear thought in mind. Before I hand him over to the police, I'm going to make this fucker pay for every bad intention he's ever had towards Harper.

His mouth will be so swollen, he won't be able to squeal. His fingers will be broken in so many places, they'll never be able to reset them well enough to creep on unsuspecting girls ever again. The dangerous side to me has flared to life, one I was convinced had stayed behind in my cell.

The deeper I trek into the woodland, the quicker I'm plummeted into pure darkness. Clouds block any hopes of light I had, forcing me to stop and take stock of my surroundings. Silence echoes around me, not even the wildlife daring to breathe.

I'm about to turn back when something slams into the back of the head. Not hard enough to hurt, but large enough to piss me off. Spinning and feeling by my feet, I find the offensive object. That bastard threw a pinecone at me.

Once again, I take off in a different direction, my patience well and truly diminished. I'm done with being taunted. Even when I'm this close to wringing his damn neck, the asshole is playing with me. This time, I ram forward with the force of a bull. My shoulders slam into tree trunks, pain I refuse to acknowledge flaring to life beneath my skin. Branches overhead shake with each assault, birds desperately flapping into the sky to get away. I don't stop, unable to decipher which shadow I'm chasing so I hunt down all of them.

Evidently, I make one huge circle back to civilization, light streaming through the trunks from another building. Straight ahead, I spot the silhouette heading towards campus and a grin spreads across my face. I've got you this time. Nothing else exists right now other than seeking vengeance on the one who's put my girl in harm's way. I fly through the woodland and burst free of the trees, slightly disorientated.

Ahead, a house looms at the end of a lawn. The tell-tale porch wraps around the exterior with a covered hot tub at one end. Rhys' house. The Beanie Bastard, as I've decided to name him, is sitting on the porch steps looking relaxed as fuck. How the hell did he get there so fast?

Spotting me, he jumps up and runs around the side garage before disappearing. I'm tired of this bullshit, but I push on. I don't have any other choice. My calves burn and my shoulders ache, but it's the tightening in my chest that has my full attention. Fuck, please let her be okay.

My feet hit the concrete of the main road, making my advances even more effective. Now we are on a smooth surface, the gap between us closes within moments. My chest heaves, my thighs pushing me even faster as he tries to slip into the courtyard. Fisting the material of his hoodie at the corner of the Dean's building, I hoist him straight off his still-running feet and throw him down onto the cemented path. He drops like a sack of shit, but I'm not done yet.

He rolls over, wide eyes staring at me in the artificial light of the windows. I drag him up, slamming him into the building hard enough to draw a pained yelp from his mouth and immediately punch him in the face. Then again, and once more for good luck. I snarl like an animal, curling my hand around his throat as I finally let the haze in my eyes clear enough to assess his features.

Upturned eyes, a thin nose, alabaster skin. His gangly frame struggles against my hold, his scrawny neck fitting snugly into the palm of my hand. I don't know this man, but he's about to know me.

"Who are you?" I growl in his face. He whimpers like a wounded animal but I'm not fooled. I raise my fist again and he flinches violently. Good, he should be scared because by the time I'm done with him, he'll be unrecognizable to his own mother. I pull my arm back further to drive my fist home in his face when something makes me pause.

"P-p-please, wait!" he stutters, tears springing free from his scrunching eyes. "It was j-just a joke your f-friend wanted to play on you." My brows pinch, a sense of dread running through my spine. Lifting a shaking hand, he points beyond my shoulder. I would ignore his attempt at distractions, if lighthearted chatter didn't filter through the rush of blood pulsing in my ears. Peering back, my blood freezes in my veins.

Behind me, filling the courtyard, are countless bodies dressed head to toe in black. They joke and laugh theatrically, every single one of them wearing a black beanie.

"What the fuck?" I mumble, vaguely aware my hand has slackened as the kid slumps into a pile of limbs at my feet. My eyes can't compute what they're seeing, my thoughts becoming scrambled. Turning, I stumble forward, confused and fatigued from my run. From the steps of the library to the edge of the fountain, bodies fill the quad. I draw closer to the throng, gaining a few appreciative glances from girls who giggle as I pass.

One in particular steps into my path with a wide smile revealing a set of straight, pearly white teeth. Blonde hair leaks out from beneath her black beanie giving me Gwen Stefani vibes.

"Hey handsome," she drawls, looking at me like a piece of meat. "You got the cargos part right, but the casting call specifically requested all black. Although I like your style a lot better." She trails her fingers up my arm on the flannel shirt, confidently squeezing my bicep. I stand there, unable to compute what's happening.

"Casting call?" I ask dumbly. Bodies bump around us, the excitement in the air tangible. Many are holding coffee cups from our open cafeteria as they seem to wait around for something. I'm a head taller than most of the crowd, able to look around the sea of beanies which seem to mock me.

"Yeah, you know? The casting call that brought us all here?" The Stefani-wannabe rolls her eyes as she pulls out her phone and shows me the screenshot. It's a poster made from a faded image of Waversea Academy, calling for anyone interested in a flash mob dance. Below is the date, time, and address before promising the best night of their lives. The person responsible is called **ThinkPink** with a fuchsia-haired avatar as her profile picture. One guess who that could be. Oblivious to my clenched jaw, the girl continues to talk slowly as if I'm dense.

"Everyone who commented got a DM about the dress code. Maybe it's still stuck in your message requests?" She shrugs. "Rumor has it some of the guys were given special roles to play before the show. Are you one of them?" Her eyes drink me in and she raises her hand as if tempted to touch me again. I step back, bumping into a guy who is the same size as one of those I was chasing. He ducks his head and quickly slinks out of sight, losing himself amongst the masses.

I could hunt him down and demand answers, but my gut tells me it'll be another dead end. Another alias we won't be able to decipher. The images we were trying to protect Harper from are out there now, so it's time to let the police take over. I need to be with her, to know she's okay.

The tight band around my chest returns as my feet start running again, this time taking the quick route past the hall and toward the hill beyond. Images appear in my mind, visions of the worst possible outcome trying to drown out the hope I'm clinging to. I left Wavershit in charge of saving her, and for once, I pray he's come through.

The fire alarm is no longer blaring as I stumble toward the main door, spotting the red flashes emanating from behind the building. I drag myself to the rear, discovering two fire trucks parked haphazardly. Men draped in heavy, beige uniforms are packing hoses back into the vehicles, having done their jobs. Behind, tucked into the back of an ambulance, Harper is wrapped in a silver blanket and Rhys' arms. Her cheeks are smudged black and her eyes are downcast, an occasional cough erupting from her lips as I near.

Rhys clocks me first, shoving to his feet quickly enough to alarm Harper. "Well?" he demands gruffly. I narrow my eyes on him before shoving him aside.

"We'll discuss it later." I crouch in front of Harper, cupping her cheek gently. Her green eyes settle on me with relief, but there's also an emptiness in their emerald depths. Her small smile seems to be more for my benefit than anything else, since there's a defeated slump to her posture.

"Are you okay, Beautiful?" I breathe.

She doesn't respond, and not because my microphone clip flew off at some point whilst running. Instead, she leans into my touch and closes her eyes on a sigh. I can't handle seeing her like this, not when I know I'm part of the cause. The message from the projector was directed at me, and although I don't know what I did to cause such a thing, ultimately I must be at fault for something. I'm the one being punished and selfishly dragging Harper down with me.

An EMT nudges between us, needing to check Harper's blood pressure so I take a few steps back. Rhys's shoulder bumps mine, his arms crossed and it's only now I realize his designer shirt is singed in several places.

"How bad is it?" I ask.

"She'll be fine. Some minor smoke inhalation but she'd had the good sense to wrap her sweater around her face. I assume you didn't manage to catch that shitface." His pale blue eyes slide to me, emotions hidden in their depths that he won't reveal in Harper's presence. "Pack your shit. You're all moving into my place. You, Harper and that preppy roommate of hers."

"About that," I clear my throat, keeping my voice down. "I think I have a new addition for your suspect list." Rhys' eyes darken instantly, his sharp mind catching onto my meaning without me needing to put it into words. Nodding, he runs a hand through his ash coated hair, the veins in his arm popping furiously.

"Then it's lucky she'll be in my house where I can keep an even closer eye on her, isn't it?" Rhys returns to Harper's side the moment there's space while the EMT fits an oxygen mask over her face. In my peripheral, a figure steps out from behind the fire truck, her pink hair dirty and face streaked with tears. I briefly meet her gaze, holding it long enough to send a clear message. Tread carefully Addy. We're onto you.

HARPER

CHAPTER THIRTY

I've roused enough to see sunlight peeking through the curtains, but still cling to the remnants of my dream. If I don't open my eyes, I can pretend the anxiety isn't seeping back in like liquid nitrogen flowing through my blood stream. I consider myself a strong person for the most part, but that last power move by the Beanie Bastard, as Clay has called him, has affected me more than I've let on.

There was a brief point between the smoke curling around the doorframe and me passing out that I remembered how I felt during the car crash that took my parents. Terrified, vulnerable, done for. I swear I caught a glimpse of my mom looking back at me in the mirror too, before I dropped to the ground to await my fate.

Now, wrapped in Rhys' sheets, that same terror lingers like the smoke trapped in my lungs. The scent of his cologne mixes with the faint trace of burnt hair on my skin. My throat still aches from the coughing, my nails sore from scratching at the locked door. Every time I close my eyes, I see fire licking the edges of the wood again, clawing to come inside.

Muffled voices drift up from downstairs. Clay's low, steady baritone, Rhys' clipped tone that means he's trying to stay calm, and then there's a softer, feminine one, threading between theirs like she's trying to hold the peace. I vaguely remember dipping in and out of last night, hearing parts of conversations through Rhys' mic. No one wanted to be the one to tell me, but they spoke of the video that played in front of the entire school. How my privacy was breached, my body gawked at. That's why Rhys ordered Addy to pack up our belongings under his watch while Clay stayed with me. Then they swapped over so Clay could go back to his dorm and do the same.

It should comfort me that they're all here, that we've all moved into this fortress of a frat house, but instead, it feels like we're all just waiting for the next disaster. A temporary illusion of safety before another attack comes crawling out of the shadows. Not that there's anything I can do about it. I'm on strict bed rest, since Rhys has taken the EMT's instruction to heart. But also, I need a shower.

I swing my legs over the side of the bed and instantly regret it. My head spins, and my muscles feel like waterlogged sandbags. The thought of standing under hot water should be comforting, but even that feels like a mountain I'm not sure I can climb. My chest tightens as I stare at the en suite door, the place I need to go, but can't. I tell myself it's just a shower. Not another trap, not another locked door waiting to smother me in smoke.

Picking up my phone from the nightstand, I take it with me, the mic app activated. I don't need any more surprises to catch me unaware. The floor is cold beneath my feet as I shuffle towards the same room, holding the wall for balance. Every creak of the floorboard sounds like the echo of that night. The mirror above the sink reflects a girl I barely recognize, pale, hollow-eyed, haunted. I reach for the shower handle, but my hand hesitates mid-air, fingers trembling. My reflection looks back at me like she's asking, *Are you sure you can do this?*

I'm not. Whether the smoke is still screwing with my system, or just my mind in, I'm trembling, clutching at the oversized T-shirt on my body. I know I'm safe here, but my naivety that I'm safe anywhere on this campus has caught up with me. The door opens behind me, and I flinch so hard my phone clatters to the floor. Like someone has just slammed a hammer into my skull, I collapse at the sheer volume of the noise booming into my inner ears.

"Hey, hey, it's just me," Clay says softly, kneeling to slowly pull my hands off the sides of my head. I don't attempt to stand, not trusting my legs, so I tip sideways into his chest. Clay wraps his arms around me, stroking my back and arms until they stop shaking. Once I'm ready to try again, Clay picks up my phone and steadies me with his palm at my elbow. "That's it, take it easy."

My chin wobbles, my self-pity reaching a whole new level. Clay turns on the shower, testing the water with his hand, and then reaches for a towel to drape over his shoulder. His movements are practiced and unhurried, the way they always are. Clay doesn't demand attention or affection. He's just *there*.

Leaning my hips against the counter, he lowers to his knee again, dutifully peeling off my socks and then the thong from beneath the large T-shirt. Clay makes no move to take a peek beneath the fabric, whereas Rhys' head would have already been up there. Standing to his full height, Clay smiles gently, just as the door slams open again. Speak of the devil and he shall appear.

"What the hell are you doing?" Rhys' voice slices through the steam already curling up from the running water. His expression is tight, his blue eyes intense. "She's supposed to be in bed!" Shouldering his way between us, Rhys cups my face, cataloguing the fragility of my features.

"Back off shitface. She wants a shower," Clay mutters, attempting to step between me and Rhys once again. A stubborn-off ensues, shoulders shoving and biceps barging. My head swims, another wave of dizziness passing through me. I can't deal with this macho-bullshit right now.

"Addy!" I scream out. The pair in front of me still, not bothering to hide their contempt when Addy marches in and slaps them both around the back of their heads.

"Right, you two. Out. Now."

Clayton places my phone on the counter before he leaves, an apology written all over his face. It's not his fault, nor Rhys'. They're both freaked out and caring for me in the only way they know how. I hear their bickering continue, my phone's mic picking up on fragments before Addy kicks the door shut.

"You always have to be the freaking savior, don't you?"

"You're the one who can't give her two minutes of peace."

"Well, you're the one—"

Addy taps my screen and mutes the mic, a knowing smile growing. I wish I could smile back to show her how thankful I am for her being here, but a sob breaks free of my throat. Addy clings to me, pulling me into her arms. Typing on my phone one handed, a robotic voice transcribes her message into my head.

'Let it all out, babe. Once you're out of tears and cleaned up, we're going to breakfast. No one can make us run scared.'

I press my face into Addy's shoulder, and for the first time since the fire, I stop trying to be okay. The sobs come out jagged and uncoordinated, the kind that make my whole body tremble. Addy doesn't try to hush me or feed me empty reassurances. She just holds me tighter, her fingers tracing slow circles on my spine while I crumble in her arms.

The shower continues to thunder, the stream coiling around us. It's thick, clogging my throat like the smoke did but I leave it. At least the steam won't block my airways, filling my lungs with filth.

"I keep thinking I should just snap out of this. I've done it so many times before," I rasp, "but this time, I don't know if I can. They've all seen me. Seen Rhys and Clay and me...being intimate. How am I supposed to show my face after that?" The sobs come harder. My legs buckle, but Addy lowers us both to the cool tile floor. Giving me a light shake, she forces me to watch her hands move.

"What are you ashamed of? Being a gorgeous woman who has the two hottest guys on campus crawling on their knees for her?"

I know there's logic in there somewhere, but I'm not ready to recognize it. I've always been the one who fixes, who fights, who doesn't let anyone see the cracks. But now, all I can do is tremble, cry and feel pathetic. Addy tucks my hair behind my ear, her own eyes glassy but steady as she continues to sign.

"You are strong, but strength doesn't mean pretending it didn't happen. It comes from owning it and saying, so what? I'm a badass bitch and I deserve to be here."

Again, knowing the truth and accepting it are two different things. Addy reaches for a washcloth and runs it under the warm stream of water pounding against the shower cubicle, gently wiping the tears from my cheeks and the soot marks from my neck. It reminds me of why I came in here, of how dirty I feel.

Nudging myself over, I slip into the shower with Rhys' T-shirt still on. The water pours over my head and body, the material sticking to my skin. Placing the men's shampoo, conditioner and shower gel beside me, Addy eases my head forward to kiss the top of it. Then, she stands, puts a playlist on my phone and leaves me to wallow and wash in peace.

I can't say how long I sit for, long enough for the tears to subside and for my heavy limbs to lighten. Exhaustion still calls my name, a bone deep ache that begs to be fulfilled, but it feels somewhat manageable. I drag the sodden T-shirt over my head, wash my hair and body, and wrap myself in a thick heated towel.

Addy is nowhere to be seen when I open the bathroom door. The boys shoot upright from where they'd been sitting, Rhys in an armchair and Clay on the edge of the mattress. The air still pulses with everything unsaid. Their guilt, anger, fear, and their dangerous need to prove who can save me better. I'm so tired of being caught between them, being pulled from one to the other until I feel like I'm going to be torn in half.

Fumbling with my phone to shut off the music, I toss it onto the bed before flopping on it myself. It's Clay who switches me back to the mic app, unable to stand the unknown any longer.

"How are you feeling, Beautiful?" He strokes my wet hair. In direct competition, Rhys grabs a second towel and starts to dry my legs. Through all of the self-pity and turmoil, I cringe. I haven't shaved in a while, becoming all too familiar with these men who call me pet names and treat me like their queen. Spoiled, that's what I am. And spoiled soon becomes lazy.

Batting the pair of them off, I wriggle up the bed and tuck myself beneath the covers before removing the towel. I know Clay would have looked away, respecting my privacy, whereas Rhys would have probably started dry-humping my leg. The hound in question doesn't hesitate to strip off and climb into bed next to me, despite it being morning. The material of his boxers presses against my ass, his warmth too inviting to deny.

A sigh sounds through my phone's receiver from where it now sits on the bedside table. I watch Clay's shoulders sag as he takes a step back, heading towards the door.

"I'll give you two some space," he says quietly, eyes flicking to mine for only a second. Rhys doesn't move, his chest rising and falling in evenly. He's locked in for ultimate snuggles and no fucks. Clay lowers his head, preparing to leave when my hand snaps out.

"Wait!" I shout, ignoring the grumble behind me. The last thing I want is for Clay to feel like a third wheel. He's a part of this as much as we are, whatever *this* is.

In my current state, I don't have the strength to turf them both out, preferring to be alone rather than be seen favoring one over the other. Nor do I want to let either of them out of my sight. Whether I intended to or not, I've grown attached, gifting them both a piece of my heart. And now I'm faced with the real possibility someone out there won't stop until one of us is hurt, I can't bear to let a moment pass without them by my side.

"Look, I know it's unorthodox, not to mention selfish and fucking insane. But I could have died last night and all I want is to have both of you close. Please?" I've turned my head to plead with Rhys. He's the one who refuses to bend, who won't accommodate anyone around him unless it's convenient. Those blue eyes watch me intensely, the skeletal forms inked on his chest, arms and neck seeming to reach for me. Tears swim in my vision, the vulnerability I tried so hard to trap inside a little box in my mind rising to the surface.

Reaching up, Rhys strokes my bottom lip with his thumb as it wobbles. His gaze flicks to Clay over my shoulder and back again, the cogs in his brain visually turning.

"If that's what you want." His breath fans my face and the first real smile of the morning stretches across my face. It doesn't quite meet my eyes, but it's a start.

Placing a kiss on my forehead, Rhys turns me back around, his body curving along the length of my back. Clay's onyx eyes are fixed on me, uncertainty etched into his features. I wait a moment, pressing my lips together. If he leaves now, I won't stop him, although I'll understand. As long as that's his choice. As long as he knew he was welcome. Stalling long enough for my heart to start thrashing, Clay's limbs fall limp.

"Fuck it," he breathes harshly. I watch him undress slowly, as if hoping he'll come to his senses with each piece of clothing that is removed. I know he won't. There's no such thing as sense and logic between the three of us anymore. Slipping beneath the cover, Clay's front presses against my own, any hint of tentativeness vanishing as the thickness of his thigh settles between my legs. This is the Clay I ache to see, the one who throws caution to the wind and grips my hips to pull me against his groin.

My gasp is swallowed, his tongue combating mine with a desperation I know all too well. Usually, Clay's touches and kisses are unhurried and gentle, but this is something else. It's pure and raw, the depths of his emotion being poured into me by the hand gripping my face. The other squeezing my hip does not belong to him. I shuffle to be closer, our chests crushing against one another's, and inadvertently wriggle my ass against Rhys' dick.

"Stop that right now," Rhys grunts almost painfully. I fall still but

Clay doesn't, his mouth consuming mine. Skilled hands with long, slender fingers glide over my waist and spread over my stomach. Rhys holds me there, simply waiting for Clay to settle.

Sex is out of the question, no matter how much my brain screams for it. My body isn't ready. I'm not in the right head space, and when both Rhys and Clay take me, I want to be completely lucid. Yes, it's a *when*, not an if anymore. That's for damn sure.

CHAPTER THIRTY ONE

Drumming my fingers on the kitchen island, I watch the scene before me from a distance. Watching and waiting for a hint, a clue, a slip up. Harper is curled up on the sofa under one of my cashmere blankets, her hair tied up in a lazy bun. Whilst she reads, Addy is sprawled beside her with a sketchbook balanced on her knees. She bobs her head to the music playing through her earbuds, her entire attitude far too relaxed for my liking.

After forwarding everything I know about Addy onto the hacker kid, he's repeatedly come back with blanks. No suspicious activity. Not so much as a bleep on her perfect college record. I'm not convinced. It's always the person closest who flies under the radar. The best friend, the seemingly innocent roommate.

Feeling the weight of my stare, Addy looks up and gives me a girly wave. I glare back, drawing a menacing line across my neck with my fingers. She laughs and goes back to her sketchpad. Harper is oblivious to it all, preferring to live in the world that her novel is providing for a little while. I don't blame her. I'd escape too if I could, but I've got to stay alert, ever watchful and aware of the dangers lurking around her.

Thundering beats against the ceiling, the heavy footfalls of the treadmill upstairs picking up pace. Clayton has found my private gym, and since it's easier to let him use it than have to see him stalking around all the time, I left him to it. None of us want to leave the house until Harper is ready, preferring to stay close.

It's been a couple of days since the fire. A couple of days since I laid awake at night, spooning her long after Clayton had left to go back to the spare room. The thought of closing my eyes, of something else happening to her, I could barely breathe thinking about it.

When I saw Harper being pulled from the smoke, the fragility of life hit me like a ton of bricks. I held her in the ambulance, whispering confessions she'll never hear. It seemed appropriate at that moment, but the reality is I can't give her something I don't possess, and a heart is on that list.

Luckily, things have sort of smoothed out. We've managed to avoid all of the gossip being published online and the reporters waiting at the bottom of my pathway. That is, until a knock sounds. I ignore it, figuring one of those pests has become impatient enough to grow a pair of balls. It sounds again and again, each time doubling in intensity. Soon, the pounding threatens to take the door off its hinges.

Addy looks across the open plan rooms, her eyes filling with worry as they lock with mine. Harper senses the shift in the air too, her head popping up and hunting for the vibrations she can feel through the floor and sofa. Whoever it is has disturbed my girl's peace, and I won't stand for that.

Unsheathing a butcher's knife from the block, I storm down the hallway, intent on giving those reporters something to really write about. In this case, an obituary. My bare feet are silent against the wooden floorboards. I glance through the narrow frosted panel beside the door, but all I see is a tall shadow in a long coat. Gripping the knife's handle tight, I throw the door wide open and hold it to the neck of a man who has the same icy blue eyes as I do. My father's gaze flicks down then back up to my face, not a hint of surprise crossing his features.

"I hardly think that's necessary," he states coldly. Stepping through me, his hand knocks my numb one aside as he invades my hallway. The door behind him stays open, a clear indicator that he's not staying.

My mouth hangs open, a chill of trepidation causing my spine to go rigid. It's usually this way when I see him, but something about him being here, in my domain and close to Harper has my throat closing in on me. Dressed in a black wool coat, I glimpse the immaculate dark suit underneath. Straightening his tie with fingerless leather gloves, my father doesn't blink as he scans the area. His gaze skims me, from my wrinkled T-shirt to my sweatpants and bare feet, and a snarl of disgust curls his top lip.

"Make yourself presentable. We're having dinner." I just about resist flinching, the cutting sound like shrapnel slicing through the small presence of calm I'd managed to find here.

"I'm not going anywhere," I rasp out. Realizing my head is slightly inclined, I shoot back upright and paint a look of indifference across my face. A skill I've learned from the man before me. My father doesn't answer right away. Instead, his eyes flicker past my shoulder, toward the living room where Harper and Addy are sitting. I side step to block his view, remembering that we're the same height now. I'm no longer that timid little boy he can look over and pretend doesn't exist.

"This isn't up for negotiation. The car will wait for twenty minutes." Turning on his heel, my father stops in the doorway and looks over his shoulder, his tone remaining flat. "And you're bringing the girl."

My blood burns, every vicious retort I should have spat now coming to mind. It's too late. He's halfway down the path, flashes of cameras assaulting him from every angle until he slides into the black limousine. A small hand touches mine and this time, I do flinch and instantly hate myself for it. Every. Damn. Time. I'm reverted back to a person I've spent years running from. Harper apologizes, as if she could do anything to wrong me, and I pull her into my arms. The edge of her receiver presses against my bicep and I sigh.

"You're not coming," I hiss sharply. Harper doesn't even react, although her stubbornness is palpable. "You're not ready."

Releasing her, I walk up the stairs with obligation making each step heavier. I only have myself to blame. If I was focused, my father would be under a mountain of debt and scrutiny by now. As it stands, he's as arrogant and powerful as ever, which is the only reason I enter my bedroom to shower and change. If he has his sights set on Harper, then I need to play along and keep him distracted.

As standard though, Harper has her own ideas. By the time I thump back down the stairs like a man walking to his own noose, she's waiting there in a dress I've never seen before. It's soft blue, the color of summer rain, slipping down her frame in a way that's both elegant and unintentional. The neckline dips just enough to reveal the faintest curve of her collarbones, her skin glowing against the delicate fabric.

Her hair is swept up and pinned with a few loose strands curling around her cheeks, and her makeup is light. Her eyes appear impossibly wide, her lips flushed a gentle rose. She looks like she belongs in my father's world far more comfortably than I do. I stutter to a stop, my brain strangling to catch up.

"How the hell," I frown. Surely I didn't take that long in the shower. "Where did you even get that?" I gesture to her dress. Harper takes great pleasure in my reaction.

"Most people just say, wow you're stunning," she smiles knowingly. If I hadn't seen her moping around for the past few days, I'd never believe this is the same girl who was shaking in my arms after the fire.

"It's Addy's," Harper answers my initial question, brushing her hands down her front and smoothing out visible creases. The girl in question is back to her sketchbook but throws up a deuce with her fingers. I drag a hand down my face and sigh, the fight bleeding out of me.

"You don't have to do this," I plead, quickly losing the will to fight.

"You're not facing him alone. Not after everything he's done."

Harper lifts her chin, defiant as ever. Damn, I respect her so much for that.

She'd walk straight into the lion's den just to stand beside me. I want to tell her no, that I can handle my father's games on my own, but the truth is selfish and clawing at my chest. I don't *want* to go without her. The idea of walking into one of my father's orchestrated ambushes alone makes my stomach twist. At least if she's there, I'll remember what I have to fight for.

"Fine," I mutter, shoving my hands into my smart trouser pockets. "But stay close. Don't say anything unless I tell you to." Harper's lips quirk with faint amusement, and the dread spirals in my gut. This is already a terrible idea.

"You say that like I'm good at taking orders. Speaking of which," her eyes flick to the top of the stairs beyond my head. I turn, and immediately regret looking. Clayton is striding down, his hair damp and slicked back, and he's wearing one of my suits. One of my *tailored* suits. The seams strain across his shoulders, his tie crooked, and the pants button looks like it's about to ping off and take my eye out. I stare at him, dumbfounded for a long moment.

"You're not invited."

"Not by you," Clayton tugs at his cuff. Striding past me, he wraps an arm around Harper's waist, the pair looking like they're running for prom king and queen. Pinching the bridge of my nose, I don't even have it in me to argue. Screw it, let's just get this over with.

The restaurant is one of those places my father uses to remind the world he doesn't eat with the commoners. That he's above all others. Glass walls and gold lighting surround the table we had to be moved to when my father realized our party size had doubled. Waiters in crisp uniforms glide between tables like trained shadows, a pianist in the corner playing a classical piece. The notes are delicate, almost afraid to be heard by the elite who dine in their midst.

Curling a hand around a crystal glass of wine that's probably older than I am, I glance around the table. Harper is by my side, my father directly ahead and Clayton to his right. Brave man. Let's hope the scallops aren't overdone tonight, or Clayton might find himself in the firing line of a plate being smashed onto the white tablecloth.

"You've caused quite the stir, son," my father says finally, setting down his own glass. His voice cuts through the low murmur of other diners like a polished knife. "Reporters camping outside your house. The university board calling me twice a day. If I didn't know better, I'd think you were trying to embarrass me." His tone is calm, almost conversational, but his intention is venomous. It's all a dance with him, careful placements of words, precise flicks of his wrist, every breath measured to the rhythm of his intention.

Harper's hand twitches in her lap, twisting into the fabric of the dress. She needs to be careful not to seethe so openly. I catch her knuckles beneath the table, squeezing in silent reassurance.

"I'm not responsible for your reputation," I reply coolly and somewhat ironically. In fact, I've made it my life's mission to fuck with my father's reputation, but it's too soon for him to know that. My comment earns me the smallest lift of his eyebrow, the sort of restrained reaction he saves for moments when he's mildly amused by my defiance. The same expression he used when I was a kid and accidentally bled on one of his Persian rugs.

"Perhaps the company you keep is unfamiliar with the legacy you are due to inherit. You can have your fun, your tattoos and your women," he flicks a careless hand at Harper and I grit my teeth, "but when we're facing a public scandal, I'm afraid I must intervene."

Ahh, so this is about the video. Not the fact that Harper nearly died, or that someone is terrorizing the three of us. All that matters is the squeaky clean appeal our last name has to those who are on the outside looking in. I don't get to voice any of these thoughts, as Harper straightens her back and speaks with distinct clarity.

"I'm sorry if the campus gossip inconveniences you, Mr. Waversea," she starts. I squeeze her fingers to the point of pain, willing her to stand down. Unfortunately, Harper has that glint in her eye that won't be denied. "I didn't ask for any of this attention. I'm simply trying to keep my head above water."

A flare of surprise flashes across his face before it's quickly dissolved. I smirk then, pride swelling in my chest. He thought she couldn't hear him. That she was here for show, but he doesn't know the tenacity of my girl. Where others might wilt, she thrives. She finds ways to become the version of herself she was always meant to be.

"I will get to you, *Miss Addams*," my father bites back. "The disorder you've brought into my son's life has not gone unnoticed."

"With all due respect, you named him as my mentor," Harper quips straight back. She shakes off my grip before I break her hand, preferring to place her palm on my jittering thigh. The last thing I want is for Harper to have a target on her back, especially from a man with the resources and influence my father has.

Our first course is served, preselected from an a la carte menu, and for a moment, it's just the soft scrape of silverware and the pianist's delicate tune filling the air. I can't stomach food, but I push it around and nibble for show. Without such reservations, my father cuts into his food neatly, as though the act itself is a statement.

Unaccustomed to an affluent palette, Clay picks at the fish, waiting for Harper to finish hers before he swaps their plates over. Her small smile is bright with affection. My father notices in an instant. The tension zips between us like a live wire. Harper tries to ease the stiffness of my actions with a gentle brush on my arm, under the careful watch of my father. His eyes are laser focused, watching the subtle interactions around the table.

I want to tell him to stop. To leave her out of his games, but my tongue feels glued to the roof of my mouth. He knows exactly what he's doing. He leans back, the picture of effortless composure, and turns his attention fully on Harper.

"So the rumors are true." To my surprise, it's Clayton that bristles and jumps to Harper's defense first.

"If you have something you want to say, Mr. Waversea, then just say it."

"Call him Phillip. No need for the formalities," I pitch in, knowing it will take the heat off Clayton and bring it back to me. The quickest way to piss off my father is to strip him of the name he holds so dear. I don't pause to think too much on how having Clayton here is a bolster I didn't know I needed. The resolve to not show him my weak side is reinforcing the strength to stand up for myself.

"I do have something to say," my father smiles faintly, though his gaze cuts through me like a razor blade. "Or more rather, something to announce." The groan I want to release stays trapped in my head. Nothing that's about to come out of his mouth can be good, and I brace myself as if his next words might physically spear me. "My annual gala is fast approaching as I decided this year, we will hold it on your twentieth birthday."

"That's at the end of this month," I frown. Usually, my father spends months planning his galas, inviting the entire student and governing body, the faculty, the investors. It's a huge 'look-at-me, I'm-better-than-you,' soiree that I've been attending long before I was an actual student. My father smiles faintly, and there's no kindness in it.

"I've managed to distract the media with the promise of another story. The choice Miss Addams is going to make that evening."

"I don't want any part of what you have planned," Harper states boldly. My father's smile doesn't slip, but his grip on his knife and fork tighten slightly. It's those minuscule clues I'm used to looking for to know when his patience is truly being tested. When it runs out, we can't be anywhere nearby. My father's eyes are on Harper's, and though she doesn't falter, I have the urge to put myself between them.

"Yet you are a part of it. You're bringing humiliation to my doorstep, and I can't ignore that. On the night of Rhys' birthday gala, you will choose a date. There will be a double page spread in every tabloid filled with images of you and your chosen. The other man will walk away, never to interact with you again." His words are careful, pre-rehearsed and laced with a threat. Clay's brow twitches as he stares at the table.

"What makes you think—" Harper starts, her food forgotten. I stop her this time, curling my body into her side and muttering into her receiver to not push this. Just wait it out and we can discuss it later. My father finds my behavior amusing.

"You three have formed your very own love triangle. It would be a tragedy not to capitalize on it."

"And if I refuse?" Harper tilts her head. A strand of her pink hair dips onto my collar, my body still close enough to hers to be considered a shield. My father's expression doesn't change. He merely dabs at his mouth with a napkin before speaking.

"Then your little academic record, the one you've worked so hard to preserve, will be reviewed under the college's new conduct policy. I imagine a headline scandal wouldn't work in your favor."

His cold eyes watch her reaction carefully, hunting for the cracks she refuses to show. Later, in the privacy of my room, we'll break together, but not here. Not now, and especially not for him. Desiring a more direct approach, my father leans his elbows on the table and threads his fingers.

"If you refuse to make a choice, at least you will be expelled. Whatever future you thought you had will evaporate. I can't speak for the others at this table."

Unknown to the other diners, a stilted quiet falls over the table. Clay is yet to move, as if he's an outsider at this table, simply taking whatever threats are thrown his way. Harper's eyes glisten, but she doesn't let the tears fall. As much as I beg her with my expression to not raise to his bait, her chin remains held high, her posture disobedient.

"You three have decided to invite the world into your private lives, and the gala is to be your final stage." My father laps up the heat in her green eyes, like a new challenger has entered his ring. I hate to think, regardless of the choice she's being forced to make, that he won't be satisfied simply breaking her. He'll want to crumble her into dust beneath his dress shoe. "Welcome to the limelight, Miss Addams. Let's see if you fit in."

There it is. The threat. The trial he knows she will want to attack head-on. My mind spins, the variables around me tumbling out of control. Regaining some composure, I twist towards my father, yet keep my arm around the back of Harper's chair.

"And if she doesn't choose me?" I call his bluff. Harper's soft intake of breath sounds beside my ear. "Won't that further humiliate the reputation you spoke of?"

My father hums, the sound filled with contempt and curiosity in equal measure. Surely gambling on Harper's sharp mind is a fool's move. But as his mouth curves around his wine glass before he dips it back, taking his time to drink, I start to put the pieces together. He isn't worried about Harper humiliating us, he's counting on it. My blood runs cold, my heart doing that palpation thing where it feels like I might go into cardiac arrest if I stay here any longer.

"We're done here," I toss my napkin into the barely touched plate of food. Rising to stand, Harper and Clayton do the same. Using a hand on the small of her back, I guide Harper around her side of the table to keep as much distance between her and my father as possible. This steers her directly into Clayton's embrace, his arm wrapping around her shoulders and leading her to the exit.

I take up the rear, intent on not looking back until my name is barked. Freezing in place, I spin on my heel and grimace. There's nothing else to be said, hence no reason to stay any longer.

"One last thing," my father says, clearly having other ideas. His gaze drags over my face, my neck tattoos, my suit, and at last the full weight of his disdain for me rises to the surface. "When she doesn't pick you,

you will become exclusive with Klara Kavanagh, and marry her upon your graduation.”

“What—” I start but my father holds up a hand, silencing me with the same quiet authority that once ruled my entire childhood.

“I’ve let you have your fun, hoping you’ll screw it out of your system, but all you’re doing is making a mockery of us. It ends after the gala or so help me, there will be consequences.”

The word *consequences* hangs between us, so thick that I can taste it. The same word he used when he cut my mother off from her family. The same word he whispered before he made sure my first mentor was transferred halfway across the country. This is no bluff, and I don’t want to know what punishment he would think up for me. I’m the one he hates the most, because I don’t even try to bend to his whims. I don’t fit the perfect mold he set up for me, hoping I’d one day step into his shoes and take over his dirty work.

I stare at him, this man who somehow manages to look perfectly composed while dismantling me in public, and realize there’s no room left for the both of us. It’s him or me, a task I need to get back to soon. If my father reads my mindset as easily as he claims, he doesn’t show it. He’s already turning his attention to the waiter, waving for the bill like the conversation’s concluded.

Harper and Clayton are halfway down the street by the time I catch up to them, standing beneath the wash of an amber streetlight. Wrapping her arms around herself, Harper puffs off small clouds of air as Clayton hails a passing cab.

She spots me just as the yellow car pulls up, Clayton popping the rear door. He enters first and her second, then I shuffle her along so I can get into the back too. I can’t stand an inch of separation right now, including sitting in the passenger seat. I bark the address and lean back, taking Harper in my arms the way I wanted to all night.

“You okay? What did he say to you?”

“Just the usual threats,” I lie, brushing the goosebumps pebbling her skin. “I’m fine. Let’s get you home.” The words slip out of me so naturally, I don't pick up on them until Clayton raises a curious brow. I've never called my house a home before. It's always been cold, no matter how many people fill it. Like a car missing its engine. Like a body missing its heart.

The cab pulls away from the curb with a slight skid of the brakes. None of us want to comment on what has transpired in the restaurant, the choice that's now hanging over our heads. I probably should be stressing at the possibility of losing Harper, the girl I've poured more of myself into than I thought possible, but it's currently at the bottom of the list.

What's circulating at the forefront of my mind is the way my father looked at her. How he was somewhat impressed and definitely angered by her determination. Whether Harper meant to or not, a new conflict with my father has begun, and this time, she's the one caught in the crossfire.

CLAYTON

CHAPTER THIRTY TWO

Standing with my arms crossed, I stare down at the bed. I've tried to sleep, but instead I lay in the dark all night overthinking. Not even the curve of Harper's ass pressed against my pajama pants or the lull of her vanilla shampoo filling my senses were enough to help me drift off. I might as well have been a ghost at dinner last night, on the outside looking in as my world was slowly torn apart. An ultimatum has been set, and it's come from the worst possible place because there's one thing Waversea's don't do, and that's lose.

Doubts swirl around my mind, the self-doubt I constantly battle with starting to take shape. It has the face of a man who scowls and smokes, who marks himself with scars and skeletons, and who's endlessly mocking me.

For the first time since I met her, I'm starting to seriously consider if Harper should be with Rhys. Not for her sake, but for his. I saw a new side to him last night, his mask well and truly slipping. I thought I was walking into a dinner with the devil and his clone, the master and his loyal heir, but that's not what I saw. For reasons unknown to me, Rhys' father makes him uncomfortable.

Yet Harper knew how to keep him calm. With that subtle, unshakable strength of hers, she defended him to a man who could make most people shrink away. She held Rhys' hand and kept him grounded, nurturing his vulnerability as if she's used to it. So now I'm left to wonder, for the sake of everyone on campus, should I just leave them be? Would the world be a better place if Rhys has his person, his focus away from causing harm and being a general shithead?

But...what about me? When is it going to be my turn for happiness, maybe even love? When do I get to be selfish and say fuck the world, I'm taking what I'm owed? I have so much to give, as well as so much to prove. Being here, surrounded by Rhys' wealth and lifestyle, it's enough to spread doubt through anyone's mind. It's that thought which draws me away from her warmth and into the mindset that I'm going to do something about it. Right now, whilst I still have a chance. Right now, before she slips through my fingers for good.

Leaving the pair to their early morning cuddle, I quietly rummage around the room to collect the items I'll need. Pacing into the bathroom, I dig through the drawers and cupboards beneath the basin. Once I have a collection of the most expensive bottles and lotions I could find, I set the jacuzzi bath running and tip in a decent amount of liquid. Scents of jasmine and white lily fill the air alongside the water cascading from an elongated tap like a waterfall.

I busy myself lighting various candles I found around Rhys' room and the lighter I stole from his jeans pocket. There's something to be said about the self-proclaimed king who has more spa products and lotions than the average princess. I make sure everything is perfect before switching off the water and returning to the darkened room.

With every step I take, my mind whispers that I could stop here. I could walk out the door, let Rhys have her, and maybe save myself the heartbreak that's crawling toward me like a slow, certain fire. But I don't move towards the door. I move towards her.

Gently smoothing my arms beneath Harper's sleeping frame, I lift her to my chest and carry her away from the monster she's been curled up with. She stirs a little, her brows pinching together as if fighting a bad dream. I'm careful not to jolt her too much, knowing she won't be able to hear around her. I could have taken the microphone from Rhys' shirt, but we don't need words. Not when she's safe in my arms instead of his.

Entering the bathroom, I pause long enough to make sure the door is firmly locked. I won't allow us to be disturbed. Sitting Harper on the marble counter beside the basin, I support her until she's woken enough to take in her surroundings. Her lashes cling together from sleep, her green eyes squinting against the candlelight, confusion flickering before recognition softens her face. She's wearing the t-shirt I insisted we put on her before she passed out last night. There was no way I was letting Rhys take advantage of her when she wasn't lucid enough to give her consent. It's caused her to smell like him, but it's better than the alternative.

Taking in the candle-lit space and spotting the heap of bubbles covering the bathtub, Harper tries to react but her brows are pinched, the slightest downturn to the corners of her mouth. I anticipated this, the pain meds I'd found on my open palm and a filled glass of water at the ready. Harper groans and presses a palm against her forehead, feeling the edge of her hangover, then accepts the meds and downs them with a thankful smile. That one small smile wrecks me. It fills me with hope that the lines haven't blurred too much, and that I can still be the hero in her story. The one who finally gives her the peace she's been longing for.

Removing the now-empty glass back from her fingers, I place it down and slowly lift the t-shirt over her head. Goosebumps rise along her skin, her breath catching as the cooler air grazes her bare shoulders. Her body is the image of perfection beneath my rough knuckles, but it's the vulnerability in the way she avoids my eyes, lashes lowering to her cheeks, that undoes me. The black thong she's wearing has bitten into her hips, a problem I happily fix by peeling the straps of material down her legs. She watches me intently through lowered lashes, her expression unreadable, making no move to rush or force me aside. It's that quiet trust that bolsters my actions and proves I've made the right choice by staying.

Feeling the heat of her gaze on my torso, I slowly push my pajama pants down over my thighs. My dick springs free, the effect her body has on me clear as ever. Kicking the material off, I lift her into my arms once more and carry her to the tub. Stepping in myself, I lower us both into the water together so that her back rests against my front, her breathing syncing with my own.

At last, I can relax. Harper's body curls slightly against mine, fitting there like it's where she belongs. I could soak in everything that is Harper, no water or tub needed. Her vitality seeps into every pore on my skin, the silent power she carries an inspiration to those of us who were so close to giving up. Who felt they had nothing left to live for.

Mr Waversea's ultimatum lingers in the back of my mind, but it won't deter me. If Harper ultimately breaks my heart, at least I can hold onto the fact that she saved me first.

Reaching for a sponge, I tentatively wash Harper's body. Her shoulders tense at first, then ease beneath my touch as if she's slowly remembering where she is. Starting with her arms, I scrub the length of them one by one, her skin turning pink under the gentle friction. It's tender and sweet, but my psyche calls for something a little more... tactile.

Retiring the sponge, I opt for rubbing the bubbles into each of her legs with my hands instead, my thumbs circling her knees, sliding down the curve of her calf. Harper's breath hitches as I work my way higher, reaching her inner thigh, her fingers curling against the rim of the tub like she's bracing for impact. My dick jumps excitedly, so I stop that course of action before I lose control. I finally have Harper all to myself, and for however long it lasts, I plan on making the most out of our time. Every second, every heartbeat, every stolen breath.

Squeezing a large dollop of shampoo into my palm, I massage it into her hair to create a lather. Her head tips forward at first, her brow furrowing, then back as my fingers find their rhythm. Has my sweet angel never been pampered like this before? I'm clearly slacking if that's the case. I work the shampoo through her scalp, slow circles turning firm, coaxing tiny sighs from her parted lips. The sound vibrates faintly against my chest.

A memory flickers across the back of my mind. My mom coming home from a twelve-hour shift at the hospital to a bubble bath run by Jeremy. He would wash her hair and paint her nails. He always said a man's only job is making sure the woman of the house is happy. I guess at least one thing he taught me has stuck.

Washing out Harper's hair, I repeat the process with a salon-branded conditioner. I hope it costs more than more people's rent, I think as I empty it into the tub. Even when I've got Harper all to myself, I can't help but chuckle a little *fuck you* at Rhys. Harper's lashes flutter when the warm water trails down her neck, her chest falling in a quiet exhale. Every fiber of my being is currently focused on showing Harper how she should be treated, how we could be. I wouldn't have all these small luxuries, but the notion is the same. Care doesn't need a price tag.

Her hand floats beneath the surface of the water until her fingertips graze my thigh, tracing a lazy pattern that makes my pulse quicken. The way her nails scrape against my skin, the way her ass presses against me. It all blurs into one clear meaning. She wants more. Harper's body softens against mine, openly trusting and wanting, and it undoes all of the discipline I've been fighting to maintain.

Cupping her jaw, I twist Harper's head to look up at me before taking her mouth with mine. Our kiss is powerful, demanding. Unlike any we've had before. She melts against my body, utterly captivated by the feel of my lips meshing with hers. Raising my hand to her breast and squeezing, I slip my tongue into her mouth on a gasp. I tease her, alternating between stroking her nipples with the backs of my knuckles and kneading her heavy breasts. She pushes them higher, firmly against my hands.

My fingers trail down the center of her cleavage and abdomen. Her legs open for me automatically as I reach the junction of her thighs, the creamy wetness I find there having nothing to do with the water surrounding us. I relish how ready she is for me. Sliding two fingers inside her, I hold them still while my thumb circles her clit. Harper wriggles impatiently but I hold still, enjoying my delicious torture far too much.

My lips paint kisses across her jaw and neck, my fingers easing in and out of her lazily. Securing her in place with my free arm, her body molds against mine. She whispers my name, begging me to make her cum. Hooking her legs over my widened thighs, she's fully exposed, and that's when I relent to her pleas.

Pumping my fingers into her, the water splashes over the side of the tub. Harper's pants fill the vast space, her nails digging into the arm locked around her. I lick a path back along her flushed neck, her face turning to take my tongue back in her mouth. She bends and writhes, eager to get closer, her hand joining mine to rub against her clit. I feel her tighten around me before she groans against my lips, her back arching and body going taut.

As soon as she's slumped against me, I cradle her and stand, taking us both out of the tub. Laying her across the thick bathmat, I stand to take in the sight before me. Harper is everything. Gorgeous, tenacious, clever, mesmerizing. Her pink-tipped hair is fanned around her, her lips parted and beckoning me. And her eyes. Those hooded, green, fuck-me eyes will forever be imprinted inside my mind.

Reaching for the condom I found in Wavershit's bedside table, I rip it open and roll it down the length of my fully erect cock while she watches hungrily. I lower the length of my body over hers, placing kisses along the length of her neck and flicking my tongue across her delectable nipples. Harper parts her legs, expecting me to make slow, sweet missionary love to her. And I will. But right now, I need to show her I can do everything the fucker behind the door can. I can be everything he is for her and more.

Rearing back on my knees, I lock her ankles together in one of my hands and rest them against my shoulder. After placing a gentle kiss on the sole of her foot, I thrust into her in one, delicious move. *Fuck, she's so tight.* Harper's back arches, a gasp mixed with a groan leaving her lips. Warmth seeps through the latex parting us, her slick juices the only reason I managed to fully sheath myself on the first thrust.

I tilt her hips and press her ass cheeks together as I slide in and out of her tight channel. She mewls and pulls at the plush bath rug, her head rolling side to side. Stars burst behind my eyes from how incredible she feels, and I already know I won't last. I've been waiting too long for this. Soon, her pleas have restarted, though this time considerably louder and more urgent. I can't deny the beauty before me, so I slam into her harder and faster.

My balls slap against her ass with each thrust, my dick ramming into her fast enough to make her breasts bounce vigorously. I take it all in, every stunning detail. The flush of her creamy skin, the pinched expression she makes just before breaking apart on a scream, her hands clawing the threads of the rug. Her pussy closes around me so forcefully, I have to push against them to make sure she doesn't sever my cock from my body. Releasing her ankles, letting her legs flop to the sides, I lean over her and go as deep as I can. Let her feel me every time she walks, every time she's with him. She'll be remembering me.

The soapy water covering our bodies mixes with sweat, my chest sliding against her breasts as I pound into her relentlessly. My eyes hold hers as I chase my own orgasm, desperate to have her the way I've been dreaming about non-stop. Her nails claw at my back, her legs locked around my hips and the screams of pleasure...I've never been so turned on in my life. My name is on her lips, and I'm determined it will always stay there.

Pressing my forehead against hers, I snap my hips back and forth, a man on a mission as banging starts to sound from behind the door.

"You sneaky fuck!" Wavershit roars. "You'd better open this fucking door!" I fight to keep the tension from my body, continuing to fuck Harper since she can't hear his shouting. Actually, it spurs me on.

Gripping Harper's jaw, I claim her mouth like a savage before dropping my head to her pierced nipple. Sucking and teasing, I force Harper's back to arch up off the floor, her hands moving to grip my hair.

"God, Clay, *yes*. Just like that," she groans. The banging on the door stalls, then intensifies. Holding her hips at just the right angle, I give her everything I've got. She cries out, trembling with pleasure, her body going rigid beneath me. The tightening of her perfect pussy is my own undoing. I snarl as the most intense and satisfying orgasm rips through me, molten hot cum spurting into the latex. Harper explodes with me, following me into the void I would never want to climb out of. I'll drown for her, so she never has to. I'll be the life raft to keep her afloat. All I want in return is for her to admit I'm enough. Just me.

Harper's breath comes in shallow waves against my chest, her body still trembling beneath my large hands. I brush my thumb over the curve of her shoulder, the reality of what just happened sinking in like a stone. For a few fleeting moments, it felt like she was mine, truly and completely mine.

But that illusion fades as quickly as the warmth leaves my skin. Rhys continues to thunder on the door, bringing me back to reality with a sudden realization. What am I doing? Falling for a girl who I fuck on the bathroom floor, her other love interest locked out merely feet away? Are these the lengths I'll go to simply to have a piece of her? These are questions I don't want to face the answers to.

So, I lie there, inside the echo of her warmth, pretending that the shudder in my chest is exhaustion and not heartbreak. I could tell her how she makes me feel human again, how every scar and jagged edge inside me feels a little smoother when she's near. But what good would it do? She'll always be caught between us. Between his chaos and my calm, between what she craves and what she needs, and I'll always be the one waiting in the shadows, taking what scraps she gives.

Harper, unaware of my inner turmoil, beams a purely satisfied grin. Her breathing evens out, her fingers tangling with mine as she rolls her head to the side and giggles. It's then I realize she can feel the vibrations of Rhys' pounding through the floor, his shadow lingering beneath the threshold.

I take solace in the fact that Harper doesn't rush to answer his call, but rather pulls me down to kiss me. Her lips glide over mine leisurely, my cock still pulsing inside of her. My body will never stop responding to her. At least, not until she makes her final decision. This ultimatum hangs over us like a dark cloud now, the clock counting down for me to make a lasting impression. I cannot fail her, and I refuse to fail myself ever again.

CHAPTER THIRTY THREE

By the time I sleep off the rest of my hangover and the pleasurable assault Clay did to my body, the man in question is nowhere to be seen.

Rhys is in the kitchen, a hand towel thrown over his bare shoulder. He's topless otherwise, an inked god moving around the appliances like it's the first time he's seeing them. I slide into a stool at the island, content to watch the flex of his muscles, the way his veins pop along the length of his arms. Even the lower V running into his gray sweatpants appears to be extra delectable today.

"Keep staring at me like that, I'll bend you over this counter and rebrand every inch that fucker dared to touch," Rhys lifts a spatula and points it at my face. I bite back a smile and openly ogle him again, just to see what he'll do.

Rhys groans, returning to his task of transferring eggs from a frying pan to two plates. My keen sense of smell picks up on the burnt underside without me needing to see it, and the toast that pops from the toaster is equally as black. If Rhys notices, he doesn't show it. At least the coffee he slides my way looks and smells heavenly, due to the machine that crafted it.

Rhys throws the pan and utensils into the basin, the view beyond the window obscured by a downfall of rain. The sky above is dark, making it difficult to judge what time of day it is. I'd guess around early afternoon. I could ask Rhys, or better yet, ask if he knows where I've left my phone. It's probably tucked between the sofa cushions and completely dead. I've become detached to the device since all forms of technology started being used to spy on me. It's rather freeing actually, but at some point, I should probably check if Aunt Marg has been trying to contact me.

"Where is Clay anyway?" I ask instead, taking a sip of my coffee.

"He ran away, said he's never coming back so you should just give yourself over to me," Rhys replies, joining my side with our ultra-late breakfasts in hand. I roll my eyes at him, before looking at the plate before me. Oh nutsacks, I'm really going to have to eat this.

Cradling my cup, I wait for Rhys to try his food first, watching the way his face pinches. His fork is thrown down with a clutter, making my receivers ring slightly.

"This tastes like horseshit," he growls, his shoulders going rigid. I laugh behind my hand, sliding my plate away to join his discarded one.

"I can't say I'm a connoisseur for animal feces, but I'll take your word for it." At Rhys' resentful snarl, I laugh harder, leaning into his side. It really is the thought that counts. "Leave the cooking to me next time." This changes his own demeanor in an instant.

"So there's going to be a next time," he grins. It takes everything in me to not let my smile slip. Thanks to Rhys' father, every little notion I give either of the guys about a possible future is like scattering bread-crumbs. What was something we were simply enjoying, coasting by on what felt right at the time, has now become an impending sentence. Both Rhys and Clay have claimed a piece of my heart. To lose one now would sever the connection and cause half of the muscle to wilt away.

Jarring me from what was due to be a long, awkward silence, the front door bangs open, followed by a yell.

"Harper Addams!" Addy screams, stomping through the house like a woman on a mission. I frown, turning on the stool to watch her approach. The stiffness of her spine doesn't match the playfulness of her purple dungarees and rainbow embellished high top sneakers. "Where the hell have you been?!"

"Um...here," I gesture to Rhys' house as if it's obvious. It's not as if she's not staying in one of the spare rooms upstairs whenever her busy schedule allows it.

"I've been trying to call you for over an hour! Have you heard the news yet?" I withhold a joke there, asking if she's mocking me, since her face is the image of seriousness. It doesn't sit right beneath her perfectly contoured make-up and artful cat eye.

Rhys, who had been clearing away the plates, steps behind Addy and effectively cages her in. His eyes are narrowed on her back, the tic in his jaw beating. He's still convinced my roommate had something to do with everything that's been happening to us. In my heart, I know there's no way. She was my first real friend and has no reason to want to harm me. Oblivious to his lingering, Addy continues in a flurry of panic.

"The police have made an arrest. They know who started the fire."

My eyes widen, the room around me falling still. As if I've switched off my implants, the sound of rain pelting the window suddenly stops. My eyebrow hitches, as does my breath, while Addy's nervousness increases.

"But?" I encourage, sensing there is more she wants to say. Addy's features clench with sympathy as if she's about to deliver bad news.

"He says he'll only speak to you."

My gut drops, nothing but air beneath my feet as I struggle to stay upright on the bar stool. A wave of nausea sweeps over me, a reality I hadn't dared to hope for starting to fabricate around me. Rhys has gone a paler shade, his nostrils flared and fists clenching at his sides. I don't want to dig any deeper into Addy's revelation, hesitant to shatter the comfort I'd found here. With Clay and Rhys both staying under this roof, with my phone shut off from the outside world, it felt safe. It felt like home.

Swallowing thickly, Rhys asks the burning question for me.

"You don't have to do this." Rhys' hand clamps down on my thigh in an attempt to keep me in his car. I stare out at the looming building beyond the passenger window, its stone façade streaked dark from the recent rain. A heavy sigh drags through me.

"Yeah, I really do," I nod. I still can't quite grasp what Addy told me. I need to see it with my own eyes, and I need answers. It doesn't make any sense. I should say goodbye to Rhys, but I already know he has no intention of letting me walk into that station alone. Officers drift down the wide steps, their badges catching the damp evening light as a few slow, clocking the Porsche parked amongst their police cars. Visitors parking is over the road, but Rhys doesn't care for convention.

Exiting, I press my back against the car and steady my breathing. The building is so tall, I have to crane my neck back to see the top of it. The last of a passing downpour sprinkles my cheeks, but that's not the reason I wrap my arms around myself. Not even my thickest, purple sweater can eradicate the chill seeping bone deep and stemming from fear. Beyond those double doors, held in an interrogation room, is the man they say tried to kill me.

Rhys' arm wraps around me and I instinctively reach for Clay's hand, before remembering he didn't come with us. I have left him several messages, telling him where we'll be should he go back to the frat house, but something tells me Clay needs some space. I'm used to his to and fro, hot and cold demeanor, but it still hurts.

Before I allow Rhys to talk me out of it, I stride up the stone steps, a female officer holding the door open for us on her way out. I instantly regret wearing my receivers. The lobby buzzes with noise and movement, phones ringing, boots skidding on tile, the faint hiss of a coffee machine somewhere in the distance. I spot a desk through the bustle and weave toward it.

A sheet of clear Perspex separates me from a hulking man on the other side, his huge shoulders crammed into a navy shirt and the wealth of facial hair covering the bottom half of his face reminding me of a bear. His pen looks tiny in his claw-like hand as he scrawls across forms. I toy with the edge of my cuff nervously, waiting for his attention before muttering the name of the person I'm here to see.

"Take a seat," he grumbles, pointing to a row of chairs with his pen. I link my fingers with Rhys' and lead him over. As soon as his butt touches the seat, I cuddle into his side. God, why am I so anxious? I'm finally going to get the answers I wanted. I'm just worried I won't like what I hear. Usually this is the point I would turn my hearing off and act ignorant, but I doubt that'll work this time.

Rhys' fingers draw patterns across my back while we wait, his other hand tapping a rhythm on my thigh. I doubt he realizes how effortlessly he's comforting me, something that would have been so unnatural to him a few months ago. As it stands, he's lost to his own thoughts and I spiral back into mine.

We're ignored for the most part, except for a few curious glances from officers. Granted, with his tattoos and scowl, Rhys looks like he's on the wrong side of the cells they have here, but there's so much more to him than the façade he prefers the world to see. My head slumps against his shoulder and I worry the bear-ceptionist has forgotten we're here until the main door bursts open.

Blond waves and muscled frame fills the doorway, relief crashing through my body and revealing a weight I didn't know was settled there. Clay spots me, sweeping me up into his arms as if we haven't seen each other for weeks. We're worlds away from where we were this morning.

"I'm sorry, Beautiful. Kenneth was freaking out, trashing our dorm. I had to talk him down from the ledge." Clay sits me back down with a kiss to my forehead. As we sit, Rhys stands, putting distance between us that feels like a void. I watch him head over to the main desk, wiping away my frown to focus on Clay.

"Is Kenneth okay?" I ask, thankful for the distraction. I don't know how much longer I can hold my tears back. I've been through an onslaught of emotions and it's not even lunchtime.

"He will be. Someone at the café swapped his lacto-free milk with full-fat dairy. I had to cream the rashes he couldn't reach on his back." Clay shudders and I wind my arm into the crook of his with an understanding nod. There's no doubt in my mind that someone intentionally messed with Kenneth's milk. He's prime bullying material, and I should have been more present. Kenneth was there for me when Clay left, but I haven't repaid the favor. After I've gotten through today, I'll make more of an effort to hang out with him.

As if by magic, and no doubt a little threatening from Rhys, a door across the lobby swings open and two men in standard slacks and shirts beckon us. After quick introductions, PC Haynes and Detective Steiner lead us toward an elevator. My head sways slightly as we head thirteen floors up and step into a hallway. The air is quieter up here, conversation fading into the distant click of keyboards as we pass rows of glass cubicles. Steiner gestures toward one near the window, dropping into his leather chair. Haynes fetches an extra seat and sets it beside the two already facing the desk.

"Thanks for coming down," Steiner starts. We take our seats, me in the center. Haynes perches on the edge of the desk, his expression kind. He's young, possibly late twenties with a light smattering of hair lining his tanned jaw. The complete opposite to his partner, who's an older gentleman with no hair to speak of and pale skin.

"It's our understanding you are....um, that you may need an interrupter?" Haynes edges carefully. I give him a wobbly smile, lifting my hair briefly for him to spot my receiver.

"That won't be necessary. Please, just tell me what you can about the fire? I need to understand why it happened." I turn to Detective

Steiner, figuring he is the lead on the case. The older man links his fingers over his rounded stomach and sighs.

"Unfortunately, we haven't managed any answers to any of those questions. It was only by the fingerprints we managed to salvage on the bathroom door handle that we were able to get a match. The why is unknown so far, as he only wants to talk to you." My pulse kicks up a beat and I swallow hard.

"So you need me to get a confession," I conclude. The boys on either side of me tense while the officers share a hopeful look. Standing, PC Haynes gestures for me to follow him.

"I can go in for you," Clay quickly offers, but I shake my head. Rhys also starts to argue, his voice a low growl. I shut him down with a look too. I decided on the way over that nothing will keep me from that room, from hearing what *he* has to say. Feeling Rhys and Clay breathing down my neck, I leave them and their reservations with Steiner in the cubicle as Haynes leads the way.

Stepping into a darkened room, the young officer keeps my attention on him.

"I'll be right here behind this one-way mirror. Anything you can get out of him, we'd be grateful for. Don't go beyond your comfort zone. We can charge him based on the evidence we've already got, but a full confession is the easiest way to prosecute."

As Haynes steps aside, my eyes land on the view beyond the mirror. The breath evaporates from my lungs, a burn filling my chest as it's unable to rise and fall. I imagined almost this exact image, but the figure slumped across a metal table still surprises me. I take a step back, bumping into Clay's hard chest for his arms to circle me.

Haynes has his hand on the handle, a reassuring smile on his face.

"Remain by the door and knock when you're done. I'll get you straight out of there." I take a steadying breath, nodding slowly. The door is pulled open and I step inside.

"Professor Peterson?" My whisper cracks. His head jerks up, the chains around his wrists rattling as he tries to get to his feet. I flinch at the clattering sound, briefly disorientated and Haynes shouts through a hidden speaker.

"*Remain in your seat,*" he barks. Peterson complies, lowering back down. He looks wrecked. His glasses are missing, his eyes wild as they search my face for I don't know what. Dark circles are embedded below, his frown lines more visible. In summary, he looks almost haunted, but also slightly relieved.

"I'm so glad you came. Thank you," the professor dips his head. I frown, remaining rooted to the spot, all my questions dying at the sight of him. I'd figured he would be transformed into a monster, spittle flying from his mouth as he shouted curses at me, finally revealing his true hatred. Instead, the desperation in his eyes jars me.

"Wh-why did you ask for me?"

"To explain. Please let me explain, I'll tell you everything." Peterson begins to sob. Actually sob, tears streaming from his eyes. The man before me is broken, hanging his head low. Slowly, I edge around the room and pull the metal seat opposite him all the way back to beneath the mirror before sitting on it. I can hear Rhys' voice in my head, telling me to get back by the fucking door.

"Okay. Explain it to me." Peterson goes quiet other than his occasional sobs. I don't want to pity him, nor do I want to notice the soreness circling his wrists. As the lack of response continues, I decide to settle for an easier question. "Did you start the fire?"

"Yes," he finally lifts his head to address me. His red eyes beg for a forgiveness I'm unable to give.

"Do you...want to kill me?" I raise a brow, hiding my trepidation behind sass. That's how I usually get by in life, and in here it's no different. Peterson's head shakes frantically, his hands shifting into a prayer.

"No, no! I never wanted to hurt you." At my confused look, Peterson shuffles the chair closer to sit upright and takes a long breath. "I'm being blackmailed. It's been going on for months. Someone hacked into my computer and....caught me with Melinda." I remain silent, my face conveying I don't know who that is.

"Melinda Hargreaves, the physiology teacher," he supplies. "We've been having an affair, and a recording was somehow made. At first, it started small with asking for money. But after a while, the real demands began. I was ordered to hand over one of your microphone clips and then the talent show...I'm so, so sorry. There were threats to show the recording to my wife. I have two daughters. I've been so worried about going home. I've been sleeping in my car."

I hold a hand up to stop his rambling. I've heard enough. A coldness churns in my stomach, but it's no longer from nerves. Peterson descends into full-on crying once again as I make my way toward the door.

"No, wait. Please don't go!" he begs. I stop and turn back to eye the pitiful sight before me. His nose is running and he desperately tries to wipe it on his shoulder. I'd been so worried about stepping into this room, but now all I feel is disgust. He's a coward who was cheating on his wife, and instead of admitting it, he attacked me. One of his students.

"Do you know who's been blackmailing you?" I ask. Peterson hangs his head with a shake, unable to speak or look me in the eye. "Then there's nothing else you have to say that I want to hear. You were so consumed by the fear of losing your wife, you put my life in danger. I could have *died*. Now, your wife will learn the truth and you'll be stuck in a cell. Great job Professor, I'll give your fuck-up an A+."

Rasping on the door, I ball my hands into fists until Haynes appears on the other side.

"I hope you got what you needed," I mutter and take off down the hall without waiting for a response. As the elevator pings open, Rhys and Clay step in by my side as I knew they would. My silent sentinels follow me aside and wait for the doors to slide closed before their arms latch around me. I gasp, shocked by my own reaction as the adrenaline fades and the tremors begin. Rhys buries his face into my neck, Clay rests his cheek on my head. Safe in their embrace, I let a single tear roll down my face.

The floor numbers tick down slowly, the hum of the machinery filling the space that's closing in around us. Three bodies, one bitter realization. We thought we'd caught him. We thought the nightmare was over, but Peterson's confession only confirms what I'd already begun to fear. He's not the one pulling the strings. He's just another pawn on the board. Whoever's behind this, whoever's watching us, they're still out there.

And the next move is ours.

RHYS

CHAPTER THIRTY FOUR

The Harper that entered the police station is not the one who stepped out. Whatever she saw and heard back there has reinstated her to her full glory. A glint of vengeance sparkles in her green eyes, the determination in her posture causing me to rearrange the position of my semi-hard dick more than once.

Said-semi is now pushed against the curve of her ass as she sits in my lap. I need a release, hard and fast and right damn *now*. The problem is I have not one, but two, cockblocks staring at me like I've pissed in their coffee. Addy and Clayton seem very friendly with each other as they watch me from across the kitchen, muttering over the rims of their cups.

Neither Harper nor I can hear them from the sofa, but I have no doubt they're conspiring against me. The entire car ride back, Harper was adamant Addy couldn't have played any part in the blackmail. That the dancer doesn't even know science professors or have the time to hound and harass them. I'm not ruling her out, especially not now Addy seems to have Clayton on side. Easily influenced fool. But he's smart, I'll give him that. If Clayton has the backing of Harper's best friend, the one I've openly hated and suspected, then Harper will surely choose him in the end. I'm furious I didn't think of it first.

Instead, I do what little I can and bury my face in her neck, holding her waist tighter like that alone might stop me from losing her. My father's ultimatum, insisting that Harper makes a choice on my birthday, has ramped up the stakes and added to the strain of trying to show Harper what I can be, who I can be for her.

But I do have a plan. I'm going to catch the bastard who's been messing with us and give Harper what Clayton never could. Sweet revenge. I'll string the fucker up and let her decide what happens next. And if she's merciful enough to let him walk away with his voice box intact, I'll take the blame. I can afford the best lawyers in the country. I'll take the bail, the fines, whatever headline they want to make out of me. Given the same chance, Clayton would talk her out of it and tell her to let the police handle things.

My girl doesn't take the pussy's way out. Then, once she's fully avenged and free to move on with her life, she'll fall for me once and for all. Me being the true hero. The sinner who's willing to do whatever it takes in the name of her happiness. The only man she sees when she walks into a room. The one she looks for when I'm not there. No, scratch that. I'll always be there.

Although right now, that means I have to do the impossible and leave her in Clayton's care. Gently moving her off my lap and setting her beside me on the sofa, my hands linger on her arms. I lean in and press my lips to hers, a soft touch with just enough bite to remind her who she belongs to.

"I'm going to check something out," I say quietly but clearly so she can read my lips. It takes every last drop of restraint to stand, because she insists on batting those thick lashes over her wide, green eyes, eyes that keep flicking between my mouth and my gaze. Fuck what I'd give to drag her upstairs and remind her exactly how I can make her tremble. But now's not the time. I need to put an end to the shadow that's hanging over us once and for all.

Straightening my Gucci hoodie, I glance toward Clayton and sneer.

"Stay with her until I get back. Don't leave this house, for anything." The growl in my voice is aimed at both of us. I hate leaving her at the best of times, but now, with her safety in his useless hands, it feels like walking away from a loaded gun with the safety off.

I head out the back door and into the side garage. The Porsche sits gleaming under its tarp, but I don't even glance at her. Whipping the cover off Nina, my Kawasaki Ninja, I drag my hand down her sleek, black frame in my usual ritual. She purrs for me, waiting to be used like the filthy slut she is.

The garage door slides open as I swing a leg over and start the engine. The roar of the bike between my legs vibrates through my chest like a second heartbeat. Finally, something I can control. Sunlight bleeds through low clouds that recently coated the world in rain. The air's heavy, thick with the promise of another storm, but I don't care. My mind is centered around one simple objective. Get in. Get the information. Get back to Harper.

I take the turns hard, cutting through the quiet streets that wrap around the campus. The wind claws at my helmet, the smell of wet asphalt rising in waves as the bike hums beneath me. The faster I go, the quieter my mind gets, until I pull into the narrow alley behind the admin block and kill the engine. Tugging off my helmet, I leave it on the seat. There's no one around, but I pull up my hood anyway.

Jogging up the building's stone steps, I ignore the intercom and push through the red door that's always unlocked anyway. The air is imbedded with the scent of burnt coffee and cheap paper. The shiny, bald circle on Mitch's head shoots up as I enter, his round frame being dragged down by the chair when he tries to stand to greet me.

"Master Waversea! It's so good of you to come in person," he fumbles while tugging his strained shirt over his gut. I stop a few steps past the desk, my sneakers skidding sharply against the tiles. I take a single, deliberate step back until my hip hits the counter, resting one arm casually on the polished wood.

"Say that again," I demand. Mitch freezes, his eyes darting between the floor, the wall, his desk, and finally back to me like a mouse cornered by a snake.

"I was just... all I meant was... it's nice for you to come in person these days." I tilt my head, fighting the snarl that's threatening to rise. My patience is a loaded gun, and this idiot keeps pulling the trigger.

"I always come explosively, thank you very much." I scoff at him. Sweat beads his upper lip, the increasing pants leaving his lungs probably the most exercise he's had in years. I lean further over the counter, forcing Mitch to take a step back and fall into his leather chair. My shadow swallows him whole as I drum my fingers on the surface.

"Start talking."

"Well, there's just that guy. You know, the one you've been sending to do your... dirty work," he whispers the last part, his eyes glancing to the cameras and back. Inside of me, something snaps. My pulse spikes, but I keep my face carved from stone, ignoring the screams ricocheting around my skull.

"See that's where we have a problem, Mitch." I drag out his name, savoring the way it makes him squirm. "No one knows I come here, nor did I send anyone on my behalf. So, you'd better start talking. What does this guy look like and what's he been doing under the pretense of my name?" The color drains from Mitch's face, his jaws trembling as dread settles in. I can already tell this is going to be bad.

"Well, he's real nice. Tall and skinny. Always wears a black beanie hat. I don't know what he does, but he brings me a soya caramel macchiato every time he visits though."

I pinch the bridge of my nose, turning slightly so the cameras catch nothing but my back and shoulder. I already know without checking the surveillance footage that the imposter would have known to do the same. My lungs ache from the effort it takes to keep breathing evenly. I roll my shoulders, loosening the tension crawling up my spine.

"You've spoken to him?" Mitch nods enthusiastically, picking up on the crumbs of usefulness he's still able to offer me. "Did he give a name? Or anything that I can use to hunt him down?"

Mitch hesitates, then wheels his chair forward with a screech and starts tapping at his keyboard. The rhythmic clatter scrapes against my nerves. My fingers twitch against the counter. By the time he finally smiles, I'm one second away from reaching over and smashing his face into the keys.

"Ahh, I knew I noted it down somewhere. His name's Dekken."

"Dekken," I drawl unbelievingly. Mitch nods, the sweat dripping down the side of his face like condensation on glass.

"Dekken. H. Cornstone, to be exact."

"Mitch, that doesn't even sound like a real fucking name. You didn't think to call me and ask?"

"But...you said if I ever reached out, you'd make me wear my intestines like a necklace." He's got me there. I push off the counter and head for the elevator, my jaw tight enough to crack. The soles of my shoes strike the floor in a steady, violent rhythm. I stop just short of the doors and twist my head over my shoulder. The scowl that crosses my face promises murder.

"I've been paying you a thousand dollars for your silence, and he's been giving you fucking macchiatos?!" A thick silence follows as Mitch drops his gaze to his lap. Dragging a hand through my hair, I stalk into the elevator and let the doors slide closed. Mitch is getting fired, plain and simple. He's lucky that's all I have time for.

The elevator takes forever to ascend to floor three, my irritation bleeding to the surface like thousands of pins and needles beneath my skin. My fists ache to hit something, anything nearby. Aside from drinking the drug that wasn't intended for me, this is the first time I've been directly affected by the hacker, unless it is a team of people. Who fucking knows anymore? The doors slide open with a ping and my feet eat up the lino flooring.

Like all of the other floors, glass separates each office cubicle and there are far more potted plants than necessary. If someone needs this much green in their lives, admin is the wrong fucking job for them. Luckily, there's not many people in today, unless they're all on lunch. Just a random goody-two-shoes who's typing away at a desk and paying me no attention.

I head for the office farthest from the others, slumping into the chair behind the desk to gather my thoughts. If it's money this guy wants, then make the demand already. I'd hand over a briefcase of cash if it meant keeping Harper out of harm's way. And when the bastard shows up to collect, I'll cave his skull in with a rock. I don't mind getting my hands dirty to give karma a day off. Coincidentally, Karma is the name of one of my father's long-time secret lovers.

Logging into the computer, I pull up Peterson's file and records. There's nothing unusual, and definitely nothing interesting. He donates to the Samaritans every year and waves the PETA flag like he's some kind of saint. The guy's never even had a smudge on his squeaky-clean record. It's only down to my father's extensive background checks that Peterson even had his fingerprints on file.

What I need is access to his online banking to find out if he paid the stalker directly. Unfortunately there are restrictions to what I can see on the campus computers without some kind of hacking equipment or the right passwords. Throwing my head back in the chair, I'm close to giving up when opportunity walks in.

Brown hair, long legs, a tight pencil skirt, and red heels. Her matching colored lips part as she spots me sitting in what I'm presuming is her seat. Recognition flares in her dark eyes as she realizes who I am. *Perfect.* A slow grin spreads across my face.

"I have a special job for you," I state before she can say a word. "Can you access the online banking records of a staff member, or get me statements for the last two months? My father has sent me here personally to see this is done discreetly, and rumor has it, you're the best employee on this floor." I add a slow, deliberate wink that turns her cheeks crimson.

Shifting aside so she can sit down, my hand rests on the back of her chair as I lean in close. Her breath catches as she inhales the scent of my cologne and presses her thighs together under the desk. Hook, line, and fucking sinker.

I stay where I am, letting her imagination picture things that will never happen. Harper's ruined me for anyone else, and the thought of touching another woman makes my skin crawl. God, how I've changed, but if playing the charming bastard keeps Harper safe, I'll do it. Besides, maybe this poor, lonely woman needs something to think about when she's home with her vibrator later. Consider it a public service.

At my direction, Peterson's name flashes onto the screen, and she releases a small, knowing sound. She's clearly heard about the scandal that will be working its way across the academy. I can already see the headlines. *Teacher Torches Deaf Student.* The tabloids will be crawling with interviews from self-proclaimed witnesses who have no idea what is actually happening. Reporters will be swarming campus by morning. Another reason I need to get back to Harper before the world closes in on her.

The administrator's fingers fly over the keys, the mouse clicking between windows I never even knew existed. Within minutes, she's pulled up the bank's site and starts entering the passwords Peterson has used on the teacher's portal over the years. On the fourth try, she's in. She opens his most recent statement, and my eyes sweep the transactions, searching for anything off. Then I see it.

Two hundred and fifty dollars a week to a D.H. Cornstone. A very specific amount, transferred regularly for the past three months. His savings are bleeding out, not just to Cornstone but also to restaurants and hotel stays. Expensive ones. Even without Harper replaying their conversation on our way back to mine, I'd be able to conclude that Peterson is having an affair. He's draining his savings, and no doubt, his daughters' college funds.

Grabbing a pen and the nearest stack of heart-shaped post-its, I scrawl my own bank details and slide it across the desk.

"What's your name?" I ask, remembering people are supposed to have manners. Her dark brown eyes flick up to mine, her breath fanning my neck in my hunched over position.

"A–Amanda Hammond," she breathes. Lust fills her vision, an effect I'm used to having on men and women alike. I'm many people's kink, the damaged asshole everyone wants to fix. I never thought someone would actually break through my defenses and make that dream a reality though.

"Amanda. This is my personal account. See to it that every cent Peterson sent to this Cornstone person is reimbursed directly into his wife's account. Then call her and explain that her husband's a lying piece of cheating shit and that the Waverseas will take care of her family. Starting with indefinitely offering scholarships to her two children."

Amanda's eyes widen, awe replacing lust. That's when it hits me, what I've just done. Somewhere in the last minute, I slipped right into my father's role without even realizing it. The authority. The control. The power.

Only when her gaze glances back up to me, this time filled with awe, do I realize my mistake. I got so caught up in my own thoughts, I hadn't even realized the role I'd fallen into so naturally. What the fuck am I doing? I was supposed to be running the investors and the scholarship program into the ground, not offering out more spaces. The ease which that dominating tone came to me has knocked the air from my lungs. Fuck, I'm going to be just like him. I'm turning into my father, the generous CEO and founder's beneficiary. I can't let that happen.

I leave the office without another word. My feet move on autopilot, carrying me to the elevator. I pace the entire way down, cracking my knuckles, breathing through the pressure building under my skin. When the doors open, I take one long inhale and let it out through my teeth.

Okay. I'm back. There's no time for my DNA-deep rot to bleed through right now. I have to focus on the immediate threats and on holding myself together at the seams. Once this is over and I've won Harper's heart, I'll make sure to never act so responsibly again. Rational thought doesn't suit me. It rubs like sandpaper against my instincts.

I race home, slicing through traffic, cutting up cars, and flipping off a bird that swoops too close to my helmet. By the time I pull into the garage, my heartbeat is finally leveling out. I ease Nina into her spot, kissing my fingertips and pressing them to her tank before draping the cover over her.

Even from inside the garage, I can hear laughter drifting through the walls. It hits a nerve I didn't know was raw. Straightening my spine, I walk around the back porch and towards the door, every step reigniting the asshole I am and bringing it back to the surface. This is where I'm comfortable, where it's safe to hide in plain sight. Don't give anyone a reason to expect more from you, and you can't disappoint them.

Entering my house, the kitchen island is covered with empty take-away containers. Harper, shithead-one and cockface-two are sitting around the dining table. Between their plates of Chinese, my vintage Dom Perignon is uncorked and shared out between three mugs. *Champagne in mugs*, it's fucking sacrilege. Between lifting forkfuls of food to their mouths, they are practicing sign language with each other.

The sight is cozy, warm, and irritating as fuck. I'm an outsider in my own home. Spotting me standing in the doorway with my arms hanging uselessly by my sides, Harper jumps up to make her way over to me.

"Hey, we saved you some food." Her arms wrap around my middle but my gaze is on the two grinning bastards at my table.

"That was nice of you," I drawl sarcastically. Harper shrugs, leading me over to the island to hand me a plate piled high with Chinese. Her eyes dancing with a drunken glaze.

"I suppose so. We used your credit card."

A smile warms the corners of my mouth, the turmoil in my being finally starting to thaw. That's right, I can give Harper the lifestyle she deserves. I have my uses.

Addy moves into the kitchen under the guise of searching the cupboards for another bottle of champagne. I sit at the island, eating and filling Harper in on what I've found out. I don't like Addy hovering too close, eavesdropping for details I might reveal. Waiting to see if I've found something to implicate her. I know her type.

"And did this blackmail assassin have a name?" Addy finally joins the conversation, picking up on the detail I purposely omitted. She leans against the opposite counter, grinning at me as if she already knows. Her dermals stretch with the motion, catching the light as she folds her tattooed arms. Sliding my gaze to Clayton, I jut my chin out.

"Your cousin," I answer cryptically. Clayton catches on straight away, his black eyes glinting with recognition. The beanie hat, the sneaking around, the familiarity of our comings and goings. It's too much of a coincidence. The person blackmailing Peterson is the same who visited Clayton's mom in her nursing home.

"Quite the detective, aren't ya?" Addy clicks her tongue, her eyes alive with a challenge. I swear she's mocking me in plain sight, even as Harper locates the champagne and pops the cork as if this is any other friendly get together. That's a joke in itself. I don't have friends or get-togethers that include downing my most expensive liquor like water. Setting down my fork, I trap Addy in my sights and tongue my lip ring.

"You know those rom-coms when the guy asks his girl to move in, only to discover she owns one of those fugly, hairless, yappy dogs? That bitch is you."

Harper gasps as if she's scandalized, whilst Addy just laughs. Loud, unbothered, and entirely too comfortable in my kitchen. Almost as if she's been here before. She pivots with a swagger, taking the champagne from Harper and swigging straight from the bottle.

"Oh yeah? What does that make Clay then?" Addy jerks her head in his direction and bobs her eyebrows teasingly. I scoff, returning to my food.

"He already knows he's a mongrel who's overstayed his welcome," I snarl, hating the reminder these lowlifes are in my personal space. Harper pushes away from the island, all humor draining from her face in an instant.

"Would it kill the three of you to just get along? Haven't we got enough to worry about?!" The harshness of Harper's tone cuts through the room like shrapnel. Leaving with heavy footfalls, I track her movements through the house, from climbing the stairs to slamming the guest bedroom door closed, muttering under her breath the entire way. I hang my head and sigh. Blue balls for me once again. I'll be able to use them as whiskey stones when they eventually drop off.

An impish giggle sounds across the kitchen, reminding me I'm not alone.

"What's so funny?" I demand, glaring at Addy with enough venom to burn a lesser person.

"The irony," she chuckles to herself. "You've upset Harper using an analogy about canines, and landed yourself directly in the doghouse." Addy bursts out laughing, taking the champagne bottle in hand as she also starts to leave. I ball my fists and grit my teeth, repeating a mantra to myself. *I don't hit girls. I don't hit girls.*

"Yeah well....I put the anal in analogy." I blurt before she exits, internally cringing. Staying silent would have worked much, *much* better. Clayton passes by, his large hand slapping across my shoulder blade.

"That was terrible, even for you." I have the urge to break every one of his fingers, but luckily for Clayton, he puts his hands to better use and starts cleaning up. Addy's voice rings out as she climbs the stairs after her best friend.

"Sweet dreams fuckers. I'll make sure to spoon Harper extra tight for you both." Her laughter echoes around the walls, sinking into my bones.

"I hate her," I hiss through my teeth. Clayton grunts, filling the basin with water to wash the dishes. His nonchalance pisses me off just as much. "But I suppose you reckon it's better to have her on your side. Whatever helps plead your case to Harper, huh? Winning by default is like bowing to an empty room. It doesn't count."

"What are you going on about?" Clayton raises a brow at me over his shoulder. Then, the realization sets in and he turns fully, wiping his hands on a dish cloth. "Oh, you think I'm using Addy to win over Harper? Good god, you really need to get your head out of your ass sometimes."

"Well then, what's with all the whispers and smiling?" I huff out, my jaw tight enough to crack a tooth. Clayton dares to roll his eyes at me, like I'm the stupidest person in the room.

"Playing good cop," he tilts his head. "Since you've been scowling at her for every breath she takes, I'm trying a more personable approach. Getting her on our side."

"That's never going to work," I snort, looking away.

"No? Then how do I know she has an alibi for every instance Harper was attacked? She wasn't at the lab field trip, she was on the other side of the country during winter break, she's never dabbled with drugs in her life and she had hundreds of witnesses during the fire." I shake my head, having lost my appetite as I push my plate in Clayton's direction.

"But the flashmob—"

"Was meant to be some big surprise at the end of the show." He interrupts and holds up his hand as if he's taming a wild animal. "The dancers were going to filter into the crowd and perform choreography Addy had created, until someone hacked her account, changed the uniform code and gave out secret missions to individuals. She's not a part of this, Rhys."

I stare at him, my hands curling around the edge of the counter so tight my knuckles ache. Why is Clayton always so calm, so sure of himself? My top lip twitches as he turns away to wash my plate.

"It has to be her," I grumble. Clayton doesn't even face me, his chest falling heavily.

"Why? Because you don't have any other leads?" The arrow his words spear into my chest is excruciating. How can he see through me when I can hardly understand myself? Yet he's right. If it's not Addy, I'm back to square one and I can't take Harper back there. I can't help her if I can't protect her. Clayton exhales before stacking the plate on the drying rack. "You're so busy hating everyone that you can't tell when someone's actually trying to help."

"Help?" I bark out a humorless laugh. "She's a fucking distraction." Sliding off the stool, I pace in a circle, stopping myself from putting a hole through the drywall. I don't even know who I'm angrier at. Addy for being too damn ballsy, Harper for storming off, or Clay for being infuriatingly calm.

"She's helping Harper to deal with all this bullshit that's going on," Clayton says quietly, not only referring to the stalker. He's including us in that statement. "And you're making it harder every time you open your mouth."

That one hits harder than expected. My jaw locks, the pulse in my neck feeling like it's about to burst through my skin. He's not wrong, but I'll be damned if I let him see it.

"You think you're some kind of saint. You think Harper runs to you because you're calmer, more patient, more fucking *balanced*?" I spit, stalking closer. Clayton wipes his hands on his jeans and meets my stare dead-on.

"No, Rhys. I think she runs to me because you scare her. She needs to feel safe." The words cut deeper than expected, but it's the pity in his gaze that rocks me to my core. How dare he pity me. My throat goes dry, the kind of dry that burns and aches for a cigarette. My fingers twitch in time with the tic in my jaw. I want to yell, to grab him, to throw something, but all I do is stand there, breathing hard through my nose.

"You don't know a damn thing about what she needs." I vibrate with fury. I keep Harper safe, even if no one in this entire world wants to acknowledge it. As long as she does, that's all that matters. Clayton pushes off the counter and steps forward until there's barely a foot of space between us.

"Don't I?" His voice drops low, but I can see the flicker of anger under his skin. "You think this is about who fucks her better or who's name she cries out first? But it's not. It's about who will continue to fight for her when his reputation comes under fire and he stands to lose it all. Who she *trusts* to still be there when everything else is burning to the ground."

Clayton shakes his head like he's tired, and brushes past me toward the hallway. My eyes track him, my entire body rigid and ready to see this fight through to the end.

"Coming from the man who is constantly leaving her behind," I call out, stalking after him. I can't let it go, despite knowing we're going in circles. It's not in me to walk away from a fight. "I've never left. I've been here the entire time, holding down the fort while she pines for you. Do you have any idea how gut wrenching that is? How soul destroying it is to watch her fall for someone else when she's supposed to be mine?"

Clayton freezes in place, his silence heavy enough to fill every corner of the room and leave no air for breathing.

"Yeah, Rhys. I do." Continuing up the stairs until a door clicks behind him, I'm left alone with the faint trickle of water draining from the basin and my own ragged breathing. I stare at nothing, my eyes unfocused and sunken. I can't even tell what the hell I'm feeling anymore. Rage, jealousy, regret. Whatever it is, it's corrosive.

My reflection in the window catches my eye, distorted by the streaks of light. I barely recognize the man staring back. He's unusually guarded, not a smirk or drop of sarcasm in sight. Dragging a hand through my hair, tugging hard enough to sting, I lean on the counter until my shoulders ache.

The kitchen feels too quiet without Harper's laughter, without her soft humming as she moves around, her gentle pretense that soothes my rotten soul. I picture her upstairs, curled in a ball, probably crying drunken tears into Addy's arms, and my insides twist.

Deep down, I know Clayton's right. Harper doesn't need another storm seeping through her life. She needs a safe place to land, and I'll never be that for her.

CHAPTER THIRTY FIVE

"Well, no dress will look right if you're going to frown in every single one," Addy scolds. I tilt my head at my reflection in the wall of mirrors, trying to force a smile that barely makes it past my lips. It's hopeless. This is the fourth changing room of an impromptu shopping trip Addy insisted on. Apparently, wearing something I already own to Rhys' birthday gala is an unforgivable offense.

Yet even with Clay's encouragement to come and armed with Rhys' credit card, nothing feels right. *I* don't feel right. Tomorrow night, I'll have to choose between the two men who've claimed pieces of my heart without even realizing it. I have no idea what I'm going to do. I don't want to lose either one of them.

Rhys has spent the past two weeks doing everything in his power to distract me from my coursework. Anytime I'm not with Clayton in class or at the library, which is now the proud owner of all its books again, Rhys is pulling me into dark rooms or storeroom closets. That's when he even lets me leave his house at all.

Clay, on the other hand, has been patient and kind. His signing practice is coming along so well, and lately, he and Rhys have managed to eat at least one meal a day together without tearing each other's throats out.

All of which makes standing here, trapped in this dress with the weight of an impossible decision pressing down on my shoulders, feel unbearable.

"This is stupid," I huff to Addy. Stepping back into the fitting room, I whip the curtain closed and peel the blood-red satin dress from my body, letting it puddle at my feet. I knew coming to the mall was a bad idea, but Addy swore if I found the *right* dress, the rest would fall into place. That I would instinctively know what to do when the time comes. Can't I just bury my head in the sand a little longer?

Tugging on my jeans, sneakers, black crop top, and leather jacket, I peel back to curtain to face my best friend and her a smug little smirk. That bitch found her perfect dress in the first store, which she insists on twirling around in its bag stuffed with tissue paper.

"How am I supposed to shop for a dress when I don't even know who my date will be?" I groan. "I need to match *him* somehow. Whoever he is going to be...Addy, how am I going to do this?" Addy taps a finger against her chin, considering.

"Okay, well, what would you wear for each?" Dropping onto the low sofa beside her, I sigh.

"If it were for Rhys, it'd have to be black, dark red, or gold. Something sleek, expensive-looking, and probably a little too revealing." My lips curve before I can stop them. "Clay would like something softer. Maybe emerald green to match my eyes, or powder blue like the sky on our first date. He's more sentimental like that." Addy throws a hand over her heart in mock swoon. I roll my eyes and shove her lightly.

"Then we buy one of each," she declares. "You could change halfway through the night and swap dates. I'll stuff Clay in the bathroom until you give me the signal." A laugh bursts out of me despite the knot in my chest. That's Addy, always finding a way to make light of my mess. I kind of hate that she's so good at it.

Leaving the fitting room, I hand the dress back to the waiting assistant with a small, apologetic smile. Addy loops her arm through mine, tugging me toward the escalators. My eyes ache from staring at sequins, and my head feels like it's being crushed under the pressure of it all.

"Please, no more shopping," I beg. "I need coffee." Addy giggles and steers us toward the mall's central café area. The space is buzzing, bodies streaming in every direction, conversations overlapping until they blur into a low roar that presses against the sensitive edges of my hearing.

"Do you mind if I tune out?" I say quickly, gesturing toward my ears.

"No problem," Addy signs back, smiling. Sunlight pours through the domed glass ceiling, glinting off the leaves of the oversized plants that decorate the space. Four levels of glass railings rise above us like a giant atrium. At the center of it all sits a cozy café fenced in by white pickets and dotted with wooden tables. A small oasis for the weary shoppers like me.

I dart for an empty table as soon as one frees up, narrowly beating a pair of students with the same idea. Addy joins the queue, leaving me to sink into my chair and wallow in quiet misery. I hate this. I hate that Phillip Waversea is ruling over me the way he rules over his son, how he's essentially blackmailing me to put an end to my fun. Just when the boys were starting to find a way to somewhat get along, a deadline was set. Fun's over, reality is back in full force.

Addy returns, setting a tray in front of me. The smell of coffee instantly eases the tightness in my chest. Between my latte and her smoothie are two triple-chocolate muffins, still warm and gooey. I sign, *'I love you'* before taking a huge bite. It's rich and molten, and I all but melt into my seat.

"Can I take you as my date instead?" I jokingly sign with one hand, picking off smaller parts of the muffin to seem somewhat dignified. Addy chuckles, her throat and chest working in quick succession.

"You're definitely my type, but I've already accepted another invitation." I pause mid-bite.

"Who?" I ask with my hand making an L shape by my chin. Addy

avoids my gaze, her demeanor changing. I've never seen shy Addy before, but the color of her cheeks is beginning to reflect her hair and she's suddenly far more interested in her smoothie. I snap my fingers at her until she gives in.

"Nikki Oakes."

"From the cheer squad?!" I crinkle my nose, unable to hide my initial reaction. Usually, I'm never one to judge, but these girls have been blindly bullying me at Klara's instruction for months. Addy deserves my judgement for fraternizing with the enemy, so I glare at her. *Judge, judge, judge.*

"Nikki is different. She does cheer because she likes to, not for the attention." Addy sits up straight, her face unusually serious as she gets all defensive. I raise my hands in defeat.

"Fine, but you can't say shit about me liking Rhys anymore," I raise a brow. Addy gives me a deadpan look, her hands moving in a flurry.

"Yes I can! Nikki does cheerleading, Rhys steals, lies, bullies—"

"Okay enough of that," I lean across the table and slap her hands away. We're both grinning now as I sit back in my seat. *"As long as you're happy, I'm happy."*

With the coffee cup in my hands, I watch the world blur around me. There's a sale rack outside one of the stores, currently being attacked by a herd of short skirts and wedged sandals. It's only when a group of girls from my study group pass by that it occurs to me that many of the shoppers out today are female and around our age.

I look closer at the levels above, seeing more than one Waversea sweatshirt leaning against the railings. Most have their hair freshly done and are examining freshly painted nails. They're going all out, and they're not even potentially the birthday boy's date. I wish I could smile alongside them, to feel that giddiness rather than the heavy ache of my heart. Finishing the coffee, I put down the cup and shake my hand in the air for Addy's attention.

"I've just realized there's a party happening on campus tomorrow,

and you're not elbow-deep in a confetti cannon. Didn't feel like micro-managing this one?" I'd meant to tease her, but as Addy tries to keep smiling, I don't miss the flash of sadness in her eyes.

"After the disaster of the talent show, Mr. Waversea has hired a professional events company to do this one. Hopefully it's a one off. I wouldn't want my resume affected by a mishap." I frown at my jeans, a lump lodging in my throat.

It's not like I asked for my naked body to be splashed across a screen during the talent show, but I still feel guilty that my best friend is being penalized for it. Unless this is another way for Phillip Waversea to throw his weight around, proving he can control more than just my life. If I humiliate his son tomorrow, it might not only be me that suffers the consequences.

"Rhys is still convinced you're behind it all. The video, the fire, and all the rest." I smirk. Addy rolls her eyes, a small laugh coming from her.

"If I'd wanted to humiliate or hurt you, I had plenty of chances while you're snoring and drooling in the bed next to me."

"I don't snore!" I sign, throwing a piece of muffin her way. She bats it away and sticks out her tongue, hollowing out her dermals. It's laughable to think Addy could plan anything malicious around the thousands of extra-curriculars she takes on. She's going to burn out soon, and hopefully I'm in a position to support her like she has me.

Not that she's complaining about having the run of Rhys' house and feasting on take out most nights, but she's still firmly Team Clayton. If Addy has her way, we'll be back in our dorm tomorrow night, a bittersweet ending to the sordid love triangle I've managed to juggle for this long. The thought sours my mood once again. There's no winning at the end of this.

Spotting a tight mini dress through the crowd, I groan audibly. Why am I even surprised Klara and her minions are also in the mall, masses of designer bags hanging from their arms? To Addy's credit, I don't see Nikki amongst those trailing Klara like flies sticking to shit. The queen bee spots me at the same time, her lips twisting into a snarl.

Any other day, I'd stand my ground, but currently I don't have the energy for whatever bitchy thing Klara wants to say. Whatever doubt she wants to put into my head can wait. Signing to Addy that it's time to go, we stand and head to the bespoke dress store on the upper level. The air is perfumed, the air con refreshing, yet my mind has checked out.

I let Addy drag me around, holding up dresses which I sigh and shrug at. The colors blur into a mass of straps and sequins, my mood scraping along the floor. All I can think is, what if I pick the wrong dress, the wrong boy, the wrong heart? Because tomorrow, everything changes and once a decision has been made, there's no going back.

"Sure, that's the one," I relent and take a hanger out of Addy's hand. She follows me to the register, trying to sign words of encouragement but I clasp her hands together and speak out loud. "It doesn't matter, Addy. The dress, the shoes, the hair. It's all pointless. I'm going to end up heartbroken either way." Her frown reflects how I'm feeling inside as the cashier rings me up and accepts Rhys' card. Accepting the bag on my behalf, Addy spins me and digs her hand into my pocket. Presenting my receivers, she urges me to put them on, refusing to be silenced this time.

"Since when does Harper Addams do as she's told?" Her voice echoes in my head, her chocolate brown eyes darkening as she gets serious. "Just because the ball is in your court, doesn't mean it has to stay there. Pick up your racket and smack that fucker back over the net." My brow jerks, a puzzled look taking over my features.

"That's a cute analogy and everything, but I don't play tennis." Addy groans, her eyes flying to the ceiling. She grabs my arms, giving me a light shake.

"You've been too distracted by the Man-Hulk and the Menace to notice you have all the control." Again, my brow does a funny little twitch and I'm left staring at her in confusion.

"Have you been in Rhys' weed stash?"

"I'm just saying," Addy accentuates her words, pulling me down the aisle towards the mall. Her arm slips into the crook of mine, her sass coming back to life. "There are more than two choices. Expand that beautiful brain of yours. If you're not happy with the options being presented to you, do something about it."

RHYS

CHAPTER THIRTY SIX

I tug on my cuff nervously, straightening the sleeve for what must be the hundredth damn time beneath my suit jacket. The fabric feels too stiff and too heavy, like it's judging me for pretending to be someone I'm not.

Twenty years old today, and I've still yet to learn how to enjoy one of the suffocating gala nights my father organises. The endless champagne, the fake smiles, the brittle laughter, but this one's different. Tonight, it's not about donors or our family name. It's not even about my birthday. Tonight is all about Harper and the decision she's about to make.

I roll my neck, shifting my shoulders again, not that it helps. The nerves crawling under my skin are relentless. They whisper words of doubt into my ear, convincing me I'm about to lose the only thing that matters to me. There's nothing more I can do to sway Harper's heart. The choice is all hers, and I'm going to have to live with whatever she decides.

Staring into the bathroom mirror, I assess my suit with a critical eye. The shirt is crisp white and unbuttoned to my chest, standing out in stark contrast to the dark tattoos covering my neck. There's not a crease to be seen on my navy suit or a single part of my black loafers that isn't shined to perfection.

My hazelnut hair is slicked back, the sides freshly trimmed short. I've switched my piercings for black metal and bathed in the new Paco Rabanne fragrance. Yeah, I'd do me. But still, I'm worried I might be ending this night alone and broken. There'd be no coming back for me. This is my one shot at happiness, the one and only time I'm going to open myself up to rejection.

At least I tried. For once in my goddamn life, I *tried*. I made her coffee while she read, quietly corrected her essays when she wasn't looking, stayed up while she talked about everything and nothing until I couldn't keep my hands off her for one more second. I attended her classes, sat through her study sessions, learned her moods, her silences, the way her laughter always came with a hint of apology. I even gave her space when she asked for it, space that nearly drove me insane.

But even with all of that, something in her eyes still stays just out of reach. There's always a flicker of distance there, like a barrier I don't know how to scale. Like a void that needs to be filled with love I might never be able to provide. I reckon that's the part that terrifies me most. The possibility that no matter what I do, I'll never be able to give her what she deserves.

My Rolex ticks past the hour, pulling me from my thoughts. It's time. I stride out of the bathroom and lift the single, red rose from my dresser. Oh yes, I'm going all out. Leaving my room, I stare longingly down the hall and listen to the girl's soft muttering seep beneath the door before making my way downstairs. Clayton is hunched over on my sofa, his eyes downcast and a frown pulling at his eyebrows.

"You'll give yourself crow's feet before she makes it downstairs," I remark. Striding into the kitchen, I grab two whiskey glasses and pour a healthy dose into each one. "Come on, asshole. Join me for a drink. It is my birthday, after all." Clayton eyes me curiously over his shoulder as I raise a glass in his direction. The guy looks like he needs this more than I do.

Standing to his full height, I take in Clayton's suit over the rim of my glass. He's wearing a classic black tux, most likely rented if the too-tight fit is anything to go by. His shirt is buttoned up to the neck, a striped tie disappearing beneath the waistcoat. What a nerd. I slide the extra glass toward him as he approaches, his obsidian eyes glancing at the rose laying on the kitchen island.

"May the best man win," I refill my glass before lifting it. On a grunt, Clayton clinks his with mine and we down our whiskey in one. Standing on opposite sides of the island, I size up my rival. Clayton may hate me, but despite everything, the feeling isn't mutual.

We've both had to face certain trials in life, but I've never lost someone I've loved. Fuck, I've never loved anyone at all. Yet after experiencing both, he's found the strength to open up his heart to the possibilities once again. I've seen the way Clayton treats Harper, how he worships her and knows exactly what she needs and when. He's well and truly fallen for her, as have I.

Sighing, I swig from the bottle this time, trying to drown my thoughts. There's no use comparing us now. The time for overthinking is over. I've told myself whatever Harper decides, I'll respect. It's a pretty lie, and it's all that's keeping me from burying Clayton beneath the porch and pretending he went out for milk and never came back.

"You could have stopped all of this, you know," Clayton sniffs, lowering onto a stool. "You could have argued harder or done something to secure her place here. Instead, you've left her to suffer." Refilling both glasses, much to his disgust, I paint a smirk on my face.

"Why would I change a competition I'm due to win?" It's a bluff, but it's plausible. Sitting beside him, I cradle my glass in one hand and the bottle in the other. I could have stood up to my father. Or at least, I wish I could have. Something about being in that man's presence sends me back to a place in my mind I pretend doesn't exist. Harper isn't scared of him, but Harper hasn't been left bleeding on his office floor.

"What does it feel like?" I ask to distract my mind from the image, finding my knuckles have turned white around the glass. Clayton raises his eyebrow. "Loving something. Being loved by someone. What does it feel like?"

Clayton doesn't move, his ever-watchful eyes staring at me as if looking for the punchline. I have no ulterior motive this time. I'm stripped back and exposed, emotions I don't understand stirring within. Sensing that I'm genuinely curious, he leans his forearms on the marbled surface.

"I don't know much about your upbringing, but I've noticed you don't have any photos around and you've never mentioned your mother. If that's the kind of love you're asking about, it just feels warm. Like you're constantly wrapped in an embrace and there's always someone to hold you when life seems too hard to bear alone." Clayton focuses on swirling his glass in his large hand, watching the amber liquid spin in circles.

"Is there another kind?" I ask, my voice smaller than I'd like. Clayton releases a breathy laugh.

"Oh yeah, there is. But I think you already know about that one." I frown at this, putting down my glass. My leg starts to bounce, my mind struggling to decipher the meaning behind his words. The intentions of my actions are to make Harper happy, and I can't deny that I care for her, but anything beyond that is a pipedream. It's territory I don't know how to trek.

"Whatever you think you've seen, you're wrong. I'm incapable of emotions beyond anger and hate," I reply, my jaw clenching. Clayton shrugs and stands, moving to place the glass in the basin. I twist my head to watch him lean against the kitchen counter with his arms crossed.

"You're lying to yourself, but for once I believe your intentions are honorable. You know you're beneath her and that down the line, you'll end up hurting her. But I've also seen that she's good for you and makes you want to be a better person. A bigger man might stand aside and let you have her. But I can't." I nod slowly at his words, knowing that feeling all too well.

Maybe Clayton and I aren't so different after all, and maybe Harper likes the notion of fixing our broken souls. However, some things are beyond repair, and the patches over our scars will only hold for so long. No matter who she chooses tonight, she'll end up miserable. Neither of us will be enough, yet we can't walk away either.

A door bangs upstairs, the sound hitting me like a gunshot. Jolting me out of my seat, my feet move before my mind has caught up. At least a part of my brain is working and the rose is in my hand as Clay and I stop at the bottom of the stairs. Shoulder to shoulder, the light facing-off with the dark. My palms itch with the need to fidget, so I opt for pushing my free hand into my pocket. Harper appears at the top of the staircase a moment later, the air freezing in my lungs.

Holy...everything. The silver dress shimmers with each breath she takes, the fabric hugging her curves like it's worshipping her. It pools around her heels, liquid light trailing behind her. The neckline plunges dangerously low, only barely contained by the faintest layer of mesh. The delicate straps roll over her shoulders, tracing the lines of her skin before vanishing into what I know must be an open back. She's a work of art. A slice of sin. She's all I want but don't deserve.

Harper's hair is pulled back from her face and cascading down her back in a river of soft curls. Her receivers are on full display, as they should be. She's a goddess of strength, overcoming challenges with such ease, many wouldn't even know she faced them. I'm nowhere near worthy of her attention or her affection, yet I want them both.

Smoothing a hand over my styled hair, I ignore my heartbeat pounding in my ears with each step Harper takes. Each stair is one closer to me. Each soft click of her heel feels like a countdown to my own destruction. I've always been spoiled with things that don't matter. Money, cars, connections. But now the only thing I care about in this godforsaken world is walking toward me, shimmering like a dream I don't deserve. I want to grab her with both hands, pull her against me, and never let her go. To claim her. To prove that she's mine and I'm hers, no matter who's watching.

Her green eyes come level with mine, and it's like staring into the truth I've been trying to outrun. There's sadness in them. Not just sadness, but resignation. She looks between me and Clayton, and I feel my throat closing. I force myself to stay still, to not reach for her, to not say a damn word.

My tongue is a live wire in my mouth, filled with arguments, with pleas, with promises I know she's already stopped believing in. There's nothing else to say. Harper's made her decision. I can see it in the hard line of her jaw, the way her shoulders square against the weight of it.

A wave of nausea grips me, twisting deep in my gut. I've been in fights that left me bloodied, dragged across the ground, but nothing has ever felt like this. Nothing has ever hurt like this. Harper makes me want to rewrite every mistake, every cruel thing I've ever done. She makes me want to beg her to save me. But now, watching her stand there so calm and so sure, I might be about to lose her and if I do, there won't be anything left of me to save.

Addy appears at the top of the stairs, beautiful in her own right as much as I hate to think it, but my brain barely even registers her. My gaze zeroes in on the two black duffel bags in her hands.

"What's going on?" Clayton asks in a gruff bark. It breaks through my fog, registering what I have failed to understand. Harper keeps her head held high and crosses her hands in front of her, as if she's practiced what she's about to say a thousand times.

"I've been asked to make a decision, and I have." She looks at Clay first, then at me, then at some safe, neutral point between us. I brace myself. "Each of you speaks to a different side to me, but together you both make me whole. I'm just as strong as I am weak, brave as I am scared. I need my protector and my challenger." Harper smiles weakly to us both in turn before stepping on the last step to take each of our hands in hers. Her fingers are shaking, but they clench tightly as if she's clinging on in sheer desperation.

"This is what I want," Harper looks from me to Clayton and back again, tears shining in her eyes. "I can't lie to myself or ignore the pull I feel towards each of you for different reasons. When one of you isn't here, it's like a piece of my soul is missing. I understand it's unusual and incredibly selfish, so I've decided that if one of you isn't on board, then I'll walk away from you both."

"Harper," I breathe, unfamiliar with the sound of my own voice. She shakes her head, needing to finish what she's started.

"I've had a virtual meeting with Dean Lawrence about being switched onto a home learning program if it comes to it. That should appease the new policy your father has put in place. But it wasn't just about the expulsion. These threats," Harper sighs with the weight of the world on her shoulders, "I can't face the threats without you guys by my side, but I can't have one and see the other everyday either. It's unconventional, but when all the bullshit is set aside, it works. We work."

My head is shaking, my mind tripping over itself. Harper doesn't want to go back to her aunts, she wants to stay here. Where the blood rushes through my veins, threatening to burn me alive, Clayton is the image of stoic serenity. I can't gauge what he's thinking, but it doesn't matter.

"So, that's my decision. It's time for you to make yours." Refusing to let the tears fall, Harper withdraws her hands and takes a step back. Addy places Harper's bags to the side of the front door, sending a visceral pain shooting through my chest. *No.* I'm just starting to understand the strength of my feelings for Harper. I can't let her go, no matter the costs.

"I'm all in." I announce, closing the space between us to take her face in my hands. My heart forgets how to beat, as if my future happiness is hinged on this moment. "I've been a slave to you since day one. Whatever you ask of me, I'll do it. I need you in my life, Babygirl. You're it for me."

The first tear falls from Harper's beautiful emerald eyes and I catch with my thumb. She leans into my hand, allowing herself a moment before shutting off her emotions again. I step in beside her, winding my arm around her waist.

"Clay?" Harper's voice quivers, her hope and dread rolling into one. I lift my head to watch him closely, threatening with my eyes for him to not fuck this up. We will sort logistics later, I'll build him a shed in the back yard to live in. Clayton doesn't look at her at first. His jaw tightens, arms crossing like he's holding himself together. When he eventually speaks, it's a low and impassive sound.

"I've fallen for you Beautiful, way too hard. I want to be your everything, and in return I'd expect the same." His onyx black eyes lift, spearing Harper so harshly, I have the urge to step in between them. Keeping my feet rooted to the spot, I let him say his peace. I suppose it's the least he's owed.

"This isn't the future I envisioned when you gave me back the hope of having one. You can't ask me to take turns and watch him treat you like a piece of meat. I'm sorry, but in the name of making you happy, I'll be making myself miserable. You can't ask that of me. I can't…" Clayton breaks his stance to run a hand through his blond locks. "I wouldn't be my mother's son if I settled for that."

"I understand," Harper whispers as if she was expecting as much. There's a slight shake to her shoulders but she forces a bittersweet smile, pushing through the pain that's written all over her face. "Well, we're all dressed up. Shall we have one last night to remember?" Harper asks hopefully and naïvely. I can see Clayton's rejection before he shakes his head side to side.

Harper sucks in a breath and reaches for him, as if she can keep him here by force, but he moves back out of her reach. He has her answer, and it's not the one he wanted. Turning on his heel, he marches straight out of the door. Just fucking leaves us standing there, resentment and bitterness entwining. Wrapping my arms around Harper's shuddering frame, I've found a new reason to hate Clayton Michaels, and it's for breaking Harper's heart.

"We don't need him. I'll do whatever it takes, I'll be enough," I promise without the basis to back it up. All I know is the desperation crawling up my throat, leaving a burning path in its wake. Harper shifts out of my grip, jerking her chin to the pink-haired imp I forgot was standing there. Addy retrieves the bags and carries them outside without looking back. "Please, baby. Don't do this."

Harper's tears are spilling freely now. Two perfect trails cutting through her make-up, cutting directly through my soul. I swear each drop lands somewhere in the hollow space where my heart used to be. I can't breathe, I can't think. The only reason I've known for living is right here, yet she's slipping through my fingers.

"It's not fair for you to only get half of me." Harper tries to edge closer to the door, but I step into her way.

"Half is fine, I'll take half," my voice cracks. "You have to stay. You already belong to me and I think...I think I'm in love with you." My own brain explodes at the revelation, words I never thought I'd say tumbling out of me. Harper continues to shake her head, my protests falling on deaf ears, no pun intended.

"You don't know what love is, Rhys," she says far too softly. "It's not owning someone, it's setting them free with the knowledge they will always come back to you." Her words break her as much as they do me. She wishes the opposite were true, but she won't lie to me either.

"Show me," I beg, reaching for her hand but she pulls away. Losing patience, I grab her upper arms and tug her against my chest. "I can learn. Just...just stay and teach me how to love you." Blinking up, Harper looks at me with such tenderness it guts me. Such misery, that I can read her response without her needing to say a word. She knows I can't love, that it's an emotion I'm not capable of. The sympathy that pinches her features is my undoing.

"Don't fucking pity me." I snarl, yet I pull her closer. My fingers find her face, thumbs trembling against her skin as I crush my mouth to hers. The kiss isn't soft. It's a punishment, a plea and a desperate, broken promise all in one. I kiss her plump lips so savagely, I know they will bruise. This is what I'm good at, all I'm good for. ""You're not leaving," I growl against her face, nipping at her jaw. "I won't let you go."

Harper gasps against me, her hands pushing weakly at my chest before gripping my shirt, torn between resisting and falling. Finding her sweet lips again, I kiss Harper until her knees buckle and I'm all that's keeping her upright. I pour everything into our connection, every ounce of regret, every memory, every unspoken apology.

If this is the last time I'll ever touch her, then she'll damn well remember it. She'll remember *me*.

HARPER

CHAPTER THIRTY SEVEN

I stagger out the door, leaving a trail of shattered pieces of my heart behind with every step. The night air hits my face, cold and harsh, but it's nothing compared to the ache in my chest. I can't blame anyone but myself. I made my choice, and I'm sticking to it, but being determined doesn't ease the pain.

All I wanted when I came to Waversea was a chance to be normal. To feel free. To breathe without the weight of my past pressing against my ribs. But being normal...sucks. It's cruel and hollow and nothing like the dream I built in my head.

I never should've left my converted attic. I should've stayed hidden away with my books, my music, my solitude. Because now I have to go back knowing I destroyed the only two people who ever made me feel whole. There won't be anyone else like them. There *can't* be, and my heart won't forgive me long enough to find out.

Wiping the tears from my cheeks with too much force, smudging the remnants of my makeup, I finally step off the porch. Some part of me was waiting for him to run after me, for Rhys to grab me, beg me to stay, tell me he'd change. One more look in those desperate blue eyes, and I would have folded. But he doesn't come. He's probably standing in that same spot, broken in ways he'll never admit. I meant what I said. He deserves better than half of me, even if it kills me to give him up.

Addy walks quietly beside me, slipping her hand into mine. Her thumb strokes over my knuckles as we walk, forcing a silent show of strength I don't feel. Addy knows what this costs me, she was the one who's spent all day trying to talk me out of it. We've already cried and said our goodbyes. Now, all that's left is to walk away. I take one of the bags she's carrying just to keep busy, to stop myself from turning back.

"You're really not coming to the party?" she asks softly. I shake my head before she even finishes. The thought of seeing anyone right now, especially Phillip Waversea's smug grin and Klara's arrogant smile, makes my stomach twist. I'd either splinter or lash out, and I can't afford to do either.

"I know I promised I would, but I'm not up to it." My voice wobbles despite my best effort to stay composed. Addy nods and grips my hand harder. We round the tall building, the click of our heels echoing across the empty parking lot like a countdown. My Audi waits beneath the lamplight, gleaming with the promise of escape like she always is. Considering I didn't sleep a wink last night, I probably shouldn't get behind the wheel, but I'll manage until I find a layby to nap in.

I look around like an idiot, hoping to see them running after me. Hoping for some cinematic miracle, but of course, there's nothing. I asked too much of them, asked for a dream that couldn't survive in the real world. Even now, I keep imagining different endings, ones where we all find a way to make it work. Where love didn't feel like a wound that will never heal. Reality has a way of burning through fantasies.

The keys bite into my palm as I press the button, the headlights blinking twice against the fall of night. Addy pops the trunk to fill with my bags, until her head snaps up suddenly. She hears the approaching footsteps before I do, but I gasp and spin, filled with futile hope.

"Where are you going?" Kenneth's voice slices through the quiet.

Whether from the jerky movement or the crushing disappointment, my heels skid on the asphalt. Kenneth catches me before I fall, his arms surprisingly steady. I didn't know he had the strength to set me back on my six-inch heels with the ease that he does. Brewing coffee must be a good workout for the arms, and he has been putting in double shifts lately.

Beneath the streetlamp, Kenneth's orange hair almost glows, his eyes full of shock and confusion. He looks ridiculous in his oversized suit, sleeves hanging over his hands. I'm surprised he was even planning on attending Rhys' birthday gala. He hates Rhys. The thought causes my chest to squeeze, because now, Rhys hates me just as much.

"I have to go," I say quietly. Addy shuts the trunk with a thud of finality. Kenneth's attention shifts to the car, realization creeping over his features.

"Go? Go where?" His eyes glaze over almost instantly, the panic in them reminding me of what a terrible human being I am.

"I can't stay Kenneth. I'm sorry, I know I've been a shitty friend to you. We can message and write. Maybe one day you could come visit?" I offer because it seemed like the right thing to do, even if I would conveniently lose my receivers that week.

The devastation in Kenneth's face resonates with everything I'm feeling internally. The thought of facing Aunt Marg's cats and smug indifference is a punishment I deserve, not that I plan on staying for long. I have inheritance left over from my parents, a nest egg that will place me in a small apartment by the sea. Just me and the sound of the waves, pretending I'm okay while slowly rotting from the inside out. I was made to survive, not to be happy, and that's exactly what I'll do. I'll keep going, even when it kills me to do so.

"Wait, wait, hold on," Kenneth fumbles for reason. "If this has something to do with Clay—"

"No. It's me that's the problem. I've messed up and led him on. It's not fair for me to stay. It'll only cause more grief."

Addy rounds my side, her hand settling on my arm. There's some kind of signal in her eyes that I don't have the energy to decipher. She bobs her brows in Kenneth's direction, signaling it's time he moved along, but I don't rush him. People don't understand or like Kenneth, but I know what it's like to be the outcast. Either way, Kenneth picks up on the not-so-subtle cue and hesitates.

"Okay, well if you're sure I can't convince you otherwise," he mumbles, his focus on the floor. Suddenly, as if he's been electrocuted, Kenneth jolts and raises his hands so fast, I flinch. "Wait! I made you something. I was going to give it to you when I next saw you. It's at the dorm, it'll just take five minutes. Please, let me grab it?"

I don't know if it's the apprehensive gleam flickering in his eyes or the fact I don't have it in me to deny another man tonight, but I nod on a weak smile.

"Sure, I'll wait. Just...don't be long." I murmur, anxious to get on the road. The night air gnaws at my skin, biting through the thin fabric of my dress. Kenneth nods quickly and takes off between the cars, his limbs flailing in that awkward, endearing way of his. Watching him disappear gives me the first real smile I've managed in hours, though it doesn't reach my eyes. I will miss his strange mannerisms and continuous chatter, even if I barely listened to any of it.

When I turn back, Addy's already holding out her arms for me. The moment she folds me into her chest, I crumble. Her honeycomb-sweet scent fills my lungs, grounding me just enough to stop me from falling apart completely. I cling to her, fingers digging into the sequins of her dress, trying to draw strength from her warmth. There's nothing left to say that hasn't already been said. No words that will make this hurt any less. I don't know if I'm about to cry or vomit, so I pull back first, forcing a weak laugh as I rub her arms like it's her that needs comfort.

"Go on," I whisper. "Get to your date. Enjoy the party for both of us, yeah?" Addy rolls her eyes and reaches into her cleavage for her phone, frowning when she reads the screen. She tucks it away again and shakes her head, pink curls bouncing.

"It's fine. I'll wait until you've left," she insists, as stubborn as ever.

"Don't be stupid," I reply with a small smirk, trying to lighten the mood. "I'll grab Kenneth's gift and be gone before you can finish your drink. I'm a big girl." I give her a playful smack on the ass that earns me a scandalized yelp. Her hands lift, forming the rock sign with her thumb extended, signing *'I love you.'*

My throat tightens as I return the sign, mouthing the words back. I watch her walk away, the soft light of the streetlamp swallowing her figure until it's just me and the dark.

Exhaling shakily, I turn back to the car, starting at my own reflection. Luckily, my face is covered by shadow, because I'm sure I'm not ready to see my puffy eyes and smudged make-up emulating that of a sad clown's. But my dress is visible, sparkling bright and accentuating my curves. I hate it. Too tight, too formal, and too much a reminder of everything I've just lost.

Popping the trunk, I dig out a hoodie and sweatpants. As beautiful as this gown is, I'm done pretending to be the girl who fits inside it. Kicking off the heels, I slide into the fabric of my sweatpants tugging the dress up inch by inch so nothing is revealed. Not that there's anyone nearby anyway. Dragging the hoodie over my head in an awkward, arm-breaking motion, I sigh at the softness, finally able to breathe again.

The trunk slams shut, and I nearly scream as I spot Kenneth standing right behind me, silent as a ghost.

"Jesus, Kenneth!" I clutch my chest, my heart hammering. "Wear a damn bell, will you?" The words come out harsher than intended, and guilt instantly follows. Sheepishly, he ducks his head and curls his shoulders inward. Swallowing passed the pulse rocketing in my throat, I place a hand on his shoulder. "I'm sorry. It's just been a rough night."

When Kenneth looks up again, his grin is bright and boyish, all forgiveness and warmth. My heart melts slightly, the thought that he's too good for this world drifting through me. That is, until he holds out a small, flattened keyring, oval-shaped, clear resin with a swirling pattern inside. Dark brown blending into pale pink. I squint at it, tilting my head, trying to make sense of it.

"Kenneth...is that...my hair?"

"Of course not!" His voice jumps an octave as he steps back, eyes wide in shock. I let out a shaky laugh of relief. Thank goodness for that. "It's the combined strands of a long-haired rat's molting process," he explains, chest puffing out. "I weaved them together before bleaching and color matching them to you."

I blink once, twice, holding his serious stare and chewing on my inner cheek. Yeah, that's still creepy but the sincerity in his expression negates the cringe that tries to break through. Pushing the keyring into my pocket, I plaster a small smile onto my face.

"Thank you, but you *really* don't need to give me gifts." I shift my weight foot to foot as this goodbye drags on longer than I planned. I'm still working through the pain consuming my chest and need to put some distance between me and those I'm aching for. Picking up on my mood, Kenneth makes a perfect 'O' with his mouth and steps aside so I can stride to my driver's door.

"I just wanted to say," Kenneth starts. I turn back, suppressing a sigh. I really want to get out of here. "People don't like me. They think I'm weird. I *am* weird, but I can't help it. I've been alone for a long time, and I think that's something you understand. When we were hanging out before, I felt like I had a friend for a while."

I frown at myself, knowing I went back to ignoring him once Clay was back in the picture. As if I expected Clay to take on the mantle of socializing with Kenneth again so I could focus on other areas of my life. Fuck, I'm a terrible person because he's right. I do know how it feels to be alone.

"Look I..." my words get stuck, tasting bitter on my tongue. I have so much to apologize for that I can't even string together a sentence. "I don't really like goodbyes Kenneth, so let's just hug it out and then I'm going to go, okay?"

Kenneth nods enthusiastically, drawing a tiny laugh from me, his arms wide and a little unsure. I step into him, curving my arms around his back. His chest is firmer than expected, the powerful thump of his heartbeat beating against my cheek. At least by coming for Waversea, I found friends like Addy and Kenneth and I can say that I tried. I gave it my best shot, but the real world just isn't made for people like me.

CLAYTON

CHAPTER THIRTY EIGHT

Somehow, I make it back to my dorm on numb feet. Numb everything. I can't believe I let her go. She was right there, endlessly beautiful despite the devastation clouding her green eyes, and I walked away. I should take solace in the fact that I was true to myself. That I found the strength to listen to my gut, even when my heart was screaming to accept her offer. Battling with Wavershit on a short-term basis is one thing, but I couldn't commit to it long term, not when I've already seen how it ends.

Whenever the three of us are together, Rhys always pulls her into his orbit, leaving me standing on the outside, desperate for snippets of her attention. He would ensure I stayed invisible, he would make it his mission to see my self-esteem scraping the floor so I won't challenge him outright. I might not be much, but I can't accept that that's all I'm worth.

My dorm room is mercifully empty when I stagger inside. Locking the door behind me, my hands shake as I tug the tie over my head and shove it into my jacket pocket. I fumble with the shirt buttons clumsily, the frustration boiling over. If I didn't have to return this suit in the morning, or if I had the money to replace it, I'd rip the damn thing off. When I finally peel the jacket and shirt away, my chest expands, lungs burning. I drop onto the edge of the bed, burying my face in my hands, and finally let the tears flow.

I'd expected to feel rage, but what's left is worse. Emptiness. A hollow ache where hope used to live. My mind spins, what if's plaguing me now that it's too late to go back. What if I'd said yes, what if I'd done more to sway Harper in my direction, what if I can't survive the wreckage tearing me apart from inside. A slice of pain cuts across my chest, knowing I'll never see her again, never catch her shy smile, or watch her eyes light up when she's passionate about something. Her memory is going to haunt me.

I stand and pace, unable to sit still but having nowhere left to go. After staying at Rhys' place, the dorm walls are more like the confinements of a cell. Tomorrow, I'll have to brave the cafeteria and the very likely possibility of my student card being declined. Not that any of those things are at the top of my worries right now.

Has Harper gone to the party with that smug asshole? Does he get to hold her one last time? Kiss her neck and feel her curves pressed against him. Or has he convinced her to stay, to be exclusively his? The thought finally triggers the delayed anger I'd been waiting for.

Lifting the desk chair, I hurl it with all my might, the wood splintering against the wall and dropping onto Kenneth's bed. My chest heaves, my mind clouded. I've walked away. I've let Wavershit win. Kicking the singular, wonky wardrobe while clawing my hands through my hair, a solid thud reverberates through the floor, followed by a dull thud beside my shoes. The kickboard has fallen from the base, laying uselessly on the floor.

"Shit." I crouch and reach to shove it back in place, but pause when I notice the shallow groove along the top edge, just deep enough for a thumbnail. Slotting the kickboard back into place, the smoothness of the action causing my brows to pull together. Using my thumbnail in the groove, I pop it out again, repeating the action until my brain manages to catch up. The piece isn't broken, it's been designed to come out.

My pulse starts pounding as I lower onto my back, pushing my hand into the empty gap underneath. Expecting my fingers to brush against dust and lost socks, I almost flinch at the cold, hard edges they graze instead. One by one, I pull the contents free and line them up on the floor. A laptop, a thick brown folder, a photo album, a zip-lock bag stuffed with hard drives and USBs. The longer I stare, the heavier the air around me becomes.

Clicking sounds at the door, the handle being tried from the outside. I jolt, gathering up the items and stuffing them beneath my pillows. The unmistakable jingle of keys comes, low muttering following. Pushing the kickboard back in place, I manage to throw myself onto my bed as the door opens and Kenneth steps inside.

"Kenneth, what the hell are you doing here?!" I ask a little too hastily. My orange-haired roommate freezes, wide-eyed and pale. His gaze drags over my bare torso, the way my chest is shifting heavily and then sweeps the room, only briefly snagging on the kickboard before staring at the shards of broken chair littering his bed. Opening his mouth and closing it again, Kenneth 's attention returns to me, remembering I asked him a question.

"I just need to get something for the party. How come you're not there? Are you going later, as a surprise? Ohh maybe you should—"

"Just get what you need, Kenneth. I'm not in the mood for small talk," I huff, eager for him to leave. Something strange is happening around here and I need silence to sort through it all. Nodding, Kenneth rushes to retrieve something from the dresser drawer, keeping his back to me so I can't see what it is. He hurries out just as quickly, my feet following him to the door. This time, I lock and deadbolt it.

Lifting my pillows, I place the items on the dresser in a line before going back to the kickboard, wanting to check I haven't missed anything. Pushing my arm in, all the way up to the shoulder, my fingers brush over fabric, which I retract to find one of my black beanies with a phone nestled inside.

Blood rushes in my ears, my heart picking up speed as I stare at the beanie. There's no mistaking the foreign label and for a split second, I doubt myself. Is it me? Have I been sleepwalking, am I schizophrenic? Did the JDC break me in ways I don't understand, am I even here now or is this all an illusion? Holy fuck, am I in a coma?

"Snap out of it, you idiot," I mentally slap myself. Rising to stand at the desk, now that there's no chair to sit on, I hover over the items that could make up a serial killer's collection. I reach for the album first, the photos inside washed out and grainy. An image of two boys around six or seven stares back at me. Both scruffy, both smiling with the kind of closeness that only comes from growing up together. The taller one has tight black curls. The other, a mop of uneven blond hair. They wear threadbare shirts and hold each other in every shot, like brothers clinging to the last bit of good in the world.

I flip faster, growing impatient and more uneasy as I go on. I don't know these kids, but the last photo makes me stop. In baggy sweatpants, the pair stand in front of a recreation center I *know*. The old brick building downtown, the one I walked past every day growing up.

A prickle of unease runs down my spine. For a kid from my neighborhood to attend Waversea is a big deal. I thought I was the only one. Moving onto the folder, my hands tremble with urgency. It's full of newspaper articles about...me. My arrest, my trial, even a news article about Jeremy's funeral. '*Final claxon for basketball prodigy*' fills the space above his black and white picture, a huge smile tugging directly at my heart.

Breathing through the slice that threatens to split my chest open, I continue searching through the plastic sleeves looking for any kind of connection between these boys and me, until I find it.

A tiny obituary clipping glued to the corner of a page. The photograph is barely the size of a stamp, but he's older in this image. His tight black curls have become an unruly mess, his face filled out. I recognize him instantly. Antonio Langton.

'In loving memory of Antonio Langton, who died on March 4th,

aged 17. Much loved and sadly missed by his father, cousin, and friends at Croswell High.'

I stumble back, managing to drop onto my bed before the floor is whipped out from underneath me. My hands go numb, the folder slipping to the floor with a dull thud. Antonio was with me the night my life went to shit, the night I lost everything.

But why is his face here, staring up at me from the floor? Even without that answer, connections start to form in my mind. Harper's attack at the lab. Kenneth was there. Harper was drugged with a coffee. Kenneth works at a coffee shop. The day my locker was vandalized with white spray paint. Kenneth came back from work early, his body covered in white powder. He knows my mom's birthday. He steals my clothes. He's majoring in both science and veterinarian studies, giving him access to the chemicals that would start a fire, to the blood that desecrated Jeremy's sports jacket. He's the stalker.

I shoot to my feet, dragging the shirt and jacket back on without bothering to button it up. I'm out the door and down the stairs before I've even decided where to go. Should I track down Harper and Waver-shit at the dance, telling them all I've discovered? Shaking my head, I decide to take this straight to the Dean as I shove my way out of the dorm building doors and crash straight into Addy. She staggers back on a broken heel, panting with her hair stuck to her face, her eyes frantic. She's been running.

"Clay," Addy gasps, her forearms against my chest. I hold her in place, dreading whatever is about to come out of her mouth. "I didn't...I left Harper, she told me to. I was going to the dance but something felt off, so I went back."

"Addy, what's happened?" I implore, giving her a little shake, gripping her too tightly. "Where is Harper?"

"Kenneth wanted to give her something in the parking lot," Addy manages to force through her chattering lips. Her adrenaline is wearing off and the cold realization is setting in for both of us. Shrugging out of my jacket, I wrap it around her shoulders and take off, my arms pumping as I close the distance between the dorm buildings. Running the length of the parking lot, I skid to a stop at Harper's cherry red Audi. The doors are unlocked, her bags still in the trunk.

Skidding around, my dress shoe knocks something on the ground, a gentle rattle sounding as it skates beneath the car. For the second time tonight, I'm on my knees, reaching for a truth I don't want to admit to myself. My hand curls around the cylinder as I retrieve the needle, my head lowering onto the tarmac. What have I done?

Kenneth has been right under my nose this entire time. I've missed every clue, dismissed his strange ways as harmless. I've been so distracted, I couldn't see what was happening right in front of my face. And even still, I want to believe that he couldn't have done all of this alone. That he's another pawn being blackmailed, but the evidence covering our dorm room floor says otherwise. This was premeditated. It's personal. But why?

I'm back on my feet, dizzy and disorientated. Wherever Kenneth has taken Harper, he can't have gone far. Taking off in the direction of the quad, I shove passed party-goers making their way to the main hall. Naivety forces me to check each one, jogging up the line of those waiting to go inside, hunting for a silver dress. Maybe I'm wrong. Maybe he couldn't go through with it. Two smart suits lean against the building, all smirks and humor as they talk to their girl, until Huxley spots me.

"Clayton? What's wrong?" Huxley steps forward, frowning at my open shirt and distressed hair. I almost stumble into him, the relief at seeing a friend is too much to deny.

"It's Harper. She's in trouble," I start. My words are hurried and incoherent, but I manage to force a brief recount through my trembling jaw. Huxley's hands grip my face to center my focus, whilst Garrett slides in to button up my shirt. He shifts his shoulders and head in time with the music streaming from the hall, his face showing none of the malice that comes out of his mouth.

"So we find and gut the ginger bastard," Garrett smiles, his eyes devoid of emotion. If I weren't already worked up, I'd feel a trace of fear at his calm demeanor. Huxley shakes my shoulders, being the voice of reason.

"Go tell the Dean everything you've just told me. We'll round up sophomores and check the campus." I'm already shaking my head, my throat closing as the panic seeps in. We're losing too much time.

"I should be...it should be me," I start but Huxley stops me with a serious glare.

"You get help. We'll look. Is there anywhere he might have gone?" Swallowing, I reel off a list of places from the science labs to the gymnasium bathroom where the fire was set. My chest compresses at the thought that Kenneth will try to harm Harper again, that he might succeed this time. Huxley and Garrett kiss their girlfriend's forehead before running off to deliver on their promise to help me, taking my shriveled heart with them. I'm Harper's savoir. I'm the one who vowed to always save her. It should be me who finds her.

"Dean's office," the blonde demands, pushing me forward. "Now."

Time stretches on, the motions around me blurring. One minute I'm outside the gothic building, the next I'm in the Dean's doorway, shuddering and desperate. The police are called, I'm told to stay put. My foot taps on the hardwood floor, my ears pricking every time a figure steps into the room. Beyond the window, red and blue lights flash, announcing the arrival of the officers. Questions are fired, my answers vague and disconnected. All I want to hear is her voice, or the news that she's been found safe and sound.

I should be out there, searching. Rhys should be by my side, looking for the girl he claims to care for as much as I do. That bastard needs to be fighting for her too. Halfway through an interrogation, I stand and leave. The officer calls after me, but I don't stop. My legs move as if their destination has been programmed, footsteps echoing down the hallway and out of the main door.

The atmosphere on campus has shifted dramatically. Students flood the main courtyard, hundreds of bodies huddled in fancy attire.

The music has stopped, a murmur of worry and a sense of apprehension trickling through the crowd. Addy lingers on the edge of it all, her cheeks tearstained as she holds the duffle from Harper's trunk. Officers swarm the area, Harper's clothes in hand as their canines sniff and search.

Red and blue flashes bounce around the open space, uniformed officers wasting time taking interviews. No one here knows Kenneth. He flies under the radar, that weirdly awkward kid no one wants to be friends with. My gaze snags on the entrance of the hall, Phillip Waversea standing tall with his arms crossed and face twisted into a scowl as he assesses the disorder before him.

Striding forward, the hushed whispers grow louder, following me as I barrel through those who aren't quick enough to get out of my way. I don't stop to listen, refusing to add to the gossip rippling through Waversea Academy. With one destination in mind, I storm towards Rhys' frat house. It looms ahead, not a single light shining in any of the windows. Running up the porch steps, I pound my fist on the door, anger splintering against the wood. How dare he hide out when Harper needs us. He doesn't get to only love her when it suits him.

I've always considered myself a calm person. The type to predict every outcome before I act. To plan ahead in hopes of preserving a future that isn't bleak. Clayton Michaels is a survivor, a protector for the little guy when the big bad wolf comes to call. But whilst I was so focused on keeping Harper safe from Rhys, another enemy has crept in to threaten her wellbeing.

Kenneth had better run far and fast once she's back in my arms, because I will stop at nothing to repay every inch of harm caused to Harper's precious body and mind. I will kill him for this, and I'll happily serve the jail time for it. I've realized all too late that there is no future left to protect if Harper isn't in it.

When my pounding isn't acknowledged, I ram my shoulder against the door. I know Rhys is in there, otherwise he'd be front and center for the media storm that's about to hit the courtyard. Once, twice, and on the third, the door cracks from its hinges and buckles inward.

The silence that greets me is suffocating. The air inside is thick, laced with the faint tang of copper. Unable to penetrate the darkness, I flick on the hallway light and sharply intake a breath at the sight before me.

Rhys stands at the base of the stairs, exactly where I last saw him almost two hours ago. Frozen. Hollow. Red circles his sunken eyes. His shirt hangs open, half untucked, the once-crisp white now smeared and stippled with red. Blood drips lazily from his fingertips to the floor, each drop landing with a soft, wet patter that cuts through the stillness. His hands are torn to ribbons, fingernails split, skin shredded. There's blood under every nail, ground deep as if he'd clawed at himself, at the walls, at something he couldn't escape.

He doesn't move when I step closer. Doesn't flinch or jerk away like he usually would. His cold, blue gaze is locked on a vacant spot of the floor, the faintest tremor in his shoulders the only sign that he's still breathing. The self-hatred in his eyes is unbearable. An abyss of guilt and loathing so raw, it twists something in my gut.

"Rhys?" I say, my voice hoarse and too loud for the quiet around us. His gaze slowly drags up to meet mine, but it's as if he's staring straight through me. Of all the things I expected when bursting in here, this wasn't it. He's weaker than I've ever seen him, like witnessing the fall of an empire. All that's left is a heap of rubble that can't be pieced back together again.

A vibration sounds against the floorboards, Rhys' phone lighting through its cracked screen. I bend to retrieve it, noting the multiple message icons. Holding the device up, he doesn't move whilst I use his face recognition to unlock the phone. The words splintered and diffi-cult to read, but I squint, making out the letters that fill my heart with dread, and explain Rhys' fragmented demeanor. Message after message, taunting and gloating.

The latest message has an attachment, and with a trembling thumb, I open the image. Harper's head is slumped against the door of my truck, her pink-tinted hair covering her face. She's not on campus. She's growing further out of reach. Tossing the phone aside, I head towards the broken door and lift it. My biceps burn, my body screaming in protest. Just as the first news van pulls up outside, I place the door back against the frame, blocking out the world beyond.

Turning back to Rhys pitiful stance, our eyes lock, his expression blank as he watches mine twist. Whether I like it or not, this is the world I've become a part of. Both Rhys and I are to blame. We ruined Harper, we dragged her into this, and we're quickly running out of time. Closing the distance between us, I grip the back of his neck and jerk him into focus, a faint snarl hitching his top lip. Good.

"Whatever this is, snap the fuck out of it. Harper is in trouble. We need to work together," I seethe.

Forcing myself a step back, Rhys' eyes flash at last, his gaze drifting down to his crimson-coated hands as if seeing them for the first time. His lip continues to curl, causing it to re-split where his lip ring recently sat and blood to pool down his chin. He looks like a demon of vengeance, and that's what I need right now. What Harper needs.

Tilting his head one way and then the next, his neck cracks, his shoulders shuddering as if he's coming back to himself. When he glares at me, I stand tall against the promise of carnage in his cold eyes. When he finally speaks, his voice is a cracked plea.

"Tell me what to do, and consider it done."

Afterword

Thank you for stepping into the world of *Burned by Sin*. I hope you've fallen for these flawed, chaotic, and beautifully broken characters as much as I have. Writing this story has been a journey of love that burns and redemption that hurts just enough to feel real.

If you enjoyed this book, I'd be incredibly grateful if you could take a moment to leave a review. Your words mean more than you know. They help other readers discover these characters and allow me to keep creating the dark, emotional worlds you love.

Thank you for reading, for feeling, and for choosing to dive into the shadows with me.

BOOK THREE - Scarred by Desire will LIVE RELEASE in December 2025. Ensure you don't miss out by joining my newsletter and following my socials for updates!

Thank you again for your support! A special acknowledgement to Amy Perkins for proofreading, Bianca and Jenn for being my betas, and as always, Kris and Ella for being my emotional support blankets.

If you're aching for something to fill your book hangover, you can join my newsletter and download a free mini snapshot of Rose and the lengths she'll go through to get over her cheating ex. Set in Waversea Academy, this spicy one-shot will take you on a chase through the woods by a trio of masked basketball players.

You can also find the sign up link on:
www.authormaddisoncole.com

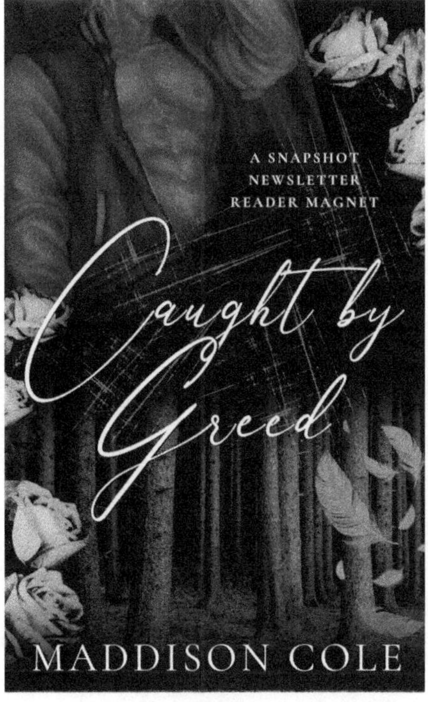

If you're a new reader to Maddison – welcome to the Mole's Burrow!!

Maddison Cole is a Why Choose Dark Romance Author hailing from the south east of the UK. She is a creative through and through, whether my medium be pencil, paint, wool or words.

In her books, you'll find a heavy dose of dark humour, men with filthy mouths, shocking twists, an abundance of spice and always a feisty female lead. When not writing, you can find Maddison hiding from her two children, two cats and husband with a dirty book and a naughty dessert.

For regular updates and a FREE spicy snapshot download, join my Newsletter , check out my website on www.authormaddisoncole.com and/or jump into my facebook readers group - **Cole's Reading Moles.**

If you'd like to keep reading from Maddison's backlist, please check out...

<u>Shadowed Souls Series – (set in Waversea)</u>

<u>RH Dark Academy Stepbrother Romance</u>

Forged by Shadows

Bound by Obsession

Haunted by Secrets

<u>The War at Waversea</u>

<u>Basketball College MFM Menage</u>

Deafened by Silence

Burned by Sin

Scarred by Desire

<u>Billionaire Brothers RH (set in Waversea) – Standalone</u>

Beautiful Delusions

<u>I Love Candy</u>

<u>Dark Humor RH - Completed Series</u>

Findin' Candy (novella)

Crushin' Candy

Smashin' Candy

Friggin' Candy

<u>All My Pretty Psychos</u>

<u>Paranormal RH with mutants, ghosts and demons - Completed Series</u>

Queen of Crazy

Kings of Madness

Hoax: The Untold Story (novella)

Reign of Chaos

<u>Bound by Fate</u>

<u>Fated Mates RH Shifter – Standalone</u>

Moon Bound

<u>A Deadly Sin</u>

<u>MMA Fighter BSDM RH - Standalone</u>

A Night of Pleasure and Wrath

<u>A Wonderlust Adventure</u>

<u>A Twisted Menage Retellling Duet</u>

Descend into Madness

Embrace the Mayhem

<u>Billionaire Badboys</u>

<u>Con Artist/Billioanire RH Romance – Uncompleted</u>

Wreckin' Amethyst

www.ingramcontent.com/pod-product-compliance
Lightning Source LLC
Chambersburg PA
CBHW070744190726
48292CB00002B/405